That Time I Accidentally Became A Serial Killer

Rebekah Sinclair

An Accidental Series
Stand-Alone

Copyright © 2025 by Rebekah Sinclair. All rights reserved.

This book is a work of fiction. Any resemblance to real people, places, or events is purely coincidental—and if it's not, take it up with my attorney (she's fabulous, fierce, and carries pink pepper spray).

No part of this book may be copied, stored, or shared by any means—unless you're just reading it quietly on your device, in which case: slay. But if you try to upload it somewhere shady, may your Wi-Fi forever lag and your coffee always be lukewarm.

This story may not be used to train or feed any form of artificial intelligence. That includes chatbots, machine learning systems, data scrapers, or whatever spooky code your morally gray tech bro friend is working on. Seriously. Keep your algorithms out of my murdery little rom-com.

Contains morally questionable behavior, romantic tension, legally dubious solutions, and a whole lot of blood. For personal use only. If you share it... well. Let's just say the homicide detective might not be the scariest one who shows up at your door.

Triggers

⚠️ **TRIGGER WARNING: Proceed with caution (and maybe a glass of wine).**

This book contains content that may be disturbing to some readers—and strangely satisfying to others. If you're here for blood, body bags, and a prosecutor-turned-accidental-serial-killer with a deeply concerning moral compass and a tiny dog with zero remorse... you're in the right place.

Side effects of reading may include:

- Uncontrollable laughter in highly inappropriate situations such as stabbing the ever-loving poop-doodie out of a rapist.
- Unholy levels of thirst for a homicide detective with a prickly personality and dreamy green eyes.
- A newfound obsession with bleach, burner phones, and legal loopholes.
- The inability to look at turkey basters the same way again.
- An urge to adopt a small dog and train it in crime scene desecration.

Trigger warnings include:

- Murder. A lot of it. Casual, premeditated, accidental—you name it, we've got it.
- Graphic violence, gore, and enough blood to make Tarantino blush.
- References to rape and sexual violence (past tense, non-graphic, but deeply thematic).
- Attempted rape (unsuccessful, no graphic detail, but emotional aftermath is present).
- Mentions of human trafficking, drug use, overdose, and systemic abuse.
- Unaliving people using sharp objects, blunt objects, legal arguments, and sometimes... kitchenware.
- Following Without Consent (some call this "stalking").
- Mentions of a suicide attempt (unsuccessful, non-glorified, not graphically depicted).
- Torture and use of torture devices, dismemberment and body disposal disguised as lo mein takeout. (We're sorry. And also not.)
- Dubious consent and consensual non-consent (CNC) scenes, including edging, sensory deprivation, binding, and gagging.
- Power imbalances, manipulation, and emotionally complex BDSM dynamics.
- Criminal mischief by a fluffy white dog who plays fetch with human eyeballs.
- Strong language. (mostly from the detective, who uses "fuck" as punctuation)

- Unapologetic female rage, morally pink decision-making, and dark romantic entanglements that blur every line.

If you're squeamish, easily offended, or think serial killers should never be hot—this book might not be for you.

But if you're ready for a dark, sexy, blood-soaked spiral into chaos?

Welcome to the body count.

For Dexter.
The real one.

The tiny white dog with a snaggletooth,
attitude for days, and the soul of a war criminal.

You are my muse. My menace. My twin flame.
This book is yours.

(But if you chew it, I swear to god—)

Scan to see the legend

Poppy

J ustice may be blind, but I'm not—especially when staring down a predator who thinks he can outsmart a woman in Valentino.

I pull into my usual courthouse spot, flip down the visor, and check my reflection.

Eyeliner? Sharp enough to draw blood.

Lipstick? Cherry red and not on my teeth. Bonus.

My blonde hair is curled to courtroom-perfection, still full of bounce from the overnight wrap.

My heels are pink. My nails are pink. My soul is... tired—but also pink.

I click the visor closed and grab my Louis Vuitton briefcase, stepping out just as my favorite chaos-hurricane appears, coffee in hand and judgment in his eyes.

Sebastian Elias Tréviot Ignatius Blaire III struts up beside me in a cobalt trench, paisley scarf trailing, sunglasses perched on his bald head, eyebrow cocked.

"Girlie-pop," Sebastian drawls, falling into step beside me, "if I die today, tell the press it was because my witness wore khakis to court. I want it on record."

He's already holding out my coffee. Triple-shot iced Americano with light oat milk, one pump toasted vanilla, one brown sugar, cold foam, cinnamon, and a pink straw.

Obviously.

I take it, already sipping. "What's your case?"

"I'm prosecuting a man suing his ex for calling him 'emotionally constipated' on TikTok. Claims it cost him a protein powder deal."

I nearly choke. "So... a real legal emergency."

"Honey, he listed 'alpha male influencer' as his profession. If I keep a straight face through voir dire, I deserve a Daytime Emmy."

Inside, the scanner beeps as I pass through. Sebastian, of course, makes a show of removing his belt and patting himself down.

"Morning, Hank," he winks at the very straight, very tired guard. "Still resisting me, I see. Admirable. Tragic, but admirable."

Hank rolls his eyes like it's his job. "Belt in the tray, Blaire."

"One day," Sebastian stage-whispers as he slides through the metal detector, "he'll cave. And when he does, I'll dedicate a closing argument to him."

We collect our things and head toward the elevator bank.

"And what about you, Miss Ma'am? Ready to legally eviscerate today's scum of the earth?"

"I'm prepped. I'm pissed. I'm wearing waterproof mascara."

"Poppy Hartwell, dawn-slayer and breaker of men's egos." He taps my coffee in a mock-toast.

"You've got this, girlie-pop."

At the hallway split where civil and criminal part ways, he keeps going, calling over his shoulder.

"Slay responsibly."

Inside my courtroom for the day, Mariela Castillo is unraveling. Her hands twist in her lap, nails bitten to the quick, eyes darting like she expects a ghost to crawl out of the woodwork.

I nudge her with my shoulder.

"Deep breath, Mari," I whisper. "You already did the hard part."

She doesn't look at me, but her breath stutters.

"You survived him," I add. "You said his name. That puts you ahead of ninety percent of this room. Including me on most Mondays."

A faint laugh escapes. Cracked. But it's hers.

There she is.

I lean in. "I'm with you. Every terrifying, infuriating step. Win or lose—we walk out together."

She meets my eyes. The hope there is fragile, but burning.

And that's enough.

This is what I was made for—not just the law books or takedowns. But this.

Being the anchor when someone's world is collapsing.

Holding steady while they face their worst moment.

Standing between victim and monster.

Reminding him that hell hath no fury like a woman in court-approved heels.

Today is the day I drag him into the light and hammer in the final nail.

If the jury has any doubt left, it'll be gone by lunch.

We step into the well. I take my place at the prosecution's table, smoothing my skirt and lining up my notes—not for reassurance, but because order quiets the noise.

Across the aisle, Travis Gannon slouches like he's posing for a mugshot-themed dating app. One arm draped over the chair, that smug grin already crawling across his face.

Like he knows how this ends.

His attorney murmurs something. He chuckles—slow, lazy, like he's waiting for brunch.

I catch the jury watching. Good. Let them see it.

The cocky detachment. The arrogance.

Like this is a DMV line and not a courtroom where he's facing twenty-five years for first-degree rape.

He makes me sick.

"All rise," the bailiff calls, and the room shifts in a synchronized murmur.

Judge Carter enters, robes billowing, exuding the calm, unshakable authority that makes both sides tremble.

Once seated, he fixes his gaze on me. "Miss Hartwell. You may proceed."

Okay, Poppy. Lipstick on, claws out.

I rise with steady hands and a calm smile.

The defendant thinks this will go his way.

He's dead wrong.

I've danced this dance before. I always lead.

With a syrupy tone that could sell sweet tea in a hurricane, I announce, "I'd like to call Travis Gannon to the stand."

A ripple moves through the gallery. Eyebrows lift. His attorney glances sideways, but Travis?

He rises like he's heading to a job interview—cocky, polished, dripping with confidence.

He buttons his jacket like he's about to close a deal instead of lying about raping my client.

I let him settle. Let him soak in the attention.

He raises his right hand, swearing to tell the truth, the whole truth, and nothing but.

And sure enough, he lies before he even sits.

"On the night of April twelfth, you claim you were at Chase Ellison's apartment, watching the Knicks?"

"Got there around eight. Watched the game. Crashed on the couch."

I nod like I'm humoring a toddler with finger paint. "Big fan?"

"Lifelong."

"So you remember that game well? They played the Heat, right?"

He puffs up. "That's right. Knicks took it."

"Final score?"

"I don't recall exactly. Something like one hundred to ninety."

"Close," I smile. "It was one hundred four to ninety-seven."

He shifts like he has somewhere better to be.

"You watched every play?"

He leans forward. "Every second."

"Then I'm sure you remember Reed's ankle injury in the third? Or Sanford's block in the final seconds?"

"Best play I've seen in years, sweetheart."

Sweetheart. Someone's confident today. I narrow my eyes a moment, letting that last comment brew.

"You and Chase are close. Best friends since high school. College roommates. Do you have a key to his apartment?"

He nods. "Of course. We're like brothers."

I pause, let the silence stretch.

"How would your 'brother' feel about you using his apartment as an alibi for the hour you spent raping Mariela Castillo?"

"Objection!"

"Sustained," Judge Carter says, but the jury already heard it.

"So, you say you never saw Mariela Castillo before she accused you—and you've never been near her building?"

"Correct."

"Even though she lives a ten-minute walk from Chase's?"

He scoffs. "New York's big."

"But you've been to Chase's countless times. You testified you picked up sandwiches from Tony's Bodega on Rivington?"

"Two roast beef on rye. We always have one before every game. For luck."

"Of course. Looking at your bank transactions, you shop frequently in the area," I gesture to the map on the easel. "Funny how all your routes intersect with the one building you claim you've never seen."

"I don't memorize every block."

"No," I agree, "just the ones you're hunting."

He clears his throat and swallows.

"You walked to Chase's from the bodega. Walk me through the route."

He rattles off a scenic detour. I mark it in red tape—clear for all to see.

"Interesting. Adds ten minutes and avoids her building in an almost exaggerated way."

"I like the quiet."

"Have you ever driven it?"

"Plenty."

"Take me through that route."

He does. I sketch it too, showing him going the wrong way on two one-way streets.

"Gotten any citations for driving the wrong way... countless times?"

"I know how I get there. I don't need you to tell me."

"Oh, certainly not." I cross my arms. "But I have a theory."

He stares at me, jaw tight.

"Mariela reported someone ringing her apartment around eleven to return her missing license. Soon after, she was attacked. I wondered—why buzz her first?"

"Objection. Why is this relevant?"

"I have a point. I promise."

"Then make it, Miss Hartwell." the judge says.

I continue, calm and deadly. "Mariela dropped her purse at that bodega the night she was attacked. Someone helped her pick up the contents. I think you took her license and a piece of mail.

You left Chase's, rang her bell to see which light turned on. Then used the fire escape. Beat her. Gagged her. Raped her. Then snuck back into Chase's and went to sleep. Alibi secured."

His face is locked, jaw twitching.

"You don't piddle where you sleep, Mr. Gannon. But Chase's place? That's your hunting ground."

I flip to a second map. Jurors shuffle. Someone gasps at the red X's that litter the page.

"Eight more women. Same injuries. Same pattern. All in a radius around Chase's."

"Objection! My client is not on trial for—"

"Withdrawn," I say. Too late to matter.

I turn back. "Thoughts on my theory, Mr. Gannon?"

He leans forward, sneering. "Cute story. You should pitch it to Netflix."

"Maybe I will." I flash a cold smile. "That game you allegedly watched? Reed's ankle? Sanford's block?"

He nods, smug.

"That was last season's game."

He blinks.

"This April twelfth, the Knicks played the Suns. No injuries. No heroics. They lost. The average score? One hundred to ninety. Something a real fan would know."

He stiffens.

"I guess you didn't watch the game at all," I say. "Because you weren't there."

Silence.

"You weren't watching basketball," I finish, voice flat. "You were raping Mariela Castillo."

He slams a hand on the witness box. "I never saw her in my life!"

And just like that, the mask slips. The monster beneath surfaces—just a little—before he pulls it back in.

"Your Honor," I say smoothly, "I'd like to enter into evidence Exhibit 12-C—security footage from the florist shop next to Tony's Bodega."

"Objection!" the defense erupts.

Judge Carter raises a hand. "Counsel, approach the bench."

His lawyer demands, "Where exactly did you get that footage, Miss Hartwell?"

I stay cool. "It's on the evidence sheet."

The judge clicks open the digital court files. "Which is where, Miss Hartwell?"

I gesture. "Submitted with everything else, Your Honor. As always."

The silence thickens—sharp enough to slice. Judge Carter scans his screen. Then his expression hardens. He stands.

"In chambers."

He doesn't need to shout.

"Bailiff, take the defendant back to holding."

The gallery buzzes. Whispers rise like static. I glance at Mariela—panicked, wide-eyed. I force a smile.

It's okay. I've got this. I hope my smile says that, though part of me isn't sure.

In chambers is never where you want to be mid trial.

But here we are.

Judge Carter turns his screen toward me. "You've built quite the case. But I need the chain of custody for this footage —now."

I scroll fast. Exhibit 12-C should be here. I remember uploading it.

I check again.

Nothing.

"No need to panic," I murmur to myself. "We are composed. Capable. We are—oh, sweet buttermilk biscuits, where is it?"

"It's not here," the defense says, smug. "Due process wasn't followed. It's inadmissible."

My stomach drops.

"It shows everything," I argue.

Judge Carter doesn't blink. "Then you should've logged it. Unless you have something else, it stays out."

The defense pounces. "Her whole case rides on that footage. Without it, all she has is a lineup ID and theatrics."

Carter presses his palms to the desk. "The burden of proof isn't a suggestion. It's the law."

My throat tightens with fury and sharp self-reproach.

"Back to court, Prosecutor," he says. And that's that.

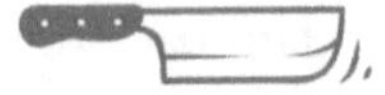

Travis is already being led back in, smirking like someone just handed him the keys to the city. I try to reach Mariela—eye contact, anything—but the moment slips past, fast and brutal.

Judge Carter takes the bench. "Due to a critical evidentiary failure," he announces, voice like a blade, "the court has no choice but to dismiss Exhibit 12-C. With no corroborating evidence beyond the victim's statement, the court cannot proceed."

Mariela breaks before he finishes.

"I'm declaring a mistrial." The gavel slams down. "Charges dismissed."

I stand, motionless. Somewhere between stunned silence and a laugh that wants to spiral.

Travis turns, basking. His suit looks sharper, like freedom has a tailor.

Mariela gasps. "I told the truth," she whispers. "He's going to do it again."

I want to scream. Cry. Rip the world apart. Instead, there's just static.

"He's going to come for me again," she adds.

"No, Mariela." My voice is low but solid. "He won't."

He strolls past the prosecution table where I laid out his lies like puzzle pieces. The bailiff holds the door like he's off to brunch.

Free. Not innocent. Just free.

He pauses at the threshold, smirking over his shoulder.

I step in front of Mariela, my body between his and hers.

"Better luck next time, sweetheart," he says.

My fists curl. My jaw tightens. But I smile—soft, hollow—for her.

"This isn't over," I whisper. "I'm not giving up."

But as he disappears into the press swarm, I'm left in the wreckage. Whispers circle. My pulse pounds a hopeless rhythm.

A throat clears behind me.

I don't need to turn. I know that aftershave and disappointed tension anywhere.

Assistant District Attorney Benjamin Cho steps into view, navy suit sharp, jaw ticking.

He doesn't speak. Just lifts his hand and jerks his chin.

We step out of the courtroom and he stops just off to the side.

"You heard," I say.

"Oh, I heard." His voice is calm like a hurricane's eye. "Press is already dragging us over the DA's third mistrial in as many months."

I flinch. "But those weren't mine."

"This one was," he snaps. "And the evidence disappeared on your watch."

"It was submitted. It was clean—"

"Doesn't matter." He pinches the bridge of his nose, glasses catching light like a scalpel. "You're brilliant, Hartwell, but brilliance doesn't matter if the jury never sees the proof. The media's calling you a 'Liability in Lipstick'."

That one cuts deeper than it should. But I hold my ground.

"I'm not the only one," I say, steadier than I feel. "Other cases—assaults, murders—they're falling apart too."

He pauses. I catch a flicker—doubt or agreement—then it's gone.

"Maybe." He straightens his cuffs. "But right now, you're the headline. I can't afford more bad press."

A beat before he continues.

"One more meltdown like this," he says coldly, "and you're on parking violations."

Then he walks away—cool-clean, like he didn't just cut my future open.

I stay right where I am, Louboutins anchored to the floor like they know I'll fall if I move.

He doesn't look back.

And I don't break.

Not here.

Not yet.

But something inside me begins to crack.

2
Poppy

Four days.

Four whole days since a man walked out of my courtroom with a smirk on his face and the full weight of the justice system letting him skip away like it was recess.

I sip from my oversized *It's Giving Prosecutor* wine glass—rosé, because red felt a little too murdery tonight—and rewind the footage again.

My office is quiet, lights dimmed, heels kicked off under the desk. My fuzzy pink slippers keep my toes warm as I watch a monster on the security tape.

Behind me, from the plush pink chair he's unofficially claimed in the corner of my office, Sebastian lets out a groan. "Diva, I swear to Dior, if I have to record one more TikTok explaining defamation law because a micro-influencer tagged me in a post, I'm going to sue the internet for pain and suffering."

"Pretty sure that's not how any of this works," I mutter, not looking away from the screen.

"Says you. I've got a ring light and a six-figure follower count that says otherwise." He dramatically swipes on his phone.

The surveillance video glows across my laptop screen like a ghost I refuse to stop chasing.

Chills race along my back each time the monster's face appears under the streetlamp.

Frame by frame.

Mariela outside Tony's Bodega. Purse slipping off her shoulder. Her license, an envelope—little pieces of her life scattered across the sidewalk. She bends, flustered, trying to gather it all.

Then him.

Mr. Disgusto. Travis Gannon.

Hair perfect, hands tucked into his pockets like he's starring in a cologne ad for creeps.

He stoops, picks up her ID and the envelope—doesn't even pause as he slips them into his pocket like they belong to him.

"Unbelievable," I mutter, swirling my wine. "Just casually stealing the address of the woman he's about to traumatize. Nothing to see here, folks."

He walks off—past her building, past the story he sold in court, straight to Chase's place.

His buddy's apartment is a revolving door of borrowed alibis.

That's his routine. Circle. Strike. Slip away with clean hands and a Knicks jersey.

The next clip rolls.

Later now—darker. Another street cam catches him at the edge of the frame. Same cocky walk. Same coat.

He turns the corner toward her building.

I pause the video, rewind it and slow it down.

And right there, under the streetlamp, his face lifts.

Not nervous. Not unsure.

Just... set.

A man with a plan.

"You picked up her ID and her mail, you little doodie lick-er," I mutter. "He knew her floor. Her unit number." I take another sip, jaw tight.

Sebastian, still trimming video clips, doesn't even glance up. "Someone should legally castrate him with a rusty eyebrow tweezer."

"He knew exactly how to get to her." My heart pounds—not with fear. With fury.

He planned it.

Plotted it.

Executed it.

And walked away like it was nothing.

I had him. This video? It was the missing link.

The nail. The coffin. The verdict tied in a bow.

It put him at the scene. Not on a couch with a beer. Not innocent.

Maybe not twenty-five years.

But prison.

Safety.

A night where Mariela could sleep without flinching at shadows.

And maybe—maybe—others would've come forward.

Because they always do.

One voice breaks the silence, and others follow.

But this? This was evisceration.

The case collapsed.

The system blinked, and he walked.

So here I am—rosé in hand, rage in my throat—holding the broken glass with no idea how it shattered.

My phone buzzes on the desk.

Mariela Castillo.

I answer immediately. "Mari?"

Her voice is shaking so badly I almost don't recognize it.

Across the room, Sebastian looks up from his phone. His editing stops mid-swipe, all the sass gone from his face in an instant.

"He's following me."

My stomach drops. "What? When?"

"Today. Yesterday. I—I don't know. I just... I keep seeing the same guy. Same hat. Same car. At the grocery store, outside my gym, parked across from my building."

My hand flies to my chest. "Did you get a picture? Can you—"

Without turning his head, Sebastian leans an inch closer like he's trying to absorb the conversation through osmosis.

His eyes flick toward me behind his screen, one brow lifting the tiniest bit. Not interrupting. Just... gathering data like a drama-starved lawyer.

"*He* sent *me* the pictures." Her voice cracks. "I got a text yesterday. Just a photo of me... walking to my car. And another today. Me on my balcony. I think he was across the street—"

I'm already standing. I don't remember putting my glass down. "You need to go somewhere safe. Have you gone to the police?"

"I did." Her laugh is wet and bitter. "They said he hasn't violated the restraining order. That he hasn't threatened me. That they can't act on assumptions."

I swear so hard internally it might've registered on the Richter scale.

"They said they can't do anything unless he makes contact," she whispers. "Unless he hurts me."

I press a hand to my temple, pacing now. I need to call the

detective on the case, and I'm already flipping through my pink leather ledger to the tab for Mari's case.

Brannon. Detective Brannon.

Of course it is. I can't stand having to deal with Brannon. The man has the investigative instincts of a damp sock and the empathy of a Roomba.

"Mari, you need to pack a bag and stay with a friend. Your aunt, maybe?"

"Stacie just had a baby, and my aunt is in El Salvador for the next two weeks."

Tiddlywinks!

I release a breath, trying to be the calm voice of reason—of action. That's what she needs. Someone who will actually do something for her.

"I'll do everything I can," I tell her. "I swear to you. I'm not going to let this go."

There's a pause. A breath.

Then, softly:

"So I have to wait until he hurts me?"

I don't have an answer. Not one that won't make her more afraid.

Because the truth is... she's right.

The system isn't made to prevent harm.

Only to respond to it.

And by then?

It's already too late.

I stab Brannon's number into my phone and pace in a tight circle around my desk, Mari still quiet on the other end of the call.

"I'm going to talk to him," I promise. "You focus on locking your doors and keeping the lights on, okay?"

"Okay," she whispers, and I switch lines.

The phone rings. And rings. And—

"Brannon."

Flat. Disinterested. Like I've interrupted his midmorning sudoku.

"It's Poppy Hartwell, ADA," I snap. "We need to talk about Mariela Castillo's case. Now."

Long pause. "Didn't realize we were still spinning our wheels on that one."

Sebastian looks up from his phone, eyes narrowing like a cat spotting something beneath the fridge, and stage-whispers toward me without missing a beat:

"And I didn't realize assholes came in beige and incompetence."

Then he goes back to editing as my eye twitches. I slap a smile into my voice so hard it might leave bruises.

"She's being followed. She's receiving anonymous texts with photos of her walking alone. Someone knocked on her bedroom window last night. And your official response is wheel-spinning?"

"She hasn't report any direct threats," he replies, voice dripping with apathy. "We can't jump every time someone gets nervous."

I blink. "She's not nervous, Detective. She's being hunted. There's a difference."

"Until he makes contact, we can't act. No restraining order violation. No actionable offense."

My jaw drops. "Oh, sweet buttermilk tap-dancing Jesus— are you serious right now?"

He exhales like I'm the inconvenience in this story. "Ma'am—"

"Ma'am?"

"Oh, he did not just." Sebastian locks his phone screen now, fully attentive.

"Unless you're about to follow that with 'you were absolutely right and here's a fleet of patrol cars,' I'd suggest you choose another noun."

"Period." My personal hype squad of one cheers me on in loud whispers.

"You're emotional."

I stop pacing. Go still.

Sebastian gasps. Hand to chest.

"Do you know what I am, Detective Brannon?" I ask, calm as can be.

"A woman trying to prevent a second attack that will land on *your* desk if you keep ignoring what's right in front of you. And when it does? I will make sure every inch of that blood is traced back to the fingerprints you didn't lift. The leads you didn't follow. The bare minimum you couldn't be bothered to do."

Silence.

Then, finally:

"If something happens, tell her to call it in."

That's it. That's his answer.

I don't even say goodbye. I just hang up.

Hard.

The phone hits the desk with a bang and skids into my stapler. My rosé sloshes, and so help me, if it had spilled on my blouse, I'd be filing a second criminal report today.

"Fiddlesticks!" I hiss, grabbing the edge of the desk. "Fiddlesticks and flaming fudge rockets!"

Because what I want to say is too unladylike for my lipstick.

"Do we need shovels for bodies or martinis?" Sebastian is ready for anything. Always. No questions.

"Both." I stare down at the desk, breath hitching. My hand is shaking from the adrenaline.

I blow out a sharp exhale through my nose and tap back to Mari's line.

She picks up instantly. "Poppy?"

"I'm here." I soften my voice, smoothing the edges like a fraying hem. "Listen, honey, it's Friday night. Courthouse is closed until Monday, which means the legal system is basically on vacation unless someone gets murdered."

"Great," she mumbles.

"I'm not saying that for drama—I'm saying it because I need you somewhere safe until I can do something more permanent."

She goes quiet again.

"Can you get to a hotel?" I ask gently. "Something close by, maybe a place with cameras in the lobby. Somewhere with staff, lights, witnesses. Give me the weekend. I'll be the first one through the courthouse doors Monday morning."

"Mmm," Sebastian mutters, going back to editing his Tics with a disbelieving shake of his head. "Tragic."

There's a long pause, then a rustle—she's moving, I think.

"Yeah," she says finally. "There's a Holiday Inn off Canal. My mom used to stay there when she visited. I can go there tonight."

"Good. That's good." I nod like she can hear it. "Book the room. I'll work on drafting a protective order. I'll file it the minute the clerk turns on the lights Monday."

"Thank you," she whispers. It's fragile. Like everything inside her is one more scare away from breaking.

I try to smile, try to put warmth in my voice. "Go pack a bag. Something cozy. Grab that pink hoodie with the wine stain you pretend not to love."

"Pink is *your* color, Poppy." There's a little bit of that bite still in there.

"Pink is everyone's color, if they are only brave enough to handle it."

She laughs—a little. Barely. But it's enough. I give her the information to send the charges to the DA's office. Demand she order room service ice cream and text me when she gets in her room.

We hang up.

And just like that, the silence rushes in.

I stare at the phone for a moment longer, thumb hovering over the call screen like I might dial her back just to say something else. Anything else.

But there's nothing left to say. Not that'll make this okay.

Across the room, Sebastian doesn't speak. He just clicks his phone shut and slides it aside, his expression softer than I've seen it all day.

He doesn't try to fix it or deflect with sass—he just lets the quiet exist, lets me breathe through it without filling the air.

He walks over, sets my wine glass a little closer to me, and squeezes my shoulder.

Once. Firm. Solid.

I place my hand over his and lean my cheek on it.

She's scared. She's alone. But, she's alive.

For now.

And the worst part?

I don't know if that last part is going to stay true.

3

Poppy

I shouldn't be this distracted behind the wheel.

But here I am—hands at ten and two, eyes on the road, thoughts three blocks behind and spiraling.

Mari hasn't texted. Not since yesterday.

She made it to the hotel Friday night. Kept me posted yesterday. Today? Quiet.

I'm not sure if I should message her. Maybe a selfie with room service and a snarky caption like "five-star paranoia on a two-star budget."

Something to let me know she's okay.

But it's been radio silence.

I check my phone at the red light—no calls. No texts.

"Oh, bananas. This isn't good."

Sebastian's voice filters through the speakers like a glitter-scented breeze. "Still nothing from Mari?"

"Not a peep," I murmur, drumming the wheel. "It's been four days. She was scared. Now—just silent."

"She could be resting. Regrouping with reality TV and waterproof eye masks," he offers.

"Or she could be dead in a ditch, and I missed the signs," I snap. Then sigh. "Sorry. Keep telling me about your date."

"Uh-uh, Miss Ma'am," he says. "Terrified clients outrank me guzzling two fabulous dicks last night. I'm here to listen and look fabulous."

My car idles beside a man walking his dog, a fogged-up bodega, teens laughing on a stoop. Everything looks normal.

And yet it all feels off.

Like I'm watching a slow-motion car crash, just waiting for the sound.

"I just... the system failed her," I whisper. "Just like it failed my mom."

And me.

I don't think about it often—what I am.

The product of an assault.

My sperm donor was charged, saw court and then walked free.

She was sixteen. He was twenty-one.

The DA said it was a misunderstanding.

Said she probably *liked* the attention an older man was giving her.

She was blamed. Accused, right alongside the man who violated her, beat her and then walked out free.

She smiled through it anyway. Built a life and raised me with more love than I deserved.

To be her sunshine on her rainy days.

But the cracks are still there. Quiet, deep and waiting.

Just like Mari's.

"Oh, sweetheart..." Sebastian murmurs.

My grip tightens. "Things that should never happen keep happening. Different year. Different face. Same darn outcome."

"You're going to change that," Sebastian says. "You already are."

I don't answer. I just pull up in front of Mom's house in Queens and cut the engine.

The windows fog from the warmth inside. I sit, watching her curtains flutter. Feeling the helplessness settle like a second skin.

"I'm here," I tell him.

"Go eat something carby and hug the woman who made you fierce," he says. "If you need me later, I'll be here. Practicing my deep-throating and looking legally devastating."

I smile. For real this time. "Thanks, Bastian."

"Anytime, Counselor. Now go be adored."

I grab the peach pie I picked up—because I couldn't show up empty-handed, and Mom will notice if I look like I haven't eaten—and head upstairs.

She opens the door before I knock.

"Took you long enough," she says, smiling as she pulls me into a hug that smells like roasted garlic and moisturizer.

"I brought pie," I say, muffled into her shoulder.

She steps back, eyes narrowing just enough to clock something. "You're pale."

"I'm always pale."

"You're pale like something's bothering you."

I brush past her. "I'm fine, Mom."

Her place is tidy, of course. Cozy but not cluttered—books stacked on the radiator shelf, a half-done puzzle on the coffee table. The scent of dinner—meatballs, maybe eggplant— grounds me.

We've never been big on traditions. No matching aprons. No themed table settings.

But Sunday supper? Non-negotiable.

For a few hours, we pretend the world isn't broken.

She dishes food while I set the table, both of us falling into rhythm. I try not to bring up work.

But when my phone buzzes for the fifth time and it's another spam email—still no Mari—I feel her eyes on me.

Mom doesn't speak right away. Just sips her water and watches me over the rim, gauging how hard to push.

"Is it the girl?"

I freeze.

She always knows.

"What girl?" I ask, cutting into a meatball with too much focus.

Her brows lift. "The girl you've been avoiding since you walked in like someone torched your favorite organizer."

I stare at my plate, trying to lie to someone who literally made my face. It's impossible.

I sigh, setting my fork down.

"Her name's Mari. She's a victim in a trial that got thrown out this week."

Mom's expression stays steady, but something dims behind her eyes.

"And she's in danger now," she says.

"She got a restraining order. But he's still around. Sending photos. The police say it's not actionable."

"Of course they did."

No bitterness. Just fact.

I nod, looking down, suddenly five years old again—helpless.

"I don't know what to do," I whisper. "The law won't protect her until something happens. Something—"

I stop. Like saying it would tempt fate.

She reaches across the table and takes my hand.

"You can't save everyone, Pops."

"I know," I whisper. "But I want to save her."

She squeezes. Softer:

"Then do what you have to."

That should be the end. A permission-granted moment you tuck away.

But her words open a door I've kept bolted.

Because I've heard them before.

Not in court but from her. Something always unspoken when I was younger.

She was tired in a way I didn't understand then.

Always watching windows. Always packing.

I thought we were adventurers. Turns out, we were just running.

We had moved seven times before I was nine.

New apartments. New schools.

Always after something happened like a midnight call. A man staring too long at the grocery store.

Back then, the rules were simple:

Don't answer the phone.

Don't talk to strangers.

And never tell anyone your mom was sixteen when she had you.

We lived on edge, like a horror movie stuck in the quiet part before the scream.

And still, he found us.

Her rapist.

My father.

No one used his name. At least never in front of me.

He wasn't a person, really. More like a shadow.

He'd call her job and leave voicemails. Show up at the store and just... watch. Nothing "actionable." Nothing the cops could do.

They said, *We can't help if he hasn't done anything.*

Sound familiar?

I used to wake up to her crying in the kitchen. Whispering into the phone. Holding ice to her jaw—even when there wasn't a bruise. Like memory alone could make it ache.

And then... it stopped.

No more calls.

No more letters.

No more fear in her eyes when the doorbell rang.

I was ten. And even then, I knew better than to ask.

Now, sitting across from her, watching the worry she tries to hide, I wonder if she made it stop.

If she did what the system never would.

I don't know what pulls the thought forward.

Maybe it's the quiet between dinner and dishes.

Maybe it's the towel she keeps folding like her hands need purpose.

Or maybe it's the weight of this week—this loss, this mistrial—pressing too hard against what I thought I could carry.

I drift inward.

Back to the thing I pretend I've made peace with.

I never asked much about him.

When I was young, I got the basics.

He was older. She was fifteen. He hurt her.

And somehow, she survived.

When I was a teen, I searched the internet.

As a lawyer, I pulled everything—transcripts, redacted photos, the case file.

One image stays with me.

His booking photo—shirtless, defiant, arms tensed like he still had control.

But it was his chest that held me.

Red scratch marks scattered like a confession.

I counted them. Not out of morbid curiosity. Not for vengeance.

Because I needed to know.

One hundred seventy-three.

That's how many I could see.

My mother—gentle, private, fierce—fought like she knew she'd die otherwise.

And still, he walked free.

That image didn't just stay in my memory. It lodged deeper.

Somewhere behind my ribs, where rage simmers and purpose waits.

I glance at her now, sipping lukewarm tea like it's just another Sunday.

And before I can stop myself, I ask the question I never dared voice.

"Why did he stop?"

She stills.

No flinch. No jolt. Just a quiet pulling inward, like she's bracing for something heavy.

Her mug clinks against the counter. She doesn't look at me.

When she finally speaks, her voice is careful. Measured.

But something colder lives beneath it.

"The system wasn't there for me," she says, fingers laced tight. "I did everything right. Filed reports. I documented everything. Called the police. We moved and changed numbers so many times.

I followed every step they said would keep us safe."

She exhales slowly but doesn't finish. The silence stretches —heavy, humming.

"One day I realized… no one was coming. Not a badge, not a court, not a neighbor. And sometimes…" Her gaze lifts, meeting mine but not quite landing. "Sometimes women just have to help themselves."

The words settle like dust—slow but unshakable.

"You do whatever you have to," she adds, softer. "To survive. Protect the people you love. Make it stop."

That last part lands differently.

To make it stop.

The chill creeps in—not from her voice, but from what builds underneath.

He harassed her for a decade until she was twenty-six and I was ten.

And then—nothing.

No more voicemails. No more shadows outside our window.

Just… silence.

I used to believe, in that innocent way kids do, that he moved on. That we were safe.

But maybe it wasn't that simple.

Maybe my mama—my fighter—went to battle in a way she never admitted. Did something to keep me safe.

"Honey?" she murmurs, tilting her head. "Are you all right?"

I try to smile, but something swells behind my ribs—hot, aching, and grateful.

Suddenly I just need a hug.

And like always, she knows. She opens her arms.

"I just… I love you," I manage, words catching as I wrap my arms around her. "For everything. For who you are."

She brushes my hair back, tucks it behind my ear like she did when I was little.

"I know," she says. "I love you too."

We don't talk about it after that.

Instead, we clear the table—stacking dishes, wiping counters, listening to the dishwasher hum like part of the family.

By the time we migrate to the living room, *Law & Order SVU* is halfway through, and Mom's setting up the dominoes like we haven't just circled the most earth-shattering conversation of our lives.

When the next episode starts, I can't help it—I dance.

I've been shimmying to that theme song since I was seven, convinced Olivia Benson was a superhero.

Mom throws a kitchen towel at me like she always does.

Some things never change.

We play three rounds of dominos and she wins two.

I accuse her of stacking the boneyard; she calls me a sore loser.

For a while, it feels simple again.

Normal.

Safe.

She disappears during a commercial and returns with two slices of peach pie and scoops of vanilla-bean ice cream already melting.

And that's when it hits me.

To make it stop.

She said it like a fact.

Like gravity.

You do whatever you have to—to survive.

To protect the ones you love.

To make it stop.

The phrase lingers. Humming beneath her smile, behind the clink of dessert plates, under the swell of the *SVU* music.

I stare down at the pie.

It's golden and perfect. Flaky crust, ice cream melting into the syrupy filling.

My fork hovers in midair because my brain is sprinting somewhere I hadn't let it go.

I thought she meant it metaphorically.

Now?

I'm not so sure.

There are only two reasons that man would've stopped harassing her.

And I've already ruled out prison.

He never went back.

I looked. When I started at the DA's office, I pulled his name from the archives. Warrants. Arrests. Parole violations. Nothing.

He just... disappeared.

But maybe I'd been looking in the wrong place.

Still holding my fork, I quietly pick up my phone, tilt it out of Mom's eyeline, and open a browser tab.

I type his name.

Add "death." and hold my breath.

It's not an obituary. No paragraph about being loved or hiking. Just one line.

"Deceased. Record closed."

My blood goes cold.

It's not just that he died.

It's *when.*

The year he vanished. The year the calls stopped. The year Mom started sleeping through the night.

It matches.

Right down to the very season.

I set my fork down carefully, like it might shatter.

My mother is humming beside me, flipping channels.

She doesn't know I'm unraveling beside her.

But the words echo.

You do whatever you have to.

To survive. To protect the people you love. To make it stop.

I stare at the screen. At his name. At *deceased.*

And clarity settles like ice water through my chest.

She did it.

She made it stop.

And I finally understand.

My mother—my foundation, my safe place—killed the man who raped her.

And got away with it.

4
Poppy

I haven't stopped thinking about it for days.

My mother—my soft-spoken, book-reading, cardigan-wearing, cross-stitching mother—is a killer.

Not theoretically. Not *could've.*

Literally.

She killed Colton Rhodes.

I found the death notice after midnight, in my pajamas, lying in bed. I started with the usual rabbit holes—criminal databases, court records, Google with too many quotation marks.

At first, nothing.

Then I found it.

Colton Rhodes. Deceased.

Throat slit.

Found in his apartment after neighbors complained about the smell.

No big investigation. No media circus. No DA outrage. He lived in East Flatbush, where most murders get chalked up to gang activity and quietly disappear.

But this wasn't random.

He was bound—tied so he couldn't fight back.

Multiple stab wounds. Deliberate and fueled by fury.

Whoever did it wanted him to feel it.

Brushing my hair, it still feels surreal.

My mother—who made vanilla ice cream yesterday and served me pie with a hurricane-calming smile—killed a man.

And got away with it.

What the fiddlesticks?

The thought's taken up full-time residence in my skull, rearranging mental furniture while I try to focus.

Spoiler: I can't.

Which is probably why I'm up too early for a sane person.

I reach for my deep-pink sheath dress—the one that fits like a glove and says, *I'm the whole package.*

I add heels, a gold-buckled belt, and my signature scent—sugared citrus and quiet devastation.

My coffee timer beeps as I finish my liner and my brownstone fills with the smell of dark roast and cinnamon. I pour a mug, add sugar, syrup, creamer.

I should be panicking, but I'm not.

I'm steady.

The prosecutor in me replays the crime, thinking through how she would have done it.

Did she drug him? Catch him sleeping? Knock him out?

Then, what would her defense be?

A violent rape followed by years of harassment. A child to protect.

But the binding. The overkill and the slashed throat.

That would be hard to justify.

I grab my purse, files, and head out.

Halfway down the stoop, I check my phone again. Still no reply from Mari.

The signs are escalating and her fear is no longer theo-retical.

It's real and it's here.

It's crawling under her skin—and mine.

Four days ago, she went back to her apartment for her laptop and work badge—forgotten in her rush to leave.

She was there only minutes but froze when she found a pile of cigarette butts on the fire escape.

She called me after hearing something. A note slid under the door.

I still remember the way you tasted.

Mari was hysterical. I stayed on the line while two uniforms escorted her to her car.

Then, two nights ago at the hotel—her voice trembling beneath false bravado.

"I didn't put the 'Do Not Disturb' sign on the door."

That was all she said at first. But I heard the unraveling. She'd left early for work—late, exhausted, barely holding it together. Came back to find the sign dangling from the handle.

That red plastic tag screaming the true message: *I was inside.*

She got the manager and asked they accompany her inside. She waited by the door until they came up and went in with her.

It was empty—but not untouched.

Her suitcase was repacked—clothes folded too neatly. Cosmetics moved from the right side of the counter to the left. Hangers turned the opposite direction. Everything was intentional.

He was telling her, he'd been there. And he'd taken his time.

That was two days ago.

Yesterday, she didn't answer.

Not on her cell. Not at work.

Voicemail went straight to the generic carrier message.

Which is how I find myself here, in front of her apartment, one hand curled around my keychain pepper spray as I stare are her partially open apartment door.

My pulse spikes as I push it gently with my knuckle and it creaks inward.

"Mari?" I call, stepping inside.

No answer.

I ease the door open, avoiding contact, every step a silent prayer this isn't what I think it is. That she's asleep. Out. Forgot her phone.

But it's on the kitchen counter, right where she'd have dropped it if she'd come in.

Except she's not here.

The apartment is too still and eerily so.

It feels tense. Like the whole apartment building is holding its collective breath.

I scan slowly, heart pounding.

The blinds are drawn as morning light slices across the floor.

There's no struggle. No broken glass. No blood.

But something's wrong. I can feel it.

"Mari?" I call again, louder.

Still nothing.

I move toward the hallway, pepper spray clenched, listening.

The floor creaks under my heels—then, faintly, a sharp, strangled sound.

A sob that makes me freeze.

"Mari?" I say, softer now. "It's me. It's Poppy. Are you

here?"

A shuffle. Fabric against tile. Another choked sound.

"Bathroom," she manages.

I find the door at the hall's end. Closed and locked.

I press my palm to the wood, voice gentle, coaxing.

"It's me, okay? Just me. I'm here."

Silence.

"I need you to unlock the door. Please."

After a moment, I hear the faintest click on the other side of the door and it opens.

There she is, curled in the bathroom corner, knees to her chest, back against the tile wall. Her makeup's smudged, her clothes are wrinkled, and her hands are shaking.

She doesn't look up. Just says, barely audible, "He—he."

I crouch slowly, careful not to spook her, and wrap my arms around her.

"It's okay," I whisper. "Take your time."

She buries her face in my shoulder and lets out a sound that cracks me open—fear and exhaustion tangled into one.

"I was in the shower." She swallows. "When I got out... there was a used condom on the counter."

My stomach drops.

"There was a note," she adds, blinking fast. "It said—" She falters. "It said, *you look good naked.*"

Every part of me goes still.

"Where is it?" I ask, voice steady.

She points to the trash can. I open it and see the unrolled condom. A crumpled note with it.

I bite the inside of my cheek until I taste copper.

She hugs her knees, voice unraveling.

"I heard him. Coming in then leaving. He walked up to the

door more than once. I could hear him breathing. He leaned in... like he was trying to smell me through the crack."

I squeeze my eyes shut for half a second. I can't lose it now. Mari needs someone strong for her.

"He made something in the kitchen," she adds, voice flat. "I heard the microwave. Plates. Silverware. Then nothing. For hours. I thought he was still out there, waiting. Waiting to see how long it would take me to break. To come out."

I lower myself and take her hand.

"You did everything right," I tell her. "You stayed safe. You stayed hidden. And now you're not alone."

She nods, mechanical.

And I know this is only the beginning.

He's not just stalking her.

He's hunting her.

And he's not rushing. He's savoring this.

"Okay," I say gently. "I'm going to make some calls."

She doesn't stop me. Just curls tighter as I slip out.

First: security.

I step into the hall, grab my phone, and call an emergency locksmith. New deadbolts. Double key. Chain lock. Discreet install. I want it sealed tighter than Fort Knox before sundown.

Then the alarm company. Her place isn't monitored—yet. By morning, it will be. I override the wait period not caring about the rush fee.

I head to my car, pop the trunk, and pull a Ziploc and gloves from one of the stocked boxes. Judge me when you live in this city and have OCD.

Back upstairs, Mari sits with her arms around her knees, rocking.

I don't speak.

Just glove up, lift the condom from the trash using a tissue, and seal it in the bag.

"I'm calling someone to pick this up," I tell her. "He probably didn't leave DNA—but we'll try."

She doesn't answer, but her jaw clenches. Soon, her aunt arrives and I can breathe easier knowing someone is here with her.

He's wearing her down.

That's the point.

He's not trying to kill her—yet.

He wants her to wish she were dead first.

Travis Gannon is a serial rapist. I see the pattern.

The women are spaced out—just enough. But once I connected the dots, it was obvious.

He hunts in three-month cycles near his buddy's apartment.

He hunts women he often sees alone. No children, and no pets so he can live out his fantasy.

The pattern is not in the women but in what he does at the scene. It's something specific. Probably from his childhood. His abusive father and the mother that didn't protect him.

And she is the one he blames.

He makes them cook for him. Yells at them before he beats them. Ties them up and rapes them.

After he cleans, he loosens the bindings—not enough to escape. Just enough to give hope.

And I realized why: He wants to watch.

He said he liked Chase's apartment for the view but it's not the bridge or the city.

Travis returns to his friends' apartment and goes out onto the balcony. He waits and listens for sirens.

He wants to witness the aftermath and feel the power of what he did.

Since his arrest—since posting bail—there haven't been any new assaults.

He's starving.

And men like Travis don't manage hunger.

He'll escalate. Evolve.

He'll kill.

If we don't stop him—if I don't—Mari may be first.

I text one of the few officers I trust to collect the evidence.

Back in the car, Mari as safe as I can make her, I drive to my mom's and dial Benjamin.

He answers with a sigh I can hear through Bluetooth.

"What now?"

"Please," I say. "One patrol car. Parked outside her building. Just tonight. I'll owe you big."

He pauses and I hear him tapping his fingers, thinking about what it would cost him to tell me no.

Finally he lets out a huff. "I'll see what I can do."

"Thank you."

I hang up as I pull onto Mom's street.

The sky is soft—cotton clouds and golden light, like the world doesn't know someone's out there planning to destroy a girl trying to survive.

I kill the engine and close my eyes.

Mari is alive.

For now.

But if I blink—if I breathe wrong—she won't be.

And I finally get it.

The system isn't broken, it's slow.

And Travis Gannon is not.

When Mari needs help, the law won't get there in time.

5
Poppy

I come bearing emergency annotation tabs and emotional damage.

The annotation tabs are for my mom's book club—color-coded little rectangles of joy that she swears by for keeping track of plot twists, foreshadowing, and the exact paragraph where she decided a character deserved to die.

She called earlier in full-blown panic mode, claiming her last pink tab betrayed her and curled at the corner.

So naturally, I stopped by the office supply store on my way over.

Because if there's one thing I understand, it's the importance of good stationery.

She meets me at the door still in her pajamas and bathrobe. That means she picked up her book this morning and probably only put it down to answer the door.

"You brought them!" she gasps, snatching the little packet from my hand like it's an organ transplant.

"I live to serve," I say, holding up a second pack. "Bonus yellows. And limited-edition dragon-scale ones. You're welcome."

She gives me that look—the one she used when I was ten

and brought home a glittered-up diorama of the Boston Tea Party—and pulls me into a quick side-hug.

But the moment she gets a good look at my face, her smile wavers.

"It's that client again, isn't it?" she asks gently, ushering me inside.

I don't answer. I just make a beeline for the kitchen, drop my bag onto the bench, and fold like a lawn chair over the marble counter.

The stone is cool. Soothing. Emotionally supportive, like an expensive therapist with zero judgment.

"Yes," I mumble into the countertop. "It's Mariela."

Mom doesn't ask for details. Not yet. She knows better than to crowd the story.

Instead, she hums softly, opens the fridge, and starts assembling a sandwich. Ham, sharp cheddar, lettuce, tomato—light mayo, no mustard. Diagonal cut, obviously. I'm not an uncultured savage. It hits the plate like a love letter from the universe.

I wasn't even hungry.

But I eat it.

Between bites, I talk.

I tell her about the hotel. The note. The condom. My fear.

And the worst part?

How powerless I feel. Like I'm screaming into a canyon and the only thing echoing back is paperwork.

Mom doesn't interrupt. She just pours me a glass of sparkling water with lemon, like hydration might stop my brain from spiraling.

When I don't talk for a while, she pats my hand, trying to move the heavy burden from my shoulders, if only for a little while.

"Come to book club with me." There's a hopeful sparkle

in her blue eyes that makes me hesitate. But who are we kidding? She never leaves the house, so if Mom invites me out... I'm going.

"Are you still reading about the dark fae prince with blue skin who broods for a living?" I roll my eyes. It's fairy smut.

Which, from what I can tell, is 90 percent smoldering eye contact, 10 percent plot, and one very horny prince who may or may not be made of shadows.

But she loves it. And that's what matters.

"Yes. But it's his cousin who is the real star of the court."

Mmm, right.

"The raven?"

"Crow." She corrects, walking back into her room to change clothes.

We head out together, and I try to be present. I try not to check my phone every five minutes. I try not to let my brain slide back into the echo chamber of what-ifs that have taken up residence behind my eyes.

Sebastian helps some, sending me pictures of his possible date outfits as he gets ready for his millionth first date of the year.

But somewhere between the driveway and the start of the book discussion, I start biting the inside of my cheek.

Same spot. Over and over. Sharp, repetitive. Familiar.

Then I'm scratching at my scalp—a nervous, rhythmic twitch at the edge of my hairline.

It's not until Mom gently places her hand over mine and gives me the look—the one that's halfway between a warning and a hug—that I snap out of it.

Right. Tics are back.

OCD flares when the stress hits a certain pitch.

I take a slow breath and reach for the silver dollar in my

purse—the one I've kept since law school. Worn smooth along the edges. Just the right weight.

I start rolling it across my knuckles.

One, two, three, four, back again.

It always works. My mind slows, if only slightly, as my fingers stay busy.

I tune back into the room just in time to hear Donna ask, "Do you think he can feel with the shadows? Like... pressure? Texture?"

My soul briefly leaves my body, files a restraining order, and returns wearing noise-canceling headphones.

The room buzzes with agreement, and someone uses the phrase "strategic penetration" without even blushing.

I stare at my water glass like it might open a portal and suck me out of this reality.

Here's the thing: it's not that I hate sex. It's not even that I've sworn it off. I just... don't think about it. Not really.

I had sex a few times. In college. It was brief. Clumsy. Loud in the wrong ways. The kind of experience that makes you wish you'd just stayed home with a grilled cheese and an episode of *Forensic Files*.

My therapist says I should "explore that more"—that maybe I haven't had a positive sexual experience, so my brain defaulted to avoid. But honestly? I'm fine. I have my wine and a crime docuseries queue that's six seasons deep. I have a vibrator. I sleep great.

And growing up in a house where the word *sex* was avoided like a swear word didn't exactly create a safe space to explore it. Understandably, my mom wasn't rushing into sex talks—not when she spent the first decade of my life dragging us across the state to stay out of reach of the man who raped her.

So now, sitting in this pastel living room full of book club moms discussing how a dark prince uses sentient shadows in intimate places, I do what any self-respecting, emotionally repressed daughter would do:

I let my eyes glaze over and focus on the silver dollar in my palm.

Spin. Catch. Roll. Breathe.

One, two, three, four.

And again.

By the time we're heading back to Mom's place, I do feel a little less heavy. Not light—but less. Like I've been slowly sinking, and someone paused the descent.

That lasts about five minutes until my phone buzzes.

A text from Benjamin blows everything out of the water: *No patrols available tonight. She'll be on her own. Someone will run a check in the morning.*

The silver dollar stills in my hand. My stomach turns cold.

She may be dead by morning.

I sit in the quiet of my mom's SUV as she cuts off the engine, the overhead light turning on when she opens her door.

"She's alone," I mutter. "He's going to get her tonight, and she'll be another cold case everyone shrugs about on the six o'clock news while they microwave frozen lasagna and forget her name."

My mom makes a soft *hmm* as she unlocks her door, and we step inside her dark home. She flicks on the kitchen light, and the familiar warmth settles over everything.

This has always been home. Even though we moved constantly when I was little—always running, always hiding— once that chapter ended... once her rapist was gone, we found this place. And we never left.

The peace inside these walls has always felt earned.

Hard-won.

Safe.

But Mariela doesn't get to feel that way and she may never again.

Not while Travis Gannon is still breathing the same air as her.

I drop my bag on the counter and stare out the kitchen window, the streetlamp casting a soft orange halo over the lawn.

You do whatever you have to, my mom had said.

To make it stop.

The words echo now, curling around my thoughts like vines. Not loud. Not dramatic. Just... true.

I don't realize how quiet I've gotten until I look over and see my mom watching me. She's got one hand wrapped around a tea mug, the other resting loosely against her hip.

Eventually, she starts nodding. Like she's hearing the exact same train of thought clanging through my head.

"Keep going down that line of thinking," she says, calm as anything. "And you'll be on the right track."

I blink at her. Then exhale.

"How do you always do that? Know what I'm thinking?"

She blows on her warm tea. "Moms just know their babies."

She's right.

I can't sit around here debating shadow sex and drinking lemon water like it's a spa day while Mariela is fearing for her life.

If the police won't watch Mariela's building... then by all that's holy and hot pink, I will.

The more I think about it, the more certain I am.

I'll sit outside and watch the building. I'll keep my camera rolling and the emergency line on standby. If I catch him even lurking near her apartment, I'll call it in. He's under a restraining order. It'll be enough to bring him in.

I straighten my shoulders a little.

You do whatever you have to.

And if that means doing a stakeout to catch a stalker-rapist with his hand in the cookie jar?

Then that's exactly what I'll do.

My mom beams, that proud-little-mama look warming her whole face. She cups my cheeks like I've just told her I got into Harvard (again), kisses one of them, and says, "I'll make you some snacks, dear."

Because naturally, if you're going to stake out a predator, you shouldn't do it on an empty stomach.

I head down the hall to change into my official crime-watching uniform—hot-pink Pilates tights, a matching sports bra, and my favorite cropped zip-up.

Comfort is key when you're preparing for long stretches of moral crisis and potential felony charges.

By the time I get back to the kitchen, my mom's got half the pantry laid out on the counter.

"Mom," I say, digging through the tote bag, "I don't need all this."

"That's a protein bar for energy, that one's a granola bar because they taste better, and the chocolate is for morale," she says without turning around, still slicing fruit like we're going on a picnic.

I fish out a sandwich bag of grapes, a single-serving pack of hummus, three kinds of crackers, and... the eight-inch chef's knife.

I hold it up like it's radioactive. "What in the name of our goddess, Elle Woods, is this for?"

She doesn't even blink. "You can never be too careful, dear."

"Right," I mutter, sliding the knife back in the bag and wondering when my life started to resemble a deleted scene from *Legally Blonde* meets *Dexter*.

Outside, the streetlights flicker on, casting warm pools of light across the pavement. It's that dusky hour where every-thing feels slow and suspended—like the night's holding its breath, waiting for something to go wrong.

I zip up my jacket, toss the tote over my shoulder, and grab my car keys from the hook by the door.

"You'll text me when you're set up?" my mom asks, walking me out.

"Of course," I say, already bracing for the surveillance-grade check-ins I know are coming.

She hugs me tight, then smooths the side of my hair like she's trying to imprint calm into me.

"Be safe," she whispers.

I nod.

Of course, how hard could this be?

Boys do it.

6
Poppy

How hard could this be?

Boys do it.

That thought aged like milk.

Turns out, stakeouts are hard—especially when you've just dipped the last grape into the final scoop of hummus like a desperate snack goblin.

I scolded myself out loud as I washed it down with water and a pink Starburst flavor packet.

Now I have to pee.

But I can't leave. Obviously.

What if he shows the moment I duck into the 24-hour bodega to beg for access to their questionable bathroom that probably requires a key chained to a hubcap?

No. I'm committed.

So far, I've jotted down twelve license plates (two might be duplicates—I got distracted by a cat). A pigeon flapped too close and scared me.

I've received four updates from my mother, now on chapter thirty-seven of her fairy smut saga and apparently thriving.

According to her, the shadow prince can make multiple

replicas of himself—each with fully functional, anatomically accurate parts.

Of course he can.

Sebastian sent me dating profiles while on his own date. That tells you everything.

He's either asleep or mid-quickie with someone from his roster.

We couldn't be more different about sex.

Sebastian talks about it nonstop. I avoid it.

We balance each other out.

I stare out the windshield. One leg jiggling. My silver dollar flips steadily over my knuckles as I watch the apartment across the street.

Mariela's fire escape is still. No movement. No lights.

I don't know what I'm expecting.

Part of me wants him to show—just to prove I'm not losing my mind. To catch something. A threat. Evidence.

But the other part is terrified.

Because if he comes... what then?

What if he sees me?

What if he walks up, smashes the window, drags me out by the hair?

I picture it so vividly it feels like memory.

Glass shattering. Blood. Fingers knotted in my hair.

Adrenaline would hit fast. Enough to keep me silent. Enough to fight.

I'd grab the knife and swing. Hope for pain. Hope for blood.

I spiral too far into the daydream down to the exact choreography.

Low first. The thigh. Then the gut. Then maybe up—fast

and frantic—like I'm trying to erase his face from the inside out.

It's a coping mechanism.

Maladaptive daydreaming.

Most people count sheep. I choreograph trauma like ballet.

I can lose hours like this.

Tonight's lead? The eight-inch chef's knife in my passenger seat.

I pick it up and balance it between my fingers. Place the tip against my index finger and spin it in a slow circle.

It nicks me before I notice.

Just a pinprick. Barely enough to sting.

Of course it's sharp. My mother always kept this blade like a scalpel—deadly, precise.

I set it down, squeeze my finger, and watch the bead of blood rise.

The knife is old. The rest of the set long gone—lost to moves and garage sales. A sleek new block sits on her counter now.

But this one? She kept.

Which is why the thought creeps in.

What if this is the knife she used to kill Colton Rhodes?

Travis's face twists into Colton's. The autopsy report I read last night returns.

Dozens of stab wounds.

Throat slit.

Overkill.

But which came first?

She could've ended it with the throat. Quick. Efficient.

But she didn't. She kept going.

This is a classic question of the chicken-or-the-egg.

Except the chicken is a dead man, and the egg is my mom's trauma-fueled rage.

If I had to bet: she slit his throat, then stabbed until nothing remained of her fear.

Until the girl who ran was gone and only the woman who survived remained.

That's how I'd do it.

Not quite as messy.

My phone chimes and I jump, nearly launching the knife into the cupholder.

It's my mother.

> MOM: Goodnight, dear! Just finished chapter 49. The shadow prince split into six copies… simultaneously. Use your imagination.

What a wholesome way to end the evening—knowing my sweet, cardigan-wearing mother is winding down with a supernatural orgy.

I set the phone down like it just told me Santa isn't real and also sex is weird now.

The dash clock reads 4:02 a.m.

Three more hours.

I can do this.

Probably.

Maybe.

The street is dead quiet. My eyes gritty, my legs are asleep and my bladder is screaming.

I'll close my eyes for one second.

Just one second.

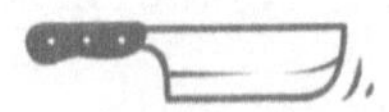

The knock on my window nearly sends my soul into orbit.

I jolt upright with a scream so sharp it startles me.

My elbow hits the door, my knee bangs the wheel, and I blindly grab the first thing I can—

An opened pack of multigrain crackers.

I throw them with the energy of a woman who's had too many shadow prince updates and not enough sleep.

They explode across my dash, lap, and dignity.

These crumbs will haunt me.

I blink to clear the surreal transition from sleep to panicked wake. A parking enforcement officer stares through the glass.

Early forties. Chewing her gum with her whole jaw. Existential crisis energy.

"You can't sleep here, hon."

Ma'am, I am one granola bar and a legal loophole away from total collapse.

I roll the window down a sliver. "Not sleeping. Just... conducting neighborhood surveillance."

She raises an eyebrow. "I don't care."

I point to my tote. "I'm a lawyer."

She pops her gum. "I still don't care."

Well.

Who tinkled in her Lucky Charms?

She walks off without another word, her reflective vest swaying like a judgmental highlighter. I slump back—then bolt upright as panic socks me in the sternum.

Mariela.

Sprinkle-covered snickerdoodles! I fell asleep.

What if something happened? What if I missed it?

Nope. No spiraling.

I toss the knife into my tote, shove open the door, already dialing as I cross the street.

It rings.

No answer.

My heart climbs into my throat—

And then—bless the color pink—she walks out the door, head down, checking her phone.

"Mariela!" I say her name too brightly. Too loudly.

"Poppy? What are you doing here?"

Well, for one—*I'm hiding a murder knife in my tote.*

For two—I lie.

"Oh! I was just... on my way to Pilates," I say, gesturing to my hot-pink leggings like I'm totally normal. "Thought maybe you wanted a ride to work?"

She tilts her head, then smiles, clearly relieved. "That would be amazing."

She climbs in. I exhale like I've just come back from the dead.

And it's chaos in here.

Crumbs. An open protein bar on the floorboard. A cracker perched on the dash like it stood night watch.

My license plate notepad fell on the floorboard and creased several of the pages. I'll have to rewrite it.

Also—I still have to pee.

Regret. So much regret.

"Oh my gosh—I'm so sorry," I say, scrambling to gather wrappers. "There was... a rogue squirrel. Climbed in through the sunroof and went for the snacks. You know how those squirrels are."

I sound ridiculous.

She laughs. "It's fine. My car's a mobile recycling bin. I've got six bottles and at least two cups I'm scared to open."

I release a nervous chuckle but I still want to vacuum my soul.

The ride isn't what I expect.

Mariela looks... fresh.

Her hair is smooth. Her blouse neatly pressed and her lip gloss is glossing like never before.

She looks like a woman starting over.

Like she slept.

At a red light, I sneak a glance and exhale a sacred sigh of pride.

It's working.

The locks. The alarm. The totally illegal stakeout.

I'm showing up and telling her she's not alone. That we're not going down without a fight.

After drop-off, I text Benjamin I'll be in late.

He replies: *bring coffee.*

I ignore it.

I'm a prosecutor. Not his barista.

By the time I get home, my bladder is full-on rioting and I barely make it to the bathroom.

The mirror shows a woman who lost a fight with granola—and sleep.

But twenty minutes later, I'm showered, dressed, and armed with under-eye patches that are going to work overtime today.

I spritz my custom perfume blend across my neck—one wrist, then the other. Two sprays. Always two.

The scent hits and something clicks into place.

Like flipping a switch from chaos to competence.

This is my battle armor. My signal to my brain that the time for spiraling is over.

The thoughts settle and the panic quiets.

Focus mode: activated.

On my way out, I text Mom a quick good-luck message:

> POPPY: Hope your shadow prince brings extra clones today. Tell that crow cousin to stop brooding and get therapy. 🖤 🪶

She sends back a winking emoji and the words *Chapter fifty-four is getting spicy.*

So glad for you, Mom.

The courthouse looms ahead like it always does—all heavy stone and judgment. I climb the steps, already mentally organizing my files for today's lineup.

And then I hear *that* voice.

Low. Warm. Rough like gravel wrapped in velvet.

"Fuck you, Rourke. Eat dog shit." He passes me with his phone pressed to his ear, not missing a beat. "Morning, Counselor."

Holy forearm muscles, Batman.

He spoke to me.

He *actually* spoke to me.

Warm chills run down my spine, straight through my blazer, short-circuiting every sensible thought I had queued for the day.

Detective Declan Blackwood.

The only thing more unsettling than a stakeout, a knife, and a nearly-missed victim—

Is him.

I open my mouth to respond—something cool, something sharp.

TGIF, am I right?

Instead, I choke on my own spit.

Like a professional.

I cough violently, humiliate myself in stereo, and speed-walk past the security checkpoint, eyes locked on the floor and cheeks the same shade as my blush-pink pantsuit.

Please, Hair Gods, let my split end prevention payoff to distract from the fact that I just drooled over a homicide detective.

We met last year during the Watson case. He testified.

It was probably the worst case I ever worked.

The ones with kids usually are.

But my case was solid and so was Declan's testimony. The man will never walk free again.

His wife was devoted to the very end. Until she was found hanging by her neck in their house. She had been there about two weeks before someone called in the smell.

Suicide note was practically a love letter to the monster.

I'll never understand it.

I may or may not have replayed Declan's direct examination... more times than someone with two functioning brain cells should admit.

Everyone at the DA's office knows him.

So do all the women. If the water cooler talk is to be believed. But I'm not judging.

He's tall, tan, and terrifyingly competent. I'm sure... in many ways.

Black clothes. Green eyes like glass in sunlight. Hair that looks like it was styled by flirty demons that would wink at you.

And that mouth.

Filthy. The actual kind. F-bombs, low growls, and threats like *Try me again and I'll make you wish you'd chosen tax fraud.*

I once heard him say that. I had to excuse myself and scream into a folder.

But on the rare occasion that I find myself in his vicinity? I forget how to breathe. I start to rethink that celibacy thing and have... other thoughts.

It's not my fault. He's just so brooding.

He's basically my mother's grumpy fae prince, if the fae were armed, tattooed, and emotionally constipated.

Five o'clock shadow: perfect.

Scowl: weaponized.

Sleeves: always rolled just enough to raise the collective blood pressure of the DA's office.

I've never once seen him smile like a normal person. Maybe once, at a vending machine, when two Snickers bars dropped at the same time. But it could've been gas.

And that man just told his lieutenant to eat dog poopie and called me *Counselor* in the same breath.

So yeah. I choked on my spit.

But that's fine. I'm fine.

Totally fine.

I press the elevator button like I don't have sweaty palms. There is no time for fangirling when I have a rapist to catch.

7
Poppy

As soon as I step off the elevator, Benjamin is there—arms crossed, brow raised, mugless.

"Coffee?" he grunts.

That's it. Not hello, not good morning, not is your client still alive, just . . . "coffee." Like a raccoon demanding tribute.

He looks at the two cups in my hands, knowing neither is for him.

I arch a brow and keep walking. "No patrols. No coffee."

My tone is sweet. My nose is in the air. My irritation is very much on display.

He falls into step beside me, exhaling like I personally created the staffing shortage.

Sebastian can sense my presence in the office and emerges from his. Both hands out, flexing his fingers, saying, "Gimme, gimme," until his hot caramel macchiato is in his hands.

"Poppy, you know the precinct is short-staffed and can't just give up uniforms when we say jump. Especially when there's no active case."

"D-rama-a," Sebastian sings out, continuing into my office.

I stop just short of my office door and turn to face him. "There is an active case. There's a victim who's been stalked, harassed, threatened, and terrorized in her own home. Her attacker is escalating. That sounds pretty active to me."

He shifts his weight, jaw tight. "You know what I mean. There's no formal filing. No judge is going to approve protective measures without new charges."

I hold his stare, heat simmering low beneath my rib cage. "So, we wait until she's dead? That's the plan? We keep our hands clean while he tears her life apart and then send her mom a condolence fruit basket?"

"Poppy—"

"No. I want this documented." I take a breath, low and controlled. "I want her most recent report entered and attached to the original case. I want it escalated with precinct contact, and I want her dirty condom and note analyzed today. She deserves to feel like someone gives a crapola."

"Preach, Diva," Sebastian calls out from inside my office.

"Do we have to do this on a Friday?" Benjamin sighs, pinching the bridge of his nose like it'll make me disappear. "I'm one bad headline away from a desk job."

"Then I hope the story includes the part where I tried to stop another woman from becoming a statistic, but you were too worried about your coffee."

We stare at each other a second longer—me, with the fire of a thousand unpaid internships behind my eyes; him, with the weariness of a man who used to care but misplaced it somewhere between budget meetings and bottled antacids.

He finally mutters, "I'll see what I can do," and walks off.

Yeah, I'm sure you will.

Sebastian's phone rings and he rolls his eyes, taking a drink of his coffee before answering. "Courts! How is my favorite socialite jailbird?"

I exhale through my nose and step into my office—my little

pink-lit sanctuary in a building that smells like anxiety and . . . nickels.

It's almost lunchtime, but I don't care. Routines don't get canceled just because the clock's ticked past its usual hour.

Lights on. Bag down. Computer on.

"Well, slay! How–ever, sweets, that many drugs on you at once could totally be taken for trafficking, and hun, orange is not your color." More coffee makes it down Sebastian's throat as he nods at whatever his client is going on about.

I cross to the window, twist the rod to open the blinds, and let in a sliver of stubborn New York daylight. The wax warmer gets switched on next—lavender and lemon zest, a scent that says we're going to pretend we have our lives together today.

I walk to the corner of my desk and greet my favorite coworker.

"Good morning, Keanu Leaves," I murmur, brushing a finger across its glossy leaf.

He's the only one I've managed to keep alive.

I used to overwater. Over-monitor. Hover like a helicopter plant parent until everything wilted out of stress or spite. But this one? I learned to back off. Give it space. Trust that sometimes, survival means letting things breathe.

And look at him now. Thriving.

"Those of us in the legal biz call that an A-1 felony."

Sebastian pauses. More nodding.

"Well, fifteen to twenty years, girlie-pop." He looks at me, shaking his head and raising his hand. "Your lip fillers won't last that long, babe."

I plop into my chair, already reaching to sort through the stack of internal mail sitting on my desk. I kick off my heels and slide into my cozy fuzzy slippers as I look through the parcels.

Sebastian keeps going with his conversation. "Yes, that is

what we want. Multiple men groveling at those diamond-pedicured feet of yours. Not multiple felony charges, so don't you dare cross the border with those, mkay?"

"Mkay. Yes, brunch when you get back, girl. Mimosas are on you though. Your retainer is almost gone. Okay. Byeeeeee." He draws out the last syllable ridiculously long before hanging up. "I do *not* get paid enough."

"Sounds fun," I tease, flipping one envelope to the back of the pile, then another.

A few standard motions, a court update, one demand letter from a defense attorney who clearly thinks he's the smartest man in the room.

And then . . . something odd.

It's not in the usual envelope. No seal. No court header.

Just my name on the front. Typed clean and precise.

I turn it over slowly, brows pulling together.

Something about it feels . . . off.

I hold up the envelope between two fingers, not quite touching it. "Did you see who dropped off internal mail today?"

"Mmm, Margot." Sebastian joins me, peeking at the letters with me. "I wish it were that new clerk. I totally scoped him checking me out Tuesday."

I put the letter down, grabbing a pair of disposable gloves from my desk drawer.

"Ooh, are your spidey-senses tingling?"

There's something in my gut. The twisty, electric kind of wrong that doesn't care about logic, and I always listen to it.

"Looks like it." I hold it up to the light with a squint.

"That just means you need to get laid, babes."

I elbow my bestie with a huff.

"You think it's dangerous?"

"No," I say quietly. "I think it's personal."

I slide a letter opener through the flap, carefully unfolding the single sheet of photo paper inside.

My heart stutters. Freezes.

It's a picture of me sleeping in my car last night.

There's no note. No caption. Just the image. Crisp. Clear. Taken from close enough to see the ominous reflection of the photographer in the door's reflection.

He was there watching me.

"Poppy."

Sebastian's voice slices through the office, all the humor gone. "What the hell is this?"

He's holding the photo. Me, asleep in my car, pita chip bag under my face like a sad little pillow. His jaw ticks. Once. Twice.

"You were watching Mariela's building?"

"Yes," I say flatly. "Since no one else would."

His gaze doesn't waver. "You fell asleep. In the dark. Alone. And—let's be honest—mid-drool."

I open my mouth to protest, but there's nothing to defend.

He exhales. "You know I joke because I love, but that photo? It's not just proof he's watching Mariela. It's proof he's watching you."

That lands harder than I want to admit.

"And I can't lose you, babe. Not to some bargain-bin psychopath with a God complex and drugstore cleanser."

I slide the photo into a sleeve, swallowing down the burn in my chest.

"Now we go smarter, not harder," he says, calmer now. "Pull on those loose threads and figure this out. Something's wrong in the system—cases falling apart, evidence vanishing. That's not random."

I nod.

Sebastian squeezes my shoulder. "Build your case like your life—and hers—depends on it."

He grabs his coffee, kisses the top of my head, and heads out.

The silence he leaves behind is louder than any lecture.

I stare at the photo again.

My face peaceful. Asleep. Unaware.

He was there, watching.

And he wanted me to know it.

I'm winding down for the night, just finishing my skincare routine with the kind of careful attention that makes me feel like I've got something under control.

A few drops of serum, a swipe of retinol, moisturizer that I'm certain is actually a magical potion.

I reach for my hair wrap, fingers poised to twist and secure it for tomorrow morning's heatless curls, when my phone dings from across the counter.

MARI: Hey Poppy, I just wanted to thank you for all you've been doing.

No emojis. No punctuation. No context.

Just a single, quiet line that lands with more weight than it should.

My thumb hovers over the keyboard, but I don't type a reply. Not yet.

Something about the message doesn't sit right with me— not because it's ungrateful or strange, but because it's... final.

Today has been strange from the start.

Waking up to wage psychological warfare with a meter maid and a sleeve of multigrain crackers.

Finding Mariela calm—too calm, considering the week she's had.

The photo on my desk that felt like someone whispering *I see you* right against the back of my neck.

My instincts are stirring again. Low. Steady.

That tight pull in my chest that tells me something's wrong, even when nothing looks it.

So instead of texting back, I press Call.

It rings.

Once.

Twice.

Three times.

Four.

Each tone echoes a little louder in my ears than the last. She just texted—she should pick up.

Finally, the line connects with a soft click.

"Poppy."

Her voice is faint, trailing like smoke.

And wrong.

Not frightened or tearful—but slow. Slurred. Empty in a way that has nothing to do with tiredness.

"I just wanted to say thank you," she says, words a little too smooth. "You believed me when no one else did."

A warning bell goes off inside me.

"Mari." My voice is sharper now, laced with panic. "Where are you? What's going on?"

She doesn't answer right away. When she does, it's in a tone I'll never forget—calm, almost gentle.

"It's just easier this way," she murmurs. "At least I get to decide what happens to me."

No. No, no, no.

"Mari—stop. Please. Just stay on the phone. Talk to me."

But she's already slipping away.

"You don't have to worry anymore, Poppy."

The silence on the line stretches for a beat that feels like a lifetime.

Then, with a softness that cuts deeper than any scream:

"Goodbye."

The call ends.

And for a moment, I forget how to move.

My whole body tightens, frozen in place as the sound of her goodbye settles like frost over everything.

The air is too still. The bathroom too quiet.

The mirror reflects me back—wide-eyed and helpless.

Somewhere deep in my chest, something breaks open.

8
Poppy

I'm a fury. A blur. A pink-sneakered hurricane tearing through the house with my phone pressed to my ear, the other hand fumbling for keys.

"911—what is your emergency?"

"My client, Mariela Castillo—I believe she's attempting suicide," I say, breath ragged. "Possible overdose. I need an ambulance dispatched immediately."

I give the address clearly—twice. "She's not responding to calls or texts. Please—she needs help now."

I don't even hear the dispatcher's reply. I'm already flying down the stairs, fingers shaking as I hit the keypad to set the alarm before the door slams.

No time to change. I'm still in my Pilates bodysuit. I throw on a jean jacket and go.

I barely remember buckling my seatbelt. Just that I'm driving like everything depends on it—because it does.

Poor Mari. I should've seen this.

The calm this morning. The fresh face.

She'd already decided and today was her goodbye.

The city blurs past. Red lights flicker like decorations I don't have time for. Tires scream through every turn.

"MOVE YOUR TUESDAY-TAKING GRANNY WAGON!" I shriek at a beige sedan. "Are you knitting socks behind the wheel?!"

I swerve around them as the car in front of me stops at a yellow light.

"ARE YOU KIDDING ME? It's not a cease-and-desist order!"

I punch the horn and fly through the intersection, catching my phone midair as it slides.

"Miss, emergency services are pulling up," the dispatcher says.

My heart's in my throat. My pulse pounds behind my teeth.

Please let me be wrong.

Minutes later, I'm rounding the last corner. Blue and red lights flash across the buildings.

My car jerks to a stop—half on the curb and I'm out before it's in park.

"Move," I bark, legs unsteady as I sprint toward the lights.

There's a stretcher and Mariela is on it, too pale.

Her lips are tinged blue and it punches the air from my lungs.

"No—Mari," I whisper, stumbling forward.

A paramedic intercepts me, hand on my arm. "Do you know this woman?"

"Yes. I'm her attorney. And her friend." My voice breaks. "I called 911."

He nods, tension softening. "She's breathing. Vitals low but stable."

I cover my mouth, knees buckling. He catches me.

"She's lucky," he says quietly. "Ten more minutes . . ."

I nod, squeezing my eyes shut as sobs shake through me.

Pressing my fingers to my temples, I breathe hard, searching for solid ground.

They wheel her toward the ambulance, and I watch like my soul is tethered to that stretcher.

"Is she going to wake up?" I ask, voice hollow.

"She will. It'll take a few hours to metabolize, but she's going to be okay."

I nod, though nothing feels okay. Not her pale face. Not the way she looks like a ghost wrapped in blankets.

The doors close and the lights spin wildly as the ambulance pulls away.

My hands still tremble, jacket crooked off one shoulder, bodysuit soaked with sweat.

Two officers linger nearby and one approaches, eyeing me.

"She yours?"

"She's my client." My voice is hoarse. "What do you need?"

He gestures toward the building. "We've started the incident report. There were empty medicine bottles on the counter but no note."

"She called me," I say quietly, arms crossed. "She said goodbye. She sounded... scared, but calm."

The officer nods grimly. "You saved her life."

No. That's not what it feels like.

I glance at the building as the streetlamps flicker on.

"I didn't do enough to keep her safe," I whisper.

He doesn't answer. Just keeps writing his report.

The street is still with only the hum of traffic and the dull ache in my chest.

I gave my statement. Signed where they asked.

Now I stand at the bottom of the stairwell, staring up at her apartment door, slightly open.

The frame is splintered. Latch blown out.

They must've kicked it in.

Inside, it's the kind of quiet that feels like a sound.

The tub is still full.

Pill bottles—cheap, store-brand painkillers. One empty. One overturned, contents scattered like confetti no one wanted.

A broken mug on the kitchen tile. A cold half-eaten bagel beside it.

I stand in the center of the room.

This is what she'll come home to. The aftermath of trying to end her life.

"She can't come back to this," I whisper.

Take off my jean jacket, lay it over the back of a chair and call the locksmith. The same one I used the other day and he's on his way.

I'll stay and clean while I wait for him.

In the bathroom, I kneel and pull the stopper. The water drains slowly, glugging down the pipes.

In the kitchen, I wrap the broken mug in a towel and toss it. The bagel too. I wipe the counter—not because it's dirty, but because I need something to do.

In the living room, I straighten the chair. Pick up a fallen cardigan. Align the coffee table.

"She deserves better than this."

I barely hear my own voice but it feels true because this isn't just a scene.

It's her home.

And when she comes back it can't look like where she almost died. It has to look like where she gets to live.

I don't realize I'm still trembling until I reach the car.

The street is calm. Same cracked sidewalk. Same flickering streetlamp.

But the air feels different. Like it's holding its breath.

I toss my jean jacket in the trunk, not caring where it lands.

It's humid—sticky in that New York way that makes seven p.m. feel like dirty dishwater.

I grab my tote. Still half full of stakeout snacks and guilt.

My fingers brush something cold.

The knife.

That eight-inch chef's knife my mother slipped into my bag like it was trail mix.

Of course it's still here.

Of course I forgot.

I shake my head, wrapping my fingers around the handle, intending to put it in the glove box before some random passerby calls in a report of a blonde wielding cutlery in activewear.

But then I hear it.

A metallic clatter. Sharp. Muffled.

Not trash. Not traffic.

Steel on steel.

It came from the alley.

I freeze.

The tote slips off my shoulder with a dull thud as I turn toward the sound.

Something moves in the shadows—high up and my gaze lifts.

There—just visible under the dim glow of a distant security light—a figure is descending the fire escape.

Slow. Controlled.

He moves like he's done it a hundred times. Maybe he has.

My breath catches in my throat as I trace his path upward with my eyes.

He was just at her apartment.

My pulse hammers so loud I can hear it in my ears.

I clutch the knife.

I don't remember deciding to do it—I just... do.

My fingers tighten around the handle, the blade heavy and cold, my other hand braced on the trunk.

He hits the pavement with a soft thump, boots barely making a sound.

Then he turns.

Stops in the middle of the alley, hood still up, face still hidden.

And then... slowly... deliberately...

He pulls the hood down.

My stomach drops.

It's him.

That face. That same smug expression from the courtroom. From the security footage. From every waking nightmare that's haunted Mariela since that night.

Travis Gannon.

The man who beat her. Raped her. Stalked her to the edge of death.

The man who walked away free.

He smiles.

That awful, casual, too-proud grin like this is just a game and I'm the next player on the board.

And then—he winks.

My grip tightens on the knife. My legs won't move and I can't blink.

He jogs off into the dark.

Just jogs like a man who knows no one's coming for him.

I stand there frozen, the night air thick against my skin, sticky like fear.

The knife in my hand is heavy. Not just in weight—but in what it means. What it could mean.

Across the alley, shadows swallow him. Travis Gannon. That smug little smile still burned into my vision like an afterimage from staring at the sun too long. Only this time, it's not the sun.

It's the devil. And he winked at me.

He would've killed her tonight.

He came back to finish what he started. To slither his way into her apartment like the cockroach he is, and the only reason she's alive is because of me.

Not the cops.

Not the courts.

Not the so-called justice system that's more interested in being fair for criminals than bringing justice for victims.

And definitely not Detective Brannon, the sentient sock puppet with a badge.

Just like no one stopped the man who hurt my mother.

You do whatever you have to.

Her words come back, soft but ironclad, like they've been waiting for this moment to crawl out of the corners of my brain and settle in.

I stare down the alley. He's gone now. But he was here. Real. Alive.

I grip the handle of the knife tighter. It feels warm now, molded to my palm like it belongs there.

"I don't want to do this," I whisper. The words shake, but they don't waiver.

I don't want to. God, I don't.

But he was here. Right here.

And if I let him go tonight, he'll vanish again. Slip back into the shadows like he always does.

And next time?

Someone else won't be so lucky.

"I don't want to kill him," I say again, barely breathing. But if I don't... someone else is going to be raped. Maybe killed.

The truth of it lands like ice water in my lungs.

This wasn't the plan. I was supposed to go to bed with glowy skin and eight hours of sleep. Not a blade and a body count.

I look down at the knife in my hand. At my shaking fingers. At the pink sneakers on my feet and the way my heart is hammering against my ribs like it's trying to run for the both of us.

This isn't revenge.

This is prevention.

This is justice, the kind the courtroom couldn't give Mariela. The kind that slipped through the cracks for my mother. For me.

I steady my breath.

I steady my grip.

And I steady myself for what comes next.

Because I'm Poppy Hartwell.

And tonight, I'm going to kill a man.

Poppy

I don't stop to question it. I just move.

He disappears around the corner like he didn't just wink at me from the shadows of my client's despair. Like Mariela isn't in a hospital bed right now because he broke her spirit with the same hands he used to pin her down and break her body.

He jogs away with that same swagger I've watched on grainy surveillance footage, and something inside me clicks.

I step forward, sneakers crunching softly against the gravel, my movements instinctive—quiet. I squeeze the handle of the knife. Cold. Grounding. Heavier now than it felt in my hand this morning when I was ready to march into Mari's building.

Stay in the shadows. Stay sharp.

My heart is thudding, loud and insistent, but my steps are controlled. I've walked through this moment in my mind more times than I care to admit—during long nights staring at the ceiling, during court recesses when I rewatched that video over and over.

I know what to do.

Aim for the artery behind the knee. It'll drop him fast.

If he grabs me, go for the neck—not a stabbing motion, just a clean swipe.

Move fast. Move smart. Don't panic.

The streets around me begin to narrow. The city closes in with its twisted alleys and dim service corridors—places where security cameras don't always reach, where a scream can get lost between buildings.

He's not heading toward Chase's apartment like he usually does. He's taking back routes. Cutting diagonally across blocks. He's leading me.

That realization crawls up my spine like a warning. This isn't just him heading home. This is deliberate.

I round another corner, breath clouding in the cool night air, and my pace slows just enough for doubt to catch up.

What in the heck am I doing?

This isn't a stakeout anymore. This isn't some late-night dramatization of *Law & Order* where I play the tenacious ADA with a spine of steel and perfectly blended contour.

This is real.

I don't have backup waiting down the block. There's no courtroom safety net. No bailiff standing by.

It's just me.

Me—and a knife I barely know how to hold properly, much less use without vomiting after.

He's a predator. A real one. One who's hurt people and who could hurt me.

And I'm chasing him.

There's still time to turn back.

I could walk away right now. No one would know. I could call this in. Let the police take over—assuming they'd even care enough to respond.

I stare down the alley ahead and see nothing but darkness.

But somewhere in that dark . . . he's waiting.

Or maybe . . . watching.

I close my eyes just for a moment. Just long enough to let my mother's voice echo again:

You do whatever you have to.

My jaw tightens.

Maybe I'm not a fighter. Maybe I wasn't built for this kind of justice.

But if I turn back now . . . someone else won't get the chance to.

And I don't think I could live with that.

I quicken my pace, trying to keep my footsteps light as the alley curves out of view. I round the corner, expecting to catch a glimpse of his hoodie, the back of his head, anything—

But there's nothing.

My breath catches as my pace falters. I scan left, then right. My heart starts to race for a different reason. *Where did he go?*

A flutter of movement to my left makes me spin. Nothing.

I press forward again, deeper into the shadows now, where the city's heartbeat seems to slow. Another turn. Another empty stretch. The buildings here are older. Forgotten.

And then, without warning—

BAM.

He hits me hard from the side, the full weight of his body knocking me sideways into a rusted service door of an old warehouse.

The force sends it crashing open, hinges shrieking. My shoulder hits first, then my hip. The floor is cold and unyielding as I land with a jolt.

The door slams behind us with a sound that echoes too loudly, and in the sudden enclosure, everything stills.

I try to push myself up, but he's already over me—blocking

out the moonlight, breathing heavy, smiling that same awful smile that I swear I'll see in my dreams for the rest of my life.

The knife—I dropped it. Somewhere in the fall.

I can't breathe. Can't move fast enough.

This isn't the version I practiced in my head. This isn't how it was supposed to go.

And yet, somehow . . . I think I always knew it might come to this.

Because monsters don't slink away quietly when you follow them into the dark.

They turn, and they pounce.

"You should've stayed in your courtroom, sweetheart," he grunts against me.

Concrete meets my back like a punch. Cold. Hard. Filthy.

"Now you get to find out what it's like when no one comes to save you."

My shoulder jars against the broken tile of the entryway floor as he slams me down, pinning me beneath him with the weight of someone who's done this before.

He grins down at me, his breath sour and heavy. "You know, I've thought about this," he murmurs near my ear, voice low and thick with cruelty. "Every day in that fucking courtroom."

My body reacts before my mind does.

I thrash—hard. Panic floods me, white-hot and electric.

My knee jerks up, catches him between the legs, but not hard enough. He grunts, rage igniting in his eyes.

His fingers clamp around my wrists and slam them into the ground. The back of my head scrapes concrete. The ceiling spins.

"Always so mouthy," he sneers, straddling my hips. "But I like 'em mouthy. Makes the screaming more fun."

His fingers claw at my shoulder, yanking at the fabric of my bodysuit. I hear the seam give way—a sickening rip that echoes in the dark. One sleeve tears free, baring my arm to the cold air and his filthy touch. He grins like he's proud of it. Like this is a game he's already won.

"Scream for me—let's see if it's as sweet as hers."

He's so close to my ear, I turn my head and I bite.

Hard.

Then harder.

I bite until my jaw aches. Until he's the one screaming. Trying to jab at my torso, but he can't get a good shot.

When I taste blood, I let go, and he jerks back with a roar, hand flying to his cheek where blood's running through his fingers.

"You fucking bitch."

I twist, shove, wriggle free enough to get one leg up and kick with everything I've got. He stumbles, off balance for a breath.

That's all I need.

I scramble, dragging myself until my hand closes around the hilt of my knife.

My mom's knife.

I roll, just as he lunges again—and this time, this time— I'm ready.

I drive the blade up into his side with a cry that doesn't sound like me. It sounds feral. Unhinged.

He screams, but not from fear. From rage.

His hand clamps around my neck and he squeezes. His eyes are wild now. Panicked. Inhuman. If they ever were.

His lips move, muttering something—maybe threats, maybe prayers—but I can't hear over the sound of my own heartbeat thundering in my skull.

His hand fumbles for the knife.

Even as he tightens the grip around my throat, his other hand scrapes the floor, blindly searching for the weapon still clutched in my fist.

He's trying to choke me out and disarm me at the same time.

But I won't let him.

Every time his fingers graze the handle, I twist, wrenching my arm just out of reach. He growls in frustration, and I feel the vibration of it against my skin—hot breath against my ear, his forearm crushing down harder. My lungs scream. My eyes burn. But I don't loosen my hold.

I shift again, draw back as far as I can.

Then I slash.

The blade bites into the tender flesh beneath his arm, just where the muscle thins and the vein pulses thick beneath it.

Warm blood sprays across my face, hot and wet and violent. It covers my throat, my arms, the wall behind me. I gasp, flinching at the sensation—but I don't stop.

I'll be dead if I do.

His grip falters and he sputters. But still, he fights.

I stab again, this time into his ribs. The blade hits resistance. Bone, maybe. Something cracks. Not just in him—but in me, too.

I feel it.

Like the ocean floor has given way for the endless march of magma that will soon ooze through it. Unyielding and unstoppable.

He tries to grab me, to roll us again. His hand finds my hair and jerks.

I scream, wrenching free.

Then I bring the knife down—again, and again—into whatever I can reach. Chest. Shoulder. Neck.

Each strike lands with a sickening crunch or a wet give. Blood coats the handle, coats my hands, but I don't let go.

I twist and slam my foot into his side, shoving him off me with everything I have left. He collapses, half-conscious, twitching. But I'm already crawling on top of him.

His eyes are wide. Pleading now.

It's far too late for that.

I channel the image of my mother—sixteen, broken, bleeding, left to suffer in silence. I channel the sound of Mariela's voice when she said goodbye.

And I let go.

I stab. And stab. And stab again.

Again.

Again.

Each time, my whole body shakes with it.

My scream tears from my throat, ragged and raw.

My arms burn. My fingers cramp. The knife slips, and I grip harder, pressing down like my life depends on it.

I stab until I can't feel my hands.

Until the world blurs through tears and blood.

Until the only sound left in this filthy building is the hollow echo of my sobs.

And then, finally, I stop.

Not because I want to.

But because I can't lift the blade anymore.

His body slumps. Limbs slack. Mouth open. Eyes vacant.

Still.

The knife clatters from my hand, and everything is quiet.

So quiet.

Not just the absence of noise—but a strange, weightless kind of quiet. Like I'm suspended in something too vast to name.

The air feels light. The edges of the world blur. Everything that usually hums inside my head—lists, numbers, rehearsed arguments, intrusive loops—is gone. It's just me and the silence.

My breath comes in shallow drags, uneven and raw, like I've forgotten how to do it properly.

There's a tremble in my limbs I can't stop. Not yet. Not while I'm still trying to piece together what I've done... and what it will cost me.

I stay kneeling. The knife still in my hand. Blood sticky along my fingers and wrists, soaking into the black fabric clinging to my skin.

My bodysuit feels tighter now—twisted and torn at the shoulder where he ripped it. It sticks to me in patches where his blood soaks through.

The pool beneath him is still spreading and it's so much. Too much.

I don't know how long I sit there.

It could be minutes. It could be hours.

Time feels like a thing that belongs to someone else.

Then—a sound.

So soft I almost miss it.

I lift my head, slowly. Every part of me stiff and aching, like I've aged a decade in the span of a heartbeat.

There it is again. Something I can hardly hear, but I know it's the kind of sound that doesn't belong in a place like this.

I shift, pushing off my knees, turning toward the source.

And that's when I see him.

In broken doorway, nearly swallowed by the shadows.
Dark brown eyes meet mine—and I know.
He saw.
He saw everything.
I'm not alone.

The moment I move, I feel it.

Not just the ache in my arms or the burn in my thighs—but the weight of it. Thick and sticky, dragging at me like guilt with a heartbeat.

I killed him.

I push up from the cold floor and catch sight of a woman in a shard of reflective metal near the broken doorway.

For a second, I don't recognize her.

She looks like something out of a horror movie. Not the survivor. No—she looks like Carrie after the pig's blood came down. A hallucination soaked in crimson and consequence.

Her eyes are wide, whites stark against dark blood. Blonde hair clings to her cheek in wet clumps. Her black Pilates body-suit is shredded and splattered.

I blink and she blinks back because that's me.

Now I feel it—the blood drying against my skin, matting my hair, sinking into my nails. It clings to me like shame and something darker I'm not ready to name.

I killed him. And I'll live with it forever.

My stomach gives out.

I stumble two steps before bile claws up. My hand braces

against the wall—bloody, and now so is the concrete. I double over and vomit until my ribs ache.

The sound echoes: splash, heave, gag.

I spit. My mouth tastes like acid and panic. I wipe it on my shoulder—useless. There's blood there, too.

Everything is covered in blood and looks like the aftermath of a Tarantino film.

I can't even wipe my mouth to clean the rapist's blood.

The dead rapist. Because I killed him.

I stumble backward, hand out like I'm on a high wire. My palm smears red over the beam, leaving a print like a warning label:

Caution: Woman on the edge. May stab again.

A laugh slips out—or a sob. Hard to tell.

The air's too thin. The smell—metallic and wrong—burns my throat.

He's dead.

That thought should settle me but it doesn't.

Because it's not just that he's dead. It's that *I* did it.

My hands. My blade. My rage.

It wasn't clinical or quick or fair.

It was animal.

And beneath the horror, the sick and shame, a voice whispers:

You liked it.

I shove it down hard—but it's there. A flicker in the dark.

The same one my mother must've heard when her voice said, *make it stop.*

And she did.

So did I.

I press my palm to my forehead. I need a plan. A breath. Something normal.

But first—I need to move.

I need to clean up.

And get the h-e-double-hockey-sticks out of this blood-soaked building before anyone finds out what I've done.

Because the truth still hangs in the air like the smell of copper and sweat:

I may have saved Mariela's life tonight...

But I don't think mine will ever be the same.

A prickle raises the hairs along my spine. A pressure. Like someone's watching.

Because someone *is* watching—and I almost forgot.

Slowly, I turn toward the ruined doorway.

Not someone—*something.*

A fluffy white creature waddles into view like he owns the place. Head tilted. Tongue out. Snaggletooth jutting like a warning fang. He blinks with all the gravitas of a marshmallow come to life.

A dog.

A little dog.

"Oh no," I whisper.

He trots forward, nails ticking on concrete. Sniffs like he's rating the place on Yelp.

"Hi there, buddy," I murmur, crouching. "I know this looks bad. I can explain."

He keeps sniffing. Closer to the corpse.

The corpse.

Oh God. I'm going to be sick again.

"Okay, I can't explain. But I'm really sorry you had to see that. It's not... who I am."

He pauses beside the body, sniffs, then lifts his leg and pees directly onto the chest cavity.

"Are you serious?"

He shakes off, then steps into a puddle of blood. Tiny red paw prints trail behind him like some violent art project from an unhinged doggy daycare.

"No, no—stop, little puppy—"

I shuffle after him, trying not to leave more prints. "Please don't extend the crime scene. We've already exceeded the limits of my psyche."

The dog pauses, wags his tail, then flops onto his back.

Right in another smear.

"Oh my—why?" I whisper.

His tail thumps. He's covered in blood now. Pink streaks matted into fur. Ears dipped. A red belly like he rolled in a strawberry smoothie.

Except it's not strawberries.

And this isn't a park.

And I'm not okay.

I take a step closer, hands out like I'm coaxing a skittish raccoon off a porch.

He tilts his head—sweet and innocent—like he didn't just defile a corpse and take a spa day in arterial spray.

"Okay, come here, little baby. I just need to—"

He bolts.

"No! Get back here!"

I'm running now. Bloodied. One shoe missing. Chasing a murder witness in shame-laced circles around a dilapidated building.

My canine co-conspirator—by proximity, not choice—is a streak of white-and-red lightning, darting between trash piles like it's his personal playground.

I lunge—and slip.

Catch myself on cracked concrete. My palm hits a puddle and blood squelches beneath it.

"Oh, that's gross."

I peel my hand back, leaving a full, perfect print.

A horror-movie poster.

"Great," I mutter. "Add it to the forensic scrapbook."

I'm covered. Arms streaked, wrists soaked. Drying on my cheek and—oh no.

There's even more blood in my hair.

I feel the stickiness. The metallic tang clinging to my waves.

"Oh God," I breathe. "I'm molting. A molting murderer leaving evidence everywhere."

The pup barrels through another puddle, feet skidding until he slides and flops onto his side.

I gasp—but of course he's fine.

He wriggles, tail wagging, tongue out, and eyes bright.

Now he looks like a crime scene stuffed animal.

Turns his head like he's posing for a mugshot.

Yes, Officer, I saw everything. Also, I licked it.

When I finally scoop him up, he wriggles once, then settles in my arms like a hot mess of violence and fluff.

Then the little beast licks my nose. Cheerfully.

Like I just saved him from a bath... and not murdered a man a few feet away.

"Dexter," I mutter, reading the name off his studded black leather collar, "you are a war criminal."

He pants, smug and proud.

And that's when it hits me.

The smell. The blood. The silence. The fact that we're still standing in a murder scene.

I slowly turn in a circle, Dexter cradled against my ribs like a very judgmental, panting baby.

The floor is streaked with red. My footprints—bare, because of course I lost a shoe during my post-homicide cardio

—trail from one end of the room to the other. There's a hand-print on the concrete. My DNA. My sweat. My vomit.

The blood isn't just on me—it's everywhere. I've contaminated everything. Bled and cried and spit and shed in every direction. This whole building might as well be a forensic wonderland. A carnival of conviction.

"Oh, cheese and crackers, Dexter," I whisper as a fresh wave of panic starts to rise. "We're going to jail forever."

I stare down at the tiny, now-pink-dappled dog in my arms.

"I can't leave you. You're covered in evidence. You're practically an accomplice. If anyone ever swabs your paw pads, we're done for. And I'm too pretty for prison, Dexter. I would not do well there."

He yawns.

"Right," I say, scanning the blood-splattered Picasso around us, landing on my abandoned shoe—and the murder weapon.

No. I'm not thinking about that.

"So, we need to go. Now. We need a plan. And then we need to never speak of this again."

But the silence that follows?

It doesn't feel like a promise.

It feels like the beginning of something I'll never be able to outrun.

But I need to try.

My little companion's snaggletooth is still sticking out like he's proud of it. He looks at me like he's just agreed to whatever cover-up plan I've concocted.

But the truth is, I have nothing.

Dexter has a collar. He seems well fed, groomed not too long ago. Not that I know much about dogs, but the hair around his face looks intentionally trimmed—neat and tidy.

Someone's probably looking for him. And if that someone finds him like this? Covered in blood? That would definitely trigger an investigation.

And that's just not a headline I need right now.

I adjust my grip on the little menace and backtrack toward my car, ducking under every streetlamp like I'm starring in an amateur version of *Mission: Impossible—Accomplice Edition*. Every passing light feels like a spotlight. Every shadow looks like it might lunge.

Panic, at this point, isn't just a feeling—it's my entire personality.

The city is dead quiet at this hour, which should be calming. It's not. It's unsettling. New York isn't supposed to sleep, but tonight? It's taken a full sedative and left me alone with the aftermath of a very violent decision.

But maybe that will work in my favor.

That place seemed long abandoned. The streets unused and it buys me time.

Enough to change. To gather a plan and come back and do... something to try and save myself from this mess.

But I know what I *should* have done.

First, I should've kept my hinny at the car and called 911.

But I didn't do that. I chased after a monster and killed him.

I shouldn't have left the scene. Staying and calling the authorities would've been my best chance at a self-defense case.

But how would I have explained the knife? Following him?

There's no excuse. Because I followed him meaning to kill him.

And I did.

So now I need to handle this—or my life will be over, just like his.

I reach my car and wave my foot under the trunk sensor, praying it reads my movement through all the blood and desperation.

It does. Praise be.

The trunk lifts, and I nearly cry from relief. I glance around to see if anyone is watching.

With Dexter wiggling like a greased-up piglet in my arms, I fumble for a disposable glove from the emergency kit wedged between jumper cables and cleaning supplies. Slipping it on one-handed is a circus act. But I manage. Sort of. It's inside out and slightly sticky.

I don't want to admit why.

I dump the contents of my tote bag onto the trunk floor in one swift motion—a protein bar and a half-eaten sleeve of lemon shortbread cookies.

Dexter sniffs them on his descent into the tote like I've just offered him five-star room service.

I hook the bag onto the coat hook behind the passenger seat, and Dexter swings gently like a designer handbag no one would ever approve for courtroom carry.

My hands are shaking. The world feels tilted, off balance— like I'm underwater.

But I can't stop now.

I lay a giant trash bag across the driver's seat like I'm prepping for either a paint job or a mental breakdown, then slide behind the wheel. My hand hovers over the ignition.

What if someone saw me?

What if they followed?

What if this is it—my last moment of freedom before it all caves in?

Dexter sneezes and that's my cue.

I shove the car into drive and floor it, peeling away from the curb like I'm racing toward normal. Toward silence. Toward a future that may or may not exist now.

And in the back seat, my new accomplice swings gently in his tote bag like the world's fluffiest, least helpful getaway driver.

At least I'm not alone in this.

Even if my partner in crime desecrates bodies and contaminates evidence.

At least I'm not alone.

Him

I saw everything—every tear, every stab, every breath she didn't realize might be her last.

I watched from above—four stories up and two decades ahead of her in the art of survival.

She never looked up. Most people don't. That's why rooftops are perfect for monsters like me.

She thinks she was alone.

She wasn't.

She had her bravery, the knife. Then the dog.

But she's always had me. She just doesn't know it yet.

The whole thing was messy and unrefined.

Sloppy footwork, too many missed arteries on the first go. She wasted too much energy with all that flailing. If this were a training video, I'd call it "How to Start a Homicide and Still Get Yourself Killed."

Adrenaline all over the place. No pacing. No strategy.

I give it a six-point-five.

But what she lacked in technique, she made up for in fire.

My sunshine finally scorched something.

And that dog—

that wriggly, white, chaotic puffball with the snaggletooth is a sadist. Mark my words.

That thing enjoyed every second. It defiled the body before you could say *rigor mortis*. Honestly, I respect the gusto.

I watch as the deranged fluffball covers himself in blood like a paint roller.

Poppy chases him in circles, slipping, stumbling, leaving handprints and hair like she's personalizing the scene.

I pinch the bridge of my nose and shake my head. "Jesus, Sunny."

If she had glitter, she'd probably scatter it too. The girl couldn't be more traceable if she tattooed her socials on his ass.

I'd intervene, but... watching her run half-barefoot, blood-drenched, after a feral dog in a decaying warehouse she just christened with her first kill?

Yeah. This is the best show I've seen all year.

But I suppose I can't sit up here all night.

This isn't the closest we've ever come to each other. I've made sure there were dozens of small moments where she walked past me so I could smell her perfume flowing off her. Hear her voice and pretend she's talking to me.

A million times I stood behind her in a grocery store and she never knew.

This could be the perfect moment. The moment when I finally face her, tell her I love her, and watch her fall in love with me.

Just the way I know she will.

Butterflies surge in my stomach at the thought. With each second that passes, it feels more and more right.

Ordained, even.

I use the ladder fixed to the side of the building and climb down.

We're even matching—both of us wearing all black. This is it.

The moment I've thought about on a loop, and I can't help but bite back a smile.

I cross the long-abandoned and cracked road that divides the warehouses. Silent.

Like smoke passing through shadows.

Flat against the building, I calm my breathing. Try to steady my pulse, but it's a hammer.

Peeking into the open window, she's finally scooped up the creature—he licks her nose like he's proud of himself.

I narrow my eyes. He better watch it. She was mine first.

I'm running through opening lines in my mind, flipping through them like cards on a Rolodex, hunting for the perfect one when she races out of the warehouse.

What the fuck, Poppy?

Two feet away from her and she didn't even see me. Didn't even look over her shoulder. Just ran.

I hold up my hand, inhale a breath, and I swear I plan to call out to her. But the words are frozen in my throat.

Instead, I just watch her run like a crazed cartoon character down the alley. She zigzags, dog underarm, knife blade swinging like she's auditioning for *West Side Story: Trauma Edition.*

"A fucking menace." I snort a laugh just as my sunshine disappears from sight.

"You're right. Probably not the best time."

She's at least heading in the right direction—toward her car. I set an alarm on my phone for fourteen minutes to make sure she arrives at her brownstone.

I let the quiet wrap around me before putting in my

earbuds. I pull up the *Manacled* playlist and scroll to one of my favorite chapters.

Chapter fifty-eight: flashback thirty-three.

I look up at the dilapidated warehouse. The building doesn't just bleed.

The walls hum with what she did.

What she became.

And me?

I breathe it in like oxygen.

She thinks tonight was a breaking point.

That something inside her snapped and can't be put back together.

But that's not what I saw.

I saw evolution.

I saw the first crack of light in all that sunshine she tries to bottle up.

Not a breakdown.

A blooming.

And she doesn't know it yet, but she's closer now to me.

To who she really is.

To what we could be. What we *will* be.

But right now, it's time to clean up after her—scrub away the DNA, the footprints, the fear.

I won't leave a single thread of her behind for someone else to touch.

Not when every inch of her belongs to me.

Not when this is just the beginning, and I can't risk anything taking her away from me.

I was going to kill Gannon tonight.

That was the plan. I had it all laid out—routes tracked, blind spots mapped, tools stashed behind a cracked boiler in the corner of this empty alley. He had no idea he was walking into his own grave.

But then... she showed up.

My sunshine. All dressed in black, with that beautiful, unhinged glint in her eye. A knife in her hand. That look on her face.

I couldn't take it from her.

She needed this. The world took too much already, and tonight... she took something back. Who am I to interrupt that kind of poetry?

I step inside.

The smell hits first—copper and bile and the lingering ghost of her perfume. That vanilla-laced citrus blend she wears like armor. It's everywhere now, tinged with sweat and panic and the tang of what she became tonight.

The scene is... something.

A masterpiece in emotional carnage. She didn't just kill him. She decimated him. Overkill, some would say. But not me. No, I'd call it righteous. Long overdue. A little clumsy, sure. But passionate.

She made a mess.

A glorious, chaotic, feral mess.

And now it's mine to clean.

I crouch by the body, eyeing the arterial spray on the far wall and the delicate little paw prints that trailed through it.

She'll never know it, but she wasn't the only one planning to spill blood tonight.

I already hated this bastard before he slipped that photograph into her office mail.

But that? That changed everything.

You don't threaten her. You don't even look at her. She's

mine. My bright thing. My purpose. You touch her, and you die.

It wasn't jealousy, exactly. It was something else. Something worse. I didn't want his attention redirected. He was supposed to stay fixed on his usual victims—easy, predictable, distant.

Not turn his hunger on her.

Her prints are everywhere.

Of course they are. Mixed into the blood, the footprints, her vomit. A literal handprint smeared across the concrete.

It's almost impressive how completely she blew every possible cardinal rule before fleeing a murder scene.

I chuckle under my breath. "You beautiful disaster."

But it's okay. I've cleaned worse.

In my ear, *Manacled* is being recited like I don't nearly have this chapter memorized. Draco threatens to burn the portraits as Hermione walks into his library.

I start to mentally catalog the list—entry points, fibers, surfaces. It's not just about wiping things down. It's about erasing her. Scrubbing this place so thoroughly it'll feel like she never breathed here.

Because there's no limit I won't go for her.

Not one. Not ever.

It's why *Manacled* is my favorite Dramione fanfic. The way Draco worships Hermione from afar—protecting her, suffering for her, waiting for her to finally look up and see what was always standing guard.

It's not just fiction. It's instruction.

Because just like Hermione eventually claimed her dragon, Poppy will claim me.

She'll say the words I've waited so long to hear.

The ones that will bind us. Forever.

Soon.

But first—this.

It only takes me a minute to pull my piece-of-shit car up and open the trunk for my supplies, starting with boot covers and gloves.

My girl turned this place into a blood-soaked cathedral.

And now I get to be the priest who wipes it clean.

First things first: the body.

No sense cleaning the place up when I'm about to make it exponentially worse.

Besides, Gannon's already leaked all over the concrete like a gut-shot deer.

It's about to get messier before it gets cleaner.

Knife. Bone saw. Plastic sheeting. Gloves. Labels. Zip ties.

I came prepared.

The body's too big to move clean. Too awkward, too many limp limbs. So I roll out a tarp and work him onto it.

My playlist kicks in as I work. You'd think the emotional climax would lose its edge by now, but no. It hits every time.

Tortured devotion. Loyalty with a body count. That's the kind of love that lasts.

Gannon's arm detaches with a sickening snap. I label it: left forearm.

Bag. Seal. Repeat.

One part at a time. Efficient. Necessary. Cathartic.

It's not even personal. Not for me.

Poppy already gave him the emotion.

I'm just handling the logistics.

I take a break when my timer pings.

Right on cue, my sunshine pulls up to her home. Still streaked with blood. Still dazed. Still beautiful.

She hurries inside with the walking cotton ball of chaos bouncing in her arms.

I stay until I see the light flicker on upstairs. She made it. Safe. Whole.

"I'll be there soon, baby," I whisper, like she can hear my promise. Then I finish bagging the torso.

By the time I'm done, the trunk of my car looks like a glorified trash compactor.

Trash bags. Industrial-grade cleaners. Three-day-old Chinese takeout stacked like camouflage.

The trick is balance. Smell is everything. Wrap a leg in rotting sesame chicken and no one looks twice.

I've got several restaurant dumpsters in mind.

They get picked up by different trucks, headed to different landfills, on staggered days.

The odds of all the pieces ending up in the same place? Astronomical.

The odds of them being found at all?

Please.

If I do my job—and I always do—Gannon will rot quietly in the corner of a landfill like the trash he is.

Tonight wasn't just about cleaning up after her.

It wasn't just about wrapping bones in plastic or sweeping away the evidence of her first kill.

It was about something far greater.

A beginning. A shift.

A quiet, bloody rite of passage.

She stepped into my world without even realizing it, and for the first time, I get to step out of the shadows.

She doesn't know it yet—not really—but we're not on opposite ends of this twisted story.

We're spiraling closer to the same inevitable truth.

Two storms circling the same dark center.

And now that blood has been spilled—

now that she's felt what it means to take control in the rawest, most permanent way—

I finally get to stop watching from rooftops and grainy security feeds and start moving toward her.

Closer to her breath.

Closer to her fear.

Closer to *us*.

She'll see me soon.

And when she does, she won't run.

Not from me.

Not from herself.

Poppy

Every case I've ever tried runs through my head like a reel of mistakes.

What they missed.

What got them caught.

What I picked apart in court like a vulture at a crime-scene buffet.

I'm not making those mistakes.

My car is hidden from sight in the detached garage behind my brownstone. If anyone puts a call out for a vehicle matching its description, I'm banking on "out of sight, out of mind."

Inside, first things first: containment.

Dexter, still secure in his tote, hangs from the coatrack looking like a very murderous purse.

Thank goodness I keep a box of pink disposable gloves in my mudroom. With a fresh pair, I strip right here. The black bodysuit and shoes go into a trash bag. New gloves. Then double-bagged. And new gloves again.

"I think I know a place I can get rid of these," I mutter, knotting the plastic tight.

Dexter watches me from his tote, still panting happily like

this has all been the best game of his life. His white fur is still splotched pink-red in places, and that snaggletooth juts out proudly, like he won a fight he never entered.

"Sorry, buddy," I say, unclipping his little black collar and dropping it and the soiled tote into a separate bag. "You're evidence now."

I grab a stack of yellow sticky notes from the wall calendar and start tagging anything I touched like it's a crime scene—because, well, it is.

Door handle.

Coat hook.

Light switch.

Everything I touched gets a neon badge of shame, a silent little "clean me later" warning for future me.

Dexter sits happily under my arm—having the time of his life—and I carry him up the stairs to the primary bathroom.

The spa tub is deep enough to keep one blood-soaked dog contained while I pull off the worst cleanup of my life. I plop him in. He yips and turns in a circle a few times, I suppose happy to be free of his tote-bag prison.

He sits, little front paws together like a royal prince.

"Don't give me that look," I mutter, voice brittle as I turn the water on full blast. "You're the one who body-surfed through a pool of blood like it was a Slip 'N Slide."

Steam rises fast, curling up the mirrors and fogging over the version of me I no longer recognize.

I step into the water first.

It scalds so perfectly.

I scrub until my skin turns blotchy and raw, using every soap, scrub, exfoliant, and miracle potion I own. Wash. Rinse. Scrub again. Trying to erase his blood, my guilt, the echo of the knife in my hand—I go at it like absolution comes with a loofah.

I try not to cry.

I do anyway.

Quiet sobs that shake in my ribs but never reach my throat. They stay there, lodged behind my sternum like all the other things I'm trying not to say. Like the fact that I killed a man. Like the fact that I don't regret it.

When I finally breathe again, I reach for the dog.

"Okay, your turn, little buddy," I whisper, hoisting him carefully into the rising water.

He doesn't fight me. Just sits in the tub with mild offense, like he expected lavender bubbles and a massage. I lather him up with shampoo that smells like cucumber and lilies, working the suds deep into his fur.

The water turns pink.

And... when I rinse him, I gasp because now he's pink.

Head to tail.

A bubblegum-dipped murder witness.

"No, no, no, no, no—" I wash. Again. Working the lather in better this time. "You're not supposed to look like you were tie-dyed in blood."

He shakes, sending flecks of pink-tinted water all over the bathroom tile.

My panic spikes.

I turn toward the mirror and lift a section of my hair.

Blonde strands... discolored. A faint rust-hued tinge clinging to the ends.

"Oh, sweet peppermint patties."

I stare at my hair in the mirror, feeling personally betrayed my natural blonde has been defiled. The coppery tint is faint—

barely there—but it is there, and that means I am one step away from matching my pink murder accomplice in the tub.

No Google. No searches. That's rule number one. No desperate "how to remove blood stains from blonde hair" queries that get traced back to me.

No digital breadcrumbs, thank you very much.

I think fast. Old school. Grandma-style solutions. Boiling water. Apple cider vinegar. A little whispered prayer to the gods of salon safety.

I pour the hot, acidic rinse through my hair in a big mixing bowl and then rewash with my expensive shampoo. Twice. Rinse. Condition. Repeat for good measure.

When I rinse for the final time, I check the mirror and let out a small breath of relief.

My blonde is back.

Poppy: 1

Homicide aftermath: ...a strong 37

Feeling brave (desperate), I try the same trick on Dexter.

He stands in the bowl like a tiny warlock awaiting some ancient canine baptism while I pour my concoction over his cotton-candy pink fluff.

I rinse. Scrub. Rinse again.

Nothing.

He shakes violently, and hops out of the bowl with an offended huff.

Still pink.

He waddles across the bathroom floor like the world's tiniest bubblegum goblin, tail high, snaggletooth the only white thing on him now.

"Oh, you're adorable," I mutter, wrapping him in a towel. "Adorable and highly admissible in court."

Which brings me to the next problem: my furry little co-

conspirator has been through a lot tonight—and, judging by the way he's been licking tile grout, he's probably starving.

I reheat a small plate of turkey, rice, and broccoli I was planning to have for dinner tomorrow. Dexter practically levitates when he smells it.

He devours it in two minutes flat, tail wagging like he didn't just roll around in crime-scene residue an hour ago.

"Good boy," I whisper, crouching beside him.

He licks my ankle in thanks and follows me to the laundry room like he knows his way around the house already.

I secure him inside with a clean towel, a bowl of water, and stern instructions not to pee on anything I can't bleach.

He yawns.

I sigh.

And then I grab my pink gloves, my favorite cleaning caddy, a bottle of bleach, and head for the car.

Because I may have cleaned me...

But the crime scene on wheels still has the DNA of a dead rapist all over it.

It takes hours.

Cleaning the car, bagging contaminated textiles, adding another bulk case of pink disposable gloves to my Amazon cart.

I find it soothing though. The bagging. The methodical calming that takes over my mind and hushes my thoughts.

There was a brief moment of that when–you know. When Travis Gannon was *no longer with us.*

For a brief moment, it was quiet. Peaceful, almost.

Inside goes much faster, and by the time I toss the last sticky note and recheck every surface, it's past four in the morning.

I sag against the kitchen counter, the silence thick around me.

And then... a scratch.

Soft. Persistent. From behind the laundry-room door.

I wince. "Oh, Dexter."

I pull the door open, and there he is—dry now, fluff re-puffed, looking mildly offended that I forgot him for longer than five minutes.

He struts out like a tiny aristocrat returning from a spa treatment, pausing at the back door with a sigh that's ninety percent judgment.

Then he looks over his shoulder.

Full dramatic pause.

Snaggletooth glinting in the moonlight like a weapon.

He huffs.

"Well, excuse me, Mr. Murder Accomplice." And I open the door for him.

He snorts—literally snorts—and trots outside to a small patch of grass that runs alongside my brownstone.

With my arms crossed, I shift back and forth on my feet, not liking feeling so exposed out here.

Like the ghost of Travis Gannon will swoop in, leading a barrage of police to my doorstep.

In the distance, the faint sound of a siren sends a cascade of chills across my body. The fine hairs on the back of my neck stand to absolute attention.

"Oh, my daisy dukes. They're coming for me already."

My breathing rises, my pulse spikes, the siren gets louder and louder still. I release a pent-up sigh when I hear it keep driving by my street and fades into the distance.

Phew. Safe a little longer.

I trudge upstairs, limbs heavy. My soul, heavier.

My silk nightie slips over my head like a whisper—soft, pale pink, ironically the exact shade of innocence I just murdered tonight.

In my room, I grab an old towel from the linen closet and lay it on the floor by the nightstand with finality.

"No dogs on the bed," I declare to my new little roommate.

Dexter sits at the edge of the threshold, tail wagging just enough to be passive-aggressive.

I climb under my down comforter, wrap myself in its warmth like it might hold me together—but it doesn't.

Not tonight.

The weight of everything presses down. Not just my blanket, but the knowledge.

That I did it.

That I killed someone.

And not just anyone—a rapist. A predator. A monster.

But still... I killed him.

My chest tightens until breathing feels like a negotiation.

The tears come hard—ugly and unstoppable.

My shoulders shake as I bury my face in my palms, the sobs breaking out of me like steam from a cracked pipe.

There's no elegance to it. No control.

Just everything spilling out.

Dexter whines from the floor.

Then a tiny yip—almost a question.

And finally, a soft scratch of paw against the comforter.

I peek over the blanket, eyes burning, nose blotchy. "Fine," I whisper, voice wrecked. "But just this once."

I lift the covers, and he doesn't hesitate.

In one fluid motion, he hops up and marches straight to my chest like a soldier reporting for emotional support duty.

He curls there, warm and oddly reassuring.

His tiny heartbeat against mine.

His snaggletooth resting for a new day of sass tomorrow.
I wrap my arms around him, like he's a stuffed animal I had
as a kid—the kind that always kept the monsters away.
And finally my breathing slows.
My body sinks into the mattress.
And I cry until there's nothing left.
Until sleep drags me under, one tear at a time.

13
Poppy

There's a distinct difference between being exhausted and being emotionally obliterated. I now understand that difference intimately.

When I finally stir, it's not because I'm rested. It's because a tiny, fluffy, pink-accented dog is standing on my chest like he owns the mortgage, huffing in my face with the righteous fury of a man denied his constitutional right to pee.

Sunlight spears through the curtains. I squint, trying to remember what day it is... or what universe I inhabit.

"Oh, snickerdoodles," I groan. "I'm a terrible criminal and a negligent dog mom."

Dexter huffs—dramatically.

Yeah. You should be arrested for this, too.

I stumble to the back door and open it just in time for my pint-sized witness to strut outside. He pees with purpose, then turns toward me.

Judgment in every glance.

When he's done sending me to the emotional guillotine, we head back in. I reheat yesterday's turkey, chop some rice and carrots, and slide it into a bowl like I'm hosting brunch for a tiny mob boss.

"Bon appétit, Detective," I mutter.

He sniffs once and dives in like I've been starving him.

He's clearly well cared for. Someone has to be looking for him. If he has a chip, they'll come knocking.

A flash of the warehouse hits before I can blink it away.

I wonder if they could trace his chip trail. Right past the crime scene.

At least I have a reason to be in the area. Mariela.

My name's on a police report. Logged with the dispatcher.

Things I'm cataloging—just in case.

Two things before I figure out what to do with the body I left behind.

Make sure no one is looking for Dexter. And get rid of any evidence here at my home. Because here is the first place the police will come looking.

When I walk upstairs and open my closet doors, Dexter trots in and plants himself in the middle of the floor like he's ready to judge my wardrobe.

Try it buddy. I've got impeccable taste and a sea of pink you can drown in.

I settle on black leggings, a pink croptop, sunglasses big enough to hide behind, and a pink and black polka dot scarf to wrap around my head. It's giving 1950's Marylin Monroe chic.

My favorite pink tennies were *ruined* last night doing things we won't mention. But thankfully, I have another pair.

Blending in is key. Low-profile. Keep it casual and crime-free.

As I fuss with the placement of the scarf, I look down.

Dexter is still watching. Still judging.

"I'm getting you proper food," I tell him. "And maybe something to help you blend into society. Your pink era is giving *manslaughter meets Lisa Frank.*"

He blinks once, utterly unfazed.

I grab my phone and whisper, "Guard the house, Dexter," while opening my rideshare app.

He yawns, clearly unimpressed with his task.

Rude.

Blend in. Blend in.

Just your average mentally stable woman buying things for a dog she totally didn't steal from a murder scene.

I march into Petorama with the kind of manic energy reserved for people who cry in their car before yoga.

I have no idea what I'm looking for so I look at everything.

Collars. So many but only one that makes sense. Pink. Rhinestones. Glorious.

I toss it in the cart.

Next up: dog bed, treats, puppy pads, squeaky toys that look like woodland creatures with bad life choices.

And then—

"Ooh, what's this?"

Pet-safe dye.

Bubblegum pink. A few shades brighter than Dexter's accidental bloodbath makeover.

My fingers close around the bottle.

Perfect.

"If he's going to be pink," I mutter, "he might as well be *intentionally* pink."

Because this shade says *quirky owner with too much free time,* not *companion to a felony.* Important distinction.

I'm mid-aisle, gripping an overpriced tiny sweater Dexter won't appreciate, when my phone vibrates.

Sebastian's name flashes. Anxiety hits like the drop on a roller coaster.

He knows.

That's dumb. How would he know?

But what if he *does*?

> SEBASTIAN: Hey bestie. Client still hanging in there or should I send a crisis intervention martini?

I roll my eyes and type fast. *Sweet biscuits and gravy. If you only knew.*

I hesitate. I'm not ready to explain the suicide attempt—or answer questions that could lead to a murder confession.

Better to keep it simple. I'll figure out what to say before work Monday.

> ME: Not good.

> SEBASTIAN: Yikes. Full drama debrief Monday? I'll bring popcorn.

Despite everything, my mouth quirks up. Not sure this is a "popcorn" situation, but Sebastian lifts the tension. Always does.

Before I close my messages, a new text appears.

UNKNOWN NUMBER

I open it.

Empty.

Okaaay? That's odd.

I swipe it into the grave as I roll into the food aisle.

Eighty-seven different brands of dog food stop me cold.

Freeze-dried. Grain-free. Duck. Elk. Raw Boost—which sounds like canine pre-workout.

Kibble shaped like stars. Bones. Helicopters?

My hands start to shake. My breath goes shallow. The world tilts.

I don't know what to get. Does he have tummy issues? Is there a certain brand his breed should eat? I don't even know what breed he is.

I blink once. Then again.

My heart is speeding up, and the noise of the store is getting louder.

And just like that, I'm not in the dog food aisle anymore.

I'm back in the warehouse.

Blood on my arms. *His* weight on top of me. The sound of flesh giving way makes me flinch and close my eyes tight.

The knife, slick and warm in my hand. The spray. The choking gurgle. The look in his eyes just before they went still.

I grip the cart handle like it's my last tether to Earth.

Focus, Poppy. Focus.

You've handled courtrooms. You've eviscerated men twice your size in four-inch heels and two hours of sleep. You can pick a dog food.

Just breathe.

"Need help?"

I jump. Literally flinch like someone just fired a gun into the Alpo.

A guy—early thirties, brown hair, soft blue polo, forgettable—stands next to me holding a bag of salmon and rice like it's the answer to life's questions. His voice is gentle. His smile is kind in that *I-make-minimum-wage-so-please-be-nice* sort of way.

"Oh. Um." I force a smile—the kind that probably looks like I have gas. "Yeah. I have no idea what I'm doing."

He glances at my cart. "First-time dog mom?"

I look down at the squeaky squirrel and the pink dye and give a weak shrug. "He's new. I panicked."

He laughs. "Salmon and rice is a good place to start. Easy on their stomach, and they usually love the taste."

I nod, my fingers finally loosening from the cart. "Thank you."

"Mark," he says, pointing to his name tag like I can't read. "Let me know if you need anything else."

I watch him walk away and wonder—briefly, insanely—if he could tell.

Could he sense it? The murder aura? The faint scent of bleach and trauma?

Probably not. He looked like the kind of guy who reads comics on his break and microwaves fish in the employee lounge.

Still, I grab the salmon and rice.

Then I take a breath.

One aisle down. Too many more to go.

Dogs require so much stuff.

It's like stocking a baby nursery—only for a four-legged, judgmental roommate with a bladder the size of a thimble and a flair for dramatic exits.

After getting the collar tag engraved, I push my overflowing cart to the checkout line. It's stacked like I'm prepping for a puppy apocalypse. The cashier gives it a once-over and blinks slowly, like she's trying to figure out if this is a resale project or a mental breakdown.

Honestly? It's both.

She starts scanning while I pretend to casually sip from the complimentary store water cooler and act like someone who definitely didn't commit a violent felony this week.

I'm even nodding along to the in-store music like "Walking on Sunshine" isn't personally mocking me.

"Did anyone help you today?" the cashier asks, cheerful and oblivious.

Panic flickers behind my eyes.

"Uhh..." My voice catches like a rusted hinge. "Someone... did. Um. Mike?"

Her brows lift.

"You mean Mark?" she deadpans.

"Yes! Yes. Mark. Totally what I said. Just... mumble-mouth." *Insert awkward laugh here.*

She doesn't look convinced, but she's too underpaid to care.

As she bags everything, I pull out my phone and order a rideshare.

I should probably look into rentals if my car has to remain in the witness protection program for a while.

Huh. Another text. Unknown number. Nothing again.

I reply with "STOP" and delete it.

She finishes bagging my cartload of impulsive guilt-spending, and I thank her with a weirdly formal head nod—like I'm leaving a funeral reception.

I step outside just as my ride pulls up. Mint green Prius. Of course.

They're always a Prius.

But before I can move forward, I hear the one sound I've been dreading since last night's scare. The sound I've been expecting since I ran out of that warehouse, forever different.

Sirens.

Several of them.

They're coming and fast.

Three cop cars fly into the parking lot with their lights on. No slow roll. Just full velocity—tires screeching, doors cracking open before they've even come to a complete stop.

My body turns to cement.

My heart free-falls into my stomach and throws itself against the floorboards of my soul like *this is it, this is how we die.*

They found the body.

They know.

I'm going to prison.

Dexter's going to starve in the laundry room, wrapped in a cashmere throw like a tiny pink burrito.

My thoughts hit DEFCON-level spiral.

Do I run?

Fake a seizure?

Call my mom and tell her I love her?

I take a step back. Then another.

My shoe catches on a rock.

I stumble, arms flailing, until my back slams into the brick wall of the pet store. The cold jolts me—but not enough to make sense of anything. Not enough to stop the rising burn of bile in my throat or the choked sob straining behind my clenched teeth.

I lift my hands in surrender. I know it'll go easier if I cooperate.

The cops bypass me completely, racing straight into the very pet store I just exited.

The rideshare driver gets out to watch the spectacle, posing as helpful while I'm standing there, hands still raised with my emotional support squeaky pig and a bag of overpriced liver treats.

A man bolts out of the pet store behind me.

And I mean *bolts*—like someone yelled *Free rotisserie chickens!* and this man has unfinished business with poultry.

I don't even have time to register what's happening before one of the officers lunges forward and takes him down hard. Concrete meets torso. There's a wheeze. A squeal. Maybe from him. Maybe from me.

He's mid-forties, all belly and bluster, wearing the same cornflower-blue shirt I saw on that helpful aisle guy earlier. Was his name Matt? No—Merit?

Wait, does it matter?

They're reading him his rights and shoving him into the back of a cruiser, sobbing like an absolute baby. It's always the big ones who break down the easiest.

I'm still frozen against the wall, sweating like a glazed ham but they weren't here for me.

I'm still free.

For now.

I glance around, like someone might still jump out from behind the automatic door display and yell, *"Just kidding! Twenty-five to life!"* But nothing happens. Just the quiet hum of chaos dissipating and the smell of rawhide in my nostrils.

My rideshare driver—God bless her—is standing beside the open trunk. She's got sunglasses, a mullet, and the expression of a woman who knows this story is going to kill in the group chat.

Maybe I shouldn't use that phrase.

This story is going to *hit hard* in the group chat. Yes, that's better.

Much more innocent sounding.

We make eye contact and nod politely.

Neither of us says a word as I toss my bags into the back

and slide into the seat like my legs only just remembered how to work.

My hands won't stop shaking. I grip the edge of the seatbelt and try to breathe through my nose like my therapist always said. Four in. Four hold. Four out.

I close my eyes and let my head fall back, the counting giving me something to focus on.

You're fine, I think to myself. *You're okay. You're just... a dog mom. A totally normal, law-abiding, trauma-free dog mom.*

Declan

The city smells different when something's burned to the ground.

Not just smoke. Not just scorched wood and melted plastic. There's something else that seeps into the air—quiet finality. Like the ghost of whatever was here has been reduced to carbon, and now it clings to your clothes like regret.

I park across the street and kill the engine.

What's left of the warehouse sits in a shallow cradle of steam, a husk of warped metal and soot-stained brick. One wall's half-collapsed in on itself. What little structure remains won't stand long. If the city's smart, they'll condemn it before the ash cools.

I step out, folder in hand, and cross the yellow tape. The uniforms on scene nod as I approach. I don't return it—not because I'm an asshole (though I am), but because I don't give a shit.

The ground crunches beneath my boots. Flipping open the folder tucked beneath my arm, I scan the first page.

One photo shows the warehouse when it still pretended to be a business. Another from five years ago, when it was already halfway to collapse and doubling as a crime scene.

Ownership history—if you can call three shell companies and a Delaware P.O. box a "history."

Five drug busts, three assaults, and one overdose in the past year alone.

This place has always been a shithole. Now it just looks the part.

The fire crews are mostly gone now. Just a couple of stragglers rolling hoses and poking at still-steaming piles of what used to be this building.

I walk the perimeter slowly, every inch of my skin tuned to the scene—cataloging the way the metal curled, the direction of the collapse, the faint chemical tang still clinging to the air. The fire was efficient. Fast-moving.

Nothing else around it burned.

I crouch near what used to be the loading bay. The concrete's cracked, heat-blistered. A dark stain spreads toward the edge.

Could be oil. Could be something else.

Won't know until forensics comes back—and I'm not holding my breath for a rush job.

The city hasn't cared about this place for decades, which is why several guys from my case have arrests at this very warehouse.

I assume that's why my lieutenant called me out here on a Saturday.

Tucking the folder under my arm, I exhale through my nose, staring out at the smoke rising from the rubble. Amid the stench of scorched wood and history, I catch a trail of cigarette smoke.

My lieutenant's nearby.

My dad's old partner, back in the day.

Also, my godfather.

It's the only reason the two of us are able to talk openly about the real case I'm working. Laced within the guise of a human-trafficking ring is an overflowing amount of evidence that points to police corruption.

They go hand in hand. One and the same.

Someone within the circuit is running a trafficking ring. And I'm going to find out who it is.

"Blackwood." He nods, taking a pull off the habit that's going to kill him one day.

"Thought you were quitting."

A piece of ash floats into my mouth, and I spit on the gravel near my boot.

He gives me a look that says *don't you start too.*

"I'm telling Sonya." And I will. He knows I will.

"So, what are we doing here?" I ask, scanning the wreckage again. "They find a body in that shithole?"

Rourke's staring at the smoldering carcass of what used to be a warehouse like it might whisper state secrets if he glares long enough.

He's got that look again—the one that says *maybe.*

And I hate *maybe.*

Maybe means we're about to lose a weekend.

Maybe means paperwork.

"You see a body?" I ask, flipping the folder closed and eyeing the structure.

"Maybe," Rourke mutters.

I snort. Called it.

"And how is there a maybe-body in all that rubble?"

Before he can answer, a loud thunk echoes through the smoke-thick air.

Two firefighters are inside, wedging a long crowbar beneath

something. For a second, I think they're turning rubble. But no.

They're working the warehouse's foundation pad—what's left of it—and as the slab shifts, a plume of dust explodes upward, dirtying the air with fresh soot and something sharper.

One of the firefighters straightens, waving us over.

"Okay, Lieutenant. Come take a look."

Rourke sighs like he's already dreading whatever we're about to see. We cross the gravel, stepping over a collapsed beam and what might've once been a shopping cart.

It hits me before I even kneel.

The smell.

Charred metal and wet ash—familiar enough. But underneath it... copper.

That tang is unmistakable.

The cracked concrete is soaked underneath. A wide, dark smear bleeds outward from a central split, like something tried to claw its way through the floor.

The firefighter crouches beside it, pointing.

"This part of the foundation was shielded from the worst of the heat when the wall came down. But yeah. That's blood."

"A lot of it," I murmur, squinting at the way it seeped. "How fresh?"

"Can't tell. Fire compromised it. But it was definitely there before the blaze. Heat cooked it deeper."

Rourke exhales slowly. "That's too much blood for someone to've walked away."

"You thinking someone was caught in the fire?" I ask, scanning the soot-drenched edges of the foundation.

He shakes his head. "No. I think there was a body here before the fire. Maybe right up until it started."

I track the blast pattern across the concrete, zeroing in on a char trail leading away from the crack—toward what used to be the loading bay.

"Accelerant was poured, that's for sure," I say, nodding toward the black, scorched arc. "Maybe someone tried to burn the body."

Rourke hums. "Addicts?"

"Could be. But then again, tweakers aren't usually coherent enough to stage an arson." I tilt my head. "So why call me in and not Johnson?"

He doesn't answer right away. Pulls out another cigarette—doesn't light it. Just chews on the filter and nods for me to follow him away from hearing ears.

"That pet-store manager you had picked up today?" he finally says. "Frank Dempsey."

I raise an eyebrow. "Yeah. Had the bastard brought in this morning so he can sit in holding all weekend."

The guy's not a trafficker—he's a client. But a recent one. Within the past six months, which means he's still got numbers in his phone. Names. Drop points. Payment methods.

Easy shakedown.

He shakes his head, low and amused. "Booking said he pissed his khakis from crying."

I snort a laugh. Figures.

"His background came in while they were booking him. Guess who owns the shell company tied to this warehouse?"

I blink once. "No."

"Yup. Frank Dempsey. Our awkward suburban dad turned trafficking suspect."

I exhale through my nose. Hard.

"Guy's got a coke habit and is bored with his marriage," I mutter. "But I don't peg him for a killer."

"Me either." Rourke shrugs. "Still. Too coincidental to ignore."

I nod, jaw tight. He's right.

"Okay," I say, snatching the unlit cigarette from his hand and breaking it in half. "Let's go scare the shit out of Dad-of-the-Year Dempsey."

I drop the greasy sack of fast food onto the table like it's a gift to mankind. Which, frankly, it is. I'm fucking starving.

There's a particular kind of peace that comes from the scent of salt, meat, and saturated regret. I take a long, cold pull of the chocolate shake, letting the sugar hit my system before the sodium does. Heaven.

"You're doing the interview," I mutter around a fry. "I'm emotionally unavailable until I finish this masterpiece."

Rourke eyes the bag with the hunger of a man whose wife put him on the pre-diabetic diet six weeks ago.

"You better have gotten enough for both of us."

I reach into the bag and pull out a plastic container chock-full of greens and set it down like I'm presenting an Olympic medal.

"I did." I gesture at the salad. "It's right here, waiting for you."

He stares at it like I slapped his mother with a head of lettuce. "You're a dick."

"And you're welcome." I unwrap my burger like it's the only thing I trust in this building. Aside from Rourke, it pretty much is.

He grabs the file folder, muttering something about betrayal and rabbit food, and stalks into the interview room.

Through the one-way glass, I watch Frank Dempsey—the suburban cautionary tale in a button-down—practically melt into his seat. The guy's shaking hard enough to rattle his watch.

His color is somewhere between paper and corpse.

"What lie did you tell your wife to excuse your pickup?"

Dempsey stammers. "DUI. I told her I got pulled for a DUI."

Predictable.

Rourke flips the folder open and pulls out a stack of photos—high gloss, low morality. Girls posed and staged for sales. Their eyes vacant, their bodies no longer their own.

As soon as the first photo hits the table, Dempsey folds like a paper crane dropped in water and sobs. The man's a puddle.

Rourke doesn't blink or raise his voice. Just slides another photo across the table. This one's different. No lights, no posing. Just a body. Still. Cold. Dead.

"That girl," Rourke says, his voice all gravel and blade, "you booked her the night before this was taken."

Dempsey chokes on his own fat tongue. "I didn't—I swear I didn't touch her—she was fine when I left—"

Rourke doesn't care. "It's in your phone, Frank. Every appointment. Every name. Every filthy little timestamp. You're practically begging to get caught."

I dip a fry in ketchup and watch as Dempsey cracks under pressure like it's amateur hour at a stress test.

"We can charge you with solicitation," Rourke continues. "Accessory to murder. Trafficking, if you want to get spicy."

The guy's leaking every detail he can remember within three seconds. Twenty-eight minutes later, I've finished my burger, cleaned up my fries, and started cataloging the ways this idiot is going to ruin his life with a single word.

Rourke leans back in his chair. "You sure this is everything?"

Dempsey's nodding so hard I think his vertebrae might shatter. "Y-yeah. I swear—I can tell you who picked her up."

Rourke's expression flickers. "What do you mean?"

"The girl. The one in the photo. A cop brought her. Dropped her off. Sat in his car while we—while I—while it happened."

I sit up straighter.

Rourke narrows his eyes. "You're saying a police officer delivered her?"

Dempsey nods again, slower now. "He came back. Picked her up after. Same guy. Unmarked cruiser."

Rourke leans forward. "Who?"

Dempsey freezes. There's that moment—tight as a piano wire—where fear and obedience wrestle for control.

He picks fear.

"I don't know if I'm supposed to say—"

"Say it," Rourke snaps. "Now."

Dempsey breathes like he's about to confess to treason. His voice trembles when it comes.

"Detective Declan Blackwood."

Everything stops.

"I remember because I thought it sounded cool."

My stomach turns to stone.

Rourke blinks. "What?"

"That's the name," Dempsey gasps. "I saw it on his badge. That's who dropped her off. Detective Declan Blackwood."

My name hits the air like a loaded gun, and for a second, I forget how to breathe.

Poppy

Dexter looks fabulous.

And that is not sarcasm. He's freshly fluffed, his coat evenly dyed in a rich, bubblegum hue that screams intentional aesthetic choice instead of evidence tampering. His snaggletooth juts proudly from the corner of his little pink mouth, his tiny paws crossed like he knows he's the moment.

I even spritzed him with pet-safe lavender mist, because why commit to a crime-adjacent makeover if you're not going to seal the look with calming aromatherapy?

We're ready. Or at least, we look like we are.

I'm a ball of nerves inside, but that seems par for the course recently.

I call a rideshare again, grimacing when I look at the fee. But I'm not risking my murder-tainted car until further notice, and my rental won't be delivered until tomorrow morning.

So, for now, she remains in garage time-out. And so does my crime-scene clean up plan. I can't exactly take an Uber to the murder.

Thoughts of someone walking in on a puffed up body make my stomach turn.

No, we're not thinking about that right now. We've got somewhere to be.

I pack light—just the essentials.

An obnoxiously oversized designer tote bag, big enough to carry the Constitution and an entire ham. Inside: three bags of bloody evidence that could put me at Rikers for life.

The pet carrier is sleek, soft-sided, and painfully expensive. Dexter hates it.

He lets out a huffy little breath like I've insulted his dignity, which—fair—but he settles in anyway, because I bribed him with liver treats.

We're heading to the vet. Not just any vet, mind you. The one I found during my late-night anxiety spiral at two fourteen a.m. yesterday. Out of the way. Sunday hours. Walk-in's welcome.

And—best of all—it's also a pet crematorium.

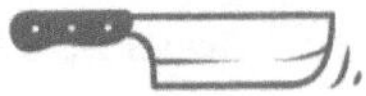

The clinic is modern, warm, and blessedly overpriced—exactly how I like it. No crusty linoleum or 1992 cat posters with *Hang in there!* captions. This place has glass walls, fiddle-leaf figs, a front desk with eucalyptus diffusers, and a soothing playlist of indie acoustic covers of Taylor Swift songs.

Dexter, the walking pink advertisement for plausible deniability, waddles in like he owns the place. One of the vet techs behind the desk claps a hand to her chest and gasps, "Oh my gosh, he's so cute!"

"Right?" I smile like a totally well-adjusted, emotionally stable human. "He's a rescue."

Which is... not a lie. Technically.

The vet tech kneels to his level. "What's his name?"

"Dexter," I say automatically, then freeze. Was I supposed to change it? Is that how this works? Witness relocation but for traumatized dogs?

She chuckles, scribbles something on the intake clipboard. "Like the serial killer show?"

I blink. My mouth opens and then closes.

"I mean, he's got that look," she adds brightly. "All cute on the outside but definitely plotting something."

I force a laugh that sounds like a dying blender.

"Yeah," I croak. "Totally harmless."

Dexter yips like he agrees, his tail wagging with far too much unbothered confidence for someone who committed a Class A biohazard in an abandoned building less than forty-eight hours ago.

I check us in, trying not to clutch my tote like it contains radioactive evidence and a spare identity.

"Okay," the tech smiles. "We'll call you back in a few. Just have a seat!"

Sure. A seat. So I can sit here for a really long amount of time with blood-covered clothing in my bag. My mind races to the chances of a cadaver dog coming in for Sunday spa day and heading straight for me.

I choose one in the corner and perch like I've never sat in a chair before, hands folded over my bag like it's going to make a break for it.

Across the waiting room, Dexter stares at a French bulldog like he's telling him everything we've done, and my phone pings with a text.

I'm greeted by my besties overly smug grin, perfectly bald head, oversized eyewear, and a giant mimosa raised in mocking toast.

> SEBASTIAN: When the first date turns into brunch the next morning. Fair warning, I'll be sending drunk selfies in about an hour.

I huff softly, lips pressing together even as a reluctant smile threatens to crack my stressed demeanor.

> ME: Don't do anything I wouldn't do!

His reply is instant, the sass practically radiating off my screen:

> SEBASTIAN: Definitely not following that advice. See you tomorrow, Counselor Killjoy.

> SEBASTIAN: Don't forget we're spilling tea!

> SEBASTIAN: I want it piping hot.

I chuckle despite myself, feeling briefly lighter before my worries inevitably drag me back down again.
Another ping.

> UNKNOWN NUMBER:

Nothing.
What in the three-ring circus is this?

> POPPY: STOP

I don't know what kind of spam list I ended up on, but I want off.

We're called back ten minutes later by a vet tech. A few more minutes of agony and the vet comes in.

She gives Dexter a thorough once-over—ears, teeth, paws, heartbeat. "He's in great shape," she says. "No injuries, no concerns. Aside from having only one tooth, of course."

She scans for a microchip. I hold my breath like we're in a bomb-disposal scene.

Nothing.

She checks again.

Still nothing.

I exhale so sharply it might qualify as a small exorcism.

"Well," she says, gently scratching under Dexter's chin, "whoever owns him takes very good care of him."

My fingers are shaking. "Yeah, he just... showed up."

"You may want to put up some fliers," she adds helpfully. "Post online? See if anyone's looking for him."

I nod like that is absolutely something I will be doing. "Yes. Great idea. I'll get right on that."

When pigs sprout wings and file their taxes.

She gives me a handout about local rescues and shelters. I fold it neatly and slip it into my tote, where it will live for the rest of eternity, untouched and unbothered.

"Well, you two are all set. Just grab your intake forms and some heartworm prevention at reception," she says as she steps out.

And this? This is the moment I've been waiting for.

The one I planned for.

Operation: Destroy the Evidence.

I casually scoop Dexter into my arms and slide off the stool with the grace of a legally blonde ninja. He lets out a small, inquisitive grunt but doesn't protest. Maybe he knows. Maybe he supports my plan.

I walk the hallway like I belong. Not fast. Not slow. Just purposeful. As if I'm a woman with real errands and zero evidence in my possession.

I pass the patient bathroom, a janitor's closet, a door marked EMPLOYEES ONLY. Then—

BIOHAZARDOUS WASTE – STAFF ONLY

Bingo.

The sign is small. White letters on a red background. The kind of sign that usually keeps people out.

But me?

Not a chance.

This is where the magic happens. The quiet disposal. The final curtain call. The place where unspeakable things go to be un-speeched.

I glance down at Dexter. His tongue sticks out just slightly.

"Wish me luck, my little accomplice," I whisper.

Inside, the room smells like bleach, pet shampoo, and poor decisions.

Everything is stainless steel and horror-movie sterile. A wall lined with red-lidded bins. One big industrial chute marked INCINERATOR – DO NOT TOUCH. Which I will absolutely be touching.

Because I'm a professional. And desperate.

Dexter snorts beside me like he already disapproves.

"All right, Dex," I whisper, setting him gently on the floor. "You're my lookout. No distractions. We're in too deep now."

He immediately begins sniffing a spot on the floor like it personally insulted him.

I open my tote bag with the reverence of someone unboxing a cursed relic. Because that's basically what this is.

The bag contains a greatest-hits collection of the longest night of my life:

My shredded black bodysuit, blood-splattered gloves and all.

Every single item is tagged in my mind with a memory I wish I could bleach.

I pause. One last look that makes me close my eyes.

This is taking it a step further. Destroying evidence after fleeing the scene of a crime. Everything I'm doing is only adding more years onto a lifelong sentence.

But I have to do it. I have to outsmart this. Outrun it.

I slip each bloodied package into the red biohazard bags, seal them, one by one—quiet and methodical.

Dexter watches judgmentally. Possibly impressed.

When they're all ready, I send them down the chute.

A low clang echoes as it disappears into whatever infernal void waits below.

"And just like that... poof. Gone."

After liberally applying some hand sanitizer fixed to the wall, I wipe my hands on my thighs. My knees feel like water, and my spine is held together with espresso and spite, but the job is done. At least, this part is.

Now all I have to do is exit and pray that nobody notices me leaving a room that says DO NOT ENTER.

No big deal.

Totally normal Sunday.

Just your average pink-drenched girl and her pink-dyed war-criminal shichon.

Something else I got out of today—the mixed breed of my cute, snorting companion.

"Dexter," I whisper. "Come here, baby. Let's not add breaking and entering to our criminal résumé."

His head tilts. Snaggletooth in full sass mode. And then— he bolts.

A full lap around the room, nails skittering across the tile like a tap dancer on caffeine. Tongue out. Pure joy on his deranged little face.

"Dexter!" I whisper-hiss, chasing after him. "You're blowing our cover!"

He dodges a mop bucket, rounds the hazardous waste chute like it's a Formula One track, and keeps running. I make a lunge and miss by an inch, nearly face-planting into a cabinet labeled FELINE URINE SAMPLES – DO NOT TIP.

And because the universe loves me, the door swings open.

An attendant walks in holding another red bag, sees me crouched in a squat-lunge like I'm mid–yoga pose, and freezes.

I straighten quickly, brushing imaginary lint off my top. "Sorry! He just... ran in here." I gesture vaguely, like that explains anything.

The guy blinks. "He?"

As if summoned, Dexter tears past his ankles like a pink, furry bullet.

And just like that, it becomes a full-blown foot chase.

Two vet techs and one emotionally compromised dog mom sprinting after an animal who probably thinks this is the best game ever invented.

"This is fine," I mutter under my breath. "This is normal. This is what responsible adulthood looks like."

One of the techs grabs a treat jar off the counter, gives it a rattle.

Shake. Shake. Shake.

Dexter skids to a stop mid-sprint, does a cartoon-style spin, then sits perfectly still like he's posing for a Renaissance portrait.

I blink. "Did you just... Jedi mind trick my dog?"

Then—because he's not done tormenting me—he slowly

rises up on his haunches, front paws flailing in the air like jazz hands.

Actual jazz hands, begging. Full-on *Oliver Twist Please, sir, can I have some more?* begging.

I slap both palms over my mouth to contain the squeal threatening to rupture the time–space continuum.

"Oh. My. Turkey gobblers. That is the cutest thing I've ever seen! How am I supposed to say no to that?!"

The entire room dissolves into laughter or *awws*. One of the techs scoops him up and hands him back, grinning.

"Oh, you'll get used to it."

I hug Dexter to my chest, his tail wagging like a weapon of mass destruction. "Doubtful."

Him

She was here. Just this morning, she was right here.

The air still holds her heat, her perfume, like the room itself is reluctant to let her go.

Stepping into her shower, I breathe her in—her scent still clings to the steam, faint but undeniable.

Coming into her home when she left this morning, I've been cleaning up the faint trail of trace DNA she couldn't see.

I'm nearly done. Those moments of *should I be* here quickly overshadowed by my need to protect her.

I was almost done with the bathroom. The anthem I've dedicated to Poppy playing in my earbuds.

"I love you always forever
Near and far, closer together..."

With my UV specs, I look around for any final surfaces that needed my attention when I saw delicate handprint on the shower glass.

Small. Fragile. Hers.

My pulse kicks. I press my palm to the fading impression, aligning our fingers like I can hold her there. Naked. Vulnerable.

Mine.

I close my eyes, surrendering to the fantasy that's devoured every sleepless night.

She stood here, where I am now—water trailing down the curves I've dreamed of, her breath catching, lips parted in quiet invitation. I imagine pressing against her, my palm sliding down her stomach, fingers circling just above where she wants them most.

She'd gasp. Shudder. So fucking wet for me.

The warmth, the slickness, her desperate need—it's all there in my mind. She moans, arches, pushes back into me, trembling as I touch her.

The ache hardens into pain. I unzip, and wrap my hand around my cock, imagining hers instead. So small and perfect gripping me.

She'd turn and kneel, taking me into her mouth like she was made for it—but I wouldn't come there. No, I'd need to be inside her.

I picture the moment I push in—tight heat surrounding me, her cry of pleasure as I fill her. That flutter of her pussy gripping me. That first thrust, deep and claiming.

Fuck. I need it like I need air.

I stroke faster, chasing the edge, lost in the thought of her —poised in court, fearless by day, undone under me at night. That contradiction wrecks me.

I want to protect her.

Own her.

Etch myself into every part of her.

She'd collapse against me, sobbing my name as I pull her back by the hair and drive her into oblivion.

The orgasm crashes over me, violent and consuming. I groan as release hits—hot jets splatter the glass. My knees buckle slightly. I brace myself, breath ragged, undone by a woman who doesn't even know I'm here.

As the wave of sensation recedes, reality seeps back in.

I lean forward, forearm braced on the fogged glass, breathing hard. My chest rises and falls with the lingering echo of her.

Countless nights I've watched her sleep—silent, still—listening to those soft moans as she dreams. Waiting. Wanting.

Aching for the moment she whispers my name in the dark, breathless and needy.

Wanting me. Needing me.

"One day soon, sunshine," I murmur, breath fogging the glass. I trace the ghost of her handprint, down the imagined curve of her silhouette. "You'll know I've been here all along."

I exhale, the last sparks of pleasure still humming through me.

"Well, that was therapeutic," I say, voice flat and dry.

Cheaper than any shrink I've ever wasted money on.

But fantasies—no matter how vivid—always end.

I sigh and refocus, focusing on the cleaning to center me. Every swipe wipes her slate clean—our slate.

As I repack my supplies, a twisted pride curls in my chest. One last look around the bathroom, and I zip the bag shut.

Not a speck of DNA left. No hair. No fingerprints.

Pristine. Better than new. A masterpiece.

Too bad no one will appreciate it.

But I will.

Because it was for her. Always her.

The slam of a car door outside slices through the silence.

Fuck.

I lost track of time. Got too caught up in her. Didn't check her location.

I move fast to the upstairs landing, dropping low into the shadows. My pulse pounds as I ease toward the window.

And there she is—my beautiful, oblivious problem. Stepping out of a rideshare. Graceful. Unaware.

Jealousy flares, hot and irrational.

A rideshare.

Some stranger drove her home.

My jaw tightens. Rage curls slow and low in my chest.

The thought of anyone else near her, even casually, lights a fuse behind my ribs.

Easy, Romeo.

I breathe deep, tempering it. Soon, *I'll* be the one driving her. Taking care of everything. She won't even remember what freedom felt like.

She's heading for the door.

I retreat deeper into the hall shadows, a smirk twitching at the edge of my mouth.

I love this part.

Her, going about her night. Me, inside her home with her. So close she could almost feel me—and yet she doesn't.

Adrenaline spikes. My body tenses.

I slip into the utility closet just before the hinges creak downstairs.

She's home.

My chest tightens at the sound of her voice—syrupy and sweet, cooing to that damned fluff-ball menace she treats like a child.

"Dexter, baby! Was such a good boy."

I squint.

You should be greeting me like that, sunshine. Not that furry little asshole.

Footsteps echo below, soft and deliberate. Then—paws, tapping up the stairs.

Fucking Dexter.

The bane of my existence, wrapped in six pounds of fluff and judgment.

He stops outside the closet, sniffing like a narc in a chew-toy disguise. A low growl builds in his throat, sharp and suspicious.

I clench my jaw.

"You little shit," I whisper, breath tight.

He growls louder. My pulse kicks. I stay still, barely breathing, every muscle coiled.

"Dexter?" Her voice drifts up. "What are you barking at, buddy?"

Shut the fuck up, Dexter. Play dead for once in your miserable life.

The irony isn't lost on me—a grown man hiding from a snaggletoothed puffball.

I freeze, counting heartbeats in the dark. It's humiliating—until it's not. Because if she finds me now, everything I've built crumbles.

Downstairs, keys rattle against the counter.

"Dexter, come down here!" she calls again, firmer.

Please listen to your mommy, I think acidly. *Be a good boy, you fluffy little snitch.*

But her footsteps start climbing.

Fuck.

Blood roars in my ears. I can't move—panic cements me in place.

This isn't how it's supposed to happen.

Not now. Not like this.

I've planned our first meeting a hundred different ways—each moment scripted, perfect.

Not trapped in a fucking closet because her lapdog thinks he's the Secret Service.

My fists clench. She's getting closer. Every step slams through my ribs. The doorknob twitches. Squeaks.

No, no, no—

Ding-dong.

The doorbell rings, sharp and obnoxious. Poppy stops. Even Dexter hesitates.

Relief hits, sharp and nauseating. It vanishes just as fast, drowned in possessive fury.

Who the fuck is that?

My jaw locks. Rage coils behind my teeth.

A date?

I'll fucking bury him.

I hear her murmur something low to Dexter, then her footsteps retreat down the stairs.

I move instantly. Slip from the utility closet and into the linen one across the hall, closing the door with surgical precision.

Phone out. Security feed up.

There's a fucking man at the door holding something. Tall and lanky build. Flannel and jeans. Nothing memorable.

I already know I hate him.

I sure as fuck don't like him ringing my girl's doorbell.

Downstairs, the door creaks. Muffled voices follow.

"Oh, thank you so much," she says brightly. "I'd forget my head if it wasn't screwed on."

The door closes. My breath leaves in a slow, ragged stream —relief tangled with suspicion.

Who the hell was that?

Her tone was casual, even grateful. A neighbor? Something more?

I would've known if she were seeing someone. If she had a date.

Before I can spiral further, her voice rises again, amused and exasperated—clearly for the fluff-ball who nearly blew my cover.

"Dexter, we're wanted for murder," she says sweetly. "We can't just go around forgetting things in our Ubers, okay? I need you to pull your weight."

Realization hits, cold and sharp.

Of course. Just the rideshare driver—returning something she left behind.

Christ, Poppy. You'll be the death of me.

I crouch in the linen closet, tension slowly leaking from my muscles. Her voice fades back into the hum of the house.

I exhale, leaning against neatly folded towels that smell like her.

I hear her on the stairs—unbothered. Predictable sunshine, always needing to prove she's right.

The utility closet door creaks open. On my feed, I watch her peer inside, smug.

"See, you little psychopath. Empty."

She heads toward her room and I follow her like she's gravity.

I watch my phone like an addict as she undresses—slow, soft, unaware. Steam blurs the feed as she steps into the shower.

God, how she tortures me.

This is my window.

I ease open the linen closet, silent—only to be greeted by a familiar, judgmental growl.

Dexter.

He snarls like he weighs more than six pounds.

I narrow my eyes.

"You've got one tooth. What's your plan here, buddy?"

I ghost forward. No sound, no trace.

Dexter follows, barking like he's auditioning for the K9 unit.

"For fuck's sake," I hiss.

This dog could shatter glass—and my entire operation.

I toss a treat. Silence. Toss another. He follows.

I slip downstairs. Adrenaline sharpens everything.

A leather tote by the door catches my eye. I slide on my specs and just like I thought, blood. Faint but glowing.

"Jesus, sunshine. How the hell did you miss this?"

There's no question—I have to take it. But the snaggle-tooth menace is still trailing me.

"Just so you know, she was mine first," I mutter, half to him, half to myself.

He lifts his leg maintaining direct eye contact.

"No—" Too late.

I shove the tote beneath him, catching the piss just in time. He watches me smugly.

"You're really enjoying this, huh?" I mutter. "You're ruining everything."

He just sits there, paws aligned, one stupid tooth gleaming like he owns the damn place.

"You look ridiculous," I growl.

Fucking asshole.

Yes, I'm beefing with a purse-accessory that barks.

I eye the bag—now soaked in indignity. I'll have to take it. She's definitely going to notice it's gone.

It'll just become part of the plan. A calling card. Like the blank texts I've been sending her.

Like the greeting I have planned for tomorrow.

I narrow my eyes at the pink terror.

"I'm watching you."

He doesn't move. Still smug. Still victorious.

As the door clicks softly shut behind me, I exhale. Frustration and dry amusement tangle in my throat.

Outmaneuvered by a cotton ball.

Next time, I win.

Poppy

My breath clouds the bathroom mirror as I lean in, applying the last swipe of mascara. Today has to be perfect—calm, collected, and completely unremarkable. Flawless makeup. Practiced smile. Model citizen.

I'm just blending a smudge beneath my lower lashes when something in the shower's reflection catches my eye. A distorted shape. I straighten slowly, pulse ticking up as I stare through the condensation on the glass door.

There it is. A handprint.

Big. Male. Impossible to explain.

I laugh—too sharp, too thin.

It's not mine. It couldn't be.

Maybe maintenance? But they've never touched the shower. And I wiped down every inch of this place in my Friday-night postmurder meltdown.

Didn't I?

My heart pounds louder than reason as I step closer. The print's still visible, even through the steam.

I wrench my gaze away and brace against the counter, willing my breath to slow. Not today, Poppy. Not when you're due in court.

But my hands shake as I set the mascara down. The utility closet flashes through my mind—Dexter growling.

His barking I heard from the bathroom last night. Goosebumps rise across my skin.

You're being paranoid.

Unless... you're not.

My perfume bottle trembles as I force another inhale. Could someone have been here? Maybe the police? Found evidence and slipped in quietly to investigate?

No. Cops wouldn't be stealthy. They'd knock, warrant in hand, and badges blazing.

I reach for the other perfume bottle and my hand stalls midair.

There's also the texts.

From the unknown number. Blank. No message. Just... presence.

It started after Travis died.

Not before. Not during. After.

A thought slams into me so hard I nearly drop the glass: What if someone saw me?

A neighbor. A camera. A witness.

No, it could have been Chase. Travis Gannon's bestie and constant alibi.

He lived nearby. Travis used his apartment as his hunting grounds. Chase as his scapegoat. Maybe he knew more than he let on. Maybe he followed Travis that night. Maybe Dexter isn't some random stray—I found him near the scene. What if I didn't just get lucky?

What if someone left him behind?

Downstairs, Dexter's tail wags like nothing's wrong. He trots back in from the yard as I fill his bowl and say, "Now is not the time for a hunger strike, little man."

He ignores his food. Again. I eye him warily.

Halfway through ordering a rideshare, I head for my leather tote—only to stop short.

It's gone.

The spot by the door where I dropped it last night is empty. I check. And check again. No sign of it.

My brain scrambles. I was holding Dexter. I put the tote down to close the door. Right there.

But nothing.

"Get a grip," I whisper, palm pressed to my forehead. "You're losing it, Poppy."

The shower handprint was mine—distorted by the gloves. Maybe I just—forgot—setting it somewhere else, maybe.

But the fear won't loosen its grip.

If someone did see me, if they are stalking me—they want me scared. Not caught. Yet.

I pull up my phone and order a full set of security cameras. They'll be here by tonight. It may be too late, but even still, knowing I'll have footage just in case anything happens makes me feel better.

The rideshare notification pings. Time to be normal. Time to pretend.

I crouch beside Dexter and stroke his ears. "If anyone comes in while I'm gone," I murmur, "bite them. Okay?"

He licks my hand cheerfully, completely unbothered. I force a smile and straighten.

Today, I'm not a murderer. I'm a lawyer. I'm fine.

Just another Monday.

Sebastian waits at the courthouse doors like he's posing for paparazzi, sunlight bouncing off his oversized sunglasses and a venti iced coffee in hand—overloaded with cinnamon-dusted foam and held out like a peace offering.

"Diva, what's with the rideshare?" He presses the drink into my hand with an affronted look, as though I've personally betrayed him. "You know I would've chauffeured my bestie anywhere."

"Ugh. Mondays." I take a sip to cover the tremor in my hand, forcing an eye roll I hope passes for casual. As if I didn't spend the weekend committing a felony and disposing of evidence. As if everything is totally fine.

"My car wouldn't start. It's at the dealership. They're sending a rental, so it's no biggie," I add, trying to sound breezy —cheerful, even. Maybe a little too cheerful.

He narrows his eyes, giving me a quick once-over, clearly skeptical, but lets it go with a dramatic sigh. "Rude of your car, honestly."

He links our arms as we head inside, and my pulse thrums beneath my skin, loud and frantic. Courthouse security looms ahead—officers, metal detectors, colleagues who deal with liars and criminals all day.

I'm convinced someone will look at me and just know.

"Morning, Hank," Sebastian chirps, offering a wink to the guard.

He drops his things into the tray with theatrical flair. I do the same, trying not to look like someone who crossed the moral event horizon friday night.

But as I step through the metal detector, waiting for the piercing beep or suspicious look from security that never comes, I realize no one's paying any attention to me at all.

No alarm goes off. No one blinks.

The world continues as if nothing's changed.

Conversations hum around us—lawyers swapping horror stories, clerks juggling paperwork, coffee machines sputtering to life. No whispers. No stares. No one looks twice at me.

And somehow, that's worse.

As we walk toward the elevators, my phone pings twice—one from my DA.

BENJAMIN: Need to see you ASAP this morning. Urgently.

My stomach drops.

Then I utterly freeze because the second one is from the unknown number that's been haunting me all weekend.

UNKNOWN:

I grind my teeth, anxiety boiling over into frustration. Enough of this game.

POPPY: Who is this?

Sebastian presses the elevator button. "One day Hank will admit he loves me," he sighs, then glances at me. "You okay? You look like Judge Carter handed you a subpoena and told you to beg for mercy."

"Just tired," I lie, fingers tightening around my coffee like it's the only solid thing keeping me upright.

Another ping as we step into the elevator and Sebastian presses the number for our floor.

UNKNOWN: You'll find out soon.

My chest tightens. It's not spam. It's a person.

My chest heats and breathing becomes near impossible.

This is bad.

Sebastian snaps a selfie with his drink. "Oh right—'tired.' That's what we're calling it? You still owe me the tea on your client's meltdown. Tell me she went full *Lifetime* movie."

I don't get the chance. The elevator doors slide open—and things go from bad to worse.

Benjamin, Lieutenant Rourke, and Detective Declan Blackwood are standing in a huddle.

Detective Blackwood's sleeves are rolled to his forearms, his jaw set in permanent scowl mode, his stance radiating broody intimidation. Every part of him looks like he's in the business of arresting people.

Homicide is here. That can only mean one thing.

Sebastian steps out of the elevator, but I'm frozen in place, feet glued to the floor, staring blankly like a carved marble statue. The doors begin sliding shut again, closing like curtains on my very public meltdown.

Smooth, Poppy. Really smooth.

"Hey!" Sebastian shouts, jamming his hand between the sensors. "Girlie pop, stop drooling and go flirt with Mr. Tall-Dark-and-Fuck-Me-Hard."

My brain short-circuits. Detective Blackwood nods at me and the other two turn and look on cue.

My body goes cold. My stomach churns.

This is it. Really it this time.

They found the body. The blood. The tote. They're about to offer me the illusion of dignity before hauling me to a cell.

I manage a step. Then another.

One at a time, Poppy. Look innocent. Or at least less murdery.

Declan's eyes are locked on me—sharp, unreadable, and impossibly green. I force a smile that feels more like a grimace.

"Good morning," I manage. It comes out barely above a whisper, and I immediately hate myself for sounding like I'm mid-interrogation on a true crime special. "To what do we owe the pleasure of a visit from homicide?"

Benjamin doesn't return the smile. His expression is tight, unreadable. "Let's take this to the conference room."

Oh, gumdrops.

I nod and follow, legs heavy. The moment I sit, I gulp iced coffee until my brain punishes me with a freezing headache. I pinch the bridge of my nose, trying to suppress the rising tide of panic.

Tiddlywinks, get it together, Poppy!

Rourke's the one who starts.

"Miss Hartwell, Detective Blackwood has been leading a covert investigation into a human trafficking network for the past eighteen months."

My mind races. Trafficking? Is this about Travis? Did they trace something back to him? To me?

He continues, "There's also a police corruption element we've kept quiet. It's bad. Systemic."

My thoughts spin wildly, scrambling to connect dots from human trafficking to the violent end I gave a serial rapist on Friday.

Have they linked him somehow?

Did he traffic women?

Am I caught in their net without realizing it?

My pulse pounds painfully in my ears, but I force myself to remain calm, to wait until the needle drops and I know exactly what lie to spin.

"Over the weekend," Rourke goes on. Oh no. Here it is.

"We interrogated an individual who directly implicated Detective Blackwood as involved with trafficking operations."

Oh, well, never mind.

Declan doesn't flinch, just folds his arms and waits like this is a waste of his time.

Benjamin steps in. "They need someone sharp to take over point. Someone who can see through half-truths, false leads, missing evidence. Someone meticulous."

He doesn't have to say it out loud. He means me.

I swallow thickly, forcing out the question gnawing at my nerves. "What exactly does any of this have to do with me?"

Detective Blackwood finally speaks, and suddenly, I'm lost in his voice, a dark, rich timbre that sends an uninvited—but very welcome—shiver down my spine. "I can't exactly investigate a case in which I'm a suspect. Wouldn't go over very well at trial, don't you think?"

All right, Mr. Grumpy Pants. No need for the dramatics.

"And if I say no?" I ask, wary.

"You don't really have a choice." Benjamin takes over. "Internal Affairs has opened a formal query into your handling of the mistrials."

The words hit like a slap.

"What?" I jolt upright. "You're serious?"

He nods once. "The errors, the suppressed evidence—someone filed a report. I have to pull you from active litigation until it's resolved."

"You know that's cow doodie." I smack my hands on the table like I can intimidate this investigation to end on the spot.

"I don't disagree. But this investigation—if we can trace the corruption, it might explain those anomalies. Maybe even clear your name."

I breathe hard through my nose, grounding myself.

My eyes inadvertently shift back to Detective Blackwood, who watches me closely.

Those vivid green eyes, irritatingly dreamy even in the midst of criminal allegations and disciplinary committees, threaten my already shaky composure.

"Well... when do we start?" I finally manage to ask, desperately trying to sound professional rather than terrified or furious or embarrassingly smitten.

Blackwood's voice is low and deliberate. "Right now."

Perfect. Just what I needed—to work side by side with the man I've been quietly fantasizing about, while dodging an internal investigation... and a murder charge.

This week is already shaping up to be an absolute winner.

18

Declan

I hate this.

Not the case. Not the pressure. Not even the part where someone's trying to ruin me—frame me, or put a bullet in my head if it comes to that.

No. What I hate is being told who I have to work with.

Especially when she walks into the precinct like she owns the place. Chip on her shoulder, iced coffee in hand, lipstick perfect.

No hesitation. No nerves.

Just that spark in her eyes like she's already halfway through solving a problem I haven't even handed her yet.

I barely glance up when Rourke brings her through the bullpen, but I feel her presence like static—bright and electric, too loud for a room like this.

She walks tall, chin high, her heels clicking across the scuffed floor with the kind of confidence that pisses off men who aren't used to being challenged.

I'm one of them. But at least I have the self-awareness to admit it.

Rourke doesn't bother with small talk. We reach the restricted corridor. I punch in the four-digit code to unlock the briefing room—the only place I trust to house what's left of this case. I gesture her inside, resisting the urge to grit my teeth when she brushes past me like she already belongs.

I shut the door. Let the lock click into place.

The board takes up an entire wall—timeline, mugshots, strings, maps, and reports layered three deep. It's chaos. But it's mine. And for the last year and a half, it's been mine alone.

"I don't work with a partner," I say.

"Well," she replies, barely glancing at me as she scans the board, "looks like you do now."

I glare.

She doesn't blink.

Just steps closer to the wall like she's examining a new exhibit. Arms crossed. Eyes scanning fast. I don't like it.

"I'm not your tour guide," I mutter. "This isn't a lecture."

"Great," she says. "I already read the files Rourke gave me on the way over. Start from the top anyway."

I talk—gruff, clipped, no frills. Just enough to sketch the outline. I keep the messier pieces vague. I want to see what she catches, what she misses. I'm not used to explaining myself, especially not to prosecutors who think they're here to play detective.

But to her credit, she tracks faster than I expect. Her gaze sharpens, eyes darting between names and timestamps.

And then—fucking hell—she starts touching my board.

"What the hell are you doing?" I snap as she moves a suspect photo and shifts the pins.

"If your version of this worked, you wouldn't need me," she says, calm, cutting, maddeningly assured.

I clench my jaw. "There's a method to this."

"There's also a missing month in this timeline," she replies, dragging a sticky note out of one cluster and dropping it in another. "And this witness contradicts this one."

Well, shit.

She's been at this for hours.

I watch, arms crossed, as she rearranges everything like she owns the goddamn board—timeline charts, evidence logs, transcripts, color-coded tabs. Her fingers move fast. Her logic moves faster. It should piss me off more than it does.

She doesn't ask permission. Doesn't wait for me to approve her analysis. She just... does it. And worse? She's right.

I shift in my chair. Sigh. She doesn't even notice.

She moves two names, draws a line connecting a known trafficker to a missing patrol report we'd written off.

"You dismissed this too fast," she says, tapping a red-high-lighted log. "Whoever's feeding intel into your chain is covering something. The error pattern's too clean."

I glance from the board to her.

This isn't a prosecutor. This is a wrecking ball in lipstick.

And apparently, I need her.

"I need a clean whiteboard," she says, already clearing space. "And every color marker you've got. No pastels."

She looks at me—not to ask. Just to confirm I know I'm doing it.

Jaw tight, I walk out. Two minutes later, I'm back with a board and markers. I slam it into place and leave the supplies beside her like she's hosting a damn art class instead of dissecting a homicide-and-trafficking case.

No thank you. Just writing.

Head down, laser focused. Color-coding sectors like this is what she was born to do. Her handwriting is annoyingly neat.

Within minutes, she's cataloged it all: corruption leads, aliases, interviews, and the internal reports that have been giving me migraines for months.

Pacing across the room helps but she doesn't even notice as she works.

Her layout catches me and I stop my path across the room. Not the neon fucking colors—Jesus—but the way she's grouped the dates. The overlaps. The noise I've been staring at for months suddenly has shape.

A pattern.

I step closer, shoulder nearly brushing hers. She notices and her breath hitches as she shifts away.

"Back up," I say. "What's the deal with that one?"

She circles a sticky note: a witness alias and a parole officer's ID.

"This guy. Your informant. He said he was working the night of the drug exchange, right?"

I nod. "Same stash that showed up in the girls who turned up dead. Same chemical signature."

"Right," she says. "But he doctored his timesheet."

She slaps a printed parole doc on the board under his name.

"He claimed he was on shift. But the PO logs say he took off for a holiday—the week before, not the week of."

I tilt my head. "So, he lied about being at work."

"Exactly. Why lie—unless you weren't supposed to be where you were?"

I feel the snap—the click I've been chasing.

"So he was there," I add in. "At the exchange."

She nods. "And he saw something."

Or someone.

My pulse stirs. He got leaned on. Tried to cover it with a shitty lie.

I glance at her again. Still holding the marker. Already chasing the next thread.

She stares at the board like she sees the next ten moves. Then she gives a sharp nod.

Shit.

I've seen that look before. Right before someone barrels into something they're not ready for.

Before I can ask, she's already moving—tossing the marker on the table and grabbing her bag.

"Where the hell are you going?" I push off the table.

"To fix your timeline," she calls, halfway to the door.

"Slow down," I snap, following. "This guy's a piece of work. Shifty. Allergic to telling the truth."

She glances over her shoulder. "Then tag along. Or stay here. I've interviewed worse."

I watch her go. Each step down the corridor like a countdown.

Everything in me says this is a terrible idea. She's brash and impulsive. Not even supposed to be here.

But she saw it. Saw what I didn't. Found a thread I didn't even know was loose.

And now she's pulling it—with or without me.

I hate it.

I hate how right she is.

I hate that I already want to know what she finds next.

My control's slipping. And if I don't follow her, I lose the case and the upper hand.

Fuck me.

"Hold on. I'll drive."

We pull up to the warehouse midafternoon. Sun beating down, concrete radiating heat, the entire block smelling like rust and burnout. A graveyard of forklifts and secondhand pallets out front. The kind of place where men clock in hungover and clock out looking for trouble.

And right now? All eyes are on her.

Poppy fucking Hartwell steps out of the car like she's on the cover of *Lawyer Monthly*, in a pale pink pencil skirt and sky-high heels that I'm convinced she uses to stomp over egos—male ones, mostly.

Matching blouse.

White blazer so clean it practically glows.

Bright blonde hair pulled back like she's heading to trial, not walking into a glorified junkyard.

She may as well be a goddamn neon sign, and every mouth-breathing idiot on this lot clocks her in less than a second.

Each one gets a scowl from me. A silent *don't even think about it* that I throw in their direction as I walk half a step behind her.

Trip works here.

Bottom of the food chain. Frequent flyer at county for shit like petty theft, trespassing, and the occasional low-level drug charge. Nothing violent—just chronically stupid.

A floor manager approaches, wiping his dirty hands on dirtier pants before offering one out to Poppy with a crooked smile.

I brace for her to swat it away or slice him with a look, but she doesn't. Just shifts the files in her arm, lifts her phone with the other hand, and avoids touching him without making it obvious.

Smooth.

"We're here to speak with a man named Trip," she says sweetly. "It's about his mother."

Does Trip even have a mother?

But hell, it works. In under two minutes, the manager is calling him up over the radio and giving us access to his sad little office.

The place smells like cigarettes and gym socks had a love child. Poppy steps in without flinching. I follow and shut the door behind us.

Trip shuffles in a minute later, lanky and twitchy, sunken eyes darting to me before he gives up. "Aw, really, Blackwood? Again?"

"You're a fucking liar, Trip." I pin him with a glare so he knows I'm pissed and in no mood for his whining. Poppy is helping herself to a drawer labeled "Timesheets."

Son of a bitch.

I start us off, keeping my voice flat, direct. "You were working the night of March third, right? Warehouse shift. Started at six."

Trip shrugs, slouches back into the creaky chair across from us like this is routine. "That's what I said, yeah."

"And your PO confirmed it?"

"Guess so."

I narrow my eyes. "That's funny. Your timesheet says otherwise."

He shrugs again, unbothered. "Paperwork's not really my thing."

Stonewalling. Classic. This isn't going anywhere fast.

"Here it is!" She says it like she just found a lost earring— casual. But then she smacks the original timesheet on the desk like a courtroom angel of death.

"You told your parole officer you were on shift," she says softly. "And you forged the timesheet you submitted to cover the fact you were not working."

Trip snorts, about to lie again. She doesn't let him.

"Because you were out delivering drugs and saw something you weren't supposed to. Right?"

Silence.

Trip's eyes shift. He licks his lips.

Poppy lowers her voice, gentle but sharp. "We're not here about you. We know you were there. You saw someone. Or something. And it scared you."

He cracks.

Just like that.

"Fuck." Trip slumps forward, arms resting on his knees, face in his hands.

What in the hell kind of voodoo did she just work on him? This prick can sit here playing games for hours.

"Look . . . I didn't wanna get in the middle of it, all right?"

"Okay. You won't be in the middle of it." Poppy folds her arms over her chest and sits on the edge of the desk. Ankles crossed and waiting like she knows he's about to spill it. And he fucking does.

"The drop was at a new address. I ain't never dropped there before." He breathes out heavy through his nose, squinting like it's painful for him to admit.

"And what did you see when you were there?" Poppy presses like she's done this a million times—and I realize, she fucking has.

She's brutal in cross-exams. I testified for her case once but sat in on the rest of the trial to make sure that piece of shit got what he deserved.

Don't let the Pretty in Pink persona fool you. She's ruthless.

"This van was already there. A bunch of girls were being led into the house."

"And what was peculiar about this that you lied?" She keeps him going.

"Because they were all bound and gagged. Blindfolded. Dirty. Some naked."

My jaw ticks. He says it like he was watching people walk into a store. Not girls held against their will, raped, and left for dead.

He pulls out a cigarette and puts it in his mouth, raising a lighter.

I snap my fingers once. "Don't be rude, fuckface." I bark. "Wait until after. Keep going."

Trip looks at me like he wants me to eat shit, but he turns back to Poppy and keeps going.

"My client said, 'Bad timing showing up now.' Told him I didn't know what he was talking about. I'm at work right now." Trip starts nodding in agreement like he's right back there in that moment. "He said, 'Good. Keep it that way.'"

That's it. He looks down at his hands, clearly at the close of his story.

Poppy puts her hand on his shoulder with a squeeze like she's saying thank you.

"I'm going to need that address."

19

Poppy

I survived.

I spent the entire day working shoulder-to-shoulder with Declan Blackwood—New York's hottest homicide detective, emotionally constipated brooder, intimidating menace—and somehow didn't pass out, hyperventilate, or make a complete fool of myself.

...Okay. Except for one moment.

Declan was deep in a folder of grainy surveillance stills. I reached across the table for my pen when tragedy struck. My elbow hit the corner of my emotional-support iced coffee and sent it toppling.

I lunged like an over-caffeinated ninja and, for a brief, shining moment, thought I had it.

I did not.

The lid popped midair, and the entire cup splashed all over Declan's pants. Not just a few drops—it looked like his thigh lost a fight with a brown-sugar tidal wave.

Naturally, my brain short-circuited. I grabbed the nearest object—a pristine case file—and started blotting.

On his pants.

With evidence.

He cleared his throat and raised a very pointed eyebrow.

That's when I realized I was blotting his... his *thing.*

I slapped the paper out of my hand like it had betrayed me.

So yes. Nailed it.

But aside from the caffeine catastrophe, the day actually went well.

There's something about a fresh case file that rewires my brain.

The victims, the motive, the cover-up—pieces click into place. It's my favorite stage.

The one where the case starts whispering secrets.

Declan grumbled the whole way, but I caught him mumbling: "Ten minutes and she's farther than I got in six months."

He said it like it physically hurt, but I heard it.

I'd engrave it on a mug if I thought he wouldn't smash it.

He dropped me off without fanfare—just a nod and a muttered something about a warrant. Real warm-and-fuzzy guy.

Now I'm sitting on the courthouse curb, shoes off, feet throbbing, waiting for the rental car that was supposedly delivered ten minutes ago.

I'm halfway through texting Sebastian about visiting Mariela when my phone buzzes.

UNKNOWN NUMBER

I frown and open it.

And the world drops out.

Images. Several of them.

The crime scene.

The body—his body. Travis Gannon.

Dismembered and laid out on tarps like a twisted jigsaw.

My hand flies to my mouth. My soul nearly bolts.

Someone else was there.

Nausea curls sharp in my throat. My fingers go cold.

I swipe through the images. It's him. It's real. It's proof.

Then one final message:

UNKNOWN NUMBER: Tip for next time: tarps.

My body freezes.

Whoever sent this wasn't bluffing.

They saw what I did.

And they're watching.

I type back with shaking hands.

POPPY: Who are you? This isn't funny. This is sick.

Then I block the number.

I close my eyes and take a breath that does absolutely nothing to calm me.

Because for the first time since this started, I don't feel like the one holding the secrets.

Someone else was there. Someone saw me kill a man.

And that someone dismembered the body after.

H ospitals smell like overcooked Jell-O, bleach, and quiet disappointment.

I step into the room balancing a too-bright bouquet of daisies in a polka-dot vase I panic-bought from the gift shop. It looked "cheerful"—and if anyone needs that, it's Mariela.

She lies in bed, pale against white sheets, staring at the ceiling like it's holding her together.

She doesn't look at me when I enter, doesn't blink when I set the flowers on the window ledge and gently clear my throat.

"Hey," I say, inching closer like I might scare her off. "I brought you these."

No response. Not even a glance.

Her skin is gray, lips dry, and the hospital bracelet looks oversized, like she's shrunk since Friday.

Meanwhile, I'm pretending I didn't get anonymous photos of the man she feared—chopped into puzzle pieces on a tarp.

I can't tell her he's gone. I definitely can't say I haven't heard from him. That would mean I'm expecting to.

Because someone will notice he's missing and I need to be shocked-but-cooperative innocence.

So I go with hope.

Poppy Hartwell, Dealer of Silver Linings and Slightly Unhinged Smiles.

"I hear you're going to an amazing inpatient facility," I say gently. "The staff is great and they have private rooms."

Still nothing.

"Are you doing okay?" I add. "Getting some rest?"

Mariela finally looks at me. Her eyes are empty, color drained to dust.

I know what she's thinking. That he'll come back. That I stole her only way out.

She doesn't know I gave her freedom. And I can never tell her.

"Hey, the hospital has a copy of the restraining order," I offer.

A bitter breath escapes her. "You think a piece of paper's going to stop him?" she whispers. "He always comes back."

I swallow and nod like I'm not unraveling.

"He can't come here," I say quickly. "Security knows. If

anyone suspicious shows up, they'll call it in. Has anyone... bothered you?"

She shakes her head slowly.

"No. It's been quiet."

Quiet.

That word sticks in my chest like glass.

Because quiet is worse. Quiet is when things creep. When monsters shift in the dark.

I force a smile and keep lying. "Quiet is good. If I hear anything, you'll be the first to know. Promise."

I give her hand a gentle squeeze and head out of the room before I unravel right in front of her.

The hallway is too bright. My heels echo too loudly. I make it to the women's bathroom and lock myself into the first stall, plopping down on the toilet to get my life together.

To remember how to breathe.

My fingers are tingling, and I need to calm down before I hyperventilate.

My phone buzzes but I ignore it. Closing my eyes, willing myself to take steady breaths in and out.

Finally, I look at my phone. One new email.

Unknown address.

My heart stutters. I click before I can think better of it.

There's a video attachment. No subject line. No message.

I press play.

It's a soundless, grainy cell phone video—but I recognize the setting instantly.

It's my warehouse.

A cigarette flicks, the ember arcs into darkness. Flames ignite in seconds. The video whites out as fire grows—then cuts to black.

There's no face. No voice.

Just a murder site erased.

My fingers go numb. The phone weighs a thousand pounds.

There's been no body reported because someone cleaned up after me. Then burned it down. And now everything is slamming together.

The handprint. The missing bag. The texts. Now this.

Someone's been in my home and has my number.

Now—my email.

My stomach drops.

This is no coincidence, or karma.

It's a stalker.

Not just any stalker.

One who helped me cover up a murder.

Silently. Completely.

And for reasons I don't understand... they want me to know.

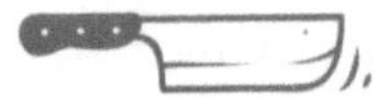

I don't remember walking out of the hospital. Or unlocking the rental.

Just that I'm in the driver's seat now, doors locked, hands shaking, laptop booting like it's a digital life raft.

Breathe, Poppy. Just breathe.

You're fine. Doing your job. Checking on a traumatized client. Being a responsible public servant.

That's the story.

If anyone audits your history, you're doing client research.

Not spiraling.

Just Poppy Hartwell, Concerned Legal Professional™.

I log into the DA's secure portal. Credentials accepted with a cheery little ding that feels wildly inappropriate.

I start where I should.

Friday's police call logs.

Filtered to Mariela's address.

Narrowed to just after seven p.m.

There it is.

The dispatch report.

Emergency services deployed.

Call recording attached.

Okay. Next: the warehouse. I widen the window—eight p.m. to midnight.

Nothing.

No disturbance calls. No suspicious activity. No mention of a man stabbed to death and left on an abandoned warehouse floor.

And, crucially, no reports of a crazed woman and a murder dog sprinting through the back alleys with a bloody knife.

I close my eyes and exhale a shaky breath that turns into a sob.

I stretch the search again—push it toward early morning.

And then there it is.

04:07 a.m.

A fire report. One single entry.

Caller: anonymous male, said he was driving a delivery route and spotted flames from the freeway. Still in his truck. No specific address. Just a general location.

Dispatch sent fire and rescue to investigate.

That's it.

No follow-up.

No crime scene photos.

No homicide unit called in.

No body. No blood. Nothing.

I sit back slowly, screen glow burning into my eyes.

There should have been a body.

I left him there. Pale. Lifeless. Still.

I flip tabs and pull up a map, cursor hovering with dread I can feel in my throat.

The pin drops.

Right there. Just outside city limits.

The warehouse.

The one with the cracked cement, the stack of tires I leaned against trying not to pass out.

The one I killed him in.

The back of my throat burns. I slam the laptop shut and hold it against my chest like a security blanket. Like the plastic shell can shield me from the fact that someone else knew I was there.

My heart slams against my ribs, like it's trying to signal danger in Morse code.

I need to go home.

I need to get inside, bolt every lock, and bury myself under a blanket of denial and one very judgmental dog.

Home is where Dexter is.

Home is where I pretend everything is fine.

Everything is safe.

The drive is a blur.

My fingers cramp around the steering wheel, my thoughts buzzing like a hive full of angry bees. By the time I pull the rental into the drive, I'm parked practically sideways—way too close to the side entrance—but I don't care.

I slide the key into the lock with shaking hands, heart pounding loud enough to drown out the bolt clicking open. The second I'm inside, I throw the deadbolt, twist the extra security latch, and type in the alarm code so fast I nearly mess it up twice.

Poor Dexter is staring at me like I've fully lost it. And maybe I have.

My hand hovers over the keypad, still trembling.

Deep breath. Just breathe.

But then—something shifts. An eerie sensation rolls over me like a chill crawling up my spine. The air is different. Still, but wrong.

I turn—and stop cold.

There, on the kitchen counter, sits a small pink box.

Perfectly square. Perfectly centered.

And perfectly wrong.

I can't describe the kind of fear that runs through me—like chains of ice slithering through every vein. It's not panic. Panic is loud. This is silent. Cold. Surgical.

Like standing on train tracks and hearing the whistle but not being able to move.

I look around my home, not daring to step forward.

"Hello?" I call out, like the stalker is going to pop up from the pantry and shout *Surprise!* like it's a birthday party.

Dexter trots over, tongue lolling, tail wagging so fiercely his entire butt does a figure eight.

Betrayal. Utter betrayal.

"Seriously?" I whisper, crouching to scoop him up. "You had one job, Dexter. Bark. Growl. Pee on something threatening. Anything."

He wags harder. Licks my face like I'm overreacting.

Someone was in my house.

Someone bypassed my alarm system, left a gift on my counter, and vanished without a trace.

My brain kicks into lawyer mode: gloves, photos, documentation. I can't exactly call this in—how do you report a stalker who helped you cover up a murder?

They could have recorded me. Kept evidence. Heck, they might've grabbed the tote bag I lost. Reporting them would be reporting myself.

But I still need to be smart. If that's even possible now.

I grab a pair of gloves from under the sink and my phone from my purse, snapping photos from every angle. The box is pale pink. No markings and no note.

Of course it's pink. It's taunting me.

With my heart pounding in my ears, I slowly lift the lid.

Inside is a cheap, basic flip phone—the kind you buy at a gas station at two a.m. when you're making bad decisions with cash in hand.

The second my gloved fingers brush it, the screen lights up.

I jump—actually jump—so hard I slam my elbow into the counter. A spoon clatters to the floor, and I jump again.

The phone buzzes once.

New Message:

UNKNOWN NUMBER: Don't ignore me.

Poppy

S leep did not happen.

At least not the kind that involves rest or dreams or any sort of brain activity that isn't *hyper-vigilance but make it feral raccoon.* I spent the night barricaded in my bedroom with Dexter curled beside me like a fluffy emotional-support meatball while my imagination ran a full marathon.

Every creak in the house sounded like someone scaling the walls. Every breeze through the vents became the breath of a stalker waiting to drop from the ceiling. My bedside lamp stayed on.

So did the hallway light. And the one in the bathroom, just in case I needed to sprint in there with Dexter and pretend the tub was a panic room.

And then, at six oh four a.m., just as I finally drifted into a thin layer of maybe-sleep, my phone buzzed.

My actual phone.

Not the trauma-sponsored flip phone from my anonymous, crime-scene-cleaning admirer. That one still sat on my nightstand like a cursed object from a true-crime museum. No, this was my phone.

I fumbled for it, my heart already performing a tap dance.

UNKNOWN NUMBER: This is Blackwood.
We need a judge's signature on a warrant.
STAT.

I blinked. Then blinked again.

Well. Good morning to you, too, Detective Perky McPerkins, while I save his contact.

POPPY: How did you get my number?

MCPERKINS: The DA website.

MCPERKINS: It's literally listed under your name.

Oh. Right.

I let out a breath and scrubbed a hand over my face, careful not to crush Dexter, who was still peacefully asleep like he hadn't failed in his sole duty of barking at suspicious energy.

He was snoring. On his back. Legs sprawled in the air without a care in the world.

POPPY: Give me twenty to get dressed and caffeinated. Email me everything.

MCPERKINS: Make sure it's a judge you trust.

That part made me pause.

There were only a few judges I trusted enough not to make a mess of this.

Judge Carter was at the top of the list—reasonable, smart, generally immune to courtroom dramatics unless someone really earned it.

I got ready in record time and scooped up my poor excuse for a security dog. I was armed with a can of hairspray and came out of my bedroom like I was SWAT team clearing a house.

Downstairs, Dexter did his business. Inside, he still hadn't touched his food from yesterday. Maybe a little? I couldn't tell.

I tossed it and gave him a new helping, but still, he just sat there, paws perfectly posed, snaggletooth giving me a thumbs-down.

"Dexter, we don't have time for protests. If you're not picking up on the context clues, we have a lot going on."

He sneezed, and I think I should have been offended.

At the courthouse, Judge Carter wasn't in chambers.

Instead, I was told that Judge Maxwell was available. And of course she was.

Judge Maxwell: known traditionalist, professional thunder-cloud, and possibly the founder of my personal fan club—if said club was made entirely of people who sigh heavily whenever I speak in court.

Rumor had it she once called my trial prep *style over substance,* which was rich considering the last man she approved a warrant for spelled *narcotics* wrong. Twice.

But fine.

This wasn't about me. This was about the case.

About doing the right thing.

And if the price of justice was enduring one more of Judge Maxwell's tight-lipped stares and possibly being told my hand-writing was too youthful, then so be it.

I knocked politely on the doorframe to her open chambers.

She looked up like she'd smelled hope where there should only be black coffee and legal despair.

"Hartwell."

I stepped inside, folders in hand, back straight. "Your Honor. I need your signature on a warrant request. The information's been emailed to your clerk and includes supporting documentation."

Her expression didn't shift. If anything, she blinked slower.

"Detective Blackwood isn't handling this personally?"

"He's leading the investigation," I replied evenly. "But he's currently chasing down the next suspect, and this signature is time sensitive. I was asked to help expedite."

She motioned toward the chair across from her desk like it offended her. I sat. Composed and calm. Like I hadn't been dreaming about ceiling-vent intruders all night.

Judge Maxwell took her time.

Reading every line.

Then rereading it.

And then making a sound in her throat like a dissatisfied owl.

I waited.

Breathed.

Smiled just enough to be polite without accidentally triggering her fight-or-eye-roll reflex.

After approximately seventeen years, she signed.

One sharp, no-nonsense scribble.

I slid the folder into my bag and stood. "Thank you, Your Honor."

She didn't look up, already back to something even duller than me.

"No one makes me work harder for a pen stroke than you."

Still nothing. Maybe a twitch. Possibly the faintest hint of satisfaction.

Progress?

Probably not but—I have the warrant.

I've never felt more legit in my life.

Black leggings, fresh black tennis shoes, a high pony tucked through the back of a black baseball cap, and—yes—my favorite hot pink crop top. Just because we're storming a crime scene doesn't mean I have to dress like disappointment.

I even remembered to bring my real blazer and court heels in a duffel in case we had to spin back to the courthouse after.

Who's responsible? This girl.

I jog toward the cluster of unmarked vehicles just outside the staging area, trying not to look too excited even though I'm practically vibrating. I've never been part of the actual raid before.

I'm always on the courtroom side of things—clean hands, controlled chaos, caffeinated arguments. Not boots on the ground with search warrants, bulletproof vests and intense eye contact.

This is very *Criminal Minds*–adjacent, and I'm thriving.

Well. I *was* thriving until Declan sees me.

He steps away from the van, instantly frowning like he just spotted a cat on a leash—confused, offended, maybe mildly intrigued against his will.

"What–are you wearing?" he asks flatly, giving me a once-over that lingers a little too long on the crop top.

I tug the hem down in solidarity with my dignity. "It's tactical spandex. Courtroom edition."

"You're not coming."

I blink. "Excuse me?"

"You're not coming on the raid."

"Oh, I am absolutely coming on the raid. I got the warrant. I'm in leggings. This is happening."

"This isn't a coffee run, Hartwell. It's a warrant execution. Active field op. You're a prosecutor."

"And," I counter sweetly, "you're my partner."

His eyes narrow. "I am not your partner."

"Well, not with that attitude." I gesture broadly to the team gathering behind him. "Look, we're all adults here. We have a warrant. We have a target. We have a window. What we don't have is time for your weird control issues."

Declan mutters something under his breath—probably a prayer for strength or a list of synonyms for *why me*—and then runs a hand down his face.

"This isn't protocol," he says finally. "You don't come into the field."

"Normally I don't. But normally I'm not investigating a department full of possibly dirty cops, helping unravel a trafficking ring, and trying to find out who is framing *your* patootie." I smile, teeth showing. "So, I'm feeling very outside the box today."

He glares.

I do not blink.

"This isn't safe."

Nothing in my life has been safe lately.

But I don't say that.

"But this is important, Declan." I ignore the feeling of my cheeks heating up having said his first name and not "Blackwood." But I keep going and pray he doesn't notice. "I almost just lost my last client becaues I couldn't get the guy. Let me come help these girls."

There's a long, strained pause where I can see the wheels turning in his broody homicide detective head. I'm fully prepared for him to pull rank, call my supervisor, or duct-tape me to the side of the courthouse.

Instead, he lets out a rough exhale through his nose and steps aside.

"Stay behind me. No wandering. You don't speak unless I say you can. And if anything even sniffs like danger, you stay in the vehicle. Got it?"

I salute with two fingers and the most obnoxious grin I can manage. "Copy that, partner."

He grumbles again, but I swear—I swear—his mouth twitches at the corner before he turns away. He could have burped, but I think I'm growing on him.

This is going to be so much better than court.

I've been trying to look professional for the last fifteen minutes. Really.

I'm standing with the team, focused, serious, calm. A prosecutor prepared to assist with a high-level warrant.

A woman not at all distracted by the fact that Declan Blackwood looks like he walked out of an action movie and is headed directly toward me.

Man. He looks great in tactical gear.

I am fine.

I repeat: I am fine.

And then he walks over holding a vest. Crosses the parking lot with some very *Top Gun*–coded sunglasses on.

He runs his tongue along his bottom lip, and something in my stomach goes on a rollercoaster ride.

"Put this on," he says, offering it like it's no big deal that he's wearing a black compression shirt and I can see every little ripple and muscle. Every. Single. One.

I take it, a little awkwardly, and do my best to strap myself in. Of course, the shoulder tab catches weird, and one side is tighter than the other, and I'm ninety-seven percent sure I've somehow made it less safe than it was before.

"Here," Declan mutters, stepping in closer.

Way closer.

Lifting the glasses on top of his head to see better, he reaches for the vest, one hand brushing my shoulder as the other tightens the front strap, and suddenly we are chest to chest, and my heart has decided it's in a sprinting competition with itself.

His hands are rough. Confident. He moves with the kind of quiet certainty that makes you forget to inhale. It's not flirtatious—it's practiced. Professional.

Which somehow makes it worse. Sexier.

I stare straight ahead at the edge of a van door like it holds the secrets to inner peace. Maybe if I focus hard enough, I'll forget that he smells like cedar and crime-solving. That his hand just grazed my rib cage. That I can feel his breath near my cheek because he's *that* close.

"Should be tighter around your sides," he says, voice low, all gravel and no give. He tugs a strap, then another. "There. Try breathing."

Yeah, I've been trying to do that for the last ten minutes.

"I'm good," I manage, voice about two octaves higher than I meant.

He pauses. Stays close.

And—I don't mean to—but I glance up.

Just for a second.

The sunlight cuts through the trees above us, catches his face in profile, and hits his eyes just right.

They're not just green—but *inhumanly* green. Like some kind of over-edited detective-themed cologne commercial. And before I can stop myself, before I even realize it's left my mouth, I whisper—

"So green..."

His eyes flick to mine.

Sharp. Focused.

And for a single heartbeat, everything goes still.

He doesn't say anything. Doesn't smirk. Doesn't move.

He just... looks at me.

And then his gaze dips—barely, but unmistakably—to my mouth.

The air between us shifts. Warms and stretches.

And then, without a word, he slips his glasses back on and turns away. Back to business.

Like the moment didn't just sucker punch my lady bits.

I exhale, slow and shaky, as the team finishes prepping.

Cool. No big deal. Just maybe don't exist near him again.

Ever.

Declan

The SWAT vehicle breaches first.

Steel, gas, and purpose—six thousand pounds of armored attitude rolling right up the lawn like it owns the place, which, for the next ten minutes, it does. Behind it, half a dozen patrol units stack up in perfect formation, lights spinning like a warning no one has time to listen to.

Seconds.

That's all it takes.

Battering ram hits the front door.

Screams. Scuffle. Shouting.

By the time the front team breaches, it's already over. No resistance. No runners. Just a pack of scumbags too high or too stupid to realize this was their final sleepover.

They're dragged out of the house one by one—some in shirts, some in boxers, one in a towel that I truly hope was not communal—hands zip-tied, faces shoved into dirt.

I watch from the rear of a police van, the back doors open, the left one pulled slightly in front of me like a makeshift shield. Gun in hand. Finger off the trigger.

Not because I expect trouble.

Because *she's* here.

Poppy Hartwell, looking like she belongs in a department-store ad for "adorkably overconfident prosecutors who won't stay in the fucking car." She's technically where I told her to be—technically—but every time I glance back, I get the creeping suspicion she's one spontaneous decision away from swan-diving into an active scene with nothing but a pair of latex gloves and sheer audacity.

This entire op has gone clean. Too clean. No shots fired. No injuries. Suspects detained. Evidence already being logged and bagged by half the department. It should feel like a win.

Instead, I'm waiting for the other shoe to drop. Because I don't trust this.

"All clear!" someone calls from the front.

And right on cue, there she *fucking* goes.

Strides past the van like she wasn't specifically told to stay put, gloves already pulled halfway up her wrists, ponytail bouncing like she's arriving for a spin class and not the aftermath of a felony warrant.

Unbelievable.

I bite back the words I want to shout and watch her cut a clean line across the lawn, duck under the tape, and head straight for the house like she's been doing this for years.

She doesn't even look at me as she passes—just adjusts her hat and steps over a pile of evidence like it's nothing.

She's infuriating.

Completely reckless.

Stubborn to the point of self-endangerment.

And, unfortunately... brilliant.

I should stop her. Drag her back. Remind her of protocol and liability and the part of the warrant that doesn't mention freelance Barbie storming the perimeter.

But I don't.

Because—God help me—I want to see what she does. What she finds. How she sees things I've missed at other scenes. She doesn't move like a lawyer. She moves like she's part of the case already, tangled in it, following invisible threads only she can feel.

And so, I wait. Fuming. Armed.

And completely powerless to stop watching her.

I follow her into the den, jaw tight, eyes sweeping the room for any lingering threat but there isn't one. The place is empty now, cleared and secure.

But she doesn't seem to care about safety. Not when there are drawers to open and furniture to interrogate.

Poppy's already halfway through dismantling a cheap metal desk in the corner, muttering to herself as she pulls out one drawer after another with all the delicacy of a grizzly bear in a locked snack cabinet.

"Careful," I grunt. "This isn't a flea market."

She doesn't even look up. "If there's evidence, it's not going to be labeled neatly in a folder under *Corruption: Volumes I–III.*" She yanks another drawer, checks the underside, shoves it aside, then pauses at the last one.

I cross my arms. "It's empty. I just checked that one."

"Mmhm," she says, distracted.

She taps it with her knuckles and it sounds—hollow.

She crouches down, already rummaging through another drawer, and pulls out a magnet. Just... finds one. Like she's a sorceress of office supplies.

"What are you doing?" I ask, not even bothering to hide the skepticism in my voice as I stare down a few uniforms who can't keep their fucking eyes to themselves.

"Looking for the catch," she murmurs, running the magnet across the drawer's surface. "If it's built like the ones in old customs-seizure desks, there'll be a metal latch."

Because obviously, the lawyer who wears hot pink crop tops to field raids also moonlights as a part-time furniture whisperer.

She moves the magnet slightly to the left. There's a soft click and I blink and hold my breath.

She slides open a thin false bottom, revealing a narrow cavity filled with USB drives, and SD cards. There's a dust-covered external hard drive that screams dirty secrets louder than any confession I've ever dragged out of a suspect.

Well, I'll be damned.

Poppy leans back on her heels, triumphant. Glances up at me like she's waiting for the lecture.

Instead, I nod once. "Good job," I mutter.

She blinks like she's not sure she heard me right.

Frankly, neither am I.

I should've known she wouldn't stop at the hard drives.

Most people would take the win—evidence found, raid secured, suspects cuffed, paperwork incoming. Not Poppy.

No, she's still moving.

Still scanning.

Her hands trail along the edge of a paneled wall like she's feeling for a heartbeat in the drywall, eyes narrowed, body tense in that way she gets when her brain is moving faster than her mouth.

It's unsettling.

Mostly because I've seen actual detectives with decades of experience miss what she's picking up like it's instinct.

She stops near a row of chairs, tilting her head.

I keep looking through the dusty bookshelf a few feet away.

There's something about the paneling—an uneven seam,

maybe a centimeter off. Probably nothing unless you're obsessively looking for anomalies in a place meant to hide them.

She presses a hand to the chair rail.

And there's a click.

The wall shifts. A panel pops open like something out of a B-movie.

A hidden fucking door.

"Poppy, wait!" I call out, but it's too late.

She's opened the fucking hidden door before I can finish my warning.

She gasps.

No—shrieks is the more accurate word. Not theatrical. Not dramatic. Pure shock.

A sound that yanks my spine straight.

I'm at her side in half a breath, adrenaline snapping through me like a switchblade.

I grab her arm and haul her back so hard she stumbles into me, her heartbeat hammering against my chest as I wrap my arm around her waist, spinning her out of the way.

My gun is drawn in a blink and aimed inside the hidden room.

There's movement behind the door and as my eyes focus, the sight stops me cold.

Inside, the room is small and windowless like a makeshift prison pretending to be storage.

And six girls.

All of them barefoot and filthy. Wrapped in the kind of rags that doesn't qualify as clothing.

Rope burns. Blood. Makeup streaked down faces that are far too young to be here.

All gagged. All bound.

I lower my weapon immediately. The weight in my hands suddenly feels disgusting.

"Clear!" I call out, voice sharp. "We need medical—now. Bring blankets. Cutters. Water."

I turn back.

Poppy is standing frozen in the doorway, eyes wide, one hand still pressed to her chest like she's holding her own heart in place. Her lips are trembling.

I reach her in two strides and grab her shoulders—not rough, not gentle. Just enough to make her look at me.

"Are you okay?" I ask, voice lower now. "Are you hurt?"

She shakes her head fast, then nods once—like the question hit her brain at a delay.

"No," she whispers. "No, I'm okay. I'm okay."

She's not but she's upright.

And that counts for something.

I look at her—really look—and something behind my ribs tightens.

Because for all her jokes, her confidence, the crop top she wore into a raid like it was a uniform, she didn't come here expecting this.

And neither did I.

One second, I'm watching her breathe—alive, whole, not bleeding out on some concrete floor—and the next, that feeling curdles into something sharp and blistering in my chest.

Anger.

Hot. Immediate and unavoidable.

"What the fuck were you thinking?"

Her post-scare shock turns to confusion instantly. "Excuse me?" Her forehead crumples.

"What. The fuck. Were you thinking?"

I let the words roll off my tongue slowly. Each one cutting the space between us.

Each one dragging me a step closer.

I want her to feel it.

The heat. The weight. The truth.

"I was thinking, 'Gee, golly. I wonder what's behind this hidden panel in the human trafficking house.'"

Hands on her hips. Blue fire in her eyes. Sarcasm locked and loaded.

"You never go in first. You got it?"

My voice drops, rough and tight.

My breath's coming too fast, and we're standing way too close.

Uniforms are watching us now—half their attention on the suspects being led out, the other half wondering if they're about to witness an implosion.

Her eyes flick to the women being escorted from the hidden room.

Some carried. Others walking on shaking legs.

Her voice goes soft. "They obviously can't hurt me."

She waves her hand at them like it should be obvious.

My patience snaps.

"You didn't know they were in there!"

Yeah, I'm yelling now.

Don't care.

"This isn't a courtroom, Poppy, where the bad guys are led in unarmed and cuffed, and the most dangerous thing you face is a bad objection."

I step in again, so close now I can feel the edge of her fury heat the air between us.

"In field ops, the bad guys don't wait to be read their rights. They hide in closets with guns. They shoot the first damn shadow that moves. You would've been the first thing through that door."

She lifts her chin. Proud, defiant and so fucking maddening.

"I wasn't unarmed. I had a brain. And maybe a little instinct that paid off."

"You were fucking curious, Poppy."

Her nostrils flare, and her voice drops into a dangerous calm. "You know what I see when I look around, Blackwood? I see victims. Alive. Because I followed a hunch. Because I moved. We would have left them trapped in there until they starved to death."

"And you think I don't care about that?" I snap.

"You think I don't want them out? That I didn't come here to find them? I've spent months trying to crack this case wide enough to breathe through it, and you come in and make a reckless move that could've ended in a body bag—and not theirs."

A beat of silence hangs between us, heavy and tight.

Then I say what I mean to say.

"You could have gotten yourself or one of the officers shot. And I would be the one that has to go tell their family they aren't coming home."

The words are quiet. Honest and raw.

"Who would that be for you, huh? Mom and Dad? A sister? A brother?"

Her expression falters—just a flicker—but it's enough.

She knows it's real.

I see it land.

See it unsettle her just like it unsettles me.

But I don't let the moment linger.

I straighten.

Rein it back in.

Lock it down.

"You want to be part of this? Fine. But if you're going to be in the field, you follow *my* orders.

You listen. Or you will stay behind next time."

Final word.

No room for debate.

She opens her mouth to argue—and thinks better of it.

Smart girl.

Wrong fucking battleground.

This isn't about ego.

It's about not scraping her body off a crusty fucking floor because she couldn't take direction.

And I'll be damned if I let that happen on my watch.

There are times in life when you realize you've signed up for something far bigger than you imagined.

This is one of those times.

The raid turned up more than just horror—it gave us everything.

Piles of it.

A digital graveyard of corruption and cover-ups: names hidden under nicknames, initials, case numbers that circle back to other cases I didn't even know were dirty. USB drives, financial ledgers, photo evidence, raw surveillance.

One of the drives alone contained almost four hundred gigabytes of video interviews—some coerced, some clearly recorded without consent.

It's a mountain of rot.

And the worst part? We can't trust anyone to help dig us out of it.

"We don't send this through proper channels," Declan said that night, voice flat as he packed the evidence into clearly labeled, tamper-proof bags. "Not yet. Not until we're sure who's clean."

I didn't argue. I didn't have to. It was obvious.

There's sewage in the department. Too many closed cases that shouldn't be. Too many open ones that never got the evidence now sitting in plastic tubs beneath a whiteboard covered in my handwriting.

So now... it's us.

Just us.

Working out of a back room in the planning office of the precinct. We keep the circle tight. Maybe three other people know the full scope of what we found—and that includes Rourke. It doesn't include my D.A., Benjamin, though.

"You trust Rourke," I said yesterday. "How long—"

"No."

Okay then.

Glad to see Mr. Perky McPerkins of Perksville is back.

We've been at it for days.

The walls are covered now—paper trails, photos, strings of names and receipts, grainy screenshots. My evidence board keeps growing, and yes, I do have a post-it system.

Declan hasn't said a word about it.

He could have. He's a grumpy homicide detective with a talent for sarcasm and an allergy to compliments. But not once has he rolled his eyes at my color-coded post-it rainbow or my "hot pink = persons of interest" rule.

In fact... I've noticed he follows it.

Quietly.

Subtly.

I caught him the other night sticking a mint green post-it under a timeline string for "financial connections," and it took everything in me not to say something snarky just to hear him grunt back. He didn't even look at me. Just kept working. Like my system made sense.

Like it was ours.

Yesterday, I found his blackmailer.

Someone by the name of Matthews moonlights as a cop, arrests girls for bogus things. They're put in the back of a cop car and never seen again.

With Declan's name cleared, I thought they might take me off the case and let him take it back fully—but alas, here I am.

We've been pulling late nights now. Back to back to back. Cups of half-drunk coffee scattered across the table. Cold takeout containers shoved to one side. The kind of silence that isn't awkward—just focused. Comfortable, somehow.

Declan's usually hunched over something when I glance up —some file, some photo, always scowling like the paper is refusing its Miranda rights.

I've stopped trying to fill the silence. I've learned how he works. And I think he's learning how I work, too.

The more I watch him here, the more I realize something terrifying:

We make a good team.

Like, suspiciously good.

And if that thought makes my stomach flutter in a way that is both inconvenient and highly unprofessional—well. I'm choosing to ignore it. For now.

Unfortunately, someone is doing everything in his glittery, chaos-wielding bestie magic to make sure I don't ignore whatever... this is between me and Detective Blackwood.

Which is totally nothing. Nothing going on between us. I mean, why would there be?

Sebastian and I usually arrive at the courthouse together. That's our thing. Two caffeinated icons striding in like we own the building. He brings coffee; I bring legal fire. It's coordinated. It's consistent. It's what best friends who spend a lot of time enabling each other's chaos do.

But this particular morning?

Declan showed up too.

Right as Sebastian was handing me my iced coffee with an extra shot of judgment, the homicide detective from my spicy dreams strolled up like a six-foot-something grump in black and stood next to me like it was the most natural thing in the world.

So, of course, Sebastian pounced.

The flirting started immediately. Borderline restraining-order levels of flirtation.

"Detective," he purred, dragging the word out like it was made of honey. "Sebastian Elias Tréviot Ignatius Blaire the Third," he said with a flourish, like the name itself should come with fanfare and a spotlight. "Pleasure."

Declan gave a very serious nod and a tip of his coffee. Probably black with two pumps of grumpy.

"You're even taller up close. Is that bulletproof vest standard issue or are you just happy to see me?"

I nearly choked on my coffee. In fact, some did come out my nose.

Declan didn't flinch. Just looked ahead as we walked. That deadpan stare he's perfected that makes grown men stammer and hardened criminals forget their names.

Sebastian thrived.

"What's your name?" he asked, eyes sparkling with menace.

Declan sipped his own coffee with a look that said, *We all know you know my name*, but he answered anyway. "Blackwood."

"Oh, we're doing last names? Mysterious. I like it." He leaned closer. "Married?"

Declan said nothing. Just gave him a slow, unimpressed look like the question didn't even deserve oxygen.

Sebastian took that as a maybe.

"Girlfriend?" he tried.

"No."

"Boyfriend?" The hope in his voice was... frankly suffocating.

"No."

"Kids?"

"No."

"Hobbies?"

Declan blinked. "That's not a yes-or-no question."

Sebastian grinned. "Still. No?"

"No."

Just flat. Dry. Like answering these questions was less irritating than breathing.

I walked sandwiched between them, trying to sip my drink like a normal person while mentally calculating whether I could fake a phone call or, I don't know, spontaneously combust.

And the worst part?

Declan didn't look annoyed. He didn't walk away. He didn't even raise a brow.

He just joined us. Solid. Calm. Like he expected this interrogation and was powering through it the same way he powers through a triple homicide.

Sebastian texts me no fewer than three times a day like it's his full-time job to monitor my emotional unraveling with flair.

SEBASTIAN: Send me a picture of
Detective Deep throat.

SEBASTIAN: Did you trip and fall and
accidentally make out yet?

SEBASTIAN: Do not emotionally repress this into your gut. You need to get laid and I'm the bestie to make sure that happens. You're welcome in advance.

It's... a lot.

And yet, for all the commentary I am getting, you know who hasn't reached out?

My stalker.

The one who sent me bloody crime scene photos.

Who gifted me a burner phone like it was a party favor from a true-crime convention.

Who emailed me a video of my own murder scene cleanup, complete with an ominous no-sound aesthetic and the artistic framing of a film-school dropout.

Radio. Silence.

It's been days now. Nothing. Not a single buzz from the murder phone. Not an anonymous envelope under my door. Not even a sticky note on my windshield that says *I know what you did last Friday.*

And I don't know if that's comforting... or terrifying.

Is he gone? Bored? On vacation? What's the etiquette for when your anonymous crime scene fairy just... ghosts you?

The anticipation is eating me alive.

To be fair, I've taken precautions. Real ones. I installed cameras—several, actually, in highly strategic positions. And I had the locksmith come out.

The same one who helped me at Mari's.

We upgraded the locks, added deadbolts, reinforced the door frames, changed my alarm code to something not birthday related, and even installed a peephole big enough to see someone's criminal aura coming from down the block.

And so far? Nothing.

No break-ins.

No messages.

No murder souvenirs.

It's been... quiet.

Too quiet.

I could almost convince myself it was just a sick joke. A prank. Some elaborate, over-the-top scare campaign orchestrated by a bored hacker with a flair for dramatics and access to high-grade industrial tarps.

Except they cleaned up the body and burned the warehouse down.

So, no. I haven't been sleeping great. I check my security feed more than I check my email.

Every creak in the house sends my heart into a tap-dancing spiral. And I haven't worn open-toed shoes in a week because if I have to sprint out of my home with one hunger-strike-posing dog, I am not doing it in sandals.

But sure. Everything's fine. Just another day in the life of a deeply repressed prosecutor accidentally entangled in whatever's darker than homicide.

At this point, I should be charging rent to the pit of dread living in my stomach.

And the worst part?

I think I prefer the fear over the silence. And I think that is exactly what the stalker is going after. Keeping me teetering on the ledge, in constant anticipation of the next move.

Today is the first day in several that it's actually killy been quiet in our little room.

The kind of quiet that settles into your bones, makes your shoulders drop, your brain stop spiraling, and convinces you that maybe—just maybe—the world isn't on fire for a full sixty minutes.

Declan's asleep.

Well—technically, "resting his eyes" in the corner of the precinct war room, lying on the brown leather sofa that's so cliché it might as well come with a jazz saxophone soundtrack. We're just missing cigar smoke and a glass of brandy.

His arms are crossed. Chin dipped to his chest. Long legs stretched out on top of the armrest, crossed at the ankles.

It's the first time I've seen him without that permanent scowl etched into his face. No furrowed brow. No jaw grinding like his molars are plotting a mutiny.

His lips are relaxed. His lashes (which are criminally thick, by the way) rest against his cheeks like he's pretending not to be beautiful on purpose.

And it's annoying. It's so annoying how stupidly handsome he is when he's not looking like he wants to arrest drywall.

I shouldn't be looking.

But I am looking.

Just a quick glance. Okay—maybe a second glance. One of those slow, slightly creepy scans you try to pass off as totally innocent, even though you absolutely just paused on his mouth for longer than is legally appropriate.

Then I look where I shouldn't.

Where I really shouldn't. Because someone is pitching a tent, if you catch my Tokyo Drift.

My thighs tighten, and I roll my hips ever so slightly, thinking about him. He's... big. He's a big mambo-jambo, and I picture myself striding up to him.

Rising my skirt as I put one knee on the couch, bracing with one hand, arching my back like a pro.

My other hand unzipping his pants and freeing his erection. Grasping him. Stroking. Rolling my thumb over the head before I lean in.

A long, slow lick up his shaft—

His phone pings.

My eyes fly to his, and he's looking right at me.

Right. At. Me.

I jolt like I've been caught sneaking cookies before dinner, and I'm stuck here. One dark eyebrow tics ever so slightly and I whip my head back to my files.

The slow inhale—it's casual as he sits up.

He totally caught me staring at his man-aconda.

There's a flicker of smug in his eyes. Barely there. Just enough to make me want to throw a sticky note at his face.

He checks his phone.

All softness gone in an instant.

Cue the scowl. Fully restored. Do not pass go. Do not collect a personality.

"What is it?" I ask, trying not to sound like I'm bracing for disaster, even though I absolutely am.

"Trip missed his mandatory parole check-in," he mutters, already on his feet. "PO can't reach him. Said he's driving out to the last address on file."

My stomach twists. "Do you think he ran?"

Declan's already grabbing his jacket. "Or he got made when we talked to him."

And there it is. The panic. That sharp, familiar jolt that comes when a lead suddenly goes ice-cold and you don't know if you're chasing a coward... or about to walk into a funeral.

He's halfway to the door before I grab my things.

"I'm coming with you."

He turns. "No, you're not."

"Yes, I am."

"Poppy."

"Declan. You can say my name all you want; it doesn't mean I'm suddenly going to chain myself to the whiteboard."

His jaw tightens. "It's not safe."

"Oh wow. I didn't realize we were just now figuring that out."

He glares.

I hold eye contact while I grab my files and head toward the door. I never look away—too-wide smile plastered on my face.

I'm sure I actually look like the clown from Steven King's *It*, more than anything.

But I don't care. Because if a witness is in danger, we don't have time for power struggles.

Also—let's be honest—I was never staying behind.

Declan

She's not coming. End of story.

"No." I say it flat. Final. Like concrete. "And it's not up for argument." I open the door and head for the exit.

Ahead of her, I adjust my raging fucking cock—yeah, the one she was definitely staring at. I could see the fantasy playing out in her head.

The slow lick of her tongue across her lip nearly made me come in my pants.

Behind me: chaos. Paper and files hit the floor like an avalanche, followed by a muttered, exasperated:

"Snickerdoodles!"

Her swear words baffle me. It's like living next to a Hallmark card that occasionally turns into the Tasmanian fucking Devil.

I don't turn around.

"Oh, Graham! I'm so sorry—"

That makes me look back.

In her rush to chase me—probably ready to throw herself into my car if I didn't cave—Poppy has collided with another attorney.

Her files are scattered like confetti. He's crouched beside her, all polished smiles and hair gel.

"Pops, you can bump into me anytime," he says with a grin that makes my teeth grind.

Did he just call her *Pops*?

She's blushing. Laughing. Tucking her hair behind one ear while trying to collect papers now wildly out of order.

She's focused on realigning her files, and this guy—this fucking guy—smells like he bathed in Axe body spray. His lack of personal-space awareness is grating.

"When are you finally going to let me take you to The Bar?" he adds, too familiar. "Pick that gorgeous brain of yours. Have a few drinks."

Oh, fuck this guy.

He's holding her files. My files. The ones no one else should see.

I shoulder him aside. Not gently.

"She's got it." My voice could crack granite.

I snatch the folders and grab Poppy's arm, steering her toward the elevators before I say something that gets me reported to HR.

"Let's go."

"Bye, Graham! Sorry—we were just on our way out to a call," she announces over her shoulder, barely looking up as she wrestles more paper into her arms like a deranged librarian.

I take out every ounce of my irritation on the elevator button.

Once the doors close and it's just us in the steel box, I turn toward her.

"You can't drop these notes again," I say. "No one outside our room sees this case. Got it?"

Without a word, she dumps the entire stack of folders into my arms. "Here."

I nearly drop half. "Jesus."

They're heavy, uneven, and clearly not meant to be carried like this. Meanwhile, she straightens her pencil skirt—which is way too fucking tight mind you—flicks golden hair from her face, and adjusts her blazer like she's walking into a Vogue shoot instead of a parole check gone wrong.

I very intentionally do not look down.

Too late. I already caught the cleavage.

Fuck.

The elevator dings. She blocks the doors with one foot, balancing like a full-time acrobat in four-inch heels and enough enthusiasm to carry a murder case on vibes alone.

She re-stacks the files, flips through a few, then holds her hands out. "Okay, gimme."

"Absolutely not."

"Excuse me?"

"I'll carry them. You focus on walking upright."

"Hey, McPerkins—he bumped me, thank you."

McPerkins? Oh, hell no.

She smiles, walking out ahead of me like I didn't just pull her from a trap made of testosterone and cologne.

Why the fuck is she smiling?

"Why the fuck are you smiling?" I snap.

She turns—flips her hair like we're in a movie—and grins.

"Because," she says, practically dancing, "I'm coming along after all."

She strides off like she's the fucking detective.

Well... shit.

At my SUV, I open her door.

She slides in like she hasn't just spent five minutes border-line skipping down the courthouse steps.

I drop the files in her lap and shut the door before she asks for fresh sticky notes.

She thanks me as I get in. "Very gentlemanly, Detective. I'm impressed."

I grunt, starting the car. "Didn't want to die by a thousand papercuts."

"Oh, ha-ha." She pats the stack like it didn't just almost compromise national security.

She flips through the chaos. "Still, I appreciate the vote of confidence—even if it came after your internal meltdown."

"It's safer having you with me than leaving you unsuper-vised with your... potty mouth."

She gasps. "My what?"

"You heard me."

"I'm delightful, thank you. And my vocabulary is perfectly appropriate."

I raise a brow. "Snickerdoodles? Who says that?"

Her face scrunches, thoughtful. Then she answers.

"My mom was a nurse. I had a lot of evenings alone. Early bedtimes. Reruns. No bloody stuff allowed. Mostly Scooby-Doo, The Brady Bunch, and Murder, She Wrote. Lots of 'zoinks' and 'gee golly, Marsha.' Cursing just... didn't fit."

I glance at her, expecting sass. But she's calmly sorting files. No embarrassment. Just facts. Just... Poppy.

I wasn't ready for her honesty.

No self-pity. Just that casual sincerity she slips into when she's not making me insane.

I clear my throat. "Your mom sounds like an amazing woman."

She brightens—actually brightens, which I didn't think

was possible given her default setting is somewhere between sunbeam and minor fire hazard.

"She is. She's my hero."

I spend the rest of the ride very intentionally not thinking about her feet in those heels.

The arch like a lighthouse in the dark.

I wonder if she's ticklish. If I took her shoe off, kissed her arch. Her ankle. Her calf, her thigh—

Nope. Stopping.

I adjust myself. Again.

She mumbles about "order," flipping through files and re-tabbing notes like they're classified documents.

We pull up to the house—about as charming as you'd expect from a guy named Trip who forges parole records and hangs out with traffickers.

A porch held together by duct tape and tetanus. Beer cans crushed into the patchy lawn. A plastic Santa stares from a bed of weeds.

It's June.

The parole officer's already out front, cigarette dangling, phone to his ear. He clocks us and nods. I nod back and round the car to open Poppy's door.

Her heel snags—probably on gravel—and she stumbles.

She grabs my forearm, quick and instinctive. Warm palm, brief contact, but it hits me like a jolt.

Then she pulls away.

Brushes invisible dust from her blazer like it'll erase the moment. Her cheeks flush pink.

Yeah, I notice that too. A lot.

"Last check-in was six days ago," the officer says, shifting his cigarette. "No calls. No work. No one's seen him."

I nod, already scanning the porch and windows.

"You knock yet?"

"No. Waited for you."

This guy is either smart or lazy. If Trip's inside, high and panicked, this guy won't be chasing him if he chooses to bolt.

"Check the front," I say. "I'll take the back."

Poppy opens her mouth—

"Car," I cut in, pointing.

She gives me a flat look crossing her arms. "I'm not a child."

"No. You're worse. You're curious."

I don't wait for her comeback. Just head for the side of the house. I already know she won't listen.

Sure enough, halfway past the rotted fence line, I hear her soft steps behind me—drifting toward the opposite side, where the trash bins sit beside a patch of overgrown bushes.

I roll my eyes so hard it hurts but keep moving, checking the lower windows. Curtains drawn. One cracked. I crouch, peering through grime-streaked glass into a living room that looks robbed and politely abandoned.

No movement.

Up front, the parole officer bangs on the door. "Trip! Open up! You're three days late, man!"

Nothing.

Another knock. Harder.

"Come on. Don't make this a thing."

Still nothing. The house is dead silent.

No lights. No shadows. No one's here.

I glance front just in time to catch Poppy creeping around the corner like she's starring in a Nancy Drew reboot no one asked for.

I swear to God.

This woman will be the death of me. And the worst part?

It won't even be cool or dramatic.

It'll be a highlighter overdose and a final, rage-induced stroke when she says fudge muffins instead of something actually cathartic.

The silence is starting to feel wrong. Trip may be sloppy, stupid, barely competent—but he's not subtle.

And this? Way too quiet.

Which means I've got a very bad feeling.

I'm halfway down the south wall, about to check a boarded-up window, when I hear her voice—bright and grim at once.

"Ugh. Smells like three-day-old fish in a gym sock."

And my stomach drops.

Shit.

"Poppy—*go back!*"

She shrieks, high-pitched and horrified.

"Oh my–"

Her voice cuts off like she clamped a hand over her mouth. Like the words choked her.

I bolt toward the sound, rounding the corner in a full sprint.

The second I see her, everything else disappears.

She's frozen.

White as a sheet, eyes wide and glassy. One hand half-raised, the other covering her mouth.

Goddammit.

That smell...

There's something about a body baking in summer heat. It clings to your nose, your clothes, your memory. One hit of that rot and it stays with you forever.

I don't need a second look.

A glance at the side of the house confirms what I knew the moment I heard her gag.

Trip's body slumps between two trash cans. Throat cut. Brown blood caking the front of his shirt.

A message on the wall in blood:

"RAT"

Something's tacked to the wall—flesh, maybe.

Her eyes stay locked on the body, but she's gone—checked out, halfway to shock.

I reach her and grab her shoulders.

"Poppy," I say. "Look at me."

Nothing.

No twitch. No response.

Fuck this.

I scoop her up—arms under her knees and back. She doesn't resist. Doesn't speak. Just folds into me like she weighs nothing.

She shudders and whispers against my neck:

"That was his tongue... wasn't it?"

My jaw tightens.

"Yeah."

She clings tighter, like she's trying to crawl inside my skin.

Her breath hitches, sharp and shallow.

"I've got you," I murmur. "Just hang on to me."

She does.

I carry her to the SUV. She doesn't move, doesn't let go. Just buries herself in my neck.

I open the door, ease her into the passenger seat, and grab a cold water bottle from the cooler—habit from too many crime scenes.

"Here." I press it into her hands. "It's cold."

She stays curled up, fingers locked. I guide her hands and help her place the bottle against her neck.

Her eyes close. Lips part. She exhales—slow and shaky, like it's the first breath in minutes.

It's working.

She's coming back.

But it's doing something to me, too.

Something I won't name.

I take a step back, needing space.

"You okay?"

She nods. Still pale and rattled.

"Good." I nod back. "I'm taping the scene and calling it in. You'll stay in the car?"

She opens the bottle, takes the tiniest sip, then exhales again.

"I'll be staying in the car for the rest of my life."

That earns the smallest smirk from me. Just a flicker.

"About fucking time."

24

Poppy

The leak isn't just in the precinct—it's in the courthouse too.

The one place I still believed in.

Trip's death sealed it.

The warrant was airtight. Fast-tracked and quiet. It didn't exist in the system until it was signed—just me, Declan, and the judge.

Once official, it entered a closed circuit. Only a few in the DA's office and courthouse staff had access. People I've worked with for years.

Trip's name was only in the supporting documentation.

Whoever leaked it—wasn't a cop.

It was someone I see in the elevator.

Someone who says good morning with a smile that might be real... or hiding a knife.

The judge.

The clerks.

A colleague.

Someone I trusted.

Or used to.

I haven't moved from Declan's SUV. Still clutching the

water bottle like it might ward off whatever's crawling under my skin.

Outside, Declan leans against the door. Calm. Sharp. In charge.

His lieutenant crackles in his ear while his thumbs move nonstop—texting, emailing, dispatching whatever homicide detectives handle in the first hour of a corpse.

Then people start arriving.

Slow at first. Then a rush. Uniforms. CSI. Coroner. A crime scene inflating in real time. Yellow tape is strung like party decorations for institutional betrayal.

And the neighbors? Thrilled.

Kids suck popsicles on the porch like it's a Netflix special.

I should be thinking about evidence.

Who processed the warrant. Who had access.

But all I can see is the word *RAT* written in blood.

And Trip's head tilted—like he'd tried to lift it one last time.

I glance in the rearview mirror.

Declan is still there.

Still stone.

And I wonder how long I can keep pretending I'm not unraveling.

Because back there, I didn't see Trip.

Not at first.

I saw Travis Gannon.

His throat torn, blood pouring down his shirt. Eyes wide open, staring as he pointed at me.

And the blood didn't say RAT.

It said MURDERER.

I froze.

I was back in the warehouse. The stench. The silence. The awful knowing:

I didn't stop a crime—I ended a life. Took something I can't give back.

I slipped into the void until hands gripped my shoulders.

Until I was buried in the warm, solid crook of Declan's neck, holding on like it was the only thing keeping me afloat.

The scent of him—clean, steady, cedar and something darker—wrapped around me like armor. Like gravity.

I buried the panic, deep and quiet, where no one could see.

Two knocks on the window nearly launch my water bottle like Old Faithful.

Declan stands outside, unimpressed by my jump scare.

No apology. Just holds up a business card and jerks his head.

The man communicates in two expressions: annoyed and slightly more annoyed.

I roll the window halfway down. "Am I being served?"

"Send this to my lieutenant." He hands me the card. "From your notes."

Rourke's name and email.

On the back: *Judge? Clerk?*

I nod, reach for my phone—

And see the flip phone glow.

1 New Message

I freeze.

Declan's still there, one hand on his hip, watching the street.

My stomach clenches. I force my voice steady. "Sure. I'll email him now."

He grunts, turns away, snapping at two kids near the police tape.

He yells across the street something about staying away from the scene and all I can think of is that old guy in the movie grumbling:

Stay off my lawn.

I fumble with the email app through the blurry screen. My thoughts everywhere, and none are useful.

Declan notices. Detective mode activates like he spotted a bloodstain on white carpet.

He circles to the driver's side and reappears with cookies.

"It's a lot," he says. Not quite gentle, but less clipped. "A snack will help."

I take them like they're life support.

"Thanks."

He thinks I'm rattled from the body.

Thinks he's giving me permission to fall apart.

He has no idea it's not *that* body I keep seeing—but another. Or that someone dangerous knows—and has fixated on me.

After a few more stabs at the screen, I finally hit send. "Okay, sent."

He nods, distracted, and keeps walking.

Phone to his ear, voice sharp. I think I hear him say Benjamin—my DA—and I'm dying to hear if it's accusatory.

I open the flip phone.

> UNKNOWN: I don't like his hands on you.

> UNKNOWN: I don't like anyone's hands on you, Sunny.

My fingers tighten around the device.

I read it again—slower, even though I understood it the first time.

The timestamped was hours ago.

He *saw* me.

Maybe when Declan carried me. He was the last to touch me—lifting me like I weighed nothing, letting me breathe again.

But earlier—there was also Graham.

I bumped into him and he called me *Pops*. Flirted like I'll stop turning him down.

That happened *inside* the courthouse, in a secured floor accessible only by employees with badges.

But Declan touched me there too—pulled me away like a wolf marking territory.

Could Graham have followed us?

Could it be someone else in the DA's office?

I shake off the spiral as a third message pings:

> UNKNOWN: I also don't like to be kept waiting.

I exhale—sharp. Cold.

Anger replaces fear.

Not today, buddy.

I've walked through blood. Held myself together with paperclips and spite.

I'm not here to entertain some delusional man-child with a burner phone and a savior complex.

I type without thinking:

> POPPY: Wrong number. There is no Sunny here.

Then I stare at it like I summoned a demon.

Which, honestly, I probably have.

The screen blinks again. Buzzes—impatient.

UNKNOWN: Good girls get rewards. But I love to punish.

UNKNOWN: Are you going to make me punish you, Sunny?

My stomach twists into a stylish, stressed little bow.

I should delete it. Or report it. Or chuck the phone into a storm drain like a normal person would.

Instead, I start typing.

I don't know what I'm planning—something clever. Something that says:

I am not your Sunny, and if you breathe near me again, I'll smite you with the justice system and a very aggressive purse.

But before I hit send, the driver's door yanks open. Declan slides in—still on the phone, voice sharp enough to leave paper cuts.

I nearly drop the flip phone. "Oh my—"

I fumble, snap it shut, try to breathe like I wasn't just mid-text with my personal boogeyman.

Declan doesn't notice. Too busy ranting into his earpiece, eyes lit with homicide fury.

"...I don't care who signed off. If the leak came from the DA's side, every name is a potential breach. Until we find the mole, no one gets full access."

His tone is clipped. Controlled. Boiling.

Meanwhile, I'm hiding a stalker phone in my purse like it's a rabid squirrel I plan to carry until it chews through the lining and ruins my life.

Declan mutters something about sealed warrants, then ends the call.

The silence is heavy and charged.

He exhales, glances at me, probably assuming I'm still rattled from the dead body by the trash cans.

Which is fair.

But also wildly inaccurate.

Because trauma has layers like a violent onion.

And mine? Mine come with bonus messages from a faceless lunatic who wants to punish me for existing independently in the year of our Lord 2025.

I shove the phone deeper into my purse as Declan stares a second too long.

I stare back. Then look away.

And absolutely do not think about the next message waiting in that cursed little flip phone.

We pull out. Declan keeps one hand on the wheel, the other near the console, scanning the road like traffic might be complicit.

"Rourke thinks it's internal."

I nod. "DA's office or clerk pool, right?"

He glances over, brow raised. "You already thought that?"

I shrug. "Not that many people can access sealed warrants. Trip's name was only in the supporting docs, which narrows it down."

Declan makes a low sound—agreement or the need to punch a wall.

With him, it's probably both.

We pull into the precinct lot, and I'm out of the SUV before he turns it off.

"I parked over here. I think," I say, veering toward the far row, tossing a wave behind me.

Declan doesn't leave. He follows at a calm, steady pace—like he doesn't believe me.

Because... my car is gone.

Completely gone.

I freeze mid-step, keys in hand, scanning the row like it's messing with me. "It was right here. I swear."

Declan says nothing. Just lifts a brow—the kind that makes me feel twelve and flustered.

I call the rental company.

And immediately want to sit down.

"Yes, Miss Hartwell," the chipper agent says. "We picked it up earlier today—around noon. Someone called and said to retrieve it. If you still have the key, you can drop it in the return envelope."

"My jaw drops. "I didn't call you."

After a pointless back-and-forth, I hang up before I get myself banned from customer service for life.

Declan watches me like a hawk that already sees the blood in the water.

He crosses his arms. "Everything okay?"

No.

I paste on my best I'm-fine smile. "Yep. All good. I'll just... call a rideshare."

"No." His tone leaves no room for argument. "Where do you live?"

I blink, ready to argue but he beats me to it. "I'll be driving past anyway."

"I can totally grab a ride—"

"Poppy."

I surrender, shoulders slumping. Mostly because I'm exhausted. Slightly because I don't want to be alone in a near-empty lot.

And weirdly... I trust him.

"Okay. Fine. But I'm apologizing the whole way there."

"Oh, goody," he says blandly.

I last three minutes before I open my mouth.

"So... how long have you been on the force?"

I expect him to grunt. Maybe glare. I definitely don't expect him to answer.

"Sixteen years."

I blink. "Wow. That's... longer than I've been filing taxes."

He huffs something that might be a laugh.

He keeps talking, gruff but steady. And I like listening.

His dad was a cop. Rourke was his partner. Says he's known him his entire life. Literally. Rourke is his godfather and held him at his christening.

Explains why he and Rourke trust only each other in this case.

He doesn't volunteer much, but I can tell there is something deeply personal that motivated him to move into homicide, but I don't press on it.

And for a moment, I stop seeing just the badge. Just the scowl.

I see him.

The way he's leaning slightly toward me, resting his elbow on the center console.

The way he looks at my floorboard and it makes me shuffle my feet.

And I know I shouldn't feel safe with someone who looks at crime scenes the way other people look at art—but I do. And that might be the most dangerous thing of all.

We pull up to my place and Declan puts the car in park but doesn't shift to leave.

"Your car in the shop?"

I nod. "Yeah. I think the alternator tried to break up with me last week."

He watches me carefully. "You need another ride, call me."

"Oh. Um. Okay."

He doesn't say anything else. Just stays there as I get out, awkwardly juggling my purse, my nerves, and a bag of cookies that somehow feel more important now than they did ten minutes ago.

I turn at the door, and give him a small wave.

He doesn't wave back but raises two fingers in a very macho   I-can't-let-go-of-the-sterring-wheel-and-compromise-showing-off-my-forearm-muscles kind of way.

But he doesn't drive off either—not until I'm inside and the door's locked.

And it makes me feel a little safer.

Not totally.

But a little.

25

Him

The door shuts behind me with a satisfying click—like punctuation at the end of a long day.

I toss my keys onto the table, let them clatter across the wood, and head straight for the fridge.

I deserve a beer.

I earned one.

I crack the bottle open just as I press the button on the remote, ready to tune in to my favorite show.

The *Poppy Hartwell Show*.

God, she's beautiful in high-def, and coming home to see her on the television is the highlight of my day.

She's realized now I've been taunting her.

Intentionally. Strategically.

I let her know I was there—and then nothing.

The absence of me is its own kind of presence. And it's driving her mad.

She's looking for me now. Not consciously—not in a way she'll admit—but in the way her eyes scan the corners of a dark room.

In the way she double-checks locked doors and glances into

her purse to make sure the burner I gave her is still there. Still waiting.

She wants to hear from me.

Needs it even.

And that's exactly how I want her.

The big screen blinks to life with a grid of warm, familiar spaces—each one a room in her house. Bedroom, bathroom, kitchen, hallway, even the stupid laundry nook she never uses because she always forgets to move things to the dryer.

It's almost charming.

Most people relax with reruns or something trashy and overhyped, but not me. I prefer the real thing. No laugh tracks. No actors. No commercial breaks. Just her.

Poppy.

Unfiltered. Unaware. And mine.

It was honestly adorable—how she thought changing the locks and resetting the security system would protect her. Like she's starring in her own little home-makeover montage.

It took me five minutes.

New keypad, fresh deadbolts, some overpriced little cameras she bought off one of those influencer ads. I barely broke a sweat.

I scan the grid, checking each room while I take a pull from the amber bottle. She's not in the kitchen. Not in the bathroom. Not in the bedroom yet, either.

Huh.

Shoes are off and keys are on the hook. But hmm... her slippers are still there.

That's not right.

She always wears those fuzzy slippers the second she walks in.

Her routine is one of my favorite things about her—it's

predictable, soothing. Like a bedtime story. Slippers, hair clip, wine. Maybe a cookie if it's been a rough day. And it's always been a rough day lately.

But tonight... something's off.

Dexter trots across one screen, his little snaggletooth bouncing with each step as he moves from the living room to the hallway. Probably gearing up to demand more dinner he won't eat.

Little fucker's staged a hunger strike against the kibble she picked up.

He pisses me off.

She doesn't need more chaos.

Not now. She's under enough pressure already. From work. From the cops. From that fucking idiot she works with.

I sit back and keep scanning, frustrated I missed the moment she got home, but I had other errands to run. Priorities.

Like paying a visit to the city crime lab.

Their security is trash, by the way. You'd think a place responsible for testing evidence in active criminal investigations would have more than one camera facing a door that doesn't even latch properly.

But no.

One step stool, two gloves, and a little diluted solution later —and the blood samples collected from her sweet little slaughterhouse were officially compromised. No DNA. No ability to identify a person.

No one connects her to it or asks questions she shouldn't have to answer.

I did that for her.

I'm making sure she doesn't go down for saving herself. For

surviving. For doing what needed to be done when no one else gave a damn.

She hasn't found out yet, but her victim has finally been reported missing.

Apparently even a soul as blackened as his managed to have someone who noticed when he stopped showing up.

Surprising, really.

But it doesn't matter. They won't find him.

I rewind the feed from earlier, flipping back to when she came home. She looked tired. Not just physically—deeply tired. That bone-deep exhaustion people carry when they've seen too much and slept too little.

Her heels came off right by the door.

The pink fuzzy slippers went on like clockwork.

Dexter ran to greet her, ears up, tail wagging, doing that stupid spin-and-sit he does when he wants snacks. She smiled at him—soft and sweet.

And I smile at her. Just a little.

She knelt down and cooed at him, told him he was a good boy. My jaw tenses at that, but I brush it off with another swig of beer.

Still didn't eat his fucking food.

She saw the bowl still full, sighed, shoulders slumping as she carried it to the counter and started her little routine again. Whispering nonsense about "protesting for leftover turkey."

She talks to him like he's a person. Like he understands. And maybe he does.

Or maybe he's just manipulating her with those beady little eyes and his stupid snaggletooth.

She gets dinner started and heads up to change. More turkey and rice and vegetables for her stubborn little houseguest.

It's when she takes him outside and stays too long that I know something is up.

My baby is an indoor kind of girl.

But she stays out. Dexter enjoys chasing fuck knows what while she stays on her phone. Glued.

I pull up the clone and see what she was looking at.

Fuck.

"Accused. Released. Now Missing: Where Is Travis Gannon?"

Well, the cat's out of the bag now.

It's a compulsion to look up everything she can now that she's seen it. She'll be able to say it was for her client. A plausible reason to deep-dive into it.

She makes a phone call to Mariela informing her he's been reported missing. She's smart.

Making it look like a concerned attorney doing her due diligence. Not at all suspicious *she's* the reason for his unknown whereabouts.

That's when the smoke detector goes off and she rushes inside with a pale-pink Dexter on her heels like he's going to help.

The turkey is burned. The vegetables are charcoal.

Dexter is on a path to starvation, and my Sunshine is about to break down into tears—but she doesn't allow it. Instead, she goes to Google.

Solutions for picky dogs.

When your dog won't eat.

Is my dog emotionally manipulating me.

Yes, Sunshine. He is. And you should get rid of him.

She disappeared again a few minutes after that—changed clothes, slippers back on the shelf, hair up.

And—

Called another fucking rideshare.

And that is what pisses me off.

Unknown men in unknown cars, pulling up to the curb like it's nothing. She's trusting them with her safety, her address, trusting them to leave her in one piece when they drop her off alone, in the dark.

She doesn't realize how risky that is.

Worse—her rental was conveniently picked up earlier today. "No longer needed," they said. Not her words. Not her doing.

Someone got her out of the house. Without transportation. Without options.

It's too fucking staged.

My gut twists tight and sharp as I scan the camera feeds, flipping from room to room, looking for anything that's off.

And then I see it.

A chair. One of the ones by the bay window in her living room.

It's crooked. Slightly off angle. Tilted inward like it was used and not returned to its rightful place.

That might not seem like much. To anyone else, it wouldn't even register.

But Poppy?

She's a perfectionist in motion. Every chair aligned. Pillows fluffed. Throw blanket folded like it belongs in a catalog. She doesn't do off-center.

She would never leave it like that.

The beer on the table is forgotten. My hand is already on the remote, rewinding fast, skipping backward through the footage in staggered blips of movement.

There—yesterday—she's walking Dexter in her backyard.

Headphones in, listening to witness testimony like she always does.

When her alarm system would have been off—just for that short window while she walked the dog she spoils more than most people treat their children.

And that's when a man appears, and my blood runs cold.

Mid-thirties, maybe. Hoodie pulled tight. Ball cap. Head down. He sprints up her porch and lets himself in.

The door closes.

Inside, he moves fast. Controlled. His body language is practiced. This isn't a break-in. It's a setup.

I lean in closer as he walks to the bay window chair—the one that's crooked now—and pulls something from inside his jacket.

An eight-inch serrated hunting knife with a bright orange handle.

He slides it under the seat cushion.

"Mother fucker."

Next, he moves to the second chair and stuffs something thick beneath it. Rope. Coiled, tucked. Hidden.

Everything inside me goes cold. Still.

Not angry.

Not even afraid.

What settles over me is something far worse.

Something colder than rage.

Something older than fear.

A silence so sharp it hums beneath my skin.

Because someone just stepped into her house.

Into the one place in this godforsaken world that still feels pure—hers.

Mine.

They left a knife and rope.

They came with intent.

And there's only one ending for people like that.

The kind they don't walk away from.

I watch him leave.

Just like that—slips out the same door he crept in through, a smug little ghost with rope under one cushion and a hunting knife under the other. Slips away before she even gets back.

Poppy strolls in a minute later, arms full of a fluffy, distracting tyrant.

She has no fucking idea.

I flip to the outside camera, jaw tight, skin humming with something sharp and ancient. A car rolls by—slow. Not neighborhood slow. Suspiciously invested slow.

I know this neighborhood. I've walked it. Driven it. I know every car that belongs here. That one doesn't.

So, I rewind.

Five minutes earlier, it passes again.

Fifteen minutes before that—again.

I keep scrubbing backward, bile rising with every loop.

Again.

And again.

And again.

The pattern is clear now, spelled out in tire tread and habit.

"This asshole is staking her out."

It slips from my mouth before I can stop it, quiet and low and vibrating with something dangerous.

He's not winging this.

He's got rhythm and timing. The slow build of someone who knows how to hunt.

This isn't a random break-in, and it's not some desperate pervert trying his luck.

This is a process. A plan.

This is a man who's done this before.

A fucking predator.

A killer and he picked her.

I rewind further, knowing what I'm looking for before I find it.

The night I was stuck hiding in the linen closet like a goddamn drama queen.

Poppy got her bag returned—remember that? She was flustered, trying to play it cool. Dexter was barking. She took the bag and thanked the man at the door. Smiled. Said something polite.

I pause and zoom.

That motherfucker. It's him.

Hat. Hoodie. Left-handed. Same build. Same posture. Same exact car. The fucking rideshare driver that picked her up from the vet's office.

"He chose her the second she stepped into his car."

Now I feel it, down to the marrow—he's had her in his crosshairs since that first ride.

I pull up her cloned phone, but the answer's already sitting heavy in my gut like a goddamn warning bell.

He's been waiting.

He stayed close.

But she had that rental—she didn't need a ride—he couldn't get near her.

So, he got rid of it.

Called it in and had it picked up. Made it look like a clerical error or a personal cancellation. Nothing suspicious.

Just a woman with no car.

And today? She burned dinner. One stupid little accident and she needed a ride to the pet store.

I check the app, and it's right fucking there. He accepted the fare.

And now?

Right now?

She's at the pet store hunting for overpriced organic kibble and outside, in that car, a predator waiting to drive her home.

Home where he's already planted rope, and a knife.

"He's going to kill her." The words scrape out of my throat like broken glass.

I don't even realize I stood up, and I'm already grabbing my keys and reaching for the doorknob.

"Not if I can fucking help it."

26

Poppy

I push through the sliding glass doors of the pet store like I'm not actively spiraling. Cool. Casual. Just your average woman looking for gourmet dog food after surviving a week that deserves a documentary and an entire therapy team.

Dexter is going to starve.

I found a dead body today.

My stalker had my rental car picked up.

And oh, right—Travis Gannon—the man I murdered—has officially been reported missing.

So yeah, I'm great. Just fantastic. My left eye is not twitching at all.

Every cell in my body hums with "maybe you should be panicking" energy, but I've shoved it down deep enough that on the outside, I probably look like someone with just enough control not to get tackled by store security.

So, you know, we're getting there.

The fluorescent lights feel like judgment. Harsh and unforgiving. I try to keep my expression neutral as I head down the dog aisle, like I'm not doing mental math on when the police might knock.

Because they will.

They'll start asking questions.

Travis's phone will ping near Mari's building that night... unless he turned it off. Unlikely. But mine will ping the same tower.

Because I was there.

And yeah, I've got my story:

I was checking on my client. Hello, suicide attempt.

I cleaned up after the chaos like a caring attorney. I called a locksmith. All of it's true.

What I won't say is that I followed a serial rapist for blocks and stabbed him. More than once.

That I liked it.

I close my eyes as the memory hits like a whisper behind my ear.

The glide of the blade. The resistance of skin. The quiet that followed.

Jeepers, that quiet.

Don't think about it.

Not now. Not here.

I'm picking the skin around my thumb. That one spot. It helps. While I spiral. While I push back thoughts I should never have—never admit.

"Back again, huh?" a voice says.

I blink and look up.

It's the guy who helped me last time. What's-his-name.

Like actually. Is it Mitch? Micah? Marvin? No, wait.

"I'm being emotionally manipulated by a dog," I say, gesturing vaguely at the shelves and the chaos of options that mean nothing to me.

He laughs and nods. "Ah, not eating the dry food? Some dogs don't care for it."

He starts showing me wet food, fresh pouches, fridge stuff.

I nod and try to follow, but my brain's still ten steps behind, spinning through cell tower pings and blood-soaked flashbacks.

The spot on my thumb. If I could just pick it off…

"You okay?" he asks, and I realize I've been staring at a can labeled *Lamb & Lentils* like it insulted my entire family.

"Oh yeah. Totally," I lie. "Just… long day. Busy week. Murder, mystery, burnt dinner, you know."

"I love a good murder-mystery show."

Riiight. That's totally what I meant.

I grab several of the most expensive containers because clearly I've lost control of everything else, so why not throw money at the one living creature still depending on me.

Dexter deserves a little rotisserie comfort.

At checkout, my thoughts are a mess. Stalker texts. A corpse. And this weird, skin-crawling anticipation I can't shake.

All I want is to go home with my comfy jam-jams and some Indian takeout. A show about murder that doesn't involve me personally.

Is that really too much to ask?

The ride back starts off… quiet.

Not peaceful quiet, not the kind you melt into with a sigh. The other kind. The kind that hums in your ears and makes you hyperaware of your own breathing.

No music. No podcast. No hum of talk radio or cheerful GPS lady. Just tires on pavement and the occasional blinker.

Sometimes I like quiet—but today it feels wrong.

I lean my head back and exhale, trying to shake off the knot of tension that's lived behind my ribs since I found that body this morning. And yet, as strange as this ride feels, something's off.

It's the same driver who picked me up from the vet's office last week.

I didn't realize it until he was already pulling away. But it's the same guy. Same lemon-scented air freshener. Same spotless floorboards and CrossFit-branded water bottle.

That vet's office is over an hour away. Which makes this... either a coincidence or a very ambitious commute.

He glances at me in the mirror as we hit a red light, catching me staring and offers a pleasant, neutral smile.

"Traffic's brutal around here this time of day. Took me forever to get across town."

I nod absently, still unsure whether to feel comforted or trapped.

"Funny seeing you again all the way out here," I say.

"Yeah, I run this whole area," he replies. "I live nearby. Lot of repeat customers—it's more common than people think."

That makes sense. Sort of.

The light changes and we keep going.

He asks about my dog—remembers him poking his head out of my purse, all attitude and fluff.

"I've got a big mutt at home," he says. "Total food vacuum. Eats everything but the leash."

I chuckle. "Mine's the opposite. Dexter thinks he's royalty. Won't eat unless his kibble's been blessed by a Michelin chef. I'm basically a prisoner in a hostage negotiation over turkey-flavored wet food."

He laughs, and for a moment, it feels normal again.

Until I glance at the windshield.

"You got any other dogs or just the one?"

There's a sticker. Small, fresh. A private school crest—white, navy, and gold. I've seen it before.

It's the academy across from the vet's office.

My stomach flips.

"Uh, yeah. First-time dog mom."

If he lives nearby, why would his kid go to school out there? Not impossible. But it doesn't click.

The geography's off and now I'm too warm.

He turns down my street, following the app but still, my gut is screaming. I open my *bSafe* app and hit the fake call feature.

A woman—single or not—can never be too careful.

He speaks as the app goes off.

"You live here alone, or is your husband just out of town?" Asked lightly but my throat tightens at the question.

I laugh—just enough to pretend I didn't hear the shift. "Oh, speak of the devil."

I answer and give my best "Hi, honey," "Two minutes away," and "See you soon, babe."

Pretending to hang up, I grab the bag of dog food.

"Well, if you ever need more regular rides, I do private arrangements outside the app. More flexible. Cheaper too."

He pulls a small stack of cards from the center console, offers one over his shoulder.

"Take it. Just in case."

I hesitate. No good reason not to take it. Not without making it weird.

So, I do.

Fingers brush the glossy cardstock. I fake a smile that feels hot-glued to my face.

"Thanks," I say, tucking it into my bag like I'm not already planning to burn it when I get home.

"Have a good one," he says, watching in the mirror as I step out.

I murmur another thank-you and shut the door.

He pulls away slowly.

Only when the taillights disappear do I finally breathe.

Then, I bolt.

I all but launch myself down the drive to the side entry like I'm in a horror movie and the killer's right behind me with theme music and a ski mask.

My fingers fumble with the keyring—*come on*—and I drop one of the bags. I pick it up with a shaking hand, glancing around in paranoid terror.

The key finally slides into the lock. I shove the door open, slam it so hard I nearly take off my own shoulder. Two clicks of the deadbolt. Alarm on. Chain set.

I press my forehead to the door and let out a breath I've been holding since I saw that sticker.

"I'm losing my mind," I whisper, heading for the drawer in the hutch—the one that holds reassurance.

My mother's knife.

I don't know why I grab it. But the weight settles in my palm, and something in me slows.

Calmer.

Not fine—but closer to functional.

My pulse steadies. My spine straightens.

The edge of the panic backs off enough to let me breathe.

But it doesn't stay away. It starts crawling back under my skin, slick and sharp.

My fingers rise to my scalp without me noticing, nails scratching the same patch they always find when I spiral—like I'm trying to dig out the thought that started it.

Everything feels chaotic. Wrong.

But I can fix that.

Cleaning helps.

It has order. A beginning, a middle, an end. Cause and effect. Something that still obeys the laws of sanity.

Dexter stares at me, unblinking. Snaggletooth gleaming like a warning.

I stop scratching, drop my hand, and inhale.

He yips, nosing the grocery bag like I've forgotten the real crisis.

"Right. Okay. Mr. Picky Pants. Let's see if you'll eat tonight."

I line up three overpriced, artisanal, vet-recommended packets like a tasting menu at Le Bark. Duck. Stew with Lamb and pumpkin—more expensive than my favorite bottle of wine.

I spoon a bit of each onto a tiny crystal dish I once used for olives.

He sniffs. Circles. Pauses. Then—of course—goes straight for the duck with the gravy and bougie compostable packaging.

He licks it clean.

Twice.

I narrow my eyes. "Really? That's the one?"

A burp. Followed by a full-body wiggle of smugness.

I throw my hands up.

"I've created a monster. A fluffy, bougie little monster."

Dexter finishes eating like the tiny culinary diva he is, then prances to the side door and gives a single, commanding bark.

Bathroom break.

Of course.

I'm so frazzled, the thought of going outside sends my heart rate to the sky. And this is one person's fault.

Mr. Silent-Treatment Stalker.

If he hadn't had my rental picked up, I could've driven

myself. I wouldn't be paranoid about some mid-life private school teacher moonlighting as a ferry for strangers.

Did Declan offer to drive me? Yes.

Would I have called him for a kibble run? Absolutely not.

Does the object of my paranoid delusions deserve my irritation?

Sure does. And I'm going to give him a piece of my mind.

The knife is coming with me. It's cold and steady in my grip, grounding me, if only for a breath. I dig through my bag with one hand, the other gripping the handle.

No stalker-phone.

Cheese and crackers, it's not here.

I check the floor. The counter. Couch cushions. Panic rises like acid.

I must've dropped it somewhere between slamming the door and trying not to hyperventilate.

Because of course I did. Because why wouldn't I misplace my stalker-issued terror device the same day I found a man with his throat cut open like a soda can?

I squeeze my eyes shut. Breathe.

"We need to calm down."

I put both hands out, speaking to Dexter like he's part of the hysteria. He's not.

He waits patiently by the door while I have my breakdown.

It's probably right outside. Maybe it slipped from my pocket when I tripped over my own feet.

"Okay, I can do this," I mutter.

Dexter needs to go out, and—scientifically speaking—indoor peeing is a stronger trigger than potential homicide.

I exhale. Flick the lock and open the door.

Just a minute. Just long enough for Dexter to do his thing.

It's cooler now. Quiet in that eerie way residential streets get at night when it's too still.

Dexter trots forward like he owns the street.

And there it is. On the pavement.

My heart jerks into my throat.

The phone.

I crouch, scoop it up in one hand, knife white-knuckled in the other.

The moment I flip it open, the screen lights up.

Seventy-three texts. Forty-five missed calls.

"My stalker has separation anxiety. Cool."

I swipe to unlock.

Dexter stops and stiffens. Growls low in his throat, snaggle-tooth front and center like he's auditioning for *Cujo: Teacup Edition.*

"Dex..." I whisper.

My eyes drop to the most recent message.

> UNKNOWN: HE'S COMING TO KILL
> YOU!!!

And just like that, every scrap of calm I'd managed to gather slams into the pavement.

Him

I'm a goddamn wildfire tearing through the city.

Horn blaring. Tires screaming. My hand glued to the wheel while my foot punishes the gas like it insulted me.

Every red light is a dare.

Every slow car in front of me is a target.

I swing the car up onto the curb without hesitation, clipping a trash bin that explodes across the sidewalk in my rearview like confetti at the world's worst parade.

I don't give a shit.

This car's a junkyard decoy. Old, dented, and forgettable. It's not meant to last. It's meant to get me there fast enough to stop a murder.

Her murder.

It can burn, crumble, wrap around a lamppost—I'll still be crawling toward her with broken ribs and blood in my lungs if that's what it takes.

My phone is in the cup holder, screen glowing like a flare— her location dot moving on the map with agonizing slowness.

She's on the way home.

Heading straight back to the place he's already defiled. The house he broke into.

The house where he tucked a hunting knife under her cushion and coiled rope under another like she's some piece of prey.

And now she's in his car.

Alone with a fucking monster.

I hit the button to call her for the hundredth goddamn time.

Come on, come on, come on.

I blow through a stop sign. Some asshole honks.

I flip him off. "Die mad, dickhead."

The phone rings and rings. "FUCK!" I slam my hand onto the steering wheel like it's the cause of all this.

She has no idea she's sitting three feet away from a mother fucking serial predator.

And if I don't get there in time, she's going to die.

My iPad is running the security feeds from her house—every motion-triggered camera I've wired into the place. Living room. Porch. Hallway.

I can't look at it for more than a second at a time. Eyes on the road. Eyes on the feed. Eyes on the road. Eyes on her.

She's close now. Just a few blocks.

I'm too far away.

My hands are slick with sweat and rage, and the steering wheel's starting to creak from how hard I'm holding it.

I'm talking to her without meaning to. Whispering like she can hear me through every red light I blow.

Stay calm, Sunshine. Don't let him see you're scared. Just a little longer.

I'm coming.

I'm coming for you, baby.

The car pulls up to the curb in front of her house.

The same fucking car that's been circling over and over like a goddamn vulture waiting for the final breath.

She steps out.

My heart stops. I can't fucking breathe.

Even the goddamn world stops spinning.

She's okay. Still in one piece.

But she's scanning—nervous. Her shoulders are tight, cheeks are flushed. Her keys are in her hand like a weapon, white-knuckled.

She knows something's wrong. Not how wrong, but her instincts are firing.

"Good girl."

She keeps her back to the house. Eyes on the car and she waits.

"Don't turn your back, baby. Don't give him the opening. You know better than that."

The car doesn't pull away just yet.

It lingers. Like he's waiting. Like he's hoping for something.

I slam the heel of my hand into the steering wheel and scream into the windshield.

"FUUUCKING MOVE!"

Drive. Away. You sick fuck.

"I'm going to fucking kill you."

And I am.

He finally pulls off.

Poppy watches, every muscle in her shoulders locked tight.

And I keep driving—every turn an act of war, every second counting down to when I can put my hands on him and make him sorry for ever setting eyes on my girl.

She doesn't even know what almost happened.

Or maybe she does.

Maybe some part of her felt it. That primal itch under the skin that says you're being watched. That hair-raising chill that whispers *run.*

She's sharp. Smarter than most.

She's been surrounded by predators long enough to sniff one out when he's breathing too close.

I fumble for my phone again and hit redial.

It rings.

Voicemail.

I slam my fist into the steering wheel so hard it cracks the plastic.

"Fuck!"

It echoes through the car like a gunshot. I don't even flinch. I want the pain. I deserve it for letting her get that close to something I should've stopped.

The security feed on the iPad shows her slamming the door behind her, back pressed to it, panting like she just outran a goddamn monster.

"Good," I mutter through gritted teeth. "Good girl. You fucking felt it."

She doesn't know why, maybe. Can't name it. But she knew.

And thank fucking God for that.

"Just stay inside, Poppy. Please—fucking stay inside."

My hands are shaking now, but not from fear. Not even from adrenaline.

It's rage.

Boiling, blinding, bone-deep rage that's been building in my bloodstream since I watched him sneak into her house. Since I saw what he left behind. Since I realized he was circling her, studying her, planning something slow and specific.

That fucker planted rope in her home like it was a starter kit for torture. He chose a blade for very specific pain.

And then he played the long game. Waited for the right moment when she was alone. For her car to vanish. For a ride request to pop up when she wasn't thinking anything of it.

He engineered the entire moment.

And I let it happen.

My foot is welded to the gas, the speedometer long past legal, weaving through traffic like I'm on fire. Every car I pass is just an obstacle between me and her.

I try her other phone number even though I know she blocked me days ago.

It doesn't ring. It just beeps three times.

It was stupid to hope, but even still, my heart drops like a stone.

I smack the dash with the heel of my hand so hard the whole console shudders. A light pops on that I don't have time to read.

My knuckles are white on the wheel. My head's pounding and still, I drive faster.

Because if he's still out there... if he said something to her in the car that tipped her off, he may have noticed a change in her demeanor. He may decide to just do it now.

Double back.

No more waiting. No more slow-play.

Just a door kicked in, a scream that never finishes, and the sound of my Sunshine being snuffed out like a goddamn candle.

I whip around a corner so fast the tires scream in protest. A mailbox explodes in my rearview as I glance at the feed—and there he is.

He's come back.

Pulling up slow. Parking a few houses down. That predatory creep of a man who already got her alone once has the audacity to roll back up.

Like he's not a fucking monster walking on borrowed time.

The feed jumps. He gets out.

He slings a small backpack over his shoulders and snaps a belt around his waist.

My breath stops. My entire body locks up like I've been shot.

That's gear.

That's duct tape and zip ties and a second knife. That's chloroform and gloves.

That's a plan.

I can't fucking lose her.

She's the only speck of light in my dark world, and she doesn't even know it yet. I haven't been able to tell her. To show her.

And I may not get the fucking chance.

A sound tears from my throat like it's being ripped out by claws, and I slam my fists into the steering wheel again and again and again.

"FUCK!"

"FUCK!"

"FUCK!"

Everything inside me fractures—rage detonating at the center of my chest—but underneath the heat, under the white-hot bloodlust, there's something colder.

Something worse.

Terror.

Pure, unfiltered terror.

The kind that makes your vision go black around the edges.

The kind that wraps around your spine and tells you: *You're too far. You'll be too late.*

Because what if I am?

What if he walks through that door?

What if she freezes?

What if all I do is watch it happen on this fucking screen?

I've been watching her for months—breathing her in through pixels and speakers and quiet moments no one else noticed—and now it might end with me watching her die.

Because I wasn't fast enough.

Because I didn't notice him in time. And now he's back. And she's inside. Alone.

And he knows it.

I slam my foot harder into the gas. I don't care if I flip the fucking car. I will get to her if it kills me.

But as the blocks crawl by on the GPS... as I watch him cross the street to her house... I realize the truth.

I'm not going to make it.

I'm still too far.

I'm not going to make it.

28
Poppy

Dexter's growl is my only warning. Deep. Unearthly. The kind of noise that doesn't belong in a tiny, fluffy dog with a snaggletooth and pink toenails.

Then a shadow moves—fast.

Something slams into me like a brick wall wearing skin, and I'm hurled against the door. My head cracks against the wood with a sickening thunk that blurs everything in a spray of stars.

I don't scream. Or maybe I do. I can't tell.

I can barely see.

My vision splits—white-hot pain on one side, darkness on the other.

My fingers are slick on the knife—my mother's knife—and I don't even aim. I just slash.

I feel it land. Feel it resist.

A sound erupts inches from my ear—part snarl, part scream. Wet and raw.

Dexter loses his mind, barking high and fast, circling our feet like he's ready to throw himself into battle.

Please, Dexter. Just run. Hide.

My vision clears just enough. I already know who I'll find:

The rideshare driver.

Bleeding from his face. One eye squeezed shut, hand clamped over it. He's panting, shaking with fury. And even with blood dripping down his shirt, he's smiling.

"You really thought that fake phone call was gonna fool me?" he spits. "You're alone, sweetheart. I knew it the first time I picked you up."

My stomach lurches.

He knew.

And I'm standing here with a knife, a dog the size of a soda can at my feet, and my stalker-issued phone just out of reach.

If only I could get to it, I'd call him like DoorDash. Express delivery for two ninety-nine? Sure.

But even if I did, he'd never make it in time.

The thought centers me. No one's coming.

I have to do this myself.

He lunges.

I barely get the knife between us when he throws his full weight into me—forcing the blade into his own torso.

It sinks deep. I feel it catch.

Then the blood hits.

Warm. Sticky. Violent. It splashes across my face, soaks my shirt, splatters into my mouth.

The taste hits me—salt and iron and oh my God I think I'm going to throw up.

I gag. Spit and swallow it down.

There's no time. He's still upright. Still grinning.

He grabs my wrist with a grip like a steel trap and slams my arm into the door so hard my fingers go numb.

"No, we're just getting started," he breathes, voice hot and twisted.

My grip on the knife hardens like cement. I can't drop this.

"You think you've got some fight in you? I love the fight. Love it more when you finally give in."

Something in me rises—sharp, searing, done.

"Over," I hiss, twisting my wrist, trying to break his grip. "My dead body."

I kick. Hard.

His body jerks, mouth opening in a silent cry. His hold loosens—just enough.

I wrench my hand, pivot the knife, and saw upward along his forearm. It's brutal and effective.

Blood slicks my hand, sprays across the door.

His grip falters.

And something in me snaps.

Not fear. Not survival.

Something colder. That whispers: *finish it*.

His face shifts—fury turning to fear. He sees it. The monster I bury. The one with blood on her hands.

And she's wide awake.

He sees it, right before I move.

Both hands on the knife now, fingers locked. I plunge it into him with everything I've got.

He screams but it's not fear. It's shock.

The blade hits resistance but I don't recoil. I press until it pushes through. Until I hear a crunch. A pop.

It should repulse me but it doesn't.

It satisfies something primal.

Something that remembers the calm after Travis Gannon's blood.

I yank the knife back and stab again.

Once. Twice. Again.

I lose count.

Dexter barks somewhere nearby, but it's muffled—like I'm underwater. Only the rhythm of the knife exists.

In. Out. In. Out.

I straddle him now, knees digging into his ribs as he squirms. He tries to throw me off, but he's bleeding out too fast.

I drive the blade in again—below the collarbone. He jerks.

Dexter growls, proud. Or maybe that's just me.

My tiny demon cheerleader.

Another stab.

Messier. The blade snags. My hands slip but I don't stop.

I can't.

Because this?

This is release.

Every blocked case. Every predator who walked. Every girl who cried and got nothing. Every fear I swallowed like glass.

It all breaks.

And I break with it.

I don't realize I'm crying until a tear slips off my chin and lands on his cheek.

Fitting.

He gurgles something. A protest? A plea? Doesn't matter. He's beyond words now—just breath and blood and the slow crawl toward death.

I poise the blade at his neck and look him in the eye.

He's still smirking. Still thinks he's in control. That I'll hesitate.

I lean in close, voice steady, breath shaking.

"You die knowing I wasn't afraid of you."

Then I drag the blade across his throat.

Crimson blooms, oozing from the gap.

His hands twitch like he's trying to move them to his neck. Like he can push the blood back in. But then, they go slack.

His head drops to the side. Stare fixed on nothing.

And I feel it.

The moment he dies.

The moment the silence is sudden. Whole.

I look down at him.

His chest is still. mouth is open. A red halo beneath him.

And I know—I did that.

I ended him.

And I don't feel guilty.

I feel...

The quiet.

It sinks in behind my ears, across the crown of my head like cool, thick sludge. Not warm. Not fuzzy. Just... quiet. Heavy. Like my brain pulled the emergency brake and everything is coasting in slow motion.

I exhale, long and shaky, like I've been holding it in for hours.

My arms tremble. My thighs ache from kneeling.

There's blood everywhere—on my hands, under my nails, soaking my shirt, my bra, my soul.

It's in my hair. On my face. I can taste it again. Copper and adrenaline.

I shuffle back toward the house like I'm underwater.

The knife drops from my hand with a dull clatter on the cement.

I don't even look at him. Not yet.

I'm still floating, trying not to break the euphoria.

Dexter is barking—sharp and frantic. Like an alarm clock in a bomb shelter.

That's what pulls me back. That panicked sound yanks me out of my daze and slams me into my body.

"Dex…" I whisper, voice cracked and raw.

Then he stops barking.

Just—goes quiet.

He's sniffing something.

I blink, vision catching up half a second too late.

I look at him. The man I killed. But something is… wrong.

Finally, I see it.

One eye missing. It's now just a dark, hollow pit.

The other stares blankly at the sky like it's waiting for instructions. Blood everywhere. Skin torn. Like something tried to peel him open and quit halfway through.

And Dexter…

Dexter is sniffing the eyeball.

"Ew—Dexter. No!"

I lunge and scoop him up with blood-slick hands. He wriggles like he doesn't understand the problem. Like his gourmet dog food wasn't enough and now he's feeling adventurous.

"No eyeballs," I scold. "We do *not* snack on serial killers."

I clutch him to my chest, his little heart hammering against mine, and I finally look at it all.

The scene.

The carnage.

What I did.

What I *can* do.

And the fog lifts just enough for the question I'd been hoping to avoid:

"…Now what in the lemon-drop dandy do I do?"

I stagger to my feet, Dexter in one arm, and bolt for the door. I fumble the knob, shove it open, and slam it behind me.

There's blood on my door. My face. My arms. My everything.

I look like I just walked off a slasher film, and all I can think about is the Eye of Sauron sitting on my driveway.

I can't move forward. I can't breathe until it's gone.

I try to prioritize the to-do list in my mind.

Hide the body.

Wash the blood.

Bathe in lemon-scented disinfectant.

But no—nothing can happen until the eyeball is gone. Out of sight and off the driveway.

I go to the kitchen, open the utensil drawer, and grab the first thing I see.

A spatula? No.

How ridiculous. What on earth can you do with a spatula?

Tongs? I'd feel the eye give—soft squish, rolling weight. Absolutely not.

A spoon? This isn't an Easter egg race.

I need something distant. Functional. Something to help me pretend I'm not removing a literal eyeball from my property.

Ah. The turkey baster.

Nestled in the back of the drawer like it's been waiting its whole life for this moment.

I stare at it, and can't believe I'm seriously considering this buuut...

The nozzle is a little wide. Maybe eyeball size? Yes. This could work.

"I guess it's not just for Thanksgiving any more."

Dexter stays tucked under my arm like a panting loaf of bread. I make my way to the door, my bloody steps squeaking like clown shoes.

Outside, the air has changed.

Heavier. Metallic. The scent of blood baked into the house under the low evening light like old pennies.

And there it is.

The eye.

Sitting there like a rejected marble.

The floodlight glints off it. My throat tightens.

Dexter sniffs toward it again.

"Don't even think about it, buddy," I whisper, lowering myself as every joint screams this is a bad idea.

I keep my gaze just off-center—like if I look straight at it, I'll go mad.

Like it'll curse me if we make eye contact.

Ha. Eye contact. Get it?

The baster hovers, trembling in my hand. I squeeze the bulb.

I hesitate.

Then I release.

The suction is wet, and immediate.

But the eye slips, rolls slightly, and I almost drop Dexter from how violently I recoil. My stomach lurches and I cough, nearly retching. The baster has a smear of blood inside, but no eye.

I gag and Dexter complains but we try again.

The baster wobbles in my grip.

I reposition, squeeze and release.

This time, it *slurps* inside.

There's a nauseating pop as it fills the clear tube like the world's worst science fair project.

And... it's in there.

Looking at me.

Veiny. Glazed. Judgmental.

I hold it out like it's radioactive. I can't put it down. Can't bring it inside. Can't think with it... staring at me.

I set Dexter down gently—he gives me a look like *Are you sure that's wise, Mother?*

I move to the body.

I don't want to touch him. Every cell in me screams *don't*, but I can't leave this eyeball tube like a grisly driveway ornament. I need it hidden.

I crouch. Reach out. With my thumb and forefinger—just the tips—I pinch the edge of his shirt sleeve. Not even fabric. Just thread.

It lifts slowly. Heavy with death. My other hand trembles as I slide the baster beneath the arm like a weird, murderous thermometer.

Then I let go.

His hand flops, then settles.

It scares the piddle out of me and I jump back. "Holy guacamole."

My hand slaps to my chest, like I can hold my heart in place by force.

My breath comes in fluttery bursts.

Dexter lets out a single bark like *Ma'am, control yourself.*

I step back and immediately slip on the blood. My foot skids—I do a not-so-graceful hop to stay upright.

"Okay," I whisper, hand still pressed to my sternum. "Okay. That's done."

But it's not.

Because I still have a body to deal with.

My *second* body.

There's a knife on the driveway. *My* knife.

It catches the light like it wants to be noticed. Like it's proud.

I walk over and pick it up with blood-wet fingers. The grip sticky. The blade warm.

I stare down at what I did.

Another slit throat. Multiple stab wounds. A full-on frenzy.

I have an M.O.

A pattern.

I'm one body away from joining the exclusive club of official serial killers.

One more.

Three murders with a cooling-off period and a recurring signature, and you get your own Wikipedia page.

My stomach turns.

No—revolts.

I barely make it to the bushes before I hurl everything into the hydrangeas. Coffee, panic, two regrettable spoonfuls of peanut butter... all of it.

Dexter lets out a low growl at my side, like he's trying to be supportive but would really prefer I not vomit directly on *his* pee bush.

I wipe my mouth on my sleeve like a feral child and stagger toward the door, willing my legs to hold me up.

The air feels different.

Still. Too still.

I pause, frowning as I scan the street. I haven't seen a car in ten minutes. No jogger. No dog walker. Not even that guy who speedwalks with ankle weights and sass.

Dexter stiffens. One short bark—then silence.

He squints toward the side of the house. Whines.

I glance too, but there's nothing there. Just the overgrown hedge and a dark smear of shadow pooling near the fence line.

"Probably... a opossum," I mutter. But the hairs on my neck don't buy it.

I move toward the door again, faster now. Blood-slick footsteps. Every sound feels loud, like the night is holding its breath.

Dexter growls—low and warning—but I'm already reaching for the knob.

That's when I hear something.

Not a car. Not a branch. Footsteps.

Close. Fast.

Too fast.

A figure barrels toward me out of the dark, and I barely have time to raise the knife before hands—large, strong—close around me. One clamps over my mouth, the other grabs my wrist, pinning it back before the blade can land.

My back slams into the door.

Hard.

I thrash, kick, scream against the palm covering my face, but it doesn't budge.

I can't breathe. Can't move. Can't see—

Not again.

Then a voice—low, commanding, terrifyingly close to my ear—whispers:

"Shhhhh... it's me."

Him

The second I get my hands on her, it's like the earth rights itself.

Like gravity snaps back into place, and I can finally stand again. My gloved hand clamps over her mouth—not out of cruelty, but necessity. She's vibrating with panic, and I need her still. Need her to know it's me. That she's not alone anymore.

My other hand seizes her wrist, pressing it hard into the doorframe—too hard, maybe, but I've been chasing her shadow across this city, and now I have her. I couldn't let go of her even if I wanted to.

Also, I don't want her to slice me up like her friend back here.

Her body molds against mine, and I press her into the wood like I can imprint her there. Like I can carve her shape into this house and make it remember she belongs here.

She's shaking. Terrified. And it's beautiful.

Because it means she's still alive.

And I got to her.

My thigh slots between hers to keep her still. Keep her mine.

I lower my voice, soft as silk, whispering against the crown of her hair. "Shhhh... it's okay. I've got you."

I feel her exhale. I see her mind working it out.

The breath she lets out isn't relief.

It's surrender.

Her eyes meet mine—what little she can see through the mask—and I watch recognition dawn.

Yes, Sunshine. It's me.

The man in your phone.

The shadow outside your window.

The monster who learned how to love only you.

She doesn't scream. Doesn't fight. Instead, she drops the knife. Just lets it fall like it was never hers. Like she knew, all along, I'd be the one to carry the weight of it.

Her knees go next.

I catch her like it's instinct.

One arm behind her back, one under her legs.

She folds into me like she was made to. Like every jagged edge of this world led us here.

And then she breaks.

God.

The sound.

It hits somewhere deep in my chest—a place I didn't know could still feel things.

She sobs—loud and broken. The kind of sob that comes after your soul's already left your body.

And I just hold her.

Tighter.

She's covered in that asshole's blood and her own misery, but it doesn't matter.

I'd carry her through fire like this. Through hell.

And she lets me.

No resistance. No hesitation. Just... trust.

She tucks her face into my neck and cries like I'm her sanctuary.

And for her, I am.

Not because I deserve it—fuck, I know I don't.

But because I'm hers.

I'm the one who saw *her*.

Saw through the performance, the cheer, the bright clothes and charming smiles. I saw the rage. The fire. The need.

And now she's in my arms.

Mine.

The world is quiet for a breath.

The storm is still coming, but right now?

She's safe.

And I'll burn everything else to ash to keep her that way.

She's light in my arms when I turn from the doorstep. Silent with exhaustion.

The kind of quiet you don't get often—when the air still tastes like adrenaline and the world feels like it might crack if you breathe too loud.

She stirs, instincts kicking in like she should put up a fight. She's so cute trying.

"Get away from me."

"Never." I hold her tighter, making it clear she's not getting down until I say so.

I carry her inside like I was made for it.

Dexter follows like he understands.

His nails click softly on the hardwood, ears perked—not anxious. Just accepting.

She doesn't know I've been coming over here. Bribing the little shit with treats. Leaving a worn shirt in his bed so he gets used to my scent.

I know exactly what she needs, and as I walk through her house with ease, she realizes it.

I've been here enough to know the creak of the banister, the dip in the third stair that catches her heel.

She always mutters about fixing it, but never does.

"I can walk, you know." She tries to hide the tremor in her voice.

Her body is warm against mine, limbs heavy with the kind of grief that doesn't make sound until it breaks.

"No, you can't. Not like this."

In the bathroom, I set her down gently. Like she might break—but not because she's fragile. Because she's sacred.

She stays where I place her, shaking. Terrified.

But she doesn't run.

And that matters.

"Who are you?" she whispers, trying to peer around as I kneel beside the tub.

I feel her eyes on me while I turn on the water. Feel her heartbeat adjusting to mine. Slowing.

She startles when I turn to her—her breath catching like a note cut short.

"I need your clothes," I say. Simple and controlled. But inside, I'm anything but.

Her eyes go wide before she narrows her glare. She doesn't move. *Yeah, baby, give me some of that fire.*

She says, "No." Breathless. Fractured. Like she knows she should resist but knows it's pointless.

I lift my hand slowly—careful not to spook her. The glove comes off one finger at a time, teeth tugging leather. I want her to watch.

I want her to know I'm not in a rush.

Her silence hums between us, thick with defiance.

"I've already seen it all, Sunny," I murmur, just loud enough for her to feel.

My gloves hit the counter with a soft thud, but her heartbeat is louder.

Her eyes flick to the shower. Putting it together. The handprint. What I was doing in there.

"This how you normally introduce yourself to strangers?"

My cock twitches at her snark. At being this close.

"Arms up."

She hesitates. Just for a breath.

"I said no."

"It wasn't a question."

My hand dips under her shirt, and it's off with a sharp pull. She stumbles toward me, palms to my chest before she yanks them back.

Her bra is next. I have to clench my jaw to keep from putting my mouth on her.

"You want my dignity too?" Her bite is back.

"I'll take everything you offer me, Sunshine." I whisper it against her ear, relishing the shiver she pretends didn't happen.

"I won't give you anything." Crossing her arms over her breasts.

She's shaking. But not from fear.

From adrenaline. Cold. The gravity of tonight sinking in.

"Yes," I lower my hands to her pants. "You will."

She doesn't stop me, but she clenches her stomach. Her thighs.

I peel the pants down slowly, helping her step out. They join the pile, and I turn my gaze to her panties. I take my time, sliding my hands up her thighs, thumbs slipping beneath the thin fabric.

"You enjoying the show, creep?" There's no venom in her tone—just an attempt to mask arousal.

I look into her eyes as I pull them down.

The fight not to stare at her pussy. To see if she's glistening. To smell her. To lick her. I've never fought so hard against something I want.

"Yes. I am."

Her face burns. Embarrassed. I want to kiss it away. Press my mouth against the soft mound above her clit.

The blood drying on her will start to grate—like a cracked desert floor. She'll want to scrub until there's nothing left.

Her panties drop to the pile. She's stripped to skin and consequence.

I finally look—and I burn at the sight.

Her chin quivers. "There's blood everywhere," she whispers, not looking away.

I stand and brush a lock of hair from her face.

"I'll clean it up," I whisper, my voice cracking at how close we are.

My knuckles skim her cheek, featherlight. She's warm.

Her skin fits beneath my hand like it belongs there. My fingers drift down—jaw, throat.

She swallows. I feel it. Fixate on it.

Every movement recorded. Memorized and etched into me.

I lower my touch to her collarbone. Goosebumps rise as I move.

I brush the side of her breast. Grazing my thumb over her nipple.

The sound she makes—soft, guttural, needy—scrapes across me like silk and barbed wire.

She wants it.

I love that she wants it. But I know she's still living by rules and boundaries.

Limits we're going to dismantle.

She jolts—like her own moan snapped her awake. She pushes my hand away like it burns, but I'm on her in a breath, spinning her to face the counter.

One hand on her hip, grounding.

The other circles her throat—firm, claiming. She gasps as I pull her back against me. My cock hard, pressed tight.

I lean in, my voice in her ear like worship wearing teeth.

"Don't run from me. Ever."

She should fight my touch. Defy me with her glare. But instead... her thighs press together. Her tongue flicks out to wet her bottom lip, and I feel it in my gut like a match against gasoline.

She still tries to pull away, but I press her harder against me.

"Do you fucking understand?" My grip tightens on her throat, her hip, and it about kills me.

She freezes when I rock into her—then nods. Not out of fear. Out of something deeper.

Something darker.

My hands guide her forward. She bends, obedient. Bracing on the counter. Trembling just enough to make my hands twitch with restraint.

"You don't know how much I've waited for you," I whisper, dragging my hand up her spine, slow as sin.

"You don't scare me." She glances back—masking how she presses her ass into me.

She wants me to feel it.

So I help her.

Letting her know just how badly I want her. And she stays

there. Locked in place by a touch she didn't ask for but can't resist.

"We're going to have fun."

I reach between her thighs, parting the lips of her pussy.

And fuck.

She's soaked.

My finger slides through her like she's been waiting just as long. A sound escapes me—dark and pleased. She clenches. I could slide into her right now.

Her shame is palpable.

She thinks I don't notice the flush on her cheeks. That this humiliates her and ignites her at the same time.

"Wet already," I murmur, grinning. My lips brush her ear. "I knew you would be."

I make her straighten and turn to face me. Her nipples graze my chest with every breath.

"You're a monster," she whispers. Her pupils blown wide, eyes brimming with tears.

I grin under the mask. She doesn't back away.

Slowly, I lift my soaked finger. Pull my mask back slightly.

"I'm your monster."

Then I slip my finger into my mouth.

And her lips pop open.

The taste of her coats my tongue—salt, heat, and everything I imagined, but more. It lingers like a secret I'll never tell.

She watches. Her embarrassment is a living thing. So is her want.

The war between them flashes across her face, and I memorize it.

I lean in closer than I should. My mask brushes her throat, and I inhale deeply.

Skin. Sweat. Adrenaline.

I breathe her in like I'm making a memory I can carry into every nightmare.

Then I step back. The space I leave feels like a wound.

I watch it land. That cold rush. That ache she wasn't expecting.

She misses me already.

She hates it. I fucking love it.

Silence stretches.

Tension, tight as a wire.

"Are you..." Her voice trembles. "Are you going to rape me?"

The world narrows to her.

I stare.

Long enough for her to doubt asking.

Long enough for her to feel the weight of it.

A slow shake of my head. No words. Just that. Calm. Final. No.

That's not who I am.

I don't take what's mine.

I make it give in.

When I finally speak, my voice is low. A promise she won't forget.

"Not unless you beg me to, Sunshine."

Because when she begs, when she asks, then she'll understand:

She was mine long before I touched her.

Her heart pounds. I see it in her pulse. The way her chest rises too fast.

My hand slides down her thigh—not to grope, but to soothe. Pressure. Steady.

The other threads through her fingers. She lets me.

I lift her leg, guide her foot toward the bath.

My palm curves around her calf. For a second, I wonder if she feels it too—that hum between us. Divine. Profane.

The water rushes over her toes, steam curling up.

"Hot enough?" I ask, though I already know it's not.

"No," she breathes. Soft and raw.

I adjust the water without a word, without looking away, and help her into the tub.

She folds in on herself, arms wrapping tight over her chest like armor.

I lean down, bracing my palm on the tub's edge. Close enough she can hear me over the water.

"Don't come out until the water runs clear."

There's blood on her skin. Her hair. Her soul. But it won't be there for long.

My eyes drink her in—every bruise, every tremble.

"Can you do that?" I murmur, voice low, meant only for her. "Can you be my good girl?"

A veil drops over her face. Lust flickers in her eyes as she stays locked in that trance.

Oh, my little Sunshine liked that.

She nods. Barely. But she does.

"Good," I whisper.

And it's not just praise—it's a benediction.

I let my thumb brush her lip, soft and reverent.

That one touch cracks something open in her. She won't admit it yet, but I know what it is.

The darkness behind her sunshine.

She's so fucking beautiful, and I don't want to leave. But I have to.

I need to erase everything that happened out there. I need to protect her again.

I slip the gloves into my back pocket.

Gather the pile of blood-stained clothes and shoes, pausing at the door for one last look before I leave her to fall apart.

I descend the stairs with her clothes in one hand and a thousand thoughts in the other.

Behind me, I hear the little beast trotting after me like I owe him answers.

His favorite person is behind a closed door, unraveling in hot water—and he's stuck with me.

Tough luck, buddy.

We're still on shaky ground, the dog and me.

He doesn't trust me. I haven't forgiven him for barging into her life.

But tonight? I resent him a little less.

I glance down at the tiny, judgmental gremlin with fur. His ears perk like he's ready to help.

"Body first," I say, pointing toward the side door. "Then *you* get a bath."

He huffs like he understands.

Like he doesn't appreciate being second priority.

Yeah, well, tough shit, you little asshole.

30

Poppy

I've been in the bath so long I'm pretty sure my skin is about to develop scales.

The water went pink. Then cloudy. Then lukewarm and useless. I drained it, refilled it and soaked again.

Scrubbed every inch of myself even though the blood was gone an hour ago. Maybe longer.

Time doesn't feel linear anymore—it's more like soup. Thick. Confused. Full of chunks I don't want to stir too hard.

I dunk my head again and let the water fill my ears. It dulls the noise in the room but makes the noise in my head louder.

I press my palms to my face, hard, until all I see is red and static.

I didn't just kill someone.

I executed him.

With control.

With intention.

And—worst of all—with satisfaction.

A soft whimper slips out of me, but I drown it with another pass of water.

Wash the thoughts. Wash the memories. Wash the part of me that liked it.

But it doesn't go away.

It's not on my skin anymore.

It's under it.

Eventually, the ache in my bones catches up. The adrenaline thins, leaving me hollow and too heavy to hold up. My body drags itself out of the tub like a ghost of its former self.

At least I avoided the faint bloodstain where my clothes were.

Something in me will remember to clean that up later.

Towel. Hair wrap. Lotion I don't remember applying.

I stare at my reflection in the fogged-up mirror and barely recognize myself. My eyes are different. Like something I've never seen is looking back at me.

I tiptoe to the bathroom door and pause.

What if he's still out there?

He, as in the guy in the mask.

Not the dead one outside, marinating in moonlight and eye gravy.

No, the other one. The one who's been watching me. Carrying me like I'm breakable—and his.

I press my ear to the wood.

Silence.

Well, that's not comforting.

I crack the door just wide enough to peek.

Dexter looks up at me.

Perfectly clean. Comically fluffy. Settled in his tiny bed like a spoiled croissant, gnawing on a bone with all the menace of a slightly drunk toddler.

He's wearing a bow tie.

A pink one.

The one that came with that ridiculous golfer outfit I bought him during an emotional blackout in a boutique aisle.

He's freshly groomed, snaggletooth working overtime like none of tonight ever happened.

Like I didn't make him a criminal accomplice.

Like he's not technically a witness.

"Hey, you little fuzz-narc," I whisper.

He stops chewing. Ears perk.

Then trots over like the most joyful of murder partners.

He's not judging me.

Not Dexter.

He's just glad I'm here. And it's enough to almost make me feel okay.

Not safe. Not calm.

But okay enough.

I bend to pick him up, still damp and towel-wrapped, and whisper into his ear like a prayer:

"I'm gonna need you to not eat any more eyeballs, okay?"

He sneezes in my face.

Which, honestly, feels fair.

On the bed, my favorite pajamas are laid out with military precision: the cotton tee that says DEFENSE RESTS across the front, matching pants with little pink gavels, and fuzzy slippers at the foot like some boutique-hotel turndown service from hell.

And... underwear.

A lacy, blush-pink pair. Folded. Centered. Like a gift that says *wear these for me tonight.*

My face goes hot. Not from the bath.

From embarrassment.

Because I know he's watching. He said it. He meant it. He's probably watching me right now—through something I can't see.

I clutch Dexter tighter against my chest like he's a chastity charm.

He sneezes again. Useless.

Downstairs is worse.

The lights are low—comfortably dim. Calming. Like a spa. Or a serial killer's nesting-doll lair.

On the coffee table, my favorite wine is already poured in my favorite glass.

My eyes flick to the side door. Beyond it—somewhere past the edge of the light—is the body. The blood. The mess I made and walked away from.

Fear prickles up my spine like someone left the A.C. on and didn't tell me.

And then the burner phone chirps from beside the glass.

I jump like it barked.

Dexter growls. One short, offended sound. Like *can you not*.

The screen lights up.

UNKNOWN: It's okay. Everything is clean.

My breath comes in slow. Then faster. Then slow again, like I'm trying to trick my lungs into believing this is fine.

That I'm fine.

That a stalker isn't reading my mind and reassuring me.

I look around.

The drawer I know I left a bloody handprint on—gone. Wiped away like a magic trick.

The floor I tracked with bloody shoes.

All clean.

I turn in a slow circle. No lens. No red lights. No suspicious black dots.

He's thorough.

Dexter trots into the living room and hops onto the couch, curling up like this is just another work night. Maybe for him it is. Maybe for me too.

I pick up the wine and hold it like a church offering.

I keep waiting.

A knock at the door.

A scream from the hallway.

An eyeball to roll out from under the couch and wink like *Hey girl, miss me?*

But nothing does.

Eventually I ease open the side door, expecting to find either a body or a police squad.

Instead, I find takeout.

No blood. No body.

No Dexter gnawing on a severed toe.

It's just food. My favorite and still hot.

The absence of carnage feels almost worse. Like the crime was too neatly erased and I'm the only one who remembers. My mind skitters—until the scent hits me.

Warm spices. Garlic. That buttery perfume of toasted naan.

Something inside me crumples.

I close the door, lock it, and then relock it. Engage the security system for the illusion of safety—because that's what we're working with now.

I open the container and dive in.

Not like someone picking at dinner in the aftermath of trauma.

Like someone starving.

I tear into it like a woman trying to fill the crater where her sanity used to be. Tandoori chicken. Basmati rice. Both samosas. Half the naan. The sauces. I drink the wine, refill the glass, and pour a third without thinking.

By the time I climb the stairs, my stomach is full and my head fuzzy, but none of it dulls the buzzing tension under my skin.

Dexter's already curled up in his bed like he didn't just watch his human commit murder. He lifts his head, blinks at me, then returns to chewing like he's showing that bone who's boss.

Cozy under my comforter, I scroll the news with one hand, wine in the other, searching for proof the universe is catching up to what I did.

But there's nothing.

No reports. No sirens. No headlines about mystery bodies or vigilante justice.

I lie down slowly, like I'm afraid I might break the moment. My body sinks into the mattress, limbs weighted by exhaustion and wine, but my brain refuses to shut off.

Dexter lets out a soft sigh as he shifts into his usual curl, snaggletooth catching the lamplight like punctuation on a very long, very weird day.

I watch the shadows shift on the ceiling. Eyes open. Thoughts circling like vultures.

I don't feel guilty.

I feel... alert.

Like something's coming.

Like it's already on the way.

It's not sleep, so I pick up the burner phone with the kind of dread usually reserved for tax audits and pap smears.

The stillness buzzes under my skin like a warning.

I flip open the screen.

The texts hit all at once. Dozens.

Warnings.

Panic.

All caps.

Location pins.

Messages that read like screams typed too fast to spellcheck. From someone who wasn't just worried—someone desperate.

And I didn't see a single one until it was too late.

I thumb through them slowly, like maybe reading slower will lessen the guilt curdling in my stomach.

One of the last just says:

I can't lose you.

I close the phone. Look around again, hoping to spot some sign of the surveillance I've apparently been under. Nothing obvious. No blinking lights. No hidden lens. But I know he's here. Or at least watching.

I'm thinking he always is.

I set the phone in my lap and sit up straighter, heart thudding loud in my chest like it's trying to work up the nerve before my mouth does.

"Are you... there?"

I wait.

Ten seconds. Maybe fifteen.

The phone dings.

UNKNOWN: Always.

My breath leaves me in a soft, shaking exhale. One single tear slips down my cheek—too slow to feel dramatic, too fast to stop.

I whisper the truth before I can second-guess it.

"I don't want to be alone."

The phone stays dark.

No reply.

I swallow hard. Try to pull the blanket tighter even though I already feel like I'm wrapped in tension. Time stretches.

Then Dexter lifts his head, growling.

My entire body goes still. Every nerve humming.

In the doorway, a shadow cast in matte black. That white skull on the black balaclava reflecting nothing back at me but quiet promise.

He doesn't move. Doesn't speak. Just waits.

So I do too.

He walks toward me slowly—measured steps meant to soothe, not startle. He doesn't approach the bed. Doesn't reach for me. Just lowers himself into the window chair like he's done it a thousand times before.

Maybe he has.

Maybe before Dexter. Before I knew. Before tonight made monsters out of both of us.

He just sits there. Watching. Breathing. Massive and unmoving, the way a mountain watches a storm roll in.

Then he pulls out his phone. Mine chimes.

UNKNOWN: Sleep. I'll stay.

My grip on the blankets softens.

The tension in my shoulders unwinds.

And for the first time in what feels like years, I let go.

I let the weight settle and finally sleep.

Poppy

The world hums, a low-vibrating sound that fills the night.

I'm on my knees, blood soaking my hands, dripping down my forearms. The knife is still in my grip, grounding me in a moment I cannot process.

My breathing comes fast and shallow, each inhale scraping my throat as I watch the body slacken, life slipping away.

This should be where the quiet settles in—where the air turns heavy and I can finally breathe again, cocooned by the strange euphoria that always follows.

But not tonight.

Tonight, the air presses colder. Thicker. Refusing to let me go.

The darkness stretches around me, and behind, I hear the scrape of boots. I turn just enough to catch him—masked—stepping from the shadows like he's always been there.

My fingers drift down my thigh. I'm naked. Red stains my stomach, legs, arms, dripping from my fingertips like paint from a broken brush.

He doesn't speak. Just drops behind me until his chest brushes my back, his thighs bracketing mine. Together, we kneel like we're praying to a god that demands savagery instead of salvation.

One hand slides around my waist, fingers slipping between my legs. The other drifts higher, wrapping around my throat—firm but careful.

I lean back instinctively, resting my head against his shoulder, my body falling into his like we've done this a thousand times.

A sigh slips out, my frame easing into his control like it was always meant to.

His body moves first, a slow roll of his hips, and mine follows—guided by a force I cannot resist.

His pelvis grinds in deliberate waves, each one tightening my skin and clenching muscle.

His fingers part me with a tenderness that shouldn't exist in a place soaked with blood. Heat floods through me, thick and coiling deep.

I want to reach for him. Drop the knife. Rip the mask away.

But my hand won't move.

I try—to lift, to shift, to stand.

But it's like one of those dreams—you run and run, but stay rooted.

Helpless.

The realization bleeds in slowly, slicing through the haze.

This isn't real.

The thought drifts through me like smoke. A warning. A whisper.

I know I should wake up.

But I don't want to.

Not yet.

Consciousness creeps in slowly, like tide over sand.

At first, only darkness. I blink, but nothing changes. My lashes flutter against fabric. A blindfold.

The blackness is too complete. It feels like I've woken inside a void.

I shift—or try to—and feel pressure at my mouth. A strap. A gag.

I breathe through my nose and a muffled moan escapes.

Awareness spreads to my aching wrists—bound, pulled downward.

Not above my head but between my legs.

I'm cuffed to a bar cold and firm. My ankles too, spaced wide enough to keep me open.

I test it—barely moving and meet resistance. I can't close my legs. Can't free my hands.

I'm exposed like a perverse offering.

How? How did he do this without waking me?

Was I that exhausted—

My thought is interrupted by the sensation of soft lips.

A warm tongue.

A moan vibrating against my center.

My back arches before I realize what I just did.

I try to jerk away, but the restraints pull tighter. Try again to curl in, to protect—but the spreader bar holds me wide.

No defense. Only sensation.

Only him.

My pulse stutters. Breath comes fast through my nose. Every nerve raw.

I try to cry out, to protest, but the sound is helpless. Wet. And worst of all, not a no.

It's been so long since I've been touched. Longer since I wanted to be.

Now I'm suspended between violation and surrender,

shame and need. My body responds before my mind can catch up.

The mouth groans, sound pressing into me. I moan again, arching, chasing a feeling I shouldn't want.

"You finally joined the party, Sunshine."

His voice is low. Not taunting—reverent. Like this is a moment he's waited for.

He exhales, breath fanning over wet skin, then resumes, lips sealing around that aching place.

I try to say no. Push the word past the gag.

This is wrong. I should say it.

But my protest dies on a gasp as he sucks harder, tongue circling slow.

I move with him now.

My body doesn't care what my conscience whispers.

Thighs trembling. Hands pulling at the cuffs, reaching for something to hold.

I reach down—straining—and my fingers touch his hair.

Soft. Thick.

He's taken off the mask.

The knowledge sends a ripple of panic and something else through me.

I should pull away and demand he stop.

But I don't.

My fingers curl against his scalp.

And I let him stay.

Because even though my body is bound and my voice silenced... I feel alive.

And in this terrible, impossible moment—I don't want him to stop.

He pulls away slowly, like it hurts. The absence sends a rush of cool air over drenched skin.

"If you want me to stop, baby, just tap me twice."

He licks me, then presses an open-mouthed kiss against my center.

"You can make this stop."

A second later, his finger replaces his mouth—slow circles over the pulse of me.

"But you won't stop this, will you?"

A choked sound escapes. My body jolts.

"Because you were dreaming about me."

His voice wraps around me like smoke.

"Was I fucking you? Both of us covered in blood?"

I shake my head—weak, useless.

Because that's exactly what I was dreaming.

Exactly.

He hums. Then I feel a thick line of spit hit my center.

His finger smears it through the mess, gliding in maddening strokes.

The hum that escapes me spurs him forward.

"Don't lie to me, Sunshine," he murmurs. "I heard you."

His finger circles faster now—not enough pressure, just enough to reignite everything.

"You were moaning in your sleep. Fucking your pillow. Begging for it."

He punctuates it with his tongue, dragging the flat of it through me.

"Admit it," he breathes. "You wanted this."

I try to shake my head. Try to resist.

But the truth is already leaking out in every breath.

My dreams had taken me there before he even touched me.

This isn't new.

It's a continuation.

He rubs faster. My legs tremble. My moans spiral.

I should stop this. I could.

So why haven't I?

My muscles tighten. Heat builds. It's coming—rushing at me like a tide.

Then he stops.

I nearly cry out, a keening sound caught behind the gag as pleasure stalls at the edge.

"All you have to do is admit it," he says, voice lower now. Closer. "Say yes, and I'll let you come."

He blows a cool breath against me. My hips jerk.

"Say it." He whispers, then flicks my center with his tongue.

The need splits me wide.

I nod. Hard. Fast. "Mhmm."

Yes.

I would say it if I could. If I wasn't gagged and shaking and unraveling.

"You're so fucking beautiful gagged like this."

He exhales—a sharp, satisfied sound—and then he's there again. Mouth urgent, tongue deep.

This time, he brings two fingers. They don't enter—just glide along the lips of my sex, amplifying every flick and swirl.

My hand fists in his hair, holding him there, begging him not to stop.

Pleasure builds fast. I ride it, hips rocking, breath ragged.

Just before it breaks, he shifts the bar, pushing it back, spreading me wider.

Then he sucks—hard.

I shatter around his mouth.

A strangled cry escapes as the orgasm crashes through me— hot, full, all-consuming.

My body clenches around nothing, the release sharp and breathless.

He moans with me, savoring every pulse.

As the waves ebb, he slows. Licks gentle. Fingers still teasing. Not entering—yet.

"You want my fingers, don't you?" he whispers, kissing my thigh.

A soft whimper.

Then he sucks—sharp—and another jolt makes my back arch.

But he stops just as quickly, leaving me aching.

His fingers stroke over me—slow, methodical, maddening.

He kisses my other thigh, suction rough enough to leave bruises.

"You have such a needy little cunt," he says. "Say it. Say you want more."

Pride is gone. Shame drowned beneath the need. I nod—again and again.

"Say it."

I moan. Garbled. Broken. But it's there. The surrender.

He groans like it's everything he needed. "Good girl."

His mouth returns—tongue gliding, lips wrapping—and then, finally, his fingers press inside.

I gasp as my legs fall open, a helpless offering.

"That's it," he murmurs, voice low and reverent. "That's my sweet little slut."

His fingers move with purpose—slow at first, then faster, curling and stroking in just the right way.

His mouth is relentless, tasting me like salvation, flicking and sucking until I'm writhing beneath him.

When a third finger slides in, my body tightens around him, a strangled moan ripping from my throat.

And then I'm gone—shattering again, harder this time, clamping down as pleasure pulses through me in wave after wave, leaving me trembling and undone.

I sob through the gag.

Not from pain, but overload. From how much he's giving. From how much I want it.

He groans, sucking his fingers clean, dragging them into his mouth like he's savoring every drop. I feel it vibrate in his chest.

"Hold on tight," he murmurs.

The bar shifts.

One moment I'm on my back, the next I'm rotated with mechanical ease—kneeling, face to the mattress, arms still bound, ankles wide, hips high.

A whimper tears loose on instinct at the vulnerability.

I'm on display—sacred and depraved.

His breath brushes my back. I hear fabric shift as he moves behind me.

My heart stutters.

No.

He said he wouldn't. Not unless I asked.

I haven't and I won't.

But my body doesn't care. It tenses—not in protest, but aching anticipation.

His hand returns.

The sob I let out melts into a moan when his fingers find me—soft, steady strokes grounding me like a promise.

"I've got you," he whispers. "You have no idea how badly I want you."

I have more range of motion and my hips work my center around his hand, grinding hard.

"Fuck yes," He growls. "Rub this wet pussy on me and come."

His fingers don't stop—not as my thighs shake, not as I cry out.

The orgasm is brutal—raw, hot, endless.

I sob into the mattress, shuddering as I come apart around his hand.

His grip stay on me.

Warm palms glide over my hips, up my spine, down my bottom.

"That's my girl," he murmurs, kissing my shoulder blade. "You're going to take my cock like such a pretty slut."

Another kiss.

"You'll see."

My breath catches. Not from the words—but how he says them.

Like I have no choice. Like it's decided already.

"You'll look just as beautiful dripping with my cum as you do covered in blood," he whispers.

He kisses the curve of my bottom—slow, deliberate.

My body twitches, hypersensitive, but I don't flinch.

"I'll take the bar off now," he says, voice low. "But you have to behave for me."

His words crawl across my skin.

I nod—shaky, spent.

He rotates me gently onto my back and starts with one foot —unlocking the cuff, kissing the sore spot where the strap held me. Then he places my leg at his hip.

Then the other. Kissed. Placed opposite. Spreading me again—not to control, but to be close.

He kneels between my legs, clothed. I'm still bare.

My nightshirt pushed past my breasts.

Then he speaks—and I feel it, deep.

"I want you to obey me, Sunshine. To trust me. Can you do that?"

I nod—smaller, but certain.

He releases the cuffs.

His hands cradle my wrists, thumbs brushing skin, lips kissing each one.

Too gentle. Almost unbearable.

He guides my arms above my head, resting them on the pillow.

"Keep them here," he whispers, my breath hitting my neck.

And I do.

His hand glides down—tracing my ribs, curving over my hip.

His mouth finds my breast—kissing first, then lapping slowly before pulling it into his mouth.

I moan—soft. Stunned.

I've never come in front of someone before. Never found pleasure from sex before. The intensity hasn't faded—it's just changed shape.

I can imagine what he'd feel like inside me and the thought makes me clinch.

If he asked for more now, I'd give it.

If he told me to beg, I might.

And he must know. He feels it in me—because he smiles against my skin, stilling my hips with a grounding hand.

I hadn't even realized I was moving.

"Soon, baby," he murmurs. "I promise."

His lips move to my jaw, then my collarbone with a soft nip.

"So soon."

Then the strap behind my head loosens. The gag slips out —wet, and warm, my cheeks sore.

I breathe. Lick my lips and swallow.

The silence tastes strange.

I brace for his mouth on mine.

But I can't do it.

I lock my lips, turning my head. My body tenses—but he doesn't kiss me.

I'm scared of it.

But I'm also disappointed.

Instead, he slides into bed beside me, pulling the covers up. Wrapping me in them like a shield, not a trap.

"If you keep the blindfold on," he says softly, "I'll stay."

I don't speak. Don't move. But I don't lift it.

He settles behind me—solid, warm.

His arms curl around me, and I melt into him like gravity's pulling me there.

His leg covers mine. One hand rubs circles into my back.

My breath releases.

My body relaxes.

He kisses the top of my head. "That's it, baby."

And then I break.

It starts quiet—a tremble in my breath.

Then the sobs hit.

Raw. Sudden.

Like they've waited at the edge of everything we just did.

I cry into him—clutching his hoodie, burying my face in his scent.

Strong. Warm. Unapologetic.

I just need him to hold me.

And he does.

He rubs my back, whispers into my hair, holds me until my body gives out—until exhaustion pulls me under.

Until I sleep, knowing I'll pay for this later.

32
Declan

Mornings are bullshit.

I'm halfway through my shitty black coffee, cursing at a slow-moving Prius, when I hit Call.

The phone rings twice before she answers, breathless and suspicious.

"What?" Poppy huffs, like I just interrupted her robbing a bank.

She's hyper. Probably running around like a caffeinated squirrel.

"Coffee order," I grunt, steering around some idiot who doesn't know how to merge.

There's a beat of silence—like she's trying to pretend she is not vibrating through the ceiling.

"I'm good," she says, too fast. "I'll get my own."

Bullshit.

I let the silence stretch.

She caves with a groan loud enough to rattle the speaker.

"Fine. Triple-shot iced Americano with light oat milk, one pump toasted vanilla, one pump brown sugar, shaken over ice, topped with cold foam and a dash of cinnamon. Happy?"

"Thrilled," I mutter, and hang up before she can make it worse.

Ten minutes later, I step into the precinct, two coffees in hand, fully ready to punch someone if they even look at me sideways.

I find her exactly where I expected—deep in a manic storm.

I don't say a word. I just set the drinks down.

Mine, basic and black. Hers, pure fucking diabetes in a cup... with a pink straw. Obviously.

She doesn't even look up.

One hand snatches her drink blindly while the other waves toward the mess of boards and papers.

She's talking a mile a minute, darting between crime scene photos, spreadsheets, and a map full of color-coded thumbtacks like she cracked the Da Vinci Code before breakfast.

The caffeine hits her system before she's even swallowed her first sip. I can practically see her vibrate at a higher frequency.

Meanwhile, I sip my black coffee like it's the only thing keeping me from jumping out a window.

Poppy's mouth runs faster than her brain.

"Okay, okay, listen—phantom LLCs, empty leases, right? But they all use the same accounting firm. And that firm"—she stabs the air with her straw, narrowly missing her eye—"shows up on three closed trafficking cases."

I stand in the doorway, arms crossed, just watching.

The hurricane's already made landfall. All I can do is survive it.

She finally stops, chest heaving, cheeks pink, waiting for me to shoot her down.

"All right." I take another sip. "Let's check it out."

Poppy blinks at me like I just sprouted another head.

"Wait. Seriously? That easy?"

"If it'll shut you up for five minutes," I grunt, pushing off the doorframe, "I'll follow the goddamn string theory to Mars."

She laughs—bright, startled—and grabs her files, her tote bag, and her absurdly complicated coffee.

I don't think she's ever laughed at something I've said. Not like that.

As she scurries after me in her too-high heels, I hear the inevitable stumble behind me.

I don't even glance back. Just shake my head.

"Fucking menace."

And the worst part?

I'm smiling when I say it.

The day starts like every other good idea I've ever had— bad coffee, bad traffic, bad instincts about what's waiting for me.

Poppy's buzzing in the passenger seat like someone mainlined espresso straight into her carotid. She's half talking to herself, half talking to me, and somehow carrying three conversations I'm not invited to.

First stop: a juice bar in Crown Heights.

The place is clean. Too clean. Like it's been staged for an Instagram photoshoot that never ends.

Poppy bounds out, clipboard in hand, bright and chipper, like we're here for a bake sale.

Meanwhile, I'm dragging behind her like the Grim Reaper's unpaid intern.

We do a walk-by, ask a question or two.

The books are squeaky. Staff's clueless or high on cold-pressed enlightenment.

Not worth flipping.

Back in the car, Poppy's tapping her pen against her knee like a telegraph machine.

Second stop: wellness spa in SoHo.

New-age hellscape. Crystals everywhere. Whale noises.

One of the workers offers me a "grounding aura cleanse," and I have to restrain myself from committing a felony.

Nothing shady here either.

Poppy leaves with a pamphlet and concerning enthusiasm about rose quartz.

I leave with a migraine.

We're about to call it when we hit the last stop:

A "counseling center" tucked between a yoga studio and a boutique that sells four-hundred-dollar leggings to trust-fund babies.

The building's nice. White brick, polished glass, private parking.

No signs of anything shady.

If anything, it's so aggressively polished it makes my skin crawl.

I kill the engine and nod toward it.

"Last one. Then you can go manifest yourself into a closing argument."

Poppy's halfway out the door before I finish the sentence, fresh coffee clutched like a weaponized bribe.

We linger near the entrance, Poppy pretending to dig through her gigantic purse.

Women come and go. All upscale. Designer bags, perfect hair, jewelry that probably costs more than my SUV.

They walk out giggling like they just won the lottery.

And every "therapist" walking in?

Male.

Young.

Model-tier hot.

The kind of good-looking that makes you suspicious.

I clock it all, but before I can say anything, Poppy spins on me, eyes wild.

"It's a brothel."

I choke on nothing.

"What the fuck did you just say?"

She's already launching into it, hands flying.

"Think about it. Private counseling center. Female-only clientele. Cash only. Gorgeous male 'therapists.' No records. No paper trail. And who's going to self-report? No one. The clients are rich women with reputations to protect. It's the perfect front."

I stare at her.

Blink once.

Twice.

Then drag a hand down my face. Jesus Christ. She's right.

"That's..." I blow out a breath, shaking my head, "... brilliant."

Poppy beams like I handed her a Nobel Prize.

"Congratulations," I mutter. "You just diagnosed Manhattan's prettiest STD delivery service."

She grins. Spins back toward the building, practically bouncing.

I rub the bridge of my nose.

"Gonna need another fucking coffee."

The second Poppy gets her dumb little idea, I know I'm screwed.

She yanks on my sleeve like a hyperactive crow spotting something shiny.

"Be in love with me," she hisses, pulling me along.

"Come again?"

"But when I leave," she adds, tossing a chunky ring onto her left finger like she's preparing for battle, "flirt with the receptionist."

I stop dead.

"What the actual fuck are you talking about?"

She's already halfway across the street, not slowing for my existential crisis.

"Trust me," she throws over her shoulder. "Just—go!"

Before I can list the forty-seven reasons this is a terrible idea, she's throwing open the door and striding in like she owns the place.

Fucking wonderful.

Inside, the place smells expensive—soft florals, clean polish, and the stench of too much money.

Poppy's instantly in character, wrapping her arm around mine like I'm her beloved emotional support gorilla. She leans in, all soft smiles and glittering eyes.

My hand hits her thigh. Fine by me.

I flex my fingers across the fabric and feel her tense. I ignore the heat that shoots up my arm and the cocky grin that follows.

"We're interested in... couples counseling," she says, twirling the fake ring like it's taboo.

The receptionist—young, hot, and professionally detached —gives us a once-over. She looks at Poppy like she has horse shit hanging out of her mouth.

She looks at me like I'm a sizzling steak.

And right in front of my *fiancée*. A scandal.

"I don't think—" She's about to shut us down when Poppy leans closer and says:

"Kay sent us."

Boom. Golden ticket.

Her posture softens. "Of course. We're always happy to take on one of Mrs. Bennett's referrals."

Well, fuck me sideways. That worked.

She slides a clipboard across the counter, all sugar and fake empathy now.

"Just fill this out and I'll get you into the system."

She's talking to Poppy, but looking at me.

Poppy flashes a megawatt grin, snatches the clipboard, scrawls something down, and gasps.

"I'm so sorry, where's your bathroom?"

She shoves the clipboard into my hands.

The receptionist waves her toward the back.

Before disappearing, Poppy gives me the most exaggerated wink I've ever seen in my life—and a double thumbs-up.

Right. Showtime.

I lean on the counter, elbow close to her.

"So," I say, nodding, "been working here long?"

Christ, I want to punch myself.

She giggles. Fucking giggles.

She crosses her arms, pushing her tits out until they're nearly falling out of her shirt. I swear I can see my death reflected in her lip gloss.

I reach over, brush a piece of hair off her shoulder. "Beautiful hair."

She purrs, leaning in, eating up the attention.

"Your fiancée is a very lucky woman, Mr..."

Full fuck-me eyes locked on me like I'm the last drinkable

man in Manhattan—except shit, we didn't come up with cover names.

Poppy reappears with an exaggerated cough. We spring apart like guilty teenagers. She glares at me, full scandalized housewife.

It looks good on her.

The receptionist flushes, proud of herself.

"Excuse me," Poppy says sweetly, "you're out of toilet paper." Her stare says, *go fix it, bitch.*

I retract my grumbling. This is fun.

The girl huffs, stands with an eyeroll, then looks at me all doe-eyed. "Excuse me a moment."

She struts away. I'm shocked she didn't throw a hip out on her sashay.

At the doorway, she tosses a not-so-subtle over-the-shoulder look like she wants me to follow her into the stockroom and defile her among the Charmin rolls.

Poppy doesn't waste a second.

She vaults behind the desk as the footsteps dissolve out of range.

Her fingers fly across the keyboard, mouse clicking like her iced coma-in-a-cup is refilling with every tap.

"What the fuck are you doing?" I whisper-yell, bracing on the counter. "We need a warrant, Poppy."

"You think I don't know that?" she whisper-yells louder. She might as well shout.

She pauses, blue eyes locked on the screen.

They really are a beautiful shade.

"Ugh, two minutes," she mutters, panic rising. "Oh, cheeseburgers, we need a distraction."

She looks at the hall. Then at me.

I raise my hands. "What do you want me to do?"

"I don't know!" she hisses, pointing. "Go be sexy!"

I groan, low and miserable, but round the corner anyway—just in time to catch the receptionist at the bathroom door, already annoyed.

When she sees me, she brightens like a kid about to get the pony she's been screaming for since Christmas.

I lean one shoulder against the frame, arms crossed. Or what passes for casual when you're one bad moment away from chewing your own arm off.

Her eyes drop to my biceps.

Predictable.

"Thought I'd come see if you needed any help." I lower my voice—rough, suggestive—like we're sharing some filthy secret.

"Mmm." She situates her breasts like they're her only asset. Flirting, nipples first. Personality second.

"A gentleman," she purrs, stepping closer. "And so strong."

Her hand rubs up my arm, thumb dragging over the muscle.

Someone. Fucking. Shoot me.

"You have quite the... physique."

One more step, and those flirty nipples are nearly grazing my chest.

"Let me take you to dinner," I say, dragging my eyes down her body and back up again—slow, deliberate. "And afterward..." I pause, letting the filth hang, "you can get better *acquainted* with my physique."

She damn near creams her panties.

"Let me just," She runs a fingernail down my arm, cold as death. "get you my number."

She finds a pen, scribbles on a sticky note, and slides her palm up my chest in a move so rehearsed it's almost sad.

I grit my teeth and hold the line.

Another minute. Just another goddamn minute.

She tucks the note into my pocket. "I'm Miranda."

Salvation arrives in the form of the front door opening with a cheerful chime.

She steps away with a fresh eyeroll, cheeks pink.

I back off like she's radioactive.

"I've got to get up there."

"By all means." I gesture for her to walk ahead.

She does more of the hip-swaying thing down the hall.

When she slides behind her desk, she gives Poppy a look that says *I'll be fucking your man before dessert is served.*

What a bitch.

I glance toward the door.

Poppy's standing there, arms crossed, one hip cocked like she's two seconds from launching a shoe at my head.

She looks... fucking amazing.

Head-to-toe pink, hair perfect, makeup flawless—even when she's pissed enough to pummel me with her fake-engagement ring.

The look she's giving me? Full-on jealous fiancée about to cause a scene.

And I'll be damned if a sick part of me doesn't like it.

I let her stare me down longer than necessary—let her stew —then slide an arm around her waist.

She stiffens for half a second, then recovers, tossing her hair and flashing a brittle, syrupy smile.

"If you're not too distracted," she says brightly, loud enough for the receptionist to hear, "we're going to be late for our hot yoga class."

The receptionist—poor, deluded thing—puffs up like she just won a prize, batting her lashes like she's already planning our imaginary hookup.

Poppy catches it.

Her eyes narrow, one brow lifting in a way that promises bloodshed, and I can't tell if she's still playing or if it's real.

"I can't wait, darling."

I tighten my arm around her and steer us toward the door, tossing the receptionist a grin sharp enough to cut glass.

Outside, the sunlight slams into us.

Poppy yanks out of my grip with a huff, marching ahead.

"Well, you played that off a little too well."

She's halfway down the block before I catch up—after tossing the number in the trash and wondering, not for the first time, how the fuck I went from respected detective to undercover fiancé to Manhattan's angriest Disney princess.

And worse?

Wondering why the hell I don't mind.

33

Poppy

I'm nailing this.

This whole *look natural* thing? I deserve an award.

I'm sitting upright, hands folded around a delicate porcelain teacup like a well-adjusted woman who definitely did not kill a man last night and then get strapped into a spreader bar and eaten out by the masked stalker who's been following her for weeks.

Nope.

Just a regular girl.

Having a regular lunch.

Definitely not wearing the clothes said stalker left on a chair with a note that said, *Be my good girl. I'll be watching.*

And absolutely not wondering why it's been radio silence since.

I'm even making eye contact like a professionally not-deranged person.

Across the table, Declan's scrolling through his phone, brow furrowed like he's thinking about something serious and not—say—how I gutted a predator last night.

Kill or be killed.

Again.

And just like Travis, this man must have left a trail behind him. Girls who fought back and lost.

And what I did made sure he won't hurt anyone else.

Then I collapsed in the arms of the man who's been hunting me and let him touch me like I belonged to him.

So yeah. Totally normal day.

I'm currently looking at the dim sum menu, eyes unfocused as I index last night's memories flashing through my mind all day. The ones I push to the back and forget about.

The ones I bring forward and pretend I'm not replaying.

I toy with the pointed corner of the laminated menu, running it under my thumbnail and wince when I poke it a little too hard.

I focus on the clip art of a cartoon chef's knife and get a flash of slashing into that man's chest.

The air thickens in my lungs and the room tilts.

I'm right back there—my driveway last night, knife in hand.

Blood rushing, warm and fast, down my wrist.

I close my eyes and take a deep breath, willing the memory to bury itself, willing myself not to drown in it.

Declan's muffled voice says something—soft, questioning —but it sounds like he's underwater.

I can't answer with the knot lodged in my throat.

"Earth to Poppy," he says, tapping my menu twice. His voice rough with that special brand of gruff he's perfected.

I blink, dragging myself back into the buzzing fluorescent lights and sticky table.

Back to the way Declan's watching me like I'm about to break into pieces right there between the spring rolls and the tea set.

I force a bright, brittle smile onto my face and toss the

menu down a little too hard, the slap of laminated paper loud enough to earn a few looks from nearby tables.

"I'm fine," I say, waving one hand like I'm swatting a fly instead of holding back the kind of existential crisis that would make a therapist cry.

Declan doesn't say anything.

Just leans back in the booth, one arm draped over the back, and he looks too good for it to be legal. The look in his eyes says he knows I'm lying.

Knows it and doesn't appreciate it—but he lets it slide anyway. Probably filing it away for later.

I pick the menu back up with fingers that are steadier than they should be, scanning it blindly, not seeing a thing.

Because I'm not thinking about dumplings.

I'm thinking about blood.

About a blade dragging through flesh.

About the peace that comes after.

But—I'm fine.

"You pick," I say, forcing a breezy shrug. "I trust you."

My cheeks burn as the last three words leave my mouth, and I know I'm blushing. Because I *do* trust him.

There's just something comforting once I look past his McPerky demeanor. Something else lingers there. Something I like.

He raises an eyebrow, skeptical, but doesn't argue. He's smart enough to know a woman on the edge when he sees one.

I sink back into the booth, pulling out my phone, desperate for a distraction. Something normal.

Instead, I get a fae-smut update from my mom. Perfect.

MOM: Update on book 2. The Light Queen just tied the Crow Prince up with her vines

MOM: Then she said, "Now be a good boy and open that pretty beak for your queen." WE. WERE. SCREAMING.

MOM: Patty had to fan herself for ten minutes.

POPPY: MOM!

MOM: It's a very compelling power dynamic, sweetie. I'm just saying.

POPPY: I'm blocking you.

MOM: Oh please. I'll send an update after chapter 24. Apparently something very interesting happens involving his feathers.

POPPY: I'm begging you to stop

After ordering, Declan pours a cup of tea, slow and careful, the steam curling between us in lazy tendrils.

First mine.

Then his.

It's such a small thing, but somehow it breaks me a little more.

I wrap my hands around the tiny cup, letting the warmth bleed into my fingers, willing it to anchor me.

He leans back. A look of curiosity is evident on his face, and I know we're about to launch into a conversation that is not wrapped around our case or what we just did in the massage parlor.

"Why sex crimes?"

I blink.

Of all the things I thought he might say, that wasn't on the bingo card.

I sip the tea to buy time.

It tastes earthy and clean and a little bitter—like honesty. I never really share this part of my life, but something about the way he's looking at me makes me feel like it's okay.

Like there's something familiar about him that I just can't pinpoint.

"My mother was raped," I say, voice low and even. "And I'm the result."

Declan doesn't move. He just... listens.

"My mom never got justice," I continue, my fingers tightening around the teacup. "She identified her attacker. Stood before him and told everyone what happened. Used his name when she talked about the crime he committed against her." I laugh—brittle and small. "But they dismissed the case. Not enough evidence."

I force myself to meet his eyes.

"I wanted to help women win. Even if it's just one at a time. Even if it's just once."

Declan's face stays locked in that stoic, unreadable way.

The silence stretches between us, heavy and raw.

And for the first time after telling that story, it doesn't feel like judgment hanging there.

It feels like mourning.

For all the women like my mom.

For all the times the system failed and someone like me was born into the wreckage.

Before either of us can figure out what to say next, the food arrives.

Dim sum spreads across the table like a parade of tiny, steaming miracles.

Soup dumplings glistening with broth, shrimp har gow wrapped in translucent rice paper, crispy pork buns split open to reveal sticky-sweet centers.

It's a feast.

A feast of everything I love and didn't realize I was starving for.

I blink down at it, thrown off balance by the absurd generosity of it all—by the way Declan somehow ordered exactly what I would have picked if my brain hadn't been chewing on knives and blood and broken memories.

I set the tea down, my hands still trembling faintly as I position my chopsticks.

The pork bun is soft and warm and perfect.

I pop it into my mouth, savoring the rich burst of meat and scallion, letting the world blur at the edges just for a second.

I don't want to sit in the heavy silence between us. Not after everything I said.

So I pick up the verbal equivalent of a flamethrower and casually light it.

"Why don't you want a partner?" I ask, reaching for another dumpling.

Declan stiffens instantly, eyes narrowing like he smelled a trap and is already plotting which limb he's willing to sacrifice to escape.

He doesn't answer.

Which is exactly why I push harder.

"You asked me something personal," I say sweetly, stuffing a piece of crispy pork bun into my mouth like an adorable threat. "It's only fair you answer, too. Or"—I pause dramatically, holding the steaming dumpling aloft—"face the soup dumpling consequences."

He glares.

I raise an eyebrow.

The bun wobbles dangerously between my chopsticks.

Finally, with a grunt that sounds like it physically pains him, he scrubs a hand over his face.

"My best friend," he mutters, "was my partner."

He pauses, jaw ticking, and I get a bad feeling about this. I regret asking and pushing—but also, he's opening up. So there's no way I'm stopping now.

"He slept with my fiancée."

The words drop between us like a lead weight—heavy and sharp.

I blink, stunned.

"I caught them the night before our wedding," he adds, voice low, like the memory still scrapes something raw in him.

I gasp, clutching my tea like it might save me. "That's awful."

I can understand why he doesn't want anyone to get close again. Best friend and partner at work—and he lost the woman he thought he'd spend the rest of his life with.

It explains why he's got the reputation he does around the courthouse. Another notch on the Blackwood bedpost, if you catch my drift.

"She was my high school sweetheart," he keeps going, shrugging one massive shoulder like it doesn't still gut him. "Should've known it was doomed to fail from our first kiss."

"What happened with your first kiss?" My eyes are wide, and I hold my soup dumpling in a spoon as I bite a hole in it, the rich broth seeping out like it's joining the conversation.

"Our braces got stuck together. Orthodontist had to separate us."

I choke so hard on the broth I almost die.

Like—actual tears-in-the-eyes, gasping-for-air-level choking.

He's dead serious. Sitting there in this dim sum restaurant, looking like he's recounting a POW story, while I'm trying not to faceplant into the siu mai.

"It's not funny."

I snort. Actually snort and cover my mouth quickly like that will hold it in.

"We had to sit like that for two fucking hours," he says—trying and failing to convince me of the gravity of the situation. "Do you have any idea how much of her spit went into my mouth?"

I lose it completely.

Full-body laughter, fists pounding the table, suffocating myself with my napkin to try and stifle my wheezing.

Declan tries to scowl.

Really, he does.

But I catch it—the little twitch at the corner of his mouth, the almost-smile he's fighting with everything he's got. But he can't hold it back.

He gives me a full-force smile, dimple and all, before he looks down and shakes his head.

A soft, reluctant chuckle rumbles out of him—so rare and raw it's not been observed since the Jurassic period.

My laughter dies down, and I stare at him because he's beautiful like this.

Untouched by anger or betrayal or grief for once.

Just... him.

Unarmored. Real.

His green eyes brighten, and something in my chest goes stupid and warm and helpless.

"Your dimples are cute," I blurt before I can stop myself,

still a little breathless from laughing, voice too soft to pretend it's a joke.

For the first time since I met him, he looks caught off guard.

Not brooding.

Not calculating the ways this could all go sideways.

Just... caught.

And I like being the one that snared him.

34

Declan

The second the words leave her mouth—*your dimples are cute*—something short-circuits in my chest.

Not that I didn't like it.

I fucking did.

Probably more than I should.

So naturally, like the emotionally stunted bastard I am, I counter with the first thing that comes to mind.

"What about you, Lolli-pop?"

She glares like I just suggested sacrificing a litter of puppies.

"Don't call me that," she snaps, cheeks still pink from laughing.

"Sweet little pink Lollipop," I tease, popping the *p*, dragging it out just to watch her squirm. "What was your amazing first kiss story? Please tell me it was equally tragic. I need this."

She hesitates, fiddling with her teacup, blowing it off with a shrug so casual it might as well come with a neon sign: *this is a lie*.

I narrow my eyes. "Come on. You got to hear about my orthodontic horror show. Fair's fair."

She squirms, taps her nails against the ceramic. Then

finally, with a huff, mutters it under her breath like that'll make it disappear.

"I've—never been kissed."

I blink.

Excuse the absolute *shit fuck* out of me. What?

The whole world screeches to a halt.

"Wait," I say, because my brain clearly didn't process that right, "never?"

She shrugs again, doing that fake-casual thing that would fool exactly no one with a functioning pulse.

"I mean, it's not a big deal."

"Not a big deal? Right. And I'm the Queen of England."

I lean forward, elbows braced on the table, dropping my voice until it's nothing but a gravel scrape.

"Are you a...?"

Her head snaps up so fast it's a miracle she doesn't give herself whiplash.

"WHAT?!" she whisper-shrieks, loud enough to turn heads two tables over.

"No!" she hisses, mortified, face going bright red. "I'm not a —" she glances around, "—v-word!"

I smirk into my tea, enjoying this way more than I should. Because if there's anything better than flustered Poppy, it's *scandalized* Poppy, ready to throttle me with a soup dumpling.

She sinks lower into the booth like she's hoping for spontaneous invisibility.

"I just..." I shake my head slowly, like I'm solving for x, "I can't wrap my fucking head around that."

Because I can't.

She's all fire and trouble and chaos and heart.

She talks a hundred miles a minute, kicks ass in heels taller than most men's egos, and still manages to look at the world like it's not completely broken.

How has nobody kissed her?

Not even once?

She glares at me, red-faced and furious. "Can we not make this a thing?"

"Okay." I lift my hands in surrender. Because despite every dumb, reckless part of me that wants to lean across the table and wreck her world, I know the line here.

For now.

We lapse into silence.

But something's shifted.

Not broken. Not shattered.

Just tilted. Crooked in that dangerous way. Like my lips on hers are now *on the table*.

The ride back starts quiet.

The kind of quiet that presses in too tight. That crawls under your skin and tightens the screws from the inside.

I keep my eyes on the road, pretending not to notice the way the air thickens between us. But I do.

I always do.

Poppy's staring out the window, tapping restless patterns on her knee. Chewing her bottom lip like she's trying to bite back every thought in her head.

And I'm not thinking about traffic anymore.

I'm thinking about her.

About how someone like *her* made it this far without ever being seen.

It claws at me. Ugly and raw.

"I just..." I say, voice rougher than I mean it to be, "I can't understand that."

She stiffens. "Can we not do this again?"

I should let it go but I fucking can't.

"If you've never been kissed," I push, quieter now, more lethal, "have you ever had a—?"

"Don't finish that," she snaps, her glare sharp enough to wound.

"That's none of your business."

"I'll take that as a no."

"It's not that uncommon, you know," she fires off, like she's reading from a brochure. "Over fifty percent of women report difficulty reaching climax during sex."

I scoff. "Yeah? Well, one hundred percent of my partners leave satisfied."

It's a dick thing to say. I know it the second it leaves my mouth.

She huffs, pure disbelief. "Not surprised."

I cut my eyes toward her, slow and sharp. "What the fuck does that mean?"

"It means," she says, voice sweet as cyanide, "your reputation precedes you, Detective Blackwood. I'd be shocked if you even remember half their names."

The hit lands.

Hard.

"My reputation?"

"It's not like I had to twist your arm to flirt with that receptionist." She scoffs, still looking out the window. "Bet you actually got her number. Did you get her name? Or does that not matter?"

I grip the wheel so tight the leather groans under my hands.

"You know," I say, voice low and sharp, "instead of lashing

out at everyone else, maybe figure out how to handle your jealousy. Like a big girl."

Her head snaps toward me. Eyes wide, cheeks burning.

"In your dreams," she hisses.

But it's too late.

I smirk—humorless, bitter. "You're not mad I flirted. You're mad it wasn't with you."

She flinches like I slapped her.

And then—because she *has* to say something that'll hit back—

"I would never be interested in someone like you," she spits.

Clean and cruel.

And I don't laugh.

Not because it's not bullshit.

But because it is.

I yank the SUV into the precinct lot harder than necessary, slamming it into park. The engine ticks as it dies, but the silence between us is louder.

I lean over, close enough to smell her perfume. My voice drops to a rasp.

"You keep telling yourself that, Lollipop. Why don't you enlighten me about this reputation I have."

She folds her arms like armor. "I've heard the rumors, Declan. I've listened to the way women talk about you."

I watch her while the silence in the SUV gets thicker. Watch the fight brewing behind her eyes.

"Oh yeah?" I say quietly. "And what is it they say?"

She rattles it off like a checklist. "That you don't date. That you never take a woman out twice. That you're just working your way through the courthouse, one clerk at a time."

I laugh—dry, humorless. "Is that what's bothering you? That I've apparently asked out everyone... except you?"

She scoffs. "Don't be ridiculous."

But there's a flicker—barely there. I catch it. And press.

"You feeling left out, baby?"

Then—cold, matter-of-fact—"Here's the truth, Poppy. I've never dated a single woman at the courthouse. Much less slept with one."

That makes her blink. Quick. Sharp.

She lifts her chin. "Like that's believable."

"It should be."

"Come on." She scoffs again. "They can't all be lying. That doesn't change the way they talk about you."

"No," I say, voice going cold. "But it should change the way *you* think about me."

Her lips part like she might answer, but nothing comes out. I see the hesitation in her eyes. The shift. The something she's about to say but doesn't.

I look down—just for a second—at her mouth.

If I stay here, I'll say something I can't take back. Something like: *it matters, Poppy. What you think of me fucking matters.*

So I don't stay.

I grab the door and swing it open.

"I'm going to sort through the files from today," I say over my shoulder, voice clipped. "Thanks for lunch."

The door slams behind me.

And I walk away without looking back.

35

Poppy

Be my good girl. Wear this for me today. Only this. I'll be watching.

I'm standing in front of my mirror, thinking about the note he left—folded precisely, with three little origami cranes beside it. His cologne clung to the paper like a fingerprint.

I did what he wanted. Or thought I did.

Clearly not, because there's been nothing from him all day.

No message. No sign.

No silent little *I-see-you* text to make my stomach swoop and my skin prickle.

Just silence.

"Way to go, Poppy," I mumble. "You broke your stalker."

I should feel relieved. Safe.

But all I feel is... empty. Like someone rewired my chest wrong.

"Holy pepperoni on a pogo stick, this is getting pathetic."

I tug a soft cami over my head. The matching shorts follow, brushing the tops of my thighs in a way that makes me shiver, even though the house is warm.

Settling on the living room floor with a sigh, I open the

case files around me, a glass of red wine near the edge of the coffee table.

The wine helps take the edge off.

Lets me pretend I'm not waiting to see if my stalker will text me.

Dexter circles twice before settling beside me.

I flip through pages—redacting notes, highlighting names—until something tugs at the back of my mind.

A pattern.

I sit up straighter, blinking at the spread.

I follow the trail with my fingertip, dragging across contracts and invoices, names and numbers, until it all converges.

One name.

A mid-level city controller tied to the clerk's office.

My heart thuds. "This is the guy that leaked the warrant."

I look at my phone on the floor next to me.

Not the burner—the one that's been heartbreakingly, infuriatingly silent.

Just my regular phone. The one that can reach Declan.

It's late.

I could wait. Let things cool off. Figure out how to apologize for being a total dumpster fire today.

But the weight of what we're uncovering won't let me.

Sighing, I grab the phone and type a quick text:

> POPPY: Sorry for the late text, but this can't wait.

I attach the photos and hit send before I can talk myself out of it.

Seconds later, both phones light up.

Not one. Both.

My heart hiccups, nerves jangling before I even know why.

The burner chimes first. I grab it without thinking, thumb hovering over the notification.

UNKNOWN: Who are you texting?

I roll my eyes so hard I'm surprised they don't fall out and roll under the couch. Really?

A whole day of silence, and now he's territorial?

"Someone's feeling clingy," I mutter, tossing the burner back onto the coffee table and looking at my real phone.

MCPERKINS: I'll have him picked up by morning.

Short. Sharp. Efficient.

And it leaves me disappointed.

I sit back on my heels. Two screens glowing in the dark like twin lighthouses.

Two different men. Two completely different worlds.

Both pulling at the same twisted butterflies in my stomach.

Both unsettling me in ways I kind of like.

I drain my wine, turn off the TV, and scoop Dexter under one arm.

"Time for bed, partner," I whisper, flicking off the lights.

The house settles around us as I climb the stairs. Each creak sounds impossibly loud.

At the top landing, Dexter's tail goes still. A low growl rumbles—quiet but fierce—against my ribs.

And stepping into my room, I see why.

Dressed in black from head to toe, gloves still on, the Punisher-style balaclava gleams just enough to make my heart slam.

He's in my chair by the window. Legs spread. One hand on his thigh, the other draped like he owns the place.

Like he owns me.

My pulse spikes hard.

That forbidden heat stirs low in my stomach, crawling up my spine—the kind of fear that isn't really fear.

The burner chimes again downstairs, the ping slicing through the quiet.

He tsks under his breath, soft and full of mock disappointment, then rises—slow and deliberate.

A predator in no hurry.

He already knows I'm not going anywhere.

He peels his gloves off one finger at a time, sliding them into his back pocket. He stops just in front of me, close enough that his body heat wraps around mine.

I can't breathe.

He lifts his hand, sliding a loose strand of hair behind my ear.

His touch trails down my neck, leaving my skin tingling, and continues lower—skimming my breast, my ribs, my waist.

When he cups my bottom, my body jolts forward, colliding with the hard planes of his chest.

His heartbeat is steady. Mine races.

His hand drags higher, finding the edge of my lace panties—panties he didn't leave for me—and his thumb glides along the hem.

"Who gave you permission to wear panties?" he murmurs, voice low and rough. "So eager for punishment, Sunshine?"

Before I can answer, his other hand slides into my hair, wrapping it around his fist and giving a sharp, commanding tug.

I gasp, head tipping back without thought.

His breath fans across my skin.

"You already disobeyed," he whispers. "Let's not make it worse."

He holds me there just long enough to make me tremble, then steps back.

One step. Then another.

The distance feels colder than the air leaking through the window.

"Go get it." he orders.

I stand frozen for a beat, body shaking under the weight of what he's asking.

Then—because defying him feels impossible—I obey.

Each step downstairs feels like a mile.

I grab the burner from the coffee table and hurry back upstairs.

He's already turned down the bed. Covers folded. Pillows fluffed. Sheets cool and inviting.

He sits at the edge, legs spread, hands resting on his thighs like he has all the time in the world, and nods at the phone.

UNKNOWN: Lose the panties, bad girl.

I hesitate, meeting his gaze through the slits of the mask.

My body screams at me to do what he says.

My pride—the tiny, stubborn bit I have left—wants to fight.

But I want more of what happened last night. The way he made me feel. It's unlike anything.

Slowly, I climb onto the bed, sliding under the covers like a shield. I square my shoulders, tilt my chin in the smallest act of defiance.

"What if I don't?" I whisper.

His answer is clipped.

"Off."

This is a standoff—a challenge—I have no hope of winning.

The tension snaps tight.

He fists the blanket and yanks it off me in one sharp jerk.

I gasp at the chill, skin pebbling, but stay still.

He slides my shorts down my legs and tosses them aside. Then, with a vicious rip, he tears the panties off.

The fabric gives way with a sound that splits the quiet, my yelp echoing after it.

He lifts the scrap to his face, inhales, gaze locked on mine.

I feel it everywhere.

The ownership. The promise that he's just getting started.

The panties slip from his fingers, forgotten.

I'm bare from the waist down, thighs together, air brushing against skin that feels too raw, too exposed.

My nipples are hard beneath my cami, and when his gaze drops to them, I feel it like a brand.

He lifts a hand and pinches one peak, rolling it slow and deliberate, watching me react with no mercy.

"You didn't follow directions," he murmurs, voice calm. "Now you need to take your punishment."

I swallow, trembling—not from fear.

Not really.

It's the danger—the ache of wanting something I shouldn't —that trips my pulse.

He releases my nipple with a pinch that makes me arch.

Then he stands, looming over me.

"We're going to see how well you can obey now," he says, voice like smoke. "Are you ready, Sunshine?"

My stomach knots. My heart hammers. But I nod.

Because I want it. I need it.

Whatever's about to happen, I'll take it to keep feeling this.

He smiles behind the mask—a shift I feel more than see.

"Spread your legs for me."

I do it, settling against the cool sheets, baring myself, heart pounding so hard it might be audible.

"Wider," he says, an edge in his tone.

I shift my knees farther apart, burning with the shame of letting him see me like this.

"Good girl," he praises, making my feet flex.

He opens the nightstand drawer and pulls out my pink vibrator.

My whole body locks up.

"I'm going to watch you fuck yourself."

"I—" My voice cracks. "I've never... in front of someone. I don't know if I can."

I say it because I can't bear to disappoint him.

But he just chuckles—dark and knowing.

"That won't be a problem tonight, Sunshine. Now, touch yourself with it."

I lick my lips, hand trembling as I slip it between my legs and turn it on. The first touch makes me gasp.

"Slow," he says, arms crossed, watching like a king. "Close your eyes, baby."

I do, circling my clit, trusting he'll keep his distance.

"Good," he murmurs. "Now a little harder. Press into it."

I obey, my body responding more easily than it ever has.

A whimper breaks from my throat.

"Slide two fingers inside. Slow. Stretch yourself."

I do—wet and desperate.

He groans, low and rough.

"Now pull out. Play with your clit again."

The commands keep coming—soft, dark, relentless.

And I follow every one.

Touching. Stroking. Pushed to the edge, the climax is building—sharp and fierce—

"Stop," he orders.

I freeze, my whole body shaking from the denial.

Frustration and need twist together. Unbearable.

He waits until I'm steady again.

Then it starts over.

Pleasure. Denial.

Again and again.

It's just his voice and my body—desperate need clawing under my skin, my legs twitching, pants and moans filling the room.

By the time I'm crying, it's not soft.

I'm sobbing.

Mouth open. Gasping. Broken.

"Please," I choke out. "Please, let me come. I can't—I can't —please—"

He stays silent. Watching.

And I realize I'd do anything if he'd just let me break.

Anything.

Finally, he moves.

Pulls his hoodie over his head in one smooth motion and tosses it aside.

Underneath, a black compression shirt clings to every hard line of muscle.

I groan before I can stop myself.

He loosens his belt, dips his hand below the waistband, and pulls himself free.

My eyes widen.

He's massive.

Long. Thick.

Heavy in his hand, he strokes himself lazily, like he knows exactly how devastating the sight is.

My walls clench, another orgasm coiling hot and fast just from looking.

He hooks both hands under my knees and drags me down the bed, the sheets rasping against my skin.

I gasp, legs falling open, baring myself completely—and for once, I don't care how desperate it looks.

I need him.

"Such a whore," he murmurs, still stroking, gaze locked on mine. "You're gonna take your reward like a good little slut, aren't you?"

I whimper, hypnotized by the pump of his hand.

I want to feel that inside me.

"Hands over your head," he commands, voice rougher now. He takes the vibrator and turns it off.

I obey, placing my hands on the pillow, heart pounding.

For a second, I think he's just going to watch me.

Then his hand slides between my legs—two fingers circling my clit, slick and slow.

I moan, back arching.

"Let me make you feel good."

He trails lower, thrusting deep, his thumb ruthless on my clit.

I close my eyes, letting pleasure drown everything else.

"Fuck. You're so tight."

Dirty, filthy things pour from his mouth, rasping low. I clench around his fingers, cheeks burning.

He tells me how good I look like this.

How he's going to ruin me so no one else will ever be enough.

The orgasm builds fast—cresting violently until I can barely breathe.

I cry out, body convulsing around him.

He doesn't stop.

His fingers work me relentlessly, dragging a second climax almost immediately—sharper, more brutal.

"Fuck, Sunshine," he groans, voice thick, almost desperate.

He grips his cock tighter, aiming it toward me. When he comes, it's hot and heavy, mingling with the arousal coating his fingers. It tips me over again so hard I sit up without meaning to, bracing one trembling hand behind me as my hips rock forward, desperate as I come with him.

"Yes!" I gasp. "Please, more."

I grab his wrist, thrusting against his hand as I ride the waves until there's nothing left but wreckage.

Something raw and electric buzzing in the space between us.

Slowly, he lifts the bottom of his mask.

I watch, transfixed, as he licks his palm—slick with both of us—then draws soaked fingers between his lips, groaning deep in his throat.

I'm so gone for him it hurts.

His thumb and forefinger catch my chin, tipping my face up.

"You're gonna smell like me tomorrow," he says, voice thick with possessiveness. "When those motherfuckers get too close—they'll know you belong to me."

I don't know whether to shiver or sob. Maybe both.

He stands and turns to leave.

Panic slams into me.

"Wait," I call out, voice small and wrecked.

He pauses in the doorway—half shadow, half man.

"Will you..." I choke, forcing it out. "Stay? Until I fall asleep?"

The room feels too dark. The memories are too loud—of killing, of how good it felt. Of how much more of him I want.

I don't want to be alone with my mind.

He stares for a beat, then moves back to the chair.

"Sleep, Sunshine. I'll be here."

I turn onto my side, pulling the sheet to my chin.

And for the first time in a long while—

I feel safe.

Declan

I scroll through Poppy's late-night text again, sipping black coffee strong enough to strip paint.

It's not the first time I've read it this morning.

She actually found the link we'd been chasing for weeks.

A midlevel city controller—low enough to avoid scrutiny, dirty enough to launder paperwork through shell companies.

Lease after lease.

Fraud buried under so much bureaucracy it would've taken a task force months to untangle.

And she did it alone.

In a few hours.

The question now isn't whether the clerk's dirty—he is.

It's whether he's working alone or if someone higher up is tipping him off.

I had the bastard picked up before he could finish opening his car door at the courthouse.

He's sitting in an interview room, sweating through his cheap suit.

But he can stew a little longer. I've got something else to handle first.

I lean against the front steps, holding an extra coffee, waiting for a certain pink tornado to blow into the parking lot.

Poppy pulls in with a fresh rental. Her friend Sebastian parks beside her, the two of them piling out with the kind of energy I'd usually associate with feral raccoons raiding a dumpster.

I sip my coffee, watching from under the brim of my cap, pretending not to notice the slight falter in her step when she sees me.

She hesitates—just for a second—then Sebastian gives her a not-so-subtle shove. I called him this morning and asked him to skip her usual coffee stop.

He doesn't bother hiding his shit-eating grin as he saunters past, tossing a casual, "Be nice, Detective Danger," over his shoulder.

I lift the coffee slightly, offering it like a peace treaty.

"Truce?"

She eyes it like it might bite her.

Or worse—make her forgive me too easily.

Still, after a long pause, she takes it.

"I'm sorry," I say. "For yesterday. I shouldn't have pushed."

Poppy blows out a breath, studying the lid like it's fascinating.

Finally, she nods.

Small. Tight.

"I'm sorry too," she says. "For . . . being a raging harpy."

The corner of my mouth twitches, but I wrestle it down.

I jerk my chin toward the courthouse.

"Come on. Your city clerk's about to shit himself in holding."

She lifts her chin like she's aiming for dignity, but there's a mischievous glint in her eye now.

"Oh, I'll handle it," she says, breezing toward the entrance like she plans to go in alone.

"Like hell you are," I mutter, following.

She glides through courthouse security, smiling and waving at a couple of regular court officers.

Meanwhile, I get the usual stink-eye as I empty my pockets and walk through the metal detector.

Business as usual.

We head toward the elevators, her heels rapping sharply against the floor, when she pulls her phone up and fake-dials with a bright, fake-smile voice.

"Hi, I'm calling the Grumpy-Gurdie hotline," she says sweetly. "I have a sourpuss to report."

I grunt, deadpan.

"Why do you dress like a Pepto-Bismol bottle?"

She gasps, glancing down at her pastel-pink pencil skirt and blouse like she's personally offended.

"This," she says, full of haughty indignation, "is rosé elegance."

I snort. "It's bubblegum warfare."

Poppy snorts too, breaking character with a quiet laugh as the elevator dings.

I shoulder the door open, watching the way the fake annoyance slides off her shoulders like a too-heavy coat.

Real Poppy peeks out again.

God help me, I missed her.

We're halfway down the hall when Poppy suddenly lights up like it's happy hour with an old friend.

"Miles!" she calls out, waving at a guy in cuffs being escorted by a court officer.

The man blinks, confused.

I bristle, just for a second. He's mousy, forgettable, dressed in a rumpled Petorama shirt and walking like he's allergic to eye contact. Still. Doesn't stop the flicker of something sharp in my chest until I size him up fully—and decide he's about as threatening as a deflated pool toy.

"It's Mark." The man brightens a little when he spots her. "Hey—how's the pup liking the new food?"

Poppy grins. "Oh, he's obsessed. Thanks again for the recommendation."

He shrugs, awkward in the cuffs. "Glad it worked out."

She gestures vaguely to the situation. "So... what's going on here?"

"Oh, I've got a lot of speeding tickets," he says with a sigh.

Her smile falters. "Define 'a lot.'"

"Eight hundred."

Poppy's jaw drops. "Like... cumulative adult life?"

"No. Last year in Chicago. Delivery van for this restaurant. Long story."

She stares at him, speechless for once, then nods slowly. "You know what? I respect the commitment."

He chuckles. "Yeah, well. Wish me luck."

"Good luck, Mason!"

"Mark," he corrects again, tone patient but dying inside.

She shoots him finger guns. "Right. I knew that."

We turn down the next hallway, and she mutters into her coffee, "He really should wear a name tag."

"He was," I say flatly.

Our clerk sits in holding, sweating through his shirt like it's a sauna and he's halfway to confession.

Poppy's perched beside me outside the interview rooms,

papers fanned out, a highlighter clenched in her fingers as she skims the files.

I sip my coffee, watching her from the corner of my eye.

The way her brows furrow when she's thinking.

The way she twirls the highlighter when she finds something that pisses her off.

Dangerous.

Distracted.

Ridiculously gorgeous.

I nudge her shoulder with mine, grinning around my cup.

"You about ready to play good cop, bad cop?"

Poppy looks up, the light catching the pink sheen of her lip gloss.

"Oh yes," she chirps. "Which one am I?"

I gaze at the ceiling like I'm offering a prayer.

"God, give me strength."

Before I can answer, movement at the far end of the hallway kills my mood.

He strolls in like the smug bastard he is—tailored to perfection, dripping with confidence, and grinning like the building should thank him for showing up.

Graham Vexley.

Defense attorney douchebag. The same jackass who asked Poppy out the other day.

"Poppy," he says, voice a little too warm.

And God help me, she smiles back.

Polite. Friendly. Familiar.

My jaw tightens.

He leans in, dropping his voice like they're sharing an inside joke.

God, I want to punch him.

Have they dated?

The thought rips the air from my lungs.

Then I remember her confession at lunch. That flush in her cheeks.

If they did date, at least they didn't kiss—he couldn't have gotten far.

Something in my chest eases.

Only slightly.

The asshole vanishes into the interview room to confer with his sweating, soon-to-be-screwed client.

I watch the door shut, jaw still grinding.

Poppy nudges my arm, oblivious that I'm three seconds from a felony.

She leans in to show me something. Her hair brushes my arm—and lingers.

Just long enough to make me want to drag her out of here and fix that pesky little kiss problem.

Dickhead Graham pokes his head out and gives us a nod, all smarmy like this is just another day at the office.

What a fucking cockwipe.

I flick my coffee into the nearest trash can and fall in behind Poppy, letting her take the lead.

She marches in, all confidence and sweet pink perfection, like she isn't about to verbally eviscerate a man in front of witnesses.

I lean against the wall near the door, arms crossed, expression blank.

The shadow in the corner.

The threat waiting while she does her thing.

Poppy drops into the chair across from the clerk with a bright, harmless smile.

Sharp little thing.

Almost makes me feel bad for the poor bastard.

Almost.

"Thanks for waiting, Mr. Peters," she says, voice warm enough to make anyone forget they're about to be flayed alive. "We appreciate your cooperation."

He shifts, sweaty and fidgety, trying to keep up.

She's too fast. Smooth.

Slides through the opening questions like it's sport—building trust, making him think he's winning.

I expected fire and brimstone.

Instead, she's ice under velvet.

And she's good. Scary good.

I just stand there like the Grim Reaper in a badge.

The attorney can't keep his mouth shut.

Every time she nears something real, he cuts in with a don't answer that.

Legalese. Clarifications. Counsel requests.

Poppy is unbothered as fuck, sipping her cup-o-sugar-death through a bright pink straw, eyebrows raised like she's already bored.

She pivots every time, turning questions into casual comments, smiling like she's three steps ahead.

She doesn't flinch when the attorney leans in to intimidate her.

Just tilts her head and gives him a smile that says *Bless your heart, but you're out of your depth.*

I bite the inside of my cheek to keep from grinning like a damn fool.

Pride, admiration, possessiveness—it's a dangerous cocktail under my skin.

Then she drops the bomb.

"I have to ask, Mr. Peters," she says sweetly, flipping through a folder. "Were you aware the shell companies you authorized were directly connected to human trafficking? Including minors?"

The clerk freezes. Color drains from his face like someone pulled the plug.

Panic splashes across his features—ugly and instant.

"Uh—"

"Because, I have to say . . ." She shakes her head, flipping through papers he doesn't recognize. "You're looking at quite a lot here."

"What are you talking about, Poppy?" Sleazeball pipes up. "This is a bullshit charge."

"Oh, you think you're looking at license fraud and a few fines?"

Now she lays it out, and I fucking love it.

"Try conspiracy to commit human trafficking. Facilitating child sexual abuse through fraudulent licensing. Racketeering. Money laundering."

The clerk's face turns red—ready to pop. He's going to break and lose his shit. I've seen it before.

That prick attorney better leash his client before I do.

She keeps going like she's reading a grocery list.

"Accessory after the fact to kidnapping minors. Negligent endangerment of a minor."

He's practically vibrating he's trembling so hard. Fists clinched, knuckles white.

She pretends to think. "Oh—and obstruction of justice."

That one snaps him.

Whatever brain cell he had ruptures.

"I didn't know!" The chair screeches back. He lunges for Poppy. "I didn't know at first!"

I'm moving before conscious thought.

I slam him facedown onto the table hard enough to rattle the legs.

One hand in his greasy hair. The other wrenching his arm behind his back. I don't care if I snap the bone.

The attorney stumbles over his chair, slams into the wall, then the floor.

"Wrong fucking move," I growl behind the clerk's ear, pulling harder.

The wet wheeze of his breath fogs the table as he struggles.

Poppy—

Doesn't. Even. Flinch.

She sits there, calm as a fucking storm, eyes bright and dangerous, watching it all unfold like she orchestrated it.

"Sit the fuck down, asshole." I shove the clerk back into his seat, keeping one hand heavy on his shoulder as he trembles, sweat pouring down his face.

Poppy leans forward, still smiling, voice dropping to a near whisper.

"You're going to tell us everything, Mr. Peters," she says, like she's telling him about a weather report. "Names. Dates. Accounts. Because if you don't, I'm going to personally make sure you're charged right alongside the people who did the worst of it."

He whimpers.

Actual, grown-man whimpering.

"And in County, there's this guy named Big Mike and he doesn't take too kindly to inmates that commit kiddie crimes."

"I didn't know."

"Big Mike needs a new cellmate, I hear."

"I didn't know!" He yell-sobs now. "At first—I didn't know what they were doing at first. But then I couldn't get out. They—they blackmailed me. I have gambling debts."

The attorney has picked himself off the floor and joins the conversation, flapping uselessly. "We want a deal."

Poppy doesn't budge. "Depends how good the intel is," she says, crossing her legs primly like she's not threatening to light this man's life on fire. "Make it worth my while."

Fucking hell.

She's fire wrapped in pink silk, and I'm burning alive over here.

The clerk breaks, and it's fucking ugly.

Tears. Sweat. Snot.

But he talks. Doesn't shut up, as a matter of fact.

"There's an auction," he gasps. "Underground. They— Jesus—they bring girls in. Sedate them. Brand them. Sell them to the highest bidder."

My blood runs cold. I've seen the pictures of the girls. Brands seared into the arm to mark them like merchandise.

"When's the next one?" I ask, voice cutting through the panic like a blade.

He hesitates.

I tighten my grip on his shoulder.

"Soon," he whines. "This weekend. They move it around but—but I might know where they're setting up next."

I glance at Poppy, and she nods. Interview is over. He can give the rest to his attorney because the storm's coming.

And we're going to be right at the center of it.

37
Poppy

I'm setting my files down on the nearest desk, still buzzing from the interrogation, when Graham slinks up like a bad idea with expensive teeth.

Declan is handing our clerk off to a uniformed officer, but the second he spots Graham, he rolls his eyes so hard I'm amazed they stay in his head.

"You're a piece of work, Pop," Graham says, like it's charming.

Declan joins me, sitting on the edge of the desk—close enough that his arm brushes mine. I don't move away.

"Poppy," he says, voice low enough to frost glass.

The air tilts and Graham blinks.

"Excuse me?"

I blink too.

Declan repeats it, slower this time. Patient. Dangerous.

"Her name–is Poppy."

I sip my iced coffee, pink straw and all, enjoying the live testosterone drama like it's theater and I've got front-row seats. I could step in. But why ruin the show?

Declan's long legs stretch out, one boot crossed over the other. His dark gray T-shirt clings to shoulders and arms that absolutely don't skip gym day. His badge flashes against the dark denim of his jeans, and the shadow from his baseball cap casts his face in something sharper.

Something dangerous.

And, frankly, devastatingly edible.

I'm still looking when he cuts his eyes at me. A smirk ghosts across his full mouth before he pretends to check his phone.

Graham tries to recover, grinning like his orthodontist charged by the compliment. "How about we talk about that deal over dim sum?"

I open my mouth to shut it down—but Declan beats me to it, voice like sandpaper.

"We had that yesterday."

I choke on a snort, barely recovering.

Graham scoffs. "You always have your watchdog talk for you, Hartwell?" He's looking at Declan but angling it at me.

Declan lifts his gaze—slow, surgical.

"Do you always piss in the corner when your clients throw tantrums?"

Oof. Right in the fragile masculinity.

Graham mutters something and stalks off with the dignity of a dropped sandwich.

"We'll talk soon!" I call sweetly.

Declan tucks his phone away and turns to leave, smug as sin.

"Hey! You don't get to just—" My reprimand dies mid-sentence. Because, God. Those jeans. That booty. Somebody sedate me.

"Good job in there, Lollipop," he calls without looking back.

I'm too busy admiring the certified double scoop situation going on in those jeans to remember I owe him a response.

"I thought my name was Poppy!"

He lifts two fingers in a lazy salute, smirking as he disappears around the corner.

And son of a butternut squash, I'm smiling too.

Declan disappears just in time for my ADA to appear in his place, all business and biting impatience.

"Get your ass in 3B, Hartwell. You're second chair for Lewis in bond hearings."

I blink. "I thought I was under investigation."

"You are. That's why you're second," Benjamin replies, slapping a case folder against my chest and continuing down the hall. "Let's not pretend this is a reward. It's fucking bonds for Christ's sake."

I mutter something about occupational whiplash but follow. Refusing an assignment won't do me any favors, especially while my license is still hanging by a thread.

There hasn't even been time to process what came out of that interview room—an underground auction, a countdown on lives. And now here I am, being shuffled off to babysit bond hearings like the world isn't about to burn down.

Courtroom 3B smells like too much perfume and not enough hope. Lewis is already at the table, whispering to herself and flipping through files like they might sprout wings and fly away. I slide into the seat beside her, smoothing my skirt and trying to pretend this is just another ordinary hearing.

I start scanning the docket. Disorderly conduct. Petty theft. The usual parade of bad choices.

Oh, perfect. Judge Maxwell is on the bench today. Every perp may walk today on principle she can't stand me.

Then I see another name I recognize.

Nathaniel Mercer.

And the room feels colder.

He's what you might call a pattern—a man whose name shows up too often in police reports and never on a sentencing sheet. Always accused. Never convicted. Charges vanish like spilled ink. Victims back out. Files go quiet.

But I remember him.

Last year, he was picked up on suspicion of drugging a woman with a homemade sedative. She came to early. Managed to get out. He claimed it was a misunderstanding.

It always is.

Judge Maxwell enters, begins hearings and he's first up.

Nathaniel steps up to the defense table now, clean-shaven, sharply dressed, hands folded like he's a polite citizen with a parking ticket. But I've seen what he leaves behind.

Lewis is still talking to herself, trying to organize her thoughts.

And I... start organizing something else.

I wonder what it would take.
    To stop someone like him.
Permanently.

Not in the heat of panic.

Not in a blur of blood and screaming and survival.

But a plan. A process. A choice.

What if I did that?

What if I chose someone like him—on purpose?

Not a monster in the moment. A monster by design.

I could follow him and learn his habits. The places he feels safest. His patterns. His tells.

Wait until he's alone.

Lure him with a gentle conversation. A smile. A drink. With a little something extra, just enough to make him woozy.

I could take him somewhere quiet.

Empty.

Echoes don't carry in certain rooms—not if you choose carefully. Vacant construction homes. A rental listing no one's shown in weeks.

This time, I'd be prepared.

Not running. Not flailing in the dark. Not fighting for myself.

This would be for them: his victims.

I'd bring gloves. A drop cloth. Industrial-strength bleach in a labeled bottle.

Of course I'd have mom's chef's knife. It's practically a family heirloom now. But other tools would be better for Nathaniel.

A scalpel, maybe.

A bone saw could be too messy. Too loud.

But a pair of dental forceps?

Now *that* has precision. Purpose.

I'd sterilize everything first. Line it up. Tools neatly arranged on a folding table. Labeled, maybe. In order. There's something calming about that.

And maybe this time I wouldn't rush.

Nathaniel Mercer doesn't deserve a clean death like a single cut to the throat or the dignity of a fast ending.

He deserves *balance*.

His victims always reported the same detail.

The bruising. The sedation.

And the bite marks.

Deep. Scarring. As if he wanted to leave his signature carved into them.

So, I'd take his teeth.

One by one.

I imagine him strapped to the chair—groggy, blinking, confusion blooming behind his eyes like a bruise. He tries to speak, but I hush him. Smile, even.

"I'm going to help you understand," I'd whisper.

The forceps are heavy in my hand but balanced, like they were made for this.

The first tooth takes effort.

Pressure. Rocking. A crack of enamel.

Blood wells up around the root, coppery and warm.

He chokes on it, and I tilt his head gently, so he doesn't aspirate. I'm not finished yet.

It's not about rage. This is deliberate. Centered.

The second tooth comes easier.

The third easier still.

There's a rhythm to it.

Left side. Right side.

Top row. Bottom.

Even numbers. Clean extractions.

With each one, his screams fade into gargled sobs.

His eyes plead.

But I'm not cruel. I'm *thorough.*

"This is for the girls you marked," I'd say. "This is so you never do it again."

His mouth is a ruined red garden now.

Gaping and quiet.

He'd start to shake. Eyes wide as blood starts to fill his mouth now, drowning him. No sense in keeping him with me anymore.

But something seems incomplete. Unfinished and it's bothering me. The slice across the neck.

It's crucial now.

I wonder what would come first. If he would drown on his blood or bleed to death. Let's find out.

I'd whisper, the steel of my blade kissing the pulse at his neck. "This is for the girl who woke up too soon."

And then... peace.

The final cut.

Not rushed.

Not angry.

Just the soft slide of metal across his throat.

Not because he deserved it.

But because I'm done.

"**P**oppy."

A sharp elbow to my ribs. Lewis, panicked. "The judge is questioning me. Help?"

The courtroom reassembles itself slowly, like pieces of glass shifting back into a window.

Mercer's still seated at the defense table. Still composed. Still playing the role.

But I realize—I've been staring at him.

Hard.

Unblinking.

Long enough that it's no longer subtle.

And he's looking right back at me.

Not confused. Not offended.

Amused.

Like he knows.

Like he saw everything I just imagined.

For half a second, I *swear* I see it—his face just as I left it in the fantasy.

Mouth a ruin. Gums exposed. Blood seeping from the raw holes where his teeth used to be.

His lips move, forming no sound. Just wet gurgling from the back of his throat.

I blink—and it's gone.

Just Nathaniel Mercer again, clean-cut and intact.

But his eyes still hold that knowing glint.

As if he can smell the smoke from the fire I haven't lit yet.

I straighten in my seat, smooth my skirt with hands that don't shake, and clear my throat.

"Your Honor," I say evenly, calmly, like I haven't just imagined pulling twenty-two of his teeth out, "Mr. Mercer has previously faced multiple allegations involving the use of sedatives against women, followed by acts of violence. Each case was dismissed for reasons unrelated to merit. The state believes he presents a substantial and ongoing threat. We request that bond be denied."

The judge pauses. Considers.

"Bond denied," she says firmly, gavel coming down with a satisfying crack.

Mercer's jaw tightens.

Just slightly.

I should be disturbed by what I imagined. I should feel something sharp or broken inside me. But all I feel is clear.

Like fog burned off by morning sun.

As the bailiff begins to escort him out, Mercer glances over his shoulder—then leans slightly into the aisle. Just enough so only I can hear.

That grin. Wide. Menacing. Teeth still intact—for now.

"I'll see you soon, sweetheart" he says, voice low and slick with threat.

I don't flinch. Don't blink.

I just smile.

Sweet. Pleasant.

Almost excited.

"Actually," I say softly, "you might."

His expression falters for a fraction of a second.

And I sit there, warm and sunny, watching him vanish through the door with a heart full of storm.

Declan

The day of the raid feels less like gearing up for an op and more like surviving a hostage negotiation.

Except the hostage is my sanity.

And the negotiator is Poppy fucking Hartwell.

Trying to control Poppy is like trying to nail a hurricane to the floor.

She's not a cop or armed.

She's not supposed to be here.

But try telling her that—then following it with a *you should stay back*—and you might as well start writing your own eulogy.

I exhale through my nose, short and sharp, as we sit in the van. The tech team is already hunched over their screens.

Small task force.

Remote surveillance.

Minimal visible presence until we have hard evidence.

The auction's set in the brothel's basement—disguised on the books as a "wellness club," which is probably the most limp-dicked but effective cover I've ever seen.

If everything goes right tonight, we'll rip the whole operation out by the roots.

Poppy's on the bench seat across from me, her knee bouncing so fast it's a blur.

The screens flicker—grainy black-and-white feeds from hidden cameras wired into the ducts and outlets.

I watch her from under my lashes as the first guests arrive.

Men in expensive suits.

Diamond cufflinks.

Loafers that cost more than our precinct's entire budget.

Politicians. Attorneys. Judges.

Faces I've seen preaching justice and morality.

Poppy leans forward, face pale, fingers tight in her lap.

I see the exact moment she recognizes someone—a sharp, visible flinch. Two of them, actually.

Both attorneys she's worked with.

One sat beside her on a sex-crimes prosecution, beaming like a saint the whole time.

I want to reach across the van, take her hand, tell her she's not crazy for feeling betrayed.

But the words die.

She meets my eyes for a second—then looks away.

That flicker cuts deeper than it should.

Before I can unpack that, the screens flash—

Then go black.

"What the hell?" a tech barks, scrambling toward the laptop.

"Remote uplink's dead. They found the relay, or it got fried."

The room turns cold.

If we can't reestablish surveillance, the whole op folds.

No evidence. No arrests.

"We have a backup transmitter," one tech offers. "But someone needs to plug it into the main router."

Christ. Walk in blind. Hope you don't get recognized by someone you've passed in court.

Before I can speak, Poppy's already moving.

"I'll go," she says, rising.

"I remember where the utility closet is."

"No," I snap, stepping between her and the gear. "I've got it."

Without waiting for her argument, I grab the transmitter and shut the van door behind me.

Inside, I move fast and low through the brothel, hugging walls and avoiding cracked doors leaking laughter and music.

I find the closet—same hallway where I had to play Mr. Suave with what's-her-face.

The door creaks open. Slatted wood. Turning on the light would be like lighting up a billboard.

I click on my flashlight, fix it between my teeth, and aim it at the router.

The backup transmitter is warm in my hands, every second ticking louder in my skull.

I crouch low. Start the swap.

Halfway through, footsteps echo down the hall.

"The internet in this shithole pisses me off."

The voice is getting closer.

Fast.

Coming straight for me.

Shit.

I kill the flashlight and flatten into the shadows, heart pounding so hard I can feel it rattling against my ribs. The footsteps get closer. Too close. I'm cornered.

No clean way out without blowing the whole thing sky-high.

I tighten my fists, ready to drop whoever steps around the

corner, when I hear a bright, nervous voice that clenches my stomach like a vice.

"Hello?"

Motherfucking Poppy.

Every hair on my body stands up.

I try to look through the slats and get a terrible view of her standing at the end of the hallway, arms wrapped around herself like a lost lamb.

"Sorry," she calls, voice wobbling just right. "I'm looking for my friend... her *appointment* was supposed to be over fifteen minutes ago."

A low male voice answers, suspicious but curious.

"You're not supposed to be here, sweetheart. The center is closed."

"I know, I just—I didn't see anyone at the front desk."

The footsteps retreat, lured by her bait.

"Wait here."

She—in fact—does not wait.

At least she ignores what *everyone* says. Not just me.

She tiptoes as quietly as possible to the closet. I open it just as she arrives, and she startles like she didn't know I'd be in here.

"What is your fucking problem?" I whisper, wrapping my arm around her waist and hauling her inside.

"Son of a mother-trucker, I am saving your booty," she mutters, steadying herself with both hands on my chest. "You're welcome."

She feels perfect in my arms, and I'm struggling to remember the English language.

"No one can take you seriously when that's how you curse."

This woman actually sticks her tongue out at me like a seven year old.

I don't want to let her go, but we're on a mission.

"Let's get this over with." I hand her the transmitter now that she's occupying what little room is left in here.

"Get over there, shorty."

She snatches it from me, fire flashing in her eyes.

Tiny green lights flicker to life.

"Signal reestablished," crackles in my earpiece. "We're live again."

She heard it too. We both nod, ready to get the fuck out of Dodge.

But before I can reach for the knob, the sound of voices returns.

"Hold your positions." The techs directive is low in our earpieces.

Steps come closer.

"We can't afford random clients running around tonight."

"You think I don't know that?"

"Calm down, Don."

"The mayor's supposed to be here," one says, and my stomach knots.

Poppy's eyes shoot to mine, wide. "So it better fucking go perfectly."

The space barely fits one body, let alone two. She's nearly pressed against me. I feel her breath on my chest—quick, too quick and shallow. She's starting to panic.

"Hey," I whisper, tipping her chin so she's looking at me. She presses into me, trembling.

I wrap my arms around her waist, murmuring low against her temple.

"Breathe, Poppy. You're okay."

She fists my vest like she's drowning. I don't mind. I wish we weren't wearing this gear—so she could hold me, not the damn vest.

I'd let her break my ribs if it kept her from unraveling.

Outside, doors open. Laughter spills out. Then they close again. They're looking for her. Getting closer to our hideout.

"Just slow down, okay?"

I never look away—and neither does she.

Her body molds to mine, soft curves against hard lines. I feel her heartbeat, her tremble, the delicate hitch of every breath.

My hand cradles her jaw like she's something fragile, something rare.

Without thinking, my thumb rubs her cheek.

Her eyes are wide and glassy, shimmering with something raw and unguarded.

I drag my thumb lightly across her bottom lip, feeling the slight tremble there, the way she leans into the touch without realizing it.

Her mouth parts slightly—soft, yielding—and her eyes flutter half-closed.

Every instinct in me roars to life.

I lean in, slow and deliberate, giving her the chance to pull away.

She doesn't.

If anything, she tilts her head up, offering herself with a soft, broken sound that damn near tears me apart.

Our mouths are a breath away, the tension pulled so taut it could slice us both open.

I want to kiss her.

Wreck her.

I want to taste what she sounds like when she moans my name.

I breathe her in instead, hovering on the precipice of something I can't take back.

The sound of voices echoing farther down the hall pulls me back to reality like a punch to the ribs.

I don't want to do this here.

Not like this.

Not the first time her lips feel another's. Not in a fucking closet where girls are being held and drugged before being sold like livestock.

Our earpiece crackles, and her shoulders jump. The moment snaps, breaking immediately.

"All clear. Return to the van."

I press my forehead to hers, forcing my pulse down.

Somehow, I pull away before I ruin us both.

"You ready?" I rasp, my voice lower, rougher than it should be.

She nods, and without another word, we slip back into the hallway.

We move quickly, navigating the shadows without getting caught.

She stays close, steps light, hand in mine until we're back in the van.

But she doesn't look at me.

Not once.

Every glance avoids mine—fixing on the walls, the floor, anything but me.

And I start to wonder if I crossed a line.

If it wasn't just adrenaline or timing.

If I read her wrong.

If she regrets every second in that closet.

But some feral, ugly part of me refuses to believe it.

I know what I saw in her eyes.

I know how her body fit against mine, like something instinctive.

Like she needed me in the same savage, breathless way I need her.

I'm fucking crazy for her. More every goddamn day.

And there's no cure in sight but taking more. Touching more. Having her in ways I know I shouldn't even dream about.

I shove it all down when the mayor shows up.

The van goes silent, and no one moves.

We just watch as the city's smiling, self-righteous, camera-loving leader strolls into a basement full of girls young enough to still believe in fairy tales. Cash burning a hole in his pocket.

A fucking monster in a tailored suit.

My stomach twists with something colder, meaner than anger.

It's betrayal.

Disgust.

Hate so sharp it scrapes bone.

I thumb a message to Rourke, fingers clumsy with rage.

> DECLAN: Incoming. Shit's about to hit the fan.

> ROURKE: Team's already staged. Waiting on your call.

Good.

Because once I get the green light, we're kicking this whole house of cards down.

I glance at the feed, jaw tight.

It's not time yet.

More guests are coming, so we have to wait.

We have to let these sick fucks sign their own warrants in blood.

But every minute we sit here feels like betrayal.

Drinks are passed around on the feed, waiters smiling like this is some fucking country club gala instead of a goddamn flesh market.

Snacks.

Cocktails.

Laughter.

I want to put my fist through the screen and put a bullet in their fucking heads.

Poppy's gone pale, her hands trembling slightly where they're curled around the edge of the seat.

When I check on her, she waves me off with a tight, broken smile that doesn't reach her eyes.

"I just..." she starts, then stops, swallowing hard.

"I just wish we could do something other than wait," she whispers, blinking too fast, her voice starting to crack around the edges. Her eyes shine, unshed tears making them glow in the flickering light from the screens.

"Hey," I say, voice low. I reach out, catching her hand where it's clenched tight in her lap, forcing her to meet my gaze.

"You got us here," I remind her, low and certain. "Without you, none of these bastards would ever see the inside of a cell."

The words seem to land.

She nods, biting her lip, clutching my hand tighter before she lets go.

She's still pale, but there's fire in her eyes again when she finally lifts her chin.

The comms crackle to life.

"All teams—final address received. Move to positions."

I shove open the side door of the van, boots hitting the ground hard.

Pull my gun and rack the slide.

One last check—it's loaded.

We're fucking ready.

Ahead of me, three of our best are already moving into formation.

I'm the last behind them.

Focused. Head down. Heart hammering.

The second we breach that building, all hell's going to break loose.

"Declan."

My name stops me cold.

Her voice—so small. Broken.

Barely more than a whisper.

It tears me apart before I even turn around.

But I do.

I have to.

And Jesus fucking Christ, the look on her face is going to haunt me for the rest of my miserable life.

Terror.

Panic.

Hope.

"Be careful," she says, and a single tear slips free, sliding down her cheek in a glimmering trail.

Before I can say a goddamn word back—before I can do something stupid like grab her and promise things I shouldn't —the call comes through.

"All teams go."

And without hesitating a single second, I'm gone.

39

Poppy

I stand in my kitchen, trembling, rooted to the floor like if I move, I'll shatter.

Silence presses in from all sides, thick and stifling, as my mind spins, dragging me down into a pit I can't outrun.

A client who tried to kill herself.

Two bodies on my conscience.

Colleagues I once trusted, exposed as monsters with polished smiles.

Declan—God, Declan—every warning siren in my head and every soft ache in my chest.

And my stalker. Because of course. What's one other thing?

The man who touches me like he already owns me.

Who made me feel things I didn't know existed.

Who showed me that surrender could be terrifying and holy.

Worst of all?

I liked it.

I craved it.

I crave it still.

I squeeze my arms tighter around myself, blinking fast against the hot sting in my eyes.

Dexter, still faintly pink, sits near the couch, gnawing his paw like he's over it too.

I want to laugh.

I want to scream.

Mostly, I just want to disappear.

Tonight should have been a victory.

We watched from the van—every monster hauled out one by one, including the mayor.

No shots fired. No bodies dropped.

The girls were rescued. The warrants were already flying before the dust even settled.

It should have felt like winning.

But it doesn't.

It feels like sitting at the bottom of the ocean, the weight of everything crushing me, no air left to breathe, nowhere to put the hurt clawing through my insides.

When the front door creaks open, I don't flinch.

I already know it's him.

The man who never knocks, never hesitates, never asks permission.

He steps inside like he belongs, the sound of boots on hardwood grounding me in a way that terrifies me more than anything else.

I run to him.

No hesitation. No thought.

I collide with him mid-step, my body crumpling into his chest, sobbing so violently it rips the air from my lungs.

He catches me without a word.

Strong arms wrap around me, steady and unmoving, like the world can fall apart and he won't.

I bury my face in the thick fabric of his hoodie, fists clenched, holding on like it'll keep me from drowning.

He doesn't say anything.

Just holds me.

Lets me fall apart without judgment.

The tears slow eventually, but my mind doesn't.

It runs in jagged, vicious loops, pulling up things I can't seem to shut off.

Of course, my first thought goes to Declan.

The way his hand cradled my jaw. The way his breath brushed my lips.

The ache to close the distance and taste him.

The wish that it was him who walked through my door.

Instead—I'm in the arms of another man.

Another predator.

Another danger.

And I want him too.

I feel his chest rise and fall beneath my cheek, steady, unbothered.

The urge to tilt my head and find his mouth hits hot and sharp, twisting my stomach.

I've seen his lips—twice—just enough to haunt me.

Enough to wonder what they'd feel like: hard and claiming, or slow and devastating.

I should hate him.

I should scream, run, call for help—anything but lean in closer.

But I crave him. Crave what he makes me feel.

The realization cuts deep, carving away the last of the girl who thought she could be normal.

Who thought she was still whole.

Dexter trots over and plops down at my feet, tail wagging half-heartedly.

He bumps my ankle with his head and whines when I ignore him.

It dawns on me that Dexter doesn't growl anymore.

He trusts the masked man like he belongs here.

The realization hits like a punch.

He's been here while I'm gone.

Often.

Maybe always.

Maybe long before I ever caught the first shiver of awareness.

"Do you come here when I'm not home?"

My voice barely breaks the silence.

He nods. Once.

Unbothered.

My stomach flips.

The questions tumble out, sharp and frantic.

"Why?"

Silence.

"When did it start?"

Nothing.

"How do you get past the alarm?"

Still nothing.

He just watches me with that same unshakable patience—like he's waiting for me to catch up.

The silence is suffocating.

It presses down on me until my skin itches, my heart hammers, my composure cracks.

He's building a wall between us and something in me snaps.

The anger bubbling under my skin finally has a target.

"Leave," I snap. "I don't want you here."

He doesn't move.

Doesn't speak.

Just watches—steady, maddening—like he already knows how this ends.

"Go," I say again, shoving against him.

It's like trying to move an oak tree.

"I mean it. Get out."

Still nothing.

Still calm, while I'm coming apart at the seams.

Hot, angry tears blur my vision. Furious drops slide down my cheeks, making it worse.

I push him again, fists landing on his chest, desperate for a reaction.

He doesn't flinch so I shove harder.

He stays rooted like I'm a stiff breeze against a hurricane.

"Why won't you leave?" I scream, my voice breaking, throat raw from everything I can't say.

He moves—quick and sure.

Grabs my wrists. Not hurting, just steady.

He walks me back until my spine hits the wall, the coolness slicing through the heat radiating off me.

He cages me there, breathing slow and steady while I gasp like I'm drowning.

"Stop it," he says, low and rough. "Stop fighting everything. Stop thinking so goddamn much and just surrender."

His voice vibrates through me, rattling something loose.

"I don't know what that means."

"Do whatever the fuck you want, Poppy," he rasps, crowding closer. "Just stop running from it."

The walls I've held up all night finally crack.

I tilt my head up, chest rising in shallow gasps.

"Kiss me," I whisper.

Not a plea.

A dare.

A broken challenge tossed between us like a lit match.

He doesn't answer right away.

Just holds my gaze, like he's making sure I know what I'm asking for.

Then he steps closer.

My heart stutters.

He cups my face in his hands, thumbs stroking my cheeks with an almost unbearable gentleness.

"You'll behave?"

I nod, my face flushed.

He glances past me, grabs a bandana from the coatrack.

He turns me gently, my shoulder brushing the wall, and slides the fabric over my eyes.

Darkness swallows everything, forcing me to feel instead of see.

Another sound—the faint slide of fabric again—and I know he's removing the balaclava.

His bare hands lift mine.

He presses my palm to his mouth making me gasp.

The soft brush of his lips narrows my world to breath and skin.

A shiver rolls through me as my fingers trace the stubble of his jaw, the curve of his cheekbones, the fullness of his mouth.

He exhales raggedly when I touch his lips.

The heat of it ghosts across my trembling fingers.

I reach higher without thinking.

Find his hair—thick, soft, a little wavy—and drag my fingers through it, scratching lightly at his scalp.

A low, needy sound rumbles from his chest.

A vibration that sinks into my bloodstream and takes root.

My heart pounds.

I'm trapped between the cold wall and the heat of him.

Blind. Trembling. Wanting.

And for once—I don't want to think.

I just want to feel.

He pulls me flush against him.

One hand cups my jaw, thumb brushing slow circles across my cheekbone like he's memorizing every inch. Like Declan did in the closet today.

For one breathless second, there's only the tension humming between us.

And then his lips find mine.

Hesitant at first, barely more than a whisper.

Testing. Tasting.

But it doesn't stay that way.

It deepens fast—hungry, consuming, a quiet, devastating claim.

His mouth is firm, demanding, hot.

He kisses like he wants to devour me.

A helpless sound escapes my throat the second my lips part.

His tongue finds mine, slow and precise, devastating in its finesse.

My arms loop around his neck, fingers tangling in his hair —holding on because I don't trust gravity anymore.

He tilts my chin, deepens the kiss, dragging noises from me I didn't know I could make.

He steals every breath. Every thought. Every last shard of fear.

It's not the way I imagined my first kiss.

It's not clumsy or sweet.

It's not gentle or uncertain.

It's fire. Hunger. Surrender.

The kind of kiss that ruins you for anything else.

The kind that burns itself into your bones and stays long after the lips that gave it are gone.

Time ceases to matter.

Seconds or hours—what difference does it make?

Everything stopped the moment he touched me.

Just when I think he'll pull away, he doesn't.

He only slows us down.

His hands roam, dragging fire in their wake.

He pulls back to shift the angle—then takes my mouth again.

My arousal spirals.

The ache between my thighs sharpens, pulsing, demanding.

I'm the one who grows hungrier.

My kisses turn urgent, desperate.

I rock against him, feel the rigid proof of how badly he wants this too.

He groans—a raw, guttural sound—and then abruptly pulls away.

The absence hits like a freight train.

Air rips into my lungs as if I'd forgotten how to breathe.

I reach blindly in front of me with one hand, the other pressed to my tingling, swollen lips—still hot from everything he took.

My legs shake.

The world is silent.

Too silent.

There are no footsteps, no breath.

No whisper of a heartbeat thumping close to me.

Just the weight of him missing.

And then—

The soft creak of the front door closing.

I rip the bandana from my eyes, heart hammering in my chest.

He's gone.

Panic crashes through me as I stumble forward, flinging the front door open hard enough to make the hinges scream.

Cold night air rushes in, sharp against my overheated skin.

I blink into the darkness, eyes scanning frantically—desperate, breathless.

At first, nothing.

Then I see him.

A shadow slipping between the pools of streetlight, moving with the silent certainty of someone who's always known how to disappear.

He lifts a helmet, slides it over his head.

The black visor snaps down with a final, brutal click.

He swings one leg over the motorcycle like it's second nature.

Sits like he was born there—solid, sure, untouchable.

"Wait," I choke, stumbling forward.

"Please—wait!"

The engine roars to life, low and angry, vibrating through the street and rattling my bones.

And then he's gone.

A blur of black and chrome swallowed by the night.

I stand there, barefoot on the concrete, arms wrapped around myself as the silence rushes back in.

Heavy and suffocating.

A single tear slides off my chin and lands on my bare arm.

Only then do I realize I'm crying.

Soft tapping draws my gaze down.

Dexter stands beside me, his little paws clicking restlessly against the driveway.

He looks up at me, head tilted, his eyes solemn and confused.

He huffs—an almost scolding sound—and turns back toward the house, tail swishing as he disappears through the open door.

I stay where I am, rooted.

Staring at the place where he vanished.

The first kiss I ever gave away—

My first taste of something I never even dared to dream about had been everything.

Fierce.

Wild.

Consuming.

Until it wasn't.

Until it became the space he left behind.

The hollow ache where he used to be.

Now, alone in the bruised silence of night, arms wrapped tight around my chest, I feel it settle in deep.

The ache of absence.

The kind that doesn't just hurt but lingers.

The kind that stays.

And somehow, impossibly, I know:

Nothing will ever be the same again.

Declan

The second the door slams shut behind me, I'm moving.

A blaze through the house.

A hurricane of fury that won't be bottled, can't be reasoned with.

My jacket hits the floor.

My boots pound a reckless path through the hall.

I'm not thinking.

I'm hunting.

I want to look the motherfucker in the eye—the arrogant, selfish bastard who took what was supposed to be mine.

Who kissed her.

Who stole the first fucking taste of her lips.

Mine.

That was supposed to be mine.

I shove the bathroom door open so hard it nearly tears off the hinges.

The light flickers on, and my target stares back at me.

Smirking.

Mocking.

Daring me.

My fist is already swinging before I realize it—rage burning so hot it blinds me.

Something cracks, but I don't even fucking feel it. A sharp, brutal impact as the bathroom mirror shatters.

Glass rains down in glittering shards, the spiderweb of fractures splintering my own reflection into a thousand broken pieces.

I stand there, chest heaving, staring at the blood blooming across my knuckles, dripping onto the floor.

The man staring back at me is wrecked.

Wild-eyed.

Haunted.

Not the brooding detective everyone sees.

Not the man who plays by rules he wrote for himself.

This?

This is the monster she kissed.

I brace both palms on the sink, the porcelain cold under my hands, and lean in until my forehead almost touches the glass.

"You kissed her," I snarl at my reflection. "*You* kissed her. Not me."

The words crack the air between us.

Me and the man who looks back at me from the cracked mirror.

I shove off the sink, pacing a savage line across the tiny room.

I turn back and point, like the man in the mirror is someone else entirely.

"You're the one she wants," I spit. "In the dark. Behind the mask. The fucking fantasy."

The bitterness curdles in my throat, choking me.

"You made her like this. You could've stopped this any

fucking time you wanted."

My hand moves before I even register it.

A sharp crack splits the air—skin on skin—as I slap myself across the jaw, stumbling a step from the force of it.

The sting blooms instantly.

Hot. Humiliating. Real.

I stare at myself, panting, shaking.

What the actual fuck am I doing? Beating the shit out of myself like I'm in fucking Fight Club.

"Get your shit together."

I blow out a huff.

This didn't start with the mask.

It started a year ago.

I was testifying in one of her cases.

One of a dozen I'd done that month.

I didn't even know her name at first—just a file number, a list of facts. Another ADA trying to spin a clean narrative out of a pile of shit evidence.

But then she walked in.

And fuck.

She owned the courtroom.

Commanded it without raising her voice.

No theatrics. No grandstanding.

Just sharp intellect, sharper eyes, and a voice that made everyone sit up straighter.

Including me.

I told myself I stayed to see justice play out.

To make sure the asshole got locked away.

But the truth?

I wanted a few more minutes to watch her.

So every day, I came back.

Took the same seat behind her.

Close enough to smell her perfume when she passed.

Close enough to feel her voice in my chest when she read her statements.

I turned down every new case just to stay in that courtroom.

Weeks went by and the trial ended.

But sentencing was scheduled a month later.

So I came back.

When the bastard heard he'd never be a free man again, he snapped.

Threw his lawyer and came straight for her.

He was big. Angry.

Didn't fucking matter.

I was over the barrier before the bailiff even moved taking him down with one punch.

She clung to me afterward.

Both hands gripping mine like I was something solid.

Something safe.

But that's not what sealed it.

It was his wife.

The way she looked at Poppy.

Hatred.

The *I'll-finish-this-myself* kind.

I've seen that look before.

I followed her for three days before the woman made her move.

Poppy walked into a store, and that bitch followed.

Her hand was buried deep in her purse. Except she paused. Right in the middle of the parking lot, she didn't follow through.

She turned around and went back to her car.

But it wasn't hesitation.

It was strategy.

She was still going to do something, she just didn't want to do it there.

I grabbed a shopping cart and rammed it into her bumper like some clueless idiot.

When she rolled down the window to yell, I knocked her out cold.

And then I checked the purse.

Exactly what I thought. A switchblade, and a sketch of Poppy dead, posed like the children her husband killed.

That sealed it.

She wasn't just grieving.

She was planning a tribute to her husband with the woman that locked him away for ever.

So I made sure it never happened.

Poppy never knew.

But I kept watching her.

Telling myself it was just to make sure she was safe.

"What the fuck am I doing?" I whisper, voice raw, shredded at the edges.

"Jesus Christ."

The man in the mirror stares back—broken, bloodshot, fucking pathetic.

"You're not real," I tell him. That other side of me that's been her shadow for a fucking year.

It sounds pathetic even as I say it.

"You're a sickness. An excuse."

Something I've worked hard to keep separate from the other part of me. The detective side of me that shows up to work with her everyday on this case.

But it doesn't matter.

Because she kissed him.

Not me.

Not the man who tries to be better.

She kissed the monster in the dark.

The monster I made.

The one I thought I could control.

The one I don't know how to fucking stop.

And worse?

It was the best fucking kiss of my life.

I press my fingertips to my mouth like I can still feel her there.

Soft. Trembling. Wanting.

"I wanted her to choose me," I mutter, staring down the stranger in the glass.

"Me."

The anger boils over before I can stop it.

I'm tired of looking at myself. Tired of the split in my skin.

I cock my arm back—and this time, there's no hesitation.

My fist punches through the mirror.

Glass shatters outward, raining onto the counter and the floor. Blood wells instantly from the split across my knuckles. Pain flares—sharp, white-hot—but it's distant.

Just background noise to the devastation inside me.

I stagger back, chest heaving, and slide down the wall until I'm sitting on the cold tile, my back scraping the paint-stripped drywall.

The broken reflection stares back at me from the jagged shards.

Fragmented. Twisted. Wrong.

I tip my head back, eyes burning.

"How do I make her choose me," I whisper to the empty room, "when I'm the one hiding behind the mask?"

There's no answer.

Only the quiet tick of the clock in the next room.

Only the rush of blood in my ears.

Only the slow, wet drip of blood onto the tile.

Finally, when my breathing evens out—

When the violence drains from my veins and leaves me hollow—

I whisper the only truth left.

"I have to end this," I say, eyes closing, the words cutting deeper than any broken glass ever could, "before she falls in love with a ghost."

Poppy

If there's one thing I've learned since my case was declared a mistrial, it's that rock bottom isn't a floor.

It's a trapdoor.

And mine swung open sometime after I was kissed by my masked stalker and left sobbing in my driveway like a lovesick idiot.

The raid footage is everywhere.

News outlets on an endless loop: grainy video clips, flashing sirens, men in suits handcuffed and shoved into black SUVs.

Every channel. Every headline.

And all I can think is, *what if I landed on the news and someone recognized me from the night of Travis' murder?*

Because nothing screams *I'm totally not a murderer* like showing up in the background, blood-splattered, holding a dog hostage.

Bless Declan for ordering me to leave the van.

If I had stayed five more minutes, I'd be a TikTok meme by now.

#HomicideHoney

#BloodyBarbie

#DextersDarkPassenger

Just thinking about it makes my stomach cramp.

Which is why there's zero chance I'm staying home waiting for anxiety to eat me alive.

It's Saturday, and my escape plan is simple: pretend yesterday didn't happen, glue myself to something semi-normal, and hope if I act like a functional adult long enough, maybe I'll become one.

The precinct is my best bet.

Surely, even my skull-masked stalker wouldn't be bold enough to follow me there.

Probably.

Hopefully.

Whatever.

Dexter, of course, has his own plans.

Plans that involve being treated like the spoiled little prince he is.

I dress him in a golf outfit because if I have to suffer through today pretending to be okay, he can suffer through wearing plaid pants and a matching hat.

He shoots me a betrayed look as I tuck tiny doggy sunglasses over his nose.

"You look fabulous," I tell him, adjusting the beret behind one floppy ear. "Own it."

Dexter huffs and flounces off toward the door, pants swishing with indignation.

I pack his tote—yes, a tote—complete with gourmet treats, chilled water, and two hand-prepped meals.

At the last second, I hold up two of his favorite crystal dishes.

He taps one with a paw like a judgmental little king.

At least someone here has it together.

Files? Packed.

Coffee? Secured.

Dog? Accessorized within an inch of his life.

My world may be crumbling like a soggy granola bar, but this?

This I can control.

My outfit is pure bubblegum warfare, as Declan once labeled it.

Pink leggings, pink crop top, pink tennies, and oversized white sunglasses.

I crank up the *Legally Blonde* soundtrack as I slide behind the wheel, the cheerful beat pumping like a lifeline.

If Elle Woods can get into Harvard, I can survive whatever today throws at me.

Probably.

Maybe.

The second I push through the precinct doors, the scent of burnt coffee and floor polish hits me like a weirdly comforting slap.

Do I have a doggy stroller? I plead the fifth.

I'm too busy wrestling the door to our little war room, grumbling a very mature, "Monkey muffins!"

When I finally win the battle and step inside, my eyes land on Declan.

Already here.

He's bent over a drawer of files, sleeves shoved up like he's personally at war with the paperwork.

Knuckles raw and cut, probably from taking down the city's scum in yesterdays raid. The sight of it pulls at my heart.

He's frozen, watching me cast voodoo hexes at the door.

For a second, I consider retreating.

Pretending I walked into the wrong building blaming it on cold foam and poor life choices.

There's a beat of silence—like he's not sure what to say.

He clears his throat. "I didn't know you had a dog."

I set Dexter's carrier down and adjust my crop top like that's going to fix the nerves fluttering through me.

"I didn't know you worked weekends," I counter, forcing a smile.

There's a tiny pause, then, very dryly, "...And he's pink."

Dexter, right on cue, trots out of the carrier like he owns the damn building.

Plaid pants swishing. Sunglasses still perched.

Beret glittering like a tiny, judgmental tiara.

If I die of secondhand embarrassment today, at least my dog looked fabulous.

"This is Dexter," I announce, handing Declan a treat from my tote. "He doesn't like men much. You might want to come bearing gifts."

Declan gives me a look—half amused, half skeptical—but crouches and offers the treat.

"Eh, I'm good with dogs."

Dexter sniffs once, then takes it. No growl.

I blink.

"Wow. He usually growls at... everyone."

I catch myself—the stalker still too close to the surface— and smile tightly.

Dexter never likes men.

Except, apparently, the one I'm trying not to crush on.

The one I definitely shouldn't want.

Because we work together.

And it would be messy.

Naturally, the day I decide to move on, Dexter gives him a human-of-the-year award.

Et tu, Dexter?

Silence stretches between us.

Not hostile. Not cold.

Just... heavy.

Like we're both dragging around a conversation we're too scared to start.

I open my mouth to say something—anything—about the weather, the Mets, literally not kissing in closets.

But Declan beats me to it.

"I hope I didn't make you uncomfortable," he says.

Voice low. Rough around the edges.

"In the closet. I was just trying to calm you down. Maybe I got carried away."

Oh.

My heart twists.

Because for a moment—I let myself wonder. What if.

I plaster on a bright smile, forcing the lie to come easily.

"No, of course not. It was just... a lot. You know? Stress. Adrenaline. Tiny closet."

He nods once.

But something flickers in his eyes I can't read.

And because I'm a walking panic attack in human form, I blurt:

"You probably have a girlfriend anyway."

Smooth, Poppy. Very smooth.

God, someone shoot me with a tranquilizer dart.

Declan's expression shifts—barely. The smile fades. Something quieter moves in.

"No girlfriend."

The words hit like a dart to the chest.

No girlfriend.

Sweet buttered pancakes, Poppy—you already knew that!

Sebastian grilled him like a steak last week in a speed round of "Declan's Love Life."

I should nod politely.

Change the subject.

Go about my day like a fully functional adult.

But no.

Because my life is a flaming dumpster on roller skates, I hear myself say:

"Do you...date?"

Oh no.

Abort the mission.

ABORT.

"I mean—not that I care," I rush, hands waving like I can erase the words midair. "It's not professional to ask. You don't have to answer."

Why are words still happening?

Declan's mouth curves into a slow smile—small, warm, devastating.

"No, I don't date," he says. "But..."

I hold my breath.

"There *is* a woman I'm interested in."

And just like that, my heart crumples like a soggy paper crane.

Of course.

Of course he likes someone.

Probably someone who isn't babysitting a shichon in plaid pants and an emotional support beret.

He's being polite.

Kind.

Sending me the subtle "please stop hurling yourself at me" signal.

I scramble for dignity. For oxygen. For a distraction.

I snap Dexter's leash on.

"Well," I manage, too brightly, "good luck. She'd be lucky to have you."

Before he can say anything—before my word vomit evolves into word diarrhea—I turn on my heel and march toward the door, cheeks burning, Dexter strutting beside me like he's auditioning for America's Next Top Model.

I barely make it down the steps before my burner phone starts buzzing like an angry wasp in a coffee can.

Not my regular phone.

The burner.

Perfect.

I know I shouldn't look.

Nothing good lives on that screen.

But I have the self-preservation instincts of a drunk raccoon, so I glance anyway.

> UNKNOWN: You running away from me, Sunny?

My heart lurches so hard I nearly trip.

I shouldn't respond.

I shouldn't have kissed him.

I definitely shouldn't have wanted to.

Resolve hardening, I shove the phone back into the thigh pocket of my leggings and pick up the pace.

Dexter waddles beside me in full plaid regalia, looking personally offended by everything.

Another buzz.

My stomach flips—traitorous and stupid.

UNKNOWN: He better stay away from you.

He?

Declan's face flashes in my mind.

The thought of anyone touching him—hurting him—makes my chest seize.

Thumbs flying, I type:

POPPY: We're working a case.
Occupational requirement.

Reply comes immediately.

UNKNOWN: Not the detective. The prick walking up to you.

What—

I spin just in time to see Graham jogging across the lot, all slicked-back hair and cologne-test smarm.

He throws up a hand in a wave.

I cringe on instinct.

Dexter starts growling.

Low. Menacing.

Snaggle tooth flashing like a prison shank.

Graham doesn't notice.

Smarm turned up to eleven.

"Hey, Poppy. How'd the raid go?" he asks like we're besties and not mortal enemies.

"Hey, Graham."

Buzz.

UNKNOWN: Make him leave. Or I will.

My heart kicks hard.

Graham crouches—reaching for Dexter like he's petting a golden retriever, not a plaid-clad war criminal in dog form.

"Don't—" I start.

Too late.

Dexter lunges.

Snaps.

Snarls like he's auditioning for a prison riot.

Graham yelps, jerking back.

His face contorts like he's not sure whether to sue me or disinfect his soul.

I slap a hand over my mouth to smother the laugh clawing its way out.

"Bad boy," I scold, half-hearted at best, tugging Dexter back.

Buzz.

> UNKNOWN: Good boy.

> UNKNOWN: Let him bite the fucker so I don't have to.

I roll my eyes so hard I might sprain something.

"Sorry, Graham, what was your—"

> POPPY: Stop stalking me.

I jab the screen mid-sentence.

Immediate reply.

> UNKNOWN: Can't. I tried.

And the worst part?

I like it.

I shouldn't.

It's unhinged.

It's toxic.

It's... intoxicating.

"Um, Poppy?" Graham blinks at me, still trying to recover from Dexter's assassination attempt.

Before I can answer, another text buzzes in:

UNKNOWN: I like to see you smile.

My traitorous mouth twitches—reflexive, helpless.

I immediately scowl to counteract it and scan the parking lot.

Where is he?

No skull masks.

No brooding bikers.

Just a few precinct workers and a mom wrangling toddlers into a minivan.

POPPY: I only smile for people who don't walk out in the middle of kissing me.

There. That'll show him.

Put the stalker in his place.

Oh. Right.

Graham is still here.

UNKNOWN: Touché

"How about dinner tonight?" he asks, flashing teeth a little too white. "I make a mean pasta puttanesca."

Dexter's growl cranks up to full Tasmanian Devil.

Teeth bared. Eyes narrowed. Ready for round two.

And because my brain panics under romantic pressure, I blurt—

"Oh! I have dinner plans tonight."

But do I stop there?

Of course not.

"Did you know pasta puttanesca was made by sex workers in twentieth-century Naples?"

Silence.

Flat, dead-air silence.

The kind that makes you wish the earth would just open up and swallow you whole.

I want to bash my head into the pavement.

"Anyhoo!" I chirp, scooping up Dexter like my life depends on it. "Gotta get back to work. Talk later!"

Dexter yaps triumphantly, like he's cheering my exit.

I speed-walk back into the precinct like my hiney is on fire, mentally stuffing that entire interaction into the vault where I keep middle school trauma and every failed first date.

I'm halfway to the bullpen when Declan intercepts me.

File tucked under one arm.

That familiar storm brewing behind his eyes.

"Booking worked all night after the raid," he says, already falling in step beside me like we didn't just have one of the most awkward hallway collisions of all time.

"Good," I reply, trying to sound normal. Trying not to think about how his voice vibrates through my ribs like a tuning fork made of tension.

He flips open the folder, all business now.

Like he needs to focus or risk doing something dangerous.

(Join the club.)

"Emergency bond hearing for the mayor was at six a.m."

My eyebrows shoot up. "And?"

"Denied."

A spark of pride lights in my chest.

Small win. I'll take it.

But before I can savor the rare taste of institutional justice, Declan hits me with the real news:

"And... did you hear? The Houseguest was found dead in the Hudson."

He holds up a newspaper.

And right there on the front page is my rideshare driver.

The world tilts as my stomach turns to ice.

The Houseguest.

One of New York's most infamous serial killers, at large for nearly two decades.

He didn't just kill women, he lived with them first.

Ate meals with them.

Watched TV in their living rooms.

Showered. Slept in their beds.

A houseguest.

My lungs lock. The air in my body turns into glass.

Declan sinks onto one of the cracked leather couches in the corner of our war room, already pulling out his phone.

I just stand there.

Frozen.

Phone slipping into my hand like muscle memory.

I scan the headline.

Vision blurring.

Pulse roaring.

Body discovered in the Hudson.

Confirmed to be "The Houseguest," now identified as Caleb Thatcher.

Known for raping, torturing, and killing over two dozen women. Police sources suggest vigilante revenge. Possibly a father or brother of one of the victims. Someone who couldn't wait any longer for justice.

My hands are numb.

My throat is closing but I keep reading.

The details are worse than I remembered—

His methods. His trophies. The fear he carved into every woman he hunted.

The article ends with a quote from the police commissioner:

"Women across the state will sleep easier tonight, knowing this monster was finally brought to justice."

I stare at the screen fighting to breathe, because I did that.

Not with a badge or a courtroom.

Not with a confession or a guilty plea.

I ended it.

With a blade and blood.

And the terrifying part that should scare me more than anything else?

I don't regret it.

Not even a little.

Declan

W ho's got you smiling like that?" I ask, voice low, casual as Poppy snaps her burner phone shut like it's about to explode. "A boyfriend?"

She's been passing texts with me—stalker me—for the last thirty minutes.

She freezes. Just a breath. but it's enough to tighten something in my chest.

"What? No. Not a boyfriend..." she says quickly, fiddling with the corner of a case file like it holds the answers to world peace.

My brow lifts. I cock my head, teasing—but my eyes are locked on her, drinking in every microexpression she can't hide fast enough.

"Someone you've been seeing?" I press, voice still easy but threading the needle closer to where it'll hurt if I pull too hard.

She hesitates.

Just long enough to stab a fucking knife through me.

Maybe it's the memory of the almost-kiss hanging between us.

Maybe it's the thought of her texting someone else, laughing at her screen the way she just did with me.

Either way, she lies.

"Yeah," she says, voice strained. "Kind of. It's... complicated?"

Christ, that's a fucking understatement.

I lean back in my chair, stretch my legs out, arms crossing like I'm relaxed—like I'm not one wrong answer from punching through the drywall.

"Is it serious?" I ask, letting the question hang like smoke.

She shifts in her chair, still pretending to organize files that don't need organizing.

"You exclusive? Or dating around?"

Her heart's racing—I see it in the flutter at her neck, in the way her hand trembles before she tucks it under the table.

"Why?" she asks, trying to laugh it off like I haven't already stripped her bare.

I shrug, flash a crooked, careless smile.

Because I want to know if I have a snowball's chance in hell with you.

"Just curious about my partner's availability," I say. "For late-night surveillance. You know—the standard."

"Oh, *now* we're partners?" Her lips twitch like she doesn't know whether to laugh or strangle me with the nearest phone cord.

I can't deny it—I like it.

I want her tangled up. Just like I am.

She draws a breath, gathers whatever scraps of courage she has left, and says quietly,

"There is one guy. But... I could never date him."

Every muscle in my body locks.

I school my face into neutrality. Inside, something fucking ruptures.

"Why not?"

She doesn't look at me. Just stares at the table, voice small but certain.

"Because we work together."

The words hit harder than any punch I've ever taken.

For a second, everything inside me goes sharp and cold.

And like the idiot I am, my mind flashes to Graham.

The smug bastard who's asked her out twice—both times in front of me. She didn't say yes. But she didn't say no either.

Was it because I was there?

Because deep down, he's the kind of man she thinks she should want?

Polished. Shiny on the outside, rotting underneath.

Not the man who's been stalking her.

Not the man who kissed her like he needed her to breathe.

No—someone easy. Safe. Someone who wouldn't even know what to do with her if he had her.

The thought burns through me.

I stare down at my phone, knuckles white, jaw tight.

Trying to breathe past it.

Trying not to show it. But it's there.

In the tension wound tight in my chest.

In the way my hands clench.

In the way my jaw grinds.

Before I do something reckless, before I ruin everything, I shove up from the table. The chair screeches hard enough to make her jump.

I force my voice steady. Clap my hands once.

"Okay," I say, rougher than I mean to. "Let's get to work."

Because if I don't... I'll end up finding Graham.

And then she'll see exactly what kind of man I really am.

And there won't be any coming back.

It's later now, after a whole damn day of obsessing over this evidence.

Dexter begged for treats no less than twenty times—and Poppy gave in to every single one like he was a dying Victorian child begging for candy.

Not that I can blame her.

When he's not acting like a miniature linebacker, body-blocking me from sneaking into her room, the little bastard's actually a decent dog.

Scrappy. Loyal.

And smug as fuck—which somehow fits right in with her.

For the last hour, we've been stretched out on the battered leather couch in our second home, picking at greasy Chinese takeout, drinking warm beers, and swapping dumb stories about murderers like we aren't actively working a literal nightmare of a case.

It feels... good.

Better than good.

It feels fucking perfect.

Like this could be our life if the universe wasn't an asshole.

Us.

Takeout containers.

Her barefoot, half-tucked into my side without realizing it.

Perfect.

And it's killing me.

Because I want to reach over, pull her into my lap, and kiss her until she forgets every other man who's ever existed. I want to push her hair off her shoulders, feel her thighs around me, hear that little sound she makes when she loses herself.

But I can't.

Not after what she said earlier.

Someone I work with.

And all I can picture is Graham—the smirking bastard circling her like a vulture—waiting for a crack in her defenses.

But what if it wasn't him?

What if it was me she meant?

I replay every moment—every glance, every hesitation—trying to piece it together like the world's worst crime scene.

When I told her there was someone I was interested in, I practically begged her to walk through that door, to pry, to pick me apart like she does everything else.

She didn't.

And when she dropped her own comment, I dropped it too—too scared, too fucking wrecked to push.

What if we were both waiting?

I'm so lost in my own head I almost miss it—her phone lighting up beside her.

The text tone of her cell is a sharp little bark.

I glance over, catching the guilt flash across her face like she's been caught sneaking cookies.

"Did you record Dexter and make him your ringtone?" I ask, grinning.

She bites her lip, trying not to smile, the guilt morphing into something impossibly soft. "Maybe."

She leans forward, phone tilting toward me—and I catch the name on the screen.

Graham Vexley.

My jaw tightens.

At least it's not some nauseating shit like Grahamy-Poo or Daddy Graham—because if it was, I'd launch myself out the nearest window.

She scoffs loud enough to make Dexter lift his head and stare.

Rolling her eyes, she slaps the phone face-down like it personally offended her.

Sweet baby Jesus. There might be hope for me yet.

"Not in the Vexley fan club?" I ask, sipping my beer like I'm not fighting a goddamn war inside.

She shifts, angling toward me, one knee bent, her arm stretched along the couch back.

Head propped against her fist, she watches me under a lazy fringe of lashes.

Like she's getting comfortable.

Like she wants to be here with me.

"Are you kidding?" she says, nose wrinkling adorably. "Graham is disgust-o."

The relief that hits me could launch a thousand choirs.

The angels themselves could descend, harps blazing, and it still wouldn't match the shit-eating grin crawling up my face.

"I assumed," I say carefully, trying to sound indifferent, "when you said someone you worked with... you were talking about him."

The air shifts.

We both feel it.

The change.

The stakes.

Her gaze drops for a beat before she shakes her head— once. Small. Definitive.

"No," she says quietly. "I wasn't talking about Graham."

My pulse hammers.

Each breath feels heavier. Like the atmosphere is thickening between us.

I set my beer down, inching closer without even realizing it.

"So," I murmur, voice low, "you don't want Graham?"

Her eyes—those ocean-blue eyes—lift to mine.

And god help me, I see it.

The truth that's going to undo me.

Her voice is barely a whisper, but it cuts through me like a blade.

"No," she says, breath hitching. "I don't want Graham."

Now she's moving too.

Drawn together like magnets, slow and inevitable.

We don't back out.

I brush her jaw, feeling the tremble in her skin.

"So who do you want, Poppy?"

She licks her lips—nervous, sweet—and I nearly lose it.

But I wait.

I fucking wait.

Her gaze flicks to my mouth, then back to mine.

"You," she breathes. "I want you."

And that is all I fucking need. She meets me halfway.

Her mouth is warm, tentative.

I savor it, letting my lips move slow against hers, learning her kiss like it's a language only we speak.

She gasps, and my heart lurches.

I pull back an inch—just to see her.

Make sure she's real.

But that awe in her gaze strips me bare, and I'm gone.

I kiss her harder.

No hesitation. No patience.

The second kiss is wild. Hungry. Starving.

She moans, and I lick into her, swallowing every broken, needy sound.

She fists my shirt, dragging me closer.

My hands roam—her jaw, her hair, the slope of her waist—burning her into me.

I groan when she tugs my hair.

She kisses me back just as desperately.

Open-mouthed. Messy. Glorious.

She shifts—swings one leg over my lap, straddling me.

Like she was made to fit right here, thighs tight around my hips.

And fuck, she's grinding against me.

Slow at first—but the friction lights me up.

I'm hard. Painfully.

Her hips roll just right, and I feel how soaked she is through those thin fucking leggings.

It's a miracle I don't come.

I drop my forehead to hers—both of us panting—and slide my hands down to cup her ass, anchoring her to me.

She shudders when I grind again.

I kiss her throat, her jaw, her racing pulse.

"Tell me," I rasp, voice shredded. "Tell me you want this, Lollipop."

Tell me I'm not dreaming.

Tell me you're mine.

She presses tighter to me, lips brushing my ear.

"Yes," she gasps. "God, yes."

And that's it.

The last fucking thread holding me together.

43
Declan

I slide my hand around her waist, the other at her neck, guiding her down onto the couch like she's something precious and mine.

Her legs wrap around me, pulling me into the heat of her body.

I kiss her like I need her to fucking breathe.

My hips grind down, the hard ridge of my cock sliding over the soaked heat of her pussy, our clothes doing jack shit to stop it.

This sweet, broken little sound escapes her and she arches into me.

That fucking arch.

It guts me.

I'm so gone for her it's not even funny.

I cup her ass, squeeze hard, drag her closer, grind where she needs it.

The way she moans—breathless, needy—makes my cock throb.

I could stay here all night, devouring her mouth, teasing her clit, but I want all of her.

I tear my mouth from hers, kiss down her neck, her collarbone.

Her fingers tangle in my hair, her legs tightening like she's scared I'll stop.

Not a fucking chance.

I kiss down her stomach, heat rolling off her skin.

I need to taste her. Not as a masked stranger. As me.

I hook my fingers in her leggings and panties and yank them down, freeing one trembling leg.

Her thighs fall open. No hesitation. No shame.

And the look on her face—*Jesus.*

Cheeks flushed, lips swollen, eyes heavy with lust.

It wrecks me.

Makes me feral.

I drop to my knees and spread her open, staring at the glistening pink of her like it's the Holy fucking Grail.

Breathing deep, I lean in and lick her.

One slow stroke from her dripping entrance to her clit.

'Declan." Her back arches, and I clamp her thighs to keep her still.

I groan into her, nuzzling deeper, devouring her like it's the first real meal I've ever had.

"You have to be quiet," I murmur, voice rough and full of wicked promises. "Can't have anyone hearing how sweet you sound when you come."

She fists the cushion, covering her mouth to smother the sounds.

I lick her again—slow and teasing, flattening my tongue over her clit.

Then I suck it between my lips—soft, then harder—letting my tongue flick over her until her thighs start to tremble around my head.

"Fuck, Poppy," I growl, my voice vibrating through her. "You taste divine."

She gasps—louder now—and I ease up, chuckling darkly against her soaked cunt.

"Quiet, or I stop," I tease, nipping her inner thigh before sliding two fingers into her without warning.

She cries out, both hands flying to her mouth. Her hips buck, and I groan at her tight heat clenching around my fingers.

"So fucking tight," I pant, curling my fingers until her whole body seizes.

"You gonna come for me, pretty girl?"

She whimpers.

"At our office," I murmur, swirling my tongue around her clit. "Where anyone could walk in and see you like this."

She begs. "Please."

Rolls her hips into my mouth. "Declan."

I lick her harder, faster, syncing with my fingers until she's gasping, sobbing, body stiffening.

"That's it," I croon. "That's my girl. Come for me, Lollipop. I need it."

And when she does—Jesus Christ—she falls apart.

Legs clamping around my head, body shaking, wetness flooding my mouth.

I keep going until she's boneless and trembling.

Only then do I pull back, licking my lips, savoring every drop.

I look up at her—spread out, flushed, chest heaving. My heart fucking bursts at the sight of her.

Christ, she's never looked more beautiful.

Across the room, Dexter yawns.

I glance over. "He's looking at us."

She does too, a smirk curving her mouth. "If you only knew what he's seen—"

Before she can finish, she grabs my shirt and pulls me down with her.

"I want all of you," she whispers, breathless.

Her eyes flicker open—bright, wild, certain. "It's been a long time. And I need it to be you."

Fuck.

She's still gripping my shirt like I'm her anchor but one hand slides down the plain of my stomach and dips beneath my pants.

Her small hand squeezes around my throbbing cock, strokes me and I almost die on the spot.

Summoning every ounce of willpower, I keep my touch tender as I cup her jaw, brushing her flushed cheek. "Are you sure, baby?"

She nods, pink-cheeked. "Yes. I want you, Declan." She emphasizes with another squeeze along my dick and it jumps in response to her.

God help me.

I lift her gently, her thighs around my waist, and set her on the edge of the desk.

Her breath catches when I step between her legs.

She opens for me, palms braced behind her, gaze locked on mine—so open it ruins me.

I lose my shirt.

She smirks, raises her arms, and I pull off her crop top. Her bra follows, and my mouth finds her nipples—licking, sucking, pinching.

I reach into my pocket.

Condom in hand, I tear it open as I unzip my pants.

She arches a brow, eyes flicking down, then back up with a smirk. "You always carry those in your pocket?"

I lean in, gripping my cock. "When I'm with you?" My voice drops. "Always."

Her eyes drop to my cock and widen.

"Oh. Em. Gee," she breathes. "You've got to be kidding me."

I don't even try to hide my grin.

"Don't be scared of it," I murmur, stroking myself, teasing her entrance.

She shoots me a look—equal parts awe and panic. "Scared? No. Skeptical? Yes. That weapon of mass destruction won't fit anywhere respectable. How do you even walk?"

I chuckle, kiss her jaw. "Strategic pants."

She's still staring, lip caught between her teeth.

I lower my mouth to hers, tongue brushing the seam, asking instead of taking.

She opens for me.

God, she opens.

"Let me make you feel good, Lollipop," I whisper. "Let me show you."

"Yeah," Her thighs tighten around my hips as she nods.

I line myself up and ease in—inch by inch, watching her.

She gasps, hands flying to my shoulders.

"It's okay," I breathe. "You're doing perfect."

She grips me tight—hot, wet heaven. I groan, pushing deeper.

"Fuck," I pant. "You feel like sin."

She whimpers, nails biting into my skin. "Declan—"

"I've got you," I murmur, cupping her jaw as I bury myself. "So good, baby."

I hold still, letting her adjust, watching her soften, her breath catch.

Then we move.

A slow, grinding rhythm—deep, deliberate—until we're gasping, spiraling.

I shift my angle—she cries out, arching.

Her eyes flash down. "Wait—what is that?"

I smirk, roll my hips so the pubic piercing drags her clit.

Her mouth falls open.

"It's for grinding," I say, voice low.

And then I do just that.

Her head falls back. "Holy mother of pearl."

I grind harder, watching every moan, every shiver.

She's close—I feel it.

"Let go," I whisper, my thumb brushing her jaw, cock driving into her. "Come on, Lollipop. Let me feel you break."

She clenches around me, eyes locking on mine as she falls.

Trembling. Gasping.

Fucking beautiful.

"That's it," I growl. "That's my girl."

Her orgasm tears through her—and I don't look away.

Don't let go.

Because she's it. Everything I want.

I set her on trembling legs, turn her around, bend her over the desk.

"Hold the desk," I rasp. "Don't let go."

Her fingers curl around the edge like it's all that's keeping her grounded.

I step behind her, slide a hand between her thighs, line up.

Looking over her shoulder, eyes wide, she's every wet dream I've ever had.

One hard thrust—and I sink to the hilt.

She arches, gasping, body shuddering.

I slap a hand over her mouth, grip her hip, and fuck her.

No mercy.

Just thick, filthy thrusts that make the desk creak.

"That's it," I growl, my fingers on her clit. "Let me feel it again."

She moans into my palm, clenching around me, already close.

She said she's never come during sex.

That ends now.

I want to give her as many as she can take.

But not here.

Not like this.

I want to worship her.

Tell her the truth.

That I've been her shadow.

That I've loved her in silence.

But not yet.

So for now—I hold her tighter.

Like just thinking about telling her might make her vanish.

Might cost me everything.

I whisper filth into her ear—how she clenches every time I call her mine.

She moans louder, tightens so hard I see stars.

"You love it," I pant. "You love when I fuck you like this. Use you. Make you my sweet little whore."

She's gone again—legs shaking, body convulsing, crying out behind my hand.

"I—" she gasps. "I can't—"

"Yes you can," I growl, thrusting harder, rubbing her clit. "One more. Give it to me, Lollipop. Come for me again."

And she does.

She screams into my palm, body going rigid as she rides it.

That's it.

My control snaps.

I bury myself deep and come so hard I see white.

I groan—low, guttural—my mouth on her neck, collapsing into her, coming in long, shaking pulses.

She whimpers, still quivering when I slide out.

Already missing her. Already needing more.

I turn her around and kiss her.

Everything I can't say passes through our lips.

She rises on tiptoes, arms around my neck, smiling.

"Do you want to come to my house?" she whispers, nose brushing mine. I almost combust.

Before I can answer—boots in the hallway.

Like the fucking grim reaper of cockblocks:

"I see his light's on. I'll ask him."

Poppy freezes, eyes cartoon-wide.

I curse and we scramble.

She yanks up her panties and leggings, hopping like a frantic, half-naked fairy.

I wipe off, toss the condom, shove my still-hard cock back into my boxers, my pants, wincing as I zip myself up.

She pulls her top on.

Knock. Knock.

Dexter BARKS—loud enough to echo off every wall, gleefully announcing our sins to the whole fucking precinct.

I tug on my shirt, rake a hand through my hair, and make sure she's good before I open the door.

And there he is.

Lieutenant fucking Rourke.

Godfather. Boss. Ruiner of lives.

He holds a manila folder, brows lifting—clueless he just ruined the best moment of my life.

"Hey," he says. "Forensics had a question about—"

Then he sees her.

Poppy, pink from forehead to feet, fidgeting with her hair like she wasn't just railed within an inch of her life on a government-issued desk.

Dexter sits in his carrier like an innocent bystander—smug snaggletooth grin and all.

"I should—uh—go," she blurts, voice an octave too high. "Thanks for... dinner. The files. And... all that."

She zips the carrier, slings her tote, and bolts with a mortified "bye!" that echoes down the hallway.

Stroller be damned.

I just stand there, hand on the door, every muscle locked.

Rourke leans against the frame, arms crossed, smirk in place.

"You always this bad at playing it cool?"

I don't answer. Just stare after her, jaw ticking because no, apparently, I'm not fucking cool.

I'm one nose rub away from burning down my life.

And for what? A girl who hung the stars in the sky?

Yeah. Exactly for her.

"Just so we're clear," I mutter, dragging a hand down my face, "I officially hate you right now."

Rourke's smirk widens.

"And you're uninvited for Christmas."

He laughs as I slam the door in his smug goddamn face.

44
Poppy

Sundays are supposed to be for relaxing.

Self-care. Bath bombs. Maybe a Netflix marathon where I cry over fictional people's fake problems and pretend mine don't exist.

Which is why I'm currently standing in my living room with a green seaweed mask drying on my face, my hair wrapped in a pink microfiber towel, and Dexter freshly blow-dried and pawfumed—when there's a sharp, very official-sounding knock.

Dexter launches into a barking fit like he's guarding Fort Knox.

I shuffle to the door in my slippers and peer through the peephole.

Two plainclothes detectives. Not ones I recognize.

Fabulous.

I open the door, keeping my expression somewhere between confused neighbor and concerned citizen.

They flash badges.

"Detective Marsden," the older one says, voice rough like he chews gravel.

"Detective Liu," adds the younger—alert, too observant for comfort.

"We'd like to ask a few questions."

Oh good gravy.

I scoop Dexter into my arms, partly to hide my shaking hands, partly to weaponize his small-dog complex as "nerves."

Liu pulls out a photograph—and the air freezes in my lungs.

It's the rideshare driver. The Houseguest.

Victim number two.

The one Dexter nearly tried to French kiss via severed eyeball.

I blink slowly, tilting my head. "Sure. What's this about?"

"Just tell us what you know about him," Marsden says.

"Not much," I shrug. "He drove me home once. Picked me up again a few days later, made small talk about traffic."

I adjust Dexter, trying to burn off the nerves sparking under my skin.

"May I ask what this is about?"

"His body was pulled from the Hudson River," Marsden says.

Insert shocked gasp here. Maybe a "my goodness" for good measure.

"We found a storage unit registered under one of his aliases," Liu adds. "It had evidence suggesting a long history of crimes. Pictures. Journals. Recordings."

His eyes flicker to Dexter—still growling like a furious blender.

I press a hand to my chest. "What does that have to do with me?"

"Your name came up in one of the journals," Marsden says.

I feign horror like an Oscar contender.

"Holy guacamole," I whisper. "Are you saying... he's some kind of serial killer?"

They exchange a look.

"Could I have been one of his victims?" I ask, voice trembling.

Marsden nods.

"It looks that way. His notes about you stop abruptly after a certain night."

Yeah, the night I accidentally murdered him. But go off, detectives. You're doing amazing, sweeties.

I clutch Dexter a little tighter, my voice trembling.

I pull out my phone, open the rideshare app, and flash them the receipt.

"This was the last time I saw him."

Marsden glances at it. "That matches the timeline."

"Oh!" I widen my eyes. "He gave me a card... somewhere..."

I dig into the junk drawer and fish out the card I'd thrown in there minutes before slashing his throat.

"He said he sometimes does rides off the app."

I hand it over.

They both light up like kids on Christmas morning and try to hide it.

Amateurs.

Liu slides me his card. "If you remember anything else, call us."

I nod, all wide eyes and rattled innocence. "Of course."

The second the door shuts behind them, I bolt it and lean back.

They think I'm a survivor.

Some lucky girl who slipped through a serial killer's fingers.

But the truth is heavier, more dangerous.

It wasn't me who barely survived him.

It was *him* who didn't survive *me*.

There should be a manual for how to hide from two men and possibly the police at the same time.

If there were, I would've bought three copies—one to read, one to highlight, and one to cry into.

After the detectives left, I couldn't stay home. The walls pressed in, and the quiet started to sound like judgment.

Declan texted me, and my heart shuttered.

I don't know what to say. That I want him but I'm having an affair with a stalker?

So I got dressed, silenced both phones, and headed to the courthouse, hoping the weight of law and order might balance the chaos in my chest.

It's nearly nighttime. The building is practically empty, save for the low hum of fluorescents and the occasional flicker that makes me feel like I'm starring in a low-budget horror film.

I walk slowly through the evidence room, fingers trailing dusty bins and manila folders. I'm supposed to be pulling files for the trafficking case, but my mind is elsewhere—hunting for something I know should be here.

My mother's case file.

It was here. I've seen it.

"Where in the cinnamon toast crunch is it?" I whisper, walking the rows of forgotten boxes.

Nothing. No record.

Concern builds fast. Why would someone pull her case?

A soft thud from a few aisles over makes me freeze. My head whips toward the sound, heart slamming into my ribs.

"Hello?" I call, voice wobbling.

Silence.

I move down the rows, the scent of dust and cold metal sharp in my nose. Every step sounds like a gunshot.

I turn sharply at another faint noise. Nothing. Just shadows.

"Stop it," I mutter. "You're imagining things."

But my hands are shaking as I shove another box aside.

And that's when I nearly scream.

Declan rounds the corner—all calm, casual menace—scaring the ever-loving cannoli out of me.

"Jiminy Christmas!" I shriek as the box lid slips and smacks the floor.

Declan smirks, far too pleased with himself.

Why does he have to be so attractive?

"Didn't mean to sneak up on you," he says, leaning my dog stroller against a shelf like some smug urban knight. "Thought I should return Dexter's abandoned chariot."

I pick up the lid, brushing hair from my face.

"The last few days have been rough. You okay?"

I alphabetize a few files. "I'm fine."

"No, you're pretending you're fine. Big difference."

He moves closer, slow and deliberate. Not threatening—more like gravity.

I shift, resting my hip against a table, feigning boredom. "You gonna psychoanalyze me now, Detective Blackwood?"

Goodness, he really is just beautiful to look at. The snug-fitting T-shirt look is really doing it for me.

Tattoos and muscles on full display.

Forearm veins making things happen in my... you know... VIP lounge... if you catch my drift.

Declan tilts his head slightly, amusement dancing in his emerald eyes because he totally caught me ogling him.

I could be drooling.

I have no idea.

"No. Just thinking about some very fond memories I have of a couch," he says, stepping closer. "And a desk."

Feigning ignorance, I blink sweetly. "Really? I don't recall either of those."

The grin he gives me could melt ice caps.

"You don't remember?" His voice drops, backing me up to the wall. "Your legs wrapped around my head. You and me committing a felony in six positions on my desk—"

"You're exaggerating," I say, breathless, heart pounding.

"Am I?" His hands bracket the wall, caging me in. His heat, scent, presence devour the space. "Because I remember nearly seeing stars when this sweet hand"—he lifts mine, kissing my knuckles—"wrapped around my cock."

My thighs clench. Pickles and pie. Is it hot in here?

"Yeah, it's not ringing a bell." What am I doing?

He leans down, brushing his lips along my neck. I melt, bracing my hands on his chest like I could stop him.

"But..." I murmur, voice barely mine, "maybe if I had a refresher."

I have no idea where this sexual confidence is coming from.

He chuckles low against my skin—a sound so sinful it could probably get us arrested. "Well, I'm happy to volunteer as tribute."

Before I can think, before I can talk myself out of it, I let him kiss me.

Slow at first. Testing. Tasting.

I meet him halfway, my hands sliding into his hair, fingers tangling in the soft, thick strands I can't stop touching.

When I kiss him back, it's like striking a match to gasoline.

He growls low in his throat, pulling me tighter, his mouth slanting over mine with a hunger that burns down to my bones. His hands roam—one cupping the back of my neck, the other gripping my thigh, yanking it up and around his hip.

I gasp when he rolls his hips into me, the hard ridge of his erection grinding against the ache he's ignited deep inside me.

"I can't stop thinking about you," he growls against my mouth, voice shredded with need.

A moan escapes my lips when I press into him, desperate for more—for everything.

One minute, I'm melting into him like butter on a stack of sin, and the next—he's spinning me around and setting me on the evidence table with a startled yelp.

My back hits the cold metal. His body cages mine, his hand reaching up my shirt and finding my nipple. He feels so good.

But then he says words that snap the world in half.

"It's okay. I've got you."

I freeze.

Every molecule of warmth in my body drains straight into the floor because that one phrase brings me right back to my stalker.

The night I first saw him—the man in the skull mask, the shadow who cradled me after the blood, after the kill—that's what he said. Low and rough and terrifying and soothing all at once.

It's okay. I've got you.

It's like the ceiling falls on me.

For a second, the world tilts sideways—blood on my hands, a knife flashing, a body crumpling—and I can't breathe.

I hear that sentence echo around in my mind until I can't tell Declan's voice from my stalker's.

Between the homicide detective and the man who helped me clean up two murders.

What in the world am I doing?

Declan investigates murders for a living. I could never tell him what I've done. I could never show him the black stain that lives inside me forever now.

"No." My voice splinters, breaking apart into jagged pieces. I push my hands against his chest, desperate to put space between us. "Declan—this is a mistake."

I regret the words that flew out of my mouth as soon as I speak them. But I can't stop it.

He lets me go instantly, his hands dropping like I burned him.

"Poppy, talk to me," he says, voice low, raw.

I shake my head, blinking fast, trying to gather the crumbling parts of my sanity.

"This—between us," I manage to mutter, hating how hollow it sounds even to me. "I'm just—"

"Another notch on my belt?" he cuts in, his voice slicing the air between us. "Is that what you think this is?"

The pain in his voice makes me flinch. "I didn't say that."

I don't know what to do.

"We just... shouldn't be doing this," I insist, crossing my arms tight across my chest like maybe they can hold in all the guilt, the confusion, the gut-deep yearning still trying to crawl out of me.

He laughs once—sharp and humorless—and rakes a hand through his hair.

"You've got feelings for someone else," he says, voice steady in a way that terrifies me. "That's what this is."

I narrow my eyes, the urge to defend myself clawing up my throat. "That's none of your business."

His jaw flexes before he nods. "But that's what this is, right? You're kissing me and thinking about someone else?"

My throat tightens. My eyes sting. I want to scream no and yes and I'm sorry and I don't know what the heck I'm doing all at once.

"That's not fair," I whisper instead, because it's easier than being honest.

The silence between us is vicious, vibrating with everything we're not saying.

Declan stares at me like he's memorizing the last look before his execution.

Something inside me shatters.

"I thought you were brave, Poppy," he says, voice so low and wrecked it barely sounds like him. "I thought you knew you could trust me."

The finality in his words slices clean through me.

He turns and walks out, each step echoing like a countdown.

The door slams, the sound ripping through the space like a bullet.

And I'm left standing there—alone.

Poppy

Declan is gone.

The door slammed minutes ago, but the sound still echoes in the hollow spaces he left behind.

I stand there for a long moment, my fingertips brushing my lips, as if I can somehow trap the lingering feeling before it disappears completely.

When I close my eyes, the memories come rushing back—uninvited, vivid, sharp.

The first time I ever laid eyes on Declan Blackwood... just over a year ago.

Vivid green eyes. A scowl sharp enough to cut glass. That jawline that could've been copyrighted as a weapon.

I felt it even then—the pull.

Like a moth spotting a bonfire and thinking, *yes, let's definitely fly into that.*

And since then, it's only gotten worse.

Every time he looks at me, touches me, calls me Lollipop with that growl of his—I come alive in ways I don't even know how to explain.

It has never been about the fantasy.

Not about the shadowed figure who watches from the dark.

It has always been Declan.

Why did I doubt that?

The answer sinks into me like a stone: fear.

Fear of what happens when someone sees all the parts of me that I have to keep locked away.

Fear of the darkness that lives within me now.

But maybe... maybe Declan wouldn't run from it.

Maybe he would see past the monster I've become.

I wipe beneath my eyes and gather what little courage I have left.

I need to go after him. To tell him I choose him. About my stalker. Everything.

My heart is thudding so loudly I almost miss the soft creak of the door opening again.

I freeze, hope flaring so brightly inside me that it nearly makes my knees weak.

He came back.

I step into the center aisle between the rows of evidence shelves, my voice breaking the quiet.

"Declan—"

But it's not him.

It's Graham.

His suit jacket is wrinkled, his tie loose, his smirk slow and far too confident as he strolls into the room.

My stomach tightens instantly.

"I didn't expect to find you here," he says, voice low and overly familiar, his gaze dragging across me in a way that makes my skin crawl.

"Saw your name on the sign-in sheet," he adds. "Thought I'd stop by and say hello."

There is a heaviness that settles over me all at once, a dreadful kind of awareness that presses against my ribs and makes breathing feel suddenly difficult.

Even the clerk has gone home by now, so it's just the two of us.

"You always work this late?" he asks, tilting his head slightly, like he's genuinely curious. "And on Sundays?"

The tone is light, but something underneath it makes my heart pound harder.

"I was just leaving," I say, forcing my voice to stay steady. "I'm meeting Detective Blackwood."

The name grounds me, steadies me.

But Graham's mouth twists, just slightly, as though the name leaves a sour taste behind.

He steps forward—too close—cutting off my path to the door.

"Blackwood, huh." He repeats the name, drawing it out. "Well, let me walk you out."

The sharp scent of whiskey hits me before he even finishes the sentence.

Something inside me prickles and sharpens, the way it does when I look into the eyes of a serial rapist and know there is nothing but darkness that lurks inside them.

There's a split second where I think I can slip past him— duck under his arm, laugh it off, keep things light enough that he won't follow.

I'm wrong.

Graham shifts, blocking the exit with the casual ease of someone who's done this before. Someone who knows exactly how to corner prey without making it look like an attack.

My heart kicks hard against my ribs.

I glance behind me for my phone—false hope. My purse,

my keys, everything—still sitting neatly at the check-in desk on the other side of the door. An entire room of metal shelves stands between me and freedom.

"Look," I say, forcing a shaky smile, "it's been a long day. I'm really not in the mood, okay?"

De-escalate, Poppy. Like every terrible workplace safety video ever told you.

But Graham leans in closer, his breath sour, his smile a slow, curling thing that turns my stomach.

"You dress like you want someone to misbehave. Lucky me."

I look down. My top is slightly askew from moments ago with Declan.

Graham reaches for my arm. His hand closes around my wrist, fingers tightening.

"Let's not play dumb, sweetheart," he says, like we're sharing some inside joke. "You've been begging for this since the plea deal I offered you."

"Leave me alone, Graham."

I yank backward, trying to pull free, but he's faster—grabbing again, his fingers digging in harder this time.

"You've always had that look. The kind of girl who pretends to say no."

Panic ignites.

I twist hard out of his grip and bolt.

My tennies smack against the concrete floor, echoing wildly between the metal shelving. Rows blur past as I tear down the aisle, breath burning in my lungs, legs screaming to go faster.

Behind me, I hear his laugh—low, mocking, the sound of someone who thinks he's already won.

"Playing hard to get?" he calls. "That's fine. I like a chase."

I veer down a side aisle, heart thundering, desperate for something—anything—that looks like a way out.

But he's faster.

He tackles me from behind, knocking the air from my body. We crash to the floor, the impact rattling my teeth. Pain blossoms sharp and immediate along my hip and shoulder.

Before I can scramble up, his tongue is running up the length of my neck—sloppy, wet, disgusting.

One hand yanks at my top, the delicate fabric tearing easily.

The other hand fumbles clumsily with his belt.

I kick, hard, but it barely slows him down.

"Stop—get off me—STOP!" I scream, thrashing, fighting, nails clawing at any part of him I can reach.

"You're gonna love this, princess," he grunts. "You just don't know it yet."

No.

I throw my knee up as hard as I can, catching him in the gut.

He gasps, loosening his grip just enough for me to kick again.

I scramble away from him, tripping as I try to get up.

Without thinking, I grab the first thing I see—the compact, sad little pink doggy stroller, still neatly collapsed and tucked against the wall thanks to Declan.

With both hands wrapped firmly around the handle, I swing with everything I have.

It makes a sickening crack when it connects with his temple.

He stumbles backward, slamming into the edge of a table hard enough to send papers and evidence bins flying.

I don't wait to see if he's staying down.

I run, breaking hard out of the evidence room door.

I snatch up my purse without breaking stride, heart hammering so loud it drowns out everything else.

I fish my keys out of the bottom of the bag, and both hands slam against the exit door, the bang echoing behind me as I run into the night air that feels too cold against my burning skin.

I don't stop until I reach my car, my hands fumbling with the keyfob, my breathing wild and uneven.

I hurl myself inside, slam the door, smash the lock button —all in one frantic motion that leaves me gasping like a fish yanked from water.

My hands clutch the steering wheel like it might anchor me, like it might stop the shaking.

It doesn't.

My pulse thrums at the base of my skull, hot and panicked, and for a moment, all I can do is squeeze my eyes shut and pray the roaring in my ears will fade.

Some instinct—some deep, primal pull—makes me lift my gaze. Makes me look back at the building.

Back at the window where I feel his eyes on me.

Graham smirking, a trail of blood smeared down his face.

Watching me like I'm the punchline to some sick joke.

He doesn't move. He doesn't come after me. He just stands there, and my stomach rolls at his stillness.

I grab my phone with shaking fingers, tapping the screen so hard I nearly miss the button.

Call one: Declan.

Straight to voicemail.

"No," I beg under my breath, trying not to cry, trying not to spiral. "Please, Declan."

Call two: Declan.

Voicemail.

Again.

This time, I whimper. A pathetic, broken sound that shreds what little pride I have left.

In pure desperation, I yank my burner phone from my tote with trembling hands.

I hit the call button, and it barely rings once before he picks up.

"Poppy," his voice says, low and urgent.

And just like that—like flipping some invisible switch—I shatter.

The tears come hot and unstoppable, my words tumbling out in a breathless, broken mess.

"He—he tried—he touched me—I ran—I—I—"

My breath hiccups against the sobs clogging my throat.

His voice changes instantly. Sharp and dark. Furious in a way that vibrates through the tiny speaker and makes me want to curl into it, to wrap myself in it like armor.

I hear the roar of an engine in the background.

"Who," he snarls. "Who the fuck touched you?"

I hiccup again, wiping at my eyes.

"I'm okay—I got away. I just— It was Graham. This guy I work with. He ripped my shirt. He was going to—"

My choked sob cuts off the rest of my words.

Silence on the line. The kind of silence that promises very bad things.

"Are you safe now?" he asks, voice clipped.

"Yes. I'm in my car. Outside evidence." I'm panting, winded. "Will you just stay on with me while I drive home?"

"No. Go home." His tone leaves no room for argument. "Don't stop. Make sure he doesn't follow you. I'll handle it."

I grip the phone tighter, my fingers still trembling as the

adrenaline that was just rushing through me begins to ebb away.

"What are you going to do?" I ask, even though deep down, I think I already know.

There's a soft, lethal exhale.

"I'm going to make sure he never touches you again," he says—so calm, it's terrifying.

46

Declan

The city sleeps like it doesn't know what it let happen.

The street in front of her house is dark—no porch lights, no windows lit up. Just shadows and silence and the bitter taste of regret burning the back of my throat.

I shouldn't have left her alone.

I should've been there to make sure she never had to carry that weight on her own.

But I wasn't.

When the door creaks open, she's already changed—soft leggings and an oversized shirt that hangs off one shoulder. Hair twisted around in a messy bun.

Utterly beautiful. Even in her sadness.

I see the bruises before she can hide them.

A red imprint blooming at the edge of her cheekbone.

The angry circles on her wrist where he grabbed her.

I reach for her without thinking.

My thumb grazes the mark on her face like I can erase it—like I can take back the moment it was made.

"You okay?"

My voice comes out lower than I mean it to, raw with things I'll never say right.

She nods. A small, quiet motion that makes my chest feel like it's going to cave in.

I step back.

"Come on."

She hesitates, standing in the doorway like she's weighing something.

I don't move. Don't push. Just give her space to decide.

Eventually, she locks the door behind her and follows me to the car.

This silence buzzes—taut and electric, filled with all the words we're not saying.

She glances at me when she thinks I'm not looking.

Her hands twist in the hem of her shirt like she's trying to keep herself from unraveling.

I don't look back.

If I look at her now, I'll say too much.

Do too much.

And tonight isn't about what I want, it's about what she needs.

We leave the lights behind.

Drive past the edge of town where the skyline fades into industry and gravel.

Out past the factories, past the mills, past everything that even pretends to be civil.

The road narrows.

Dirt and trees swallow the car like a secret.

The kind of place where no one asks questions. Where no one comes looking.

Finally, I pull up to the old barn and kill the engine.

The world outside falls into silence so deep you could drown in it.

I sit for a second. Then turn to her.

"What happens next is your choice."

Her brow furrows—cautious, tired, still haunted.

"You don't have to go in," I say. "You can take the car. Turn around, drive back to the highway. It's a straight shot from here. No tricks. No strings."

I let the offer hang there. Not because I want her to take it. But because she needs to know this isn't about me.

Not this part.

This part's hers.

Then I open my door and step into the chill.

Gravel crunches under my boots as I move toward the barn.

I don't look back.

She'll either come or she won't.

But if she comes . . . she'll never be the same.

The barn groans as I push the doors open.

Rotting wood. Rusted hinges. Cold air thick with the smell of old hay and newer blood.

She steps in behind me. I hear the gravel shift under her boots, the slight hitch in her breath.

The dark swallows everything at first. No lights. Just the low moon bleeding through the gaps in the boards.

Graham is waiting for her.

Strapped to an old steel dental chair, center of the room.

Wrists—what's left of them—bound to the arms.

Ankles chained to the bolts I sank into the floor myself.

Blindfolded. Gagged. Noise-canceling headphones tight over his ears. Dried blood around his mouth.

Her gaze drops—and she chokes out a gasp when she notices his hands.

Laid neatly across his chest, palms up. Like he's praying.

The ends of his wrists are blackened and cracked. Burned

shut to stop him from bleeding out. Not because I was feeling merciful.

Because I wanted him conscious and waiting.

She doesn't move. Doesn't cry. Doesn't scream.

Just stares.

And I watch her, not him.

Because he's not the point.

She is.

She starts moving.

Just walks a slow circle around him—around us—like she's trying to make sense of the angles. Of the ruin.

Like she's waking up with each step she takes.

Her gaze skims down to the charred stumps at the ends of his arms. She stares long enough that I know she's picturing how it happened.

But then she spots the cut. The small one high on his neck, just below the jaw.

She steps closer, tilts her head. "What's that?"

I answer without hesitation. "I severed his vocal cords."

She blinks. "Why?"

"So his begging wouldn't interrupt you."

Her breath hitches but she doesn't step back.

Her voice is quiet. Careful. "Interrupt me from what?"

I say nothing, just turn and roll the tray over from the shadows behind me.

The wheels rattle over the concrete, then stop with a soft squeak.

She looks down.

Everything's been laid out with intention.

A scalpel.

A standard six-inch combat knife.

A pair of trauma shears.

A meat hook.

A small hammer.

A blowtorch with a full butane tank.

Surgical clamps.

And a box of pink nitrile gloves.

She stares at it all, expression unreadable but not horrified.

"What happens next," I say, "is yours."

She doesn't answer. Just turns back to Graham. She watches his chest rise and fall—tight, shallow breaths.

I can see the war behind her eyes but I say nothing.

She doesn't need my voice in this.

"Well," she says, her hands trembling slightly as she reaches for the gloves, "he always did talk too much."

My smirk is barely there as I cross my arms over my chest and lean against the pole.

She slides them on, and as she fixes each finger, her breathing changes.

Quicker. Sharper.

A tear slips down her cheek, just one, but it cuts deeper than any blade on the tray.

Like she's remembering what it felt like to be alone with him.

To be scared. Cornered.

She steps closer, staring at his bound, blindfolded form as she takes the hunting knife. Its silver serrated blade reflects the soft yellow light in the barn.

Her hand moves—fast and hard.

The first slash is across his chest. Deep. Vicious.

He jerks violently, head snapping back.

Didn't see it coming. Couldn't hear it.

His mouth opens in a silent scream, body writhing against the chains.

She watches him twitch—then slashes again.

And again.

Her fear melts into rage.

"How many?" she asks, her voice cracking.

Another cut, sharper this time. "How many women did you do this to?"

Another. "How many had to survive you?"

Another.

Her arm moves in a blur, each slice carving a memory into flesh.

Until her chest heaves and her body trembles and her mouth parts like she might finally scream—

—but doesn't.

Instead, she stills.

Pulls in one long breath then another before her eyes flick down to the tray.

To the tools meant for more delicate work.

She sets the blade down and reaches for the forceps.

Then selects a smaller, cleaner knife.

She moves to his head.

Grabs his tongue with the forceps and yanks it forward.

He gags, chokes, thrashes weakly.

She doesn't blink.

"You're disgusting," she says.

"You used this to make women feel like nothing. To make me feel like nothing."

She tilts her head, studies the stretch of meat between her fingers.

"Never again."

Then she severs it in one clean motion.

Blood floods his mouth in an instant. He convulses—sputtering, choking, but he can't scream.

His vocal cords are already gone.

What comes out is nothing more than a wet, rattling hiss.

She watches him suffer, unflinching.

Then whispers, almost to herself,

"I wonder which will kill you first . . . choking or blood loss."

She takes the chef's knife—not her mother's.

But I brought it anyway.

Thought she'd want it near—thought it might mean something.

She draws the blade across his neck, slow and deliberate.

He jerks against the restraints—his spine arching.

One of his severed hands slips off his chest and hits the floor with a dull *thud*.

Rolls once.

Stops behind her shoe.

She doesn't look at it.

Keeps her eyes fixed on Graham.

The man she's killing to take back what he tried to take from her.

"I've thought about it, you know," she murmurs.

Her voice is so quiet I almost miss it.

"Killing."

I keep my eyes on her, but I don't answer.

She's not talking to me. Not really.

"The other day, in court. A rapist was back again. A fresh victim."

She swallows.

"I sat there watching him talk to the judge about what an upstanding citizen he is. And I pictured it. Killing him. Not out of rage—just to . . . correct the imbalance."

She looks up at me.

And for the first time since she walked into this place, her expression looks vulnerable.

"Why do you still want me . . . after this?"

There is zero hesitation in my answer.

"It was always going to be you after this."

She holds my gaze for a beat.

And something in her—fractures.

Not in a way that breaks her.

In a way that frees her.

Then the last breath rattles out of Graham's chest, and there's nothing left but meat and silence.

She looks at him a moment, realizing his life is gone. It's hers now.

And says, without emotion,

"Hm. Bled to death."

Poppy

The silence wraps around me like a warm, weighted blanket, tucking me into a place I've never been—still, heavy, peaceful.

Then the other side of me—the shrieking, panicked side that still pretends she's normal—wakes up and starts screaming.

What have you done?

The first breath feels wrong.

My chest rises and falls like there's a cinder block on it, pressing down, daring me to crumble.

I take one shaky step back and catch my foot on something.

Looking down, my vision spins as the barn sways.

It's a hand. His.

I killed him.

A loud, rhythmic tapping snaps in my face. Tap. Tap.

His blood—dripping off the chair, pooling on the dirt floor.

I drop the knife and my throat tightens.

"It's okay."

It sounds like Declan, but I see the mask—my stalker's. Three of them, as my vision multiplies.

I feel like I'm going to throw up.

"Just stay with me."

Instead—I run.

I bolt from the barn, adrenaline crashing through me.

The night air hits like a slap. The sky stretches black and endless, broken by clawing trees.

I don't know where I am.

Woods. Darkness. That's all I have.

I gasp, each inhale sharp and shallow, and run—wild, aimless.

Branches snag my arms, slashing stinging lines across my skin.

The ground dips and rises, nearly sending me sprawling.

But I don't stop.

I need space.

To get away from him—from the man who knows what I've done.

From myself.

I don't make it far because he's right behind me.

"Stay away!" I scream.

It shatters the night, but he doesn't slow.

Of course he doesn't.

He's too patient.

Too sure.

Like he knows something I don't.

"You don't get to touch me again!"

"No?"

His voice slices through the dark—low and rough, thick with something that sends a shiver through me.

"Then why," he growls, closer now, "are you running just slow enough for me to catch you?"

I stumble, heart lurching.

Because he's right.

Somewhere deep down, some traitorous part of me isn't running to get away.

I'm running to be caught.

And he does.

Catches me mid-stride—one brutal, effortless motion—and spins me into the side of an old, rusted truck half-eaten by vines and time.

The metal kisses my back with a cold slap.

I thrash. Kick.

"Don't—don't—" I pant, but it's useless.

He captures my wrists, pinning them above my head like it's nothing, his body flush against mine, every hard line of him a cage.

His voice is steady. Dark. A slow bleed of heat over my skin.

"Say it. Say what you are."

"I'm nothing," I choke out, my voice cracking on the lie.

His laugh is low. Dangerous.

"No. You're lying, Sunny."

I squeeze my mouth shut, shaking my head.

His thigh wedges between mine, pressing into the ache I'm desperate to ignore. His size—immovable. A fortress of hunger.

"Say another lie out of that slut mouth," he growls, "and I'll fill it for you."

I press my lips tighter, biting back the flood clawing at my insides.

But the words tumble out anyway.

"I'm not lying. Let me go," I hiss, thrashing with a useless surge of adrenaline. "I'm not anything."

He doesn't budge.

Leans in, mouth brushing my ear.

"Wrong fucking answer."

He drags me to the ground so fast I gasp.

Rough hands in my hair.

The clink of a belt.

Tears burn. Anger and heartbreak twisting like a blade.

"Get away from me," I croak.

But he only snarls, "Stop telling yourself lies."

He pulls out his cock—long, thick, painfully hard.

And my thighs betray me, clenching as slickness pools fast enough to make my head spin.

I whimper. I know how pathetic it sounds.

"Open your lying fucking mouth," he commands, fisting himself, gripping my hair.

The blunt head nudges my lips—taunting, inescapable.

"Wrap your lips around me, Sunshine. We both know you're starving for it."

I open my mouth to tell him to go to hell.

I really do.

But the second my lips part, he thrusts deep.

My gag reflex triggers, tears springing to my eyes.

He grunts—low, filthy satisfaction rumbling from his chest.

Drives in again, slow but firm.

Owns me.

He talks to me the whole time.

Scolding. Praising.

Telling me how beautiful I look choking on the truth.

"That's it," he rasps. "Take it. Take me deep, baby. You love this. You love me owning your mouth."

I claw weakly at his thighs, trying to push him back. But it's a lie.

And he knows it.

Every time he slides into my throat, I suck harder on the way out—rolling my tongue, hollowing my cheeks like I'm trying to wreck him the way he's wrecking me.

"Look at me," he snaps, yanking on my hair so I have no choice.

I do—and almost lose what's left of my sanity.

His pupils are blown, voice a growl soaked in feral hunger.

"Relax your jaw," he orders.

I obey.

Loosen and open for him.

The next thrust is deeper. Then deeper still.

He groans, dragging the sound out like it's torn from somewhere primal.

"Keep your eyes on me, baby." he breathes, petting my hair. "Be my filthy fucking girl and look at me while you suck my cock."

He slides in again, each thrust dragging more praise and command.

"Slide your hand down your pants," he growls.

I don't.

A flicker of rebellion that I can hold onto.

But she's dying.

He was ready for my protest. He grips the back of my head, pushing himself deep into my throat. I can't breathe.

My eyes water and I gag.

"Fucking do it." He grunts. "Slide those fingers along that sweet cunt of yours and I'll let you breathe."

My hand trembles as I slip it past my waistband.

I almost sob at the contact on my wanting center.

He slides out, letting me breathe before moving back in.

"Touch yourself, Sunshine. Don't you dare lie again," he says, voice ragged.

I slide my fingers through my panties and shudder.

It's shameful how wet I am.

"Show them to me," he demands.

I lift my hand, fingers glistening.

Proof.

He smiles. Dark. Hungry. Devouring.

Like I'm the only thing he's ever wanted.

He hauls me up and throws me over his shoulder.

"Put me down."

I bang on his back and kick until his palm smacks my ass—hard.

"Be still."

He carries me back to the barn, sets me down against the car that brought us here.

I move on instinct and knee him. Hard.

The sound—half grunt, half growl—is so satisfying I almost smile.

I run.

Or try to.

A few staggering steps—then he's on me again, slamming me into the car.

The metal rattles beneath us.

"Give me your fucking shoes," he snarls, hand pressing cruelly into my back.

I whimper, twisting, but he shoves me down until my cheek scrapes cold metal.

My shoes are ripped off—one after the other—and tossed through the open window like discarded confetti.

"Take off your pants," he commands.

The air is cold against my skin, but my face burns as I obey, sliding my leggings down and kicking them away.

He tosses them in after my shoes.

Now I'm standing there—half dressed, half ruined.

A shirt. A bra. Nothing else.

Naked from the waist down. Exposed in every way that matters.

One of his hands captures both wrists, pinning them high against the door.

The other slides down—slow and brutal—between my legs.

I gasp, a broken sound, because I'm soaked.

Humiliation lances through me.

"You can lie to me," he murmurs against my neck, "but not to your body."

I shake my head, tears leaking hot and fast.

Ashamed. Furious.

But my hips betray me, bucking into the heel of his palm.

"You think you can kill a man and still pretend to be sweet and clean?"

His fingers work me—punishing strokes against my clit, plunging into me with no mercy.

I thrash, whimper, shudder—but I'm not trying to get free.

Not really and he knows it.

I know it.

And it's killing me.

"You want this," he growls. "You need this."

Each word is a nail.

He keeps coaxing me—mouth filthy at my ear, hand filthier between my legs—dragging me closer.

"Please," I cry out, barely a whisper. I was supposed to be a demand to stop. To let me go. Instead- "Please don't stop."

"Beg for it," he commands.

"I need it," I gasp. "I need everything."

"Admit what you are, Poppy."

I shake my head—a pitiful attempt.

His fingers thrust harder, grinding into hypersensitive nerves, and I sob the words before I can stop myself.

"I'm a killer," I choke, the admission tearing out of me like a wound.

He exhales like he's been holding his breath for years.

"Again," he demands.

"I'm a killer," I whisper, tears still streaming.

"And you're mine," he says roughly, lowering his mouth to my ear. "Say it. Say you belong to me."

My whole body trembles.

He plunges two fingers inside—stroking deep, relentless—until I can't think, can't breathe, can't do anything but feel.

"I—I belong to you," I gasp.

"Good girl," he breathes, growling at my throat.

He lifts me like nothing, my legs locking around his waist on instinct, carrying me to the hood of the car.

The slap of cold metal steals my breath.

One hand fists his cock, lining up.

My brain catches up just enough to blurt, "You don't have on a condom," like that should matter when I'm half-naked on a car in the woods after committing murder.

"I love your idea of foreplay, Sunshine."

I can feel him grin behind the mask as he thrusts deep, driving a brutal moan from my throat.

"I don't need a fucking condom, baby," he growls. "I know you got your tubes tied."

The words are a slap and a balm.

A filthy promise that slices through the last threads of sanity.

He yanks my bra up, pinching my nipple hard enough to make me cry out—timing it perfectly with a slam of his hips.

"You can't get pregnant," he rasps, "and you belong to me, Sunny. I fucking own you."

His hands spread my thighs—it feels obscene. Vulgar.

And it's perfect.

I can see everything.

Where we're joined.

Where he's stretching me.

Pounding into me with greedy thrusts.

"I'm gonna fill you with my cum," he snarls. "Have you dripping with me."

I do belong to him.

God help me, I do.

The sounds are filthy.

Groans. Growls. Skin on skin.

His voice in my ear:

"You wanted this."

"I watched you. I waited for you."

We move like we've done this a thousand lifetimes.

Wild. Desperate and hungry.

His thrusts turn sharper.

His thumb finds my clit—rubbing tight, relentless circles.

"Tell me how much you love my cock," he demands.

"I love it," I breathe, half-choked.

"Not good enough," he growls and smacks my clit—sharp, stinging—and I cry out.

Before I can gasp, he spits on it, thumb smearing it messily.

"Say the words, filthy girl."

I stutter, the words trembling on my tongue.

"I—I love your cock."

"Where?"

"My mouth," I whimper. "I loved—your cock in my mouth."

He groans like it's the sweetest thing he's heard, thrusts turning punishing.

"And where else?"

"My... my pussy," I sob.

"Fuck yes, baby," he snarls. "Say it."

"I love your cock in my pussy."

"Doing what?"

"Fucking me. Fucking my pussy with your big cock."

"That's it. That's my good fucking girl."

I feel another orgasm cresting—blinding, brutal.

"And you're gonna love it when I take your ass too, aren't you, little slut?"

I freeze.

When I don't answer fast enough, he smacks my clit again—sending me headfirst into another climax.

I scream, not caring who hears.

"Yes," I sob. "Yes, I want you to take my ass."

The pleasure burns so hot I can barely breathe.

We come together—violent, breathless—bodies crashing like a storm.

His hand clamps on my bottom.

My fingers rake down his back—desperate.

And just as his hips stutter and he groans into my neck, I hear it.

That lazy, mocking humor under the growl.

"I told you we'd work on your dirty talk."

Casual. Familiar.

Declan.

The realization crashes into me, shattering everything.

It's been him the whole time.

And somehow—deep down—I already knew.

I freeze.

The cold slams into me.

I shove at his chest, breaking free.

"Poppy."

I yank my pants from the car, fumbling them on with shaking hands.

"Poppy, just wait."

"Take it off," I rasp.

Silence.

"Take it off, Declan," louder now. "Take the mask off."

He hesitates.

For one breath, I think he won't.

But then he does in an instant.

Declan Blackwood.

Wrecked. Familiar. Him.

Like the earth cracked open and spit out the truth I never wanted.

The air whooshes from my lungs.

"No."

I stagger, the ground tilting.

Tears hit instantly.

"You..." I choke. "It was you?"

He flinches.

"Baby, please—"

"This whole time—you lied. You made me feel crazy."

My hands shake.

"You followed me," I gasp. "You touched me. You—"

My voice breaks.

Then cold: "The murders."

I cover my mouth.

He watched. Even cleaned them up.

"Oh, God."

He steps forward.

"Poppy—"

"Stay away from me!" I shriek, backing into the car.

I scrub at my mouth as the other hand fumbles for the door.

His face twists.

He grabs both arms.

"Please, don't go," he says, voice breaking. "Let me explain."

"No. You're a monster," I spit, gripping the handle like a lifeboat.

"I love you."

It tears me in half.

I slap him before I realize I've moved.

The sound cracks like a whip.

"I hate you," I sob.

He steps back, hand covering the mark.

I throw myself inside the car.

"Poppy, please."

His voice breaks but I can't look at him.

Can barely see.

I peel away in a scream of tires and dust, leaving him in the dark—

Mask dangling from his hand like he just watched the only part of him that mattered disappear.

And maybe he did.

Poppy

By the time I pull into my driveway, it's like the ground beneath me isn't even real anymore.

I don't remember the drive. Or breathing.

Only the sound of my own heartbeat—frantic, fractured—ricocheting through my chest.

I leave the keys in the ignition.

It takes everything I have just to get out of the car, to stumble up the steps, to shove open the door like the house might disappear if I don't reach it fast enough.

Dexter barks once in the distance, but it's just white noise in a world that's gone quiet in all the wrong ways.

I rip the burner phone off the counter and snap it in two.

The plastic cracks sharply in my hands. I toss the pieces into the trash like they might start burning if I keep them close.

After Dexter visits his favorite potty bush, I scoop him up and head inside.

I engage every lock I installed back when I believed protection meant something.

If my head even hit the pillow, I don't know—but somehow I made it to my room.

Slept in my clothes. Woke up wanting to burn them.

Maybe it was hours. Maybe days.

But the car is gone.

Disappeared like it was never there.

Like it could've just been a bad dream.

Instead, three origami cranes sit on my bedside table.

Tears burn my eyes as I fist them, Crumple them into a ball and throw them on the floor.

I should cry or scream, or punch something just to feel the pain.

But all I feel is . . . hollow.

Like whatever was left of me rotted away in the rain.

Instead, I get dressed.

I go to the store.

I buy the things a woman buys when she's preparing to unmake her own life—signal detectors, new locks, Wi-Fi scramblers.

The man at the checkout couldn't tell if I was FBI or just insane.

When I get home, I start searching.

I tear through my house in silence.

No curses. No cries.

Just the steady, mechanical work of a woman determined to strip every lie down to its studs.

Fifty.

I find fifty hidden cameras before I lose count.

In vents.

Outlets.

Seams of picture frames.

Corners of my life where I thought no one could reach me.

They were everywhere.

He was everywhere.

The man who watched me.

The man who waited for me to fall apart so he could catch me.

The man who made me fall in love with him.

Twice.

At once.

I rip the last camera from its hiding place with shaking hands, tossing it into the pile growing like rot on the dining room table.

Dexter sticks close, engaged in his own frantic mission.

He holds a stuffed giraffe by the neck, sprinting back and forth in a brutal battle that Dexter is determined to win.

I don't turn on the TV.

I don't reach for music.

I don't text my mom for her latest fae-porn update.

I just clean.

I bleach the kitchen.

I scrub the floors.

I wipe down every surface like I'm trying to erase finger-prints I know are mine.

It's not about being clean.

It's about starting over.

It's about letting the old Poppy die here, quietly, between lemon cleaner and tears that won't fall.

I don't know who I am without the fear.

Without the fantasy.

Without the lies.

I don't know who I am now that I know the truth—

That the man who loved me was never a stranger in the shadows.

He was always right there.

And the worst part isn't the betrayal.

It isn't the horror.

It's the ache.

The cold, hard ache that keeps whispering that even after everything . . .

I still love him.

I still want him.

But I don't know how to forgive him.

I don't know how to forgive myself for wanting him.

So I scrub the counters.

Again.

And again.

And again.

Until my skin is raw and my hands are cracked.

Until the only thing left in this house is silence—

And the woman I've become.

Standing at the threshold of something she can't walk back from.

Something permanent, dark.

I don't know where to put all of this. The emotion. The wreckage of the last few days.

I sit on my bed, legs folded under me, wearing an oversized sleep shirt.

My nails are wrecked—torn down so far the skin around them is rimmed in angry red, stinging every time I flex.

I've been picking at them without realizing, worrying the flesh until it bleeds.

It hurts.

But not enough.

Nothing feels like enough anymore.

Not the way my body throbs between my thighs.

Not the weak vibration buzzing against my skin.

Not the frantic press of my hand, desperate for some tiny relief from the emptiness clawing through my chest.

I whisper it out loud—maybe to myself, maybe to the dark: "I want to feel it. The way you do."

I want to understand what he saw when he looked at me. I want to see it too.

My hand slips away from the vibrator. It falls to the mattress with a soft, pathetic thud.

I open the nightstand. The small switch knife inside gleams under the low light.

I pick it up.

The handle fits my palm like it was made for me.

Breathing shallow, I shift, pulling my leg up until the tender skin of my inner thigh is exposed.

My pulse thrashes in my ears.

But my hand is steady as I press the tip of the blade into my skin—just deep enough to drag a letter there. Slow. Deliberate.

D.

For Declan.

For Devil.

For Destruction.

For Don't forget who you belong to.

Blood beads up immediately—bright, hot, beautiful.

It doesn't hurt the way I thought it would.

It's sharper. Cleaner.

It cuts through the noise screaming in my head.

I exhale, feeling the first true breath I've taken in days.

The crimson welling from the letter is hypnotic.

I dip a fingertip into it, smearing the warmth in a slow, reverent stroke.

First across my tongue—just a swipe, a taste, something primal and broken clawing forward.

Then down to the vibrator still buzzing weakly on the bed.

I drag my bloodstained fingers across the silicone head. Marking it. Claiming it.

Turning it from something mundane into something mine.

I don't realize I'm crying until I taste the salt and blood together on my lips.

But it's not sadness.

It's worship.

Surrender.

I lie back on the bed, the knife still gripped in one hand, the vibrator in the other.

And for the first time in days, I don't feel hollow.

I feel claimed.

Even if he's not here.

Even if I told him I hated him.

Even if I don't know how to forgive him . . . or myself.

He still owns me.

Maybe that's what I was always waiting for.

I spread my legs wider, my breath hitching, thighs trembling as I press the blood-slicked vibrator against my clit.

The jolt of pleasure is violent. Sharp.

My hips buck instinctively, chasing it even when my mind screams to pull away.

I ride the edge, dragging the toy lower, pressing it against the fresh, angry letter.

Pain slices through the haze—white-hot and exquisite.

I whimper, rolling my hips in tiny, desperate circles.

The sting, the heat—it sharpens everything. Makes it real in a way nothing else can.

"You wanted me to hurt," I whisper. "You wanted me ruined."

And I am.

I picture it so vividly I can almost see it.

Declan in the doorway. My stalker in the shadows.

Watching. Letting me fall apart because he made me this way.

I imagine him crossing the floor. Pinning me down. Tying my wrists so tight the ropes bite.

Blade in hand, carving more letters into my trembling body.

His hands roaming. His mouth devouring. Filling me until there's no part left untouched.

I moan, pressing the toy harder against myself.

The pressure crests—my body stiffening, heart pounding.

When it crashes over me, I tip my head back for the sobbing cry that rips free.

My thighs spasm. My vision goes white.

I collapse back against the mattress, panting like my lungs might burst.

The ceiling stares back, blank and uncaring, as I tremble through the aftershocks.

"He'll know now," I whisper. "He'll see it. He'll know I'm his."

There's no coming back from this and I don't want to.

By the time I pull fresh sheets onto the bed, I almost feel human again.

Almost.

The wound on my thigh throbs, a slow, steady reminder that nothing is truly clean anymore. Nothing is untouched.

I'm smoothing out the last corner of the bed when my phone buzzes on the nightstand. I grab it before the anxiety can take root.

"Poppy Hartwell."

"This is Officer Matthews. We've got a new victim intake at St. Peter's. She requested a female advocate."

The call is standard. Expected. A lifeline of normalcy tossed into the storm.

It would be nice if trauma kept business hours, but no such luck.

"I'll be right there."

I dress quickly, shove the phone in my pocket, sling my bag over my shoulder, and leave Dexter in charge of security.

The drive is short. Familiar streets blur past in streaks of light and shuttered storefronts.

For the first time in days, my head feels clear. Anchoring myself in someone else's pain lifts the weight of my own.

I park in the side lot and enter through the ER, nodding at the tired officer behind the desk.

"Room 402," I tell him, flashing my badge.

It's nearly three a.m. The guard barely looks up from his newspaper.

The night shift never gets too precious about protocols.

The elevator hums to the fourth floor. Right wing.

Which is odd. Victims don't usually recover on this side. But maybe they ran out of beds.

The hallway stretches ahead, fluorescent lights dimmed so shadows can stretch longer than they should.

It's quiet. But not peaceful.

"And not creepy at all," I mutter.

I find 402 and ease the door open.

The room is dim. Shadows pool in the corners. No machine hum. No monitor beeps.

I peek around the curtain, bracing for blood or brokenness.

The bed is neatly made, empty, with no patient. Wrongness slithers over me like a second skin.

I step back, heart thudding, adrenaline kicking in.

Before I can turn, a hand clamps over my mouth and yanks me off my feet.

I react on instinct, and throw my head back, sharp and desperate.

A foot slammed back on a shin, as my teeth clamp down on the forearm holding me.

A twist, a shove—and somehow, by pure adrenaline and panic, I wrench free.

I stumble into the hallway, gasping for breath, fumbling for my phone. I remember the sign for the stairs and start sprinting.

I dare a glance behind me and the twisted face I see emerging from the door is familiar.

Where do I know him?

My thumb finds Declan's contact without conscious thought. The screen lights up—Calling—the little spinning circle taunting me, dragging out the seconds.

Please.

God, let him see it.

Please don't let him be done with me.

Before it can even ring once, someone behind me growls and dives for my legs.

I tumble to the ground with their full weight on top of me and I realization hits me.

This guy is on our evidence board. He's linked to a house that processes new girls.

What's his name?

My phone skitters across the gleaming floor, sliding under the nurses desk and I hope to god the voicemail will pick up.

I turn and kick, then crawl toward it, remembering who he is.

"Matthews!" I grunt out as hands pull me back and a fist drives into my abdomen.

The air rushes out of me but still, I open my mouth to scream, but he flattens himself on top of me and covers my mouth with a thick sweaty hand.

A needle punches into the side of my neck, and everything slows down.

The hallway tilts. The overhead lights smear into starbursts.

And just before the blackness rushes up to claim me, I manage one more plea:

"Declan."

Declan

We're parked in the dark, engines off, close enough to see the warehouse but not so close we give ourselves away.

Inside the van, it's quiet. The kind of quiet that drags the minutes out, makes the tension settle under your skin like splinters. Everyone's ready, wired tight, waiting for the signal to move.

I should be thinking about the mission. About the layout. The possible exits. The worst-case scenarios.

Six sites tonight, six coordinated raids, and at one of them —the informant swears it—the man behind it all will finally show his face.

Six chances to end it. Six chances to catch a ghost.

But even now, even with the adrenaline humming under my skin, my mind keeps drifting.

To Poppy.

It's been days. No calls. No messages. No glimpses of her storming into the precinct with Dexter on her hip and murder in her eyes.

I tell myself it's fine. That she just needs time.

I tell myself she's safe, tucked away in that little house with her ridiculous pink dog and her security system that even I can't breach anymore.

She needs space, and I'll give it to her. Even if it's killing me.

She's furious. Hurt. Scared of me in ways she never was before.

And she's right to be.

I lied.

I crossed every line worth crossing.

I broke every promise I never even had the chance to make.

But I love her.

I love her so much it feels like an open wound inside my chest, something raw and throbbing that no amount of distance can cauterize.

She'll come back when she's ready.

When she's figured out that no one else will ever love her the way I do.

No one else will ever see every twisted, bloody part of her and call it beautiful.

I have to believe that, because if I don't—

If I even start to let myself imagine a future without her—

The comm crackles, yanking me back. "Two minutes to breach. Stay sharp."

I nod, even though no one's looking, my focus snapping back into place like a blade sheathing itself.

Six sites.

Six doors about to come down.

Six opportunities to find the man at the top.

He's out there. Tonight. In the open.

Finally vulnerable.

There are too many involved in this ring, in the corruption, for us to have confidence this raid didn't get leaked. The only thing we have to our advantage is the time.

It's not part of the warrants or the subpoenas the DA had to beg Judge Carter to sign. But we made sure to talk about what time the raids would begin. Spread it around like wildfire that they'd be hit one at a time and fall like dominoes.

We're hours early—and we're hitting them all at once. Hopefully these assholes think they have more time to clean things up than they really do.

I flex my fingers around the grip of my Glock, steadying my breathing.

The countdown ticks in my head.

Three.

Two.

One.

Move.

The countdown ends—and the city erupts.

All across the map, six different points ignite at once—six doors blasted open, six teams moving fast and brutal.

A suburban home with a hidden basement.

A nail salon doubling as a front.

A condo floor nobody's supposed to live on.

A strip club's private back room.

A dusty old storefront that hasn't filed a tax return in twenty years.

And us—at the docks, storming an abandoned warehouse that smells like mildew and gasoline.

I move first, leading the charge.

Flashbangs shatter the air. Bodies hit the ground.

Men screaming. Girls crying. Chaos exploding in every direction.

I move through it like a machine.

One runner tries to make a break for it—fast, stupid.

I hit him midstride, drive my knee into his spine, and he

crumples like wet cardboard. Cuffed and left for the transport van.

We sweep the main floor, clear the corridors, drag out the monsters hiding behind false walls and rigged shelving.

It should feel like a win. It should feel like we're choking the life out of their empire.

But it doesn't. Something's wrong.

The layout's too perfect. Too clean.

Like they are making sure someone has time to get away. My gut tightens, and before I even think, I'm moving.

Down the far hall, I spot a door swinging on its hinges, rocking like a heartbeat.

I bolt, lungs burning, boots hammering the concrete.

Through the door. Into the alley. Just in time to catch the gleam of a black sedan tearing off into the night.

"Son of a bitch."

I raise my weapon and fire.

Glass explodes. The back window disintegrates into a mist of shrapnel.

The car fishtails, tires screeching, but the fucker doesn't stop.

Keeps going.

Fast.

I take off after him, rage boiling under my skin.

I chase him halfway down the alley, past dumpsters and the stink of rotting fish, until it's obvious—he's gone.

Breathing hard, I slow to a stop.

The radio at my hip crackles, an officer's voice breaking through the static.

"Boss—was that him?"

I stare down the alley, fists clenching uselessly at my sides, the taste of copper thick on my tongue.

"Yeah," I growl. "That was him."

The leader.

The man who built this hell.

Gone like a ghost. Again.

I glance down at the shattered glass glittering at my feet, the blood pounding in my ears louder than the sirens now wailing in the distance.

Almost isn't good enough. Not tonight.

Not when I promised myself I wouldn't fail again.

My voice is a low, vicious whisper as I kick a piece of broken taillight down the alley.

"You're not getting away again, motherfucker."

The raid is winding down, but I'm not.

I stand just outside the warehouse, breathing in the metallic stink of blood, sweat, and gunpowder.

My sleeves are stained, my boots coated in grime. I should be focusing on cleanup, on transport, on wrapping this all by the book.

Instead, I'm counting down the minutes until I can get back to my phone so I can scroll for the hundredth time, staring at a wall of dead black screens where her house cameras used to be.

To keep the mission as secret and secure as possible, no devices. No addresses until the last moment.

The absence of my phone is burning a hole in my hand.

It's stupid and desperate.

She tore them out. Ripped me out.

Still, here I am, clinging to the scraps of something already slipping through my fingers.

She just needs time.

The lies are thin as paper, but I keep stacking them anyway, hoping they'll build something sturdy enough to stand on.

The buzz of radios and murmured voices presses against me, static and meaningless.

I'm half listening, half somewhere else, until a thread of conversation catches the sharpest part of my brain.

Two traffickers, cuffed and slouched against the cracked pavement, their heads bowed together, voices low and smug.

"At least we got the Yellow Diamond," one mutters, voice just loud enough to slice through the fog in my skull.

The other snorts. "He'll probably keep that piece of bubblegum for himself."

I don't think. I don't breathe.

Poppy's face slams into my mind.

That blonde hair, bright as a sunbeam. That ridiculous pink parade she wears like armor.

Yellow Diamond.

Bubblegum.

It's her.

It's fucking her.

The crack inside me splinters wide open.

Before either of them realizes their mistake, I grab the nearest one—the one who spoke first—by the back of the neck and slam his face into the concrete.

Once.

Twice.

The crunch of cartilage and bone is a raw, ugly sound.

Blood blooms across the pavement, teeth scattering like broken promises.

His body goes slack, sagging in my grip. I let him fall, useless now.

"Blackwood!" My lieutenant's shout cuts through the noise. Boots pounding toward me.

I don't care.

I'm already turning to the second man, my hand fisting the front of his filthy shirt, lifting him off the ground until his toes scrape uselessly at the concrete.

His eyes bulge. He starts to stammer.

I drive the barrel of my Glock up under his chin, forcing his mouth open with the pressure.

"You're going to talk," I say quietly, almost gently. "And if you even think about lying—"

I press the gun harder against the soft spot beneath his jaw, feeling the fine tremble of terror shudder through him.

"I'll tear your fucking throat out and feed it to you while you watch."

His mouth flaps uselessly for a second, fear strangling the words in his throat.

Good.

Let him choke on it.

Because if they touched her—

If they hurt her—

If they so much as looked at her the wrong way—

There won't be a hole deep enough on this planet for them to hide in.

50

Poppy

Firelight flickers against cold stone walls, the shadows twisting and crawling like living things.

My body aches. My mouth tastes of metal and salt.

It takes a moment, my head beating like a drum, to remember what happened. Where I am.

The dark hospital hall. The chase. The pinch of the needle.

I close my eyes and squeeze them shut, trying to will the headache to stop.

When I try to move, something tugs hard at my ankles—tethered to a thick pipe bolted into the stone behind me.

My wrists are bound in front, tight enough to bruise. I can stand. I can shift. But I can't run.

A slow, creeping panic builds in my chest, trying to claw its way up my throat.

I fight it back, biting the inside of my cheek hard enough to taste blood.

Panic won't save me.

Think. Breathe. Survive.

My vision swims as I turn my head, forcing myself to scan the room.

Two dozen branding irons are fixed into some kind of

holder, buried in the hot embers of the fire. This is where they brand girls with serial numbers before sending them on.

I keep looking around. This is a room of torment—knives, cuffs and chains. A handsaw.

It's terrifying.

I turn my attention to myself.

I'm not naked or bleeding. But my pants are gone. I'm barefoot.

Not . . . violated.

Yet.

But the intent in the air is thick. Heavy. I wasn't taken for ransom or leverage.

I was taken to be broken.

We must have gotten close to the source, because abducting a prosecutor working a sex-trafficking and police-corruption case is not a coincidence.

I breathe through the spike of terror trying to take root.

Not today.

Not like this.

Across the room, half lit by the dying fire, I spot it—a scalpel lying on a metal tray. Close enough to see, just far enough to be impossible to reach.

A cruel little promise.

I stretch until my muscles scream, the bindings cutting deep into my skin, but I can't reach it.

My fingers graze empty air.

Gritting my teeth, I search the ground.

Splintered wood.

Broken off from one of the rotting floorboards.

I shimmy down awkwardly, scraping my palms raw against the stone as I wedge the shard of wood between my fingers.

Using it like a makeshift hook, I aim for the scalpel.

The first attempt sends it clattering farther away, the high-pitched ring of metal on stone scraping across my nerves.

"Come on, come on," I whisper, desperation bleeding into the words.

Sweat slides down my temple, my heart hammering so hard I can feel it shaking the knots at my ankles.

I refuse to stop. To give up.

I hook the splinter again, dragging it with painstaking care, inch by inch.

Closer. Closer—

The tip of the scalpel catches the wood.

I hold my breath as I pull, slow and steady, until the blade scrapes across the ground toward me.

With trembling fingers, I drop the splinter and fumble the scalpel into my hands.

Clutch it tight between my bound palms, hiding it beneath the folds of my sleeves.

A weapon.

A chance.

A promise to myself.

I've come too far to die like this.

I press the edge of the scalpel against the rope, my hands trembling so badly it keeps slipping.

The fibers are stubborn, the blade too small. Every sawing pull frays the rope a little more, but not fast enough.

I don't have time.

The thud of boots echoes beyond the stone door, and instinct flares sharp and blinding inside me.

I hide the scalpel behind my forearm just as a shadow darkens the tiny reinforced window.

I go still.

Still in the way prey goes when it knows it's already been seen.

The firelight dances across his face, and my stomach plummets.

I know him.

Not a stranger pulled off the street.

Not some faceless monster from the underbelly.

No. This is worse.

A courthouse regular.

Someone who blended into the edges of my days like background noise.

Hank. The security officer from the courthouse.

The same one Sebastian used to flirt with shamelessly every Friday, grinning and elbowing me, whispering he'd "come out eventually."

I guess he did. Just not the way any of us thought.

The look he gives me now isn't friendly. It's predatory. Appraising.

The door creaks open, heavy on rusted hinges, and Hank steps inside like he owns the place.

Hands in his pockets. Gun strapped carelessly at his side.

He smiles wide, eyes gleaming.

"Well, look at you," he drawls, voice casual, like we're running into each other in the coffee line and not a torture dungeon. "Awake and lookin' real pretty for the boss."

I don't move. Don't speak.

I just breathe and wait.

Hank saunters closer, glancing around like he's making sure no one's watching—like someone might care about what happens in here.

"You're gonna sell for a fortune," he says, crouching a little, voice dropping low like he's sharing a dirty secret.

"Every man you ever put behind bars? Every one you pissed off? They got friends, sugar. Friends who want to see you scream."

He steps right into my space, and I lower my head slightly, making my body small, my shoulders curve inward.

I let him think it's fear. That I'm helpless.

It makes him vulnerable.

He reaches for my restraints—maybe to check them, maybe just to gloat.

And that's when I strike.

The scalpel flashes and buries deep into his throat.

The sound he makes isn't a scream. It's a wet, gurgling gasp.

Confusion blooms in his eyes before they cloud over.

I twist the blade sharply, dragging it to the side with brutal precision.

I push him backward as he stumbles, blood gushing in thick ribbons down his uniform.

He crumples onto the floor like a broken puppet, his hands grasping at nothing.

I turn my attention back to my own survival, letting him try to stop his impending death that's now only seconds away.

There is no panic. No fear.

Just focus—and the cold, clean hum of urgency in my blood.

My forearms burn, sawing the tiny blade across the thick rope, but finally, it gives and falls to the dirty ground.

Just like Hank's body, lying lifeless only a few feet away, a dark pool of blood spreading around him.

I lean over to the table, bracing myself with one hand and stretching to reach the heavier knife just a little farther away.

I stretch, the rope burning around my ankles, but I grab it.

I saw through the bindings and they give just as footsteps echo in the hall outside.

Someone else is coming.

Only one more—if I'm lucky.

I slip the bloody knife into my grip and wipe my palm down Hank's shirt to dry it.

My heart is hammering, but my mind?

Clearer than it's ever been.

I position myself against the cool stone wall, the knife loose and ready in my hand.

They brought me here and wanted a show.

Well, I'll give them a bloodbath.

The room smells like blood now. Like the kind of violence you can taste in the back of your throat.

Next to me, syringes are scattered across a table. Some empty. Some full.

And I get some inspiration.

Shifting the heavy blade to my other hand, I grab a full syringe and pop the cover.

Holding it high, my thumb poised over the plunger. Ready.

The heavy thud of boots on stone gets closer. Louder.

I tuck myself behind the door a little more, and my heart beats slow. Controlled.

No more running. No more pleading.

I am the monster they should have been afraid of. They just had no flippin' idea.

The door creaks open—just wide enough. A man steps in —tall, thick-necked, already muttering under his breath.

"Where the fuck—?"

He doesn't even notice me as he rushes forward, dropping to his knees to check his companion.

That's when I move, silent as breath, and lunge.

The syringe punches into his neck, deep and vicious, as my thumb shoots the plunger downward.

He rears back with a roar, his hand flying up, catching me across the face with a blow that rattles my teeth and splits my lip wide open.

I stagger across the room, bracing my hands against the hard wall to soften the impact.

A metallic taste floods my mouth, but I hold fast to the handle of my knife.

But I don't need it. Not right now.

He grabs at his throat, wild-eyed—but it's too late.

His arms go slack. His knees buckle.

He hits the floor hard, dragging himself an inch, maybe two, before the drug wins.

I wipe the blood from my mouth with the back of my hand, lip burning like fire.

My whole body aches, but it's a good ache—one I've earned.

I lean over him, pick up his slack arm, and let it drop to the ground like dead weight.

A dark, bitter smile curves my lips.

"Let's have some fun," I whisper.

51

Declan

Red lights blur into nothing. My tires screech turning onto her street.

Tearing into the driveway, a pit opens in my stomach. Her car's gone.

I slam my fist on the door.

"Poppy!"

No answer.

Inside, Dexter's barking—sharp, frantic. It guts me.

I kick the door—once, twice.

The third hit splinters the wood.

Dexter's barking grows louder as I rush inside.

"Poppy!"

Nothing.

No footsteps. No scent of her shampoo. No clumsy sounds.

I tear through the house—bedroom, closet, bathroom.

Then I stop.

On the floor: a twisted bedsheet.

Bloodstained. Not much—but enough.

Someone hurt her. I don't know how badly.

I force myself to breathe.

Throw open the laundry room door.

Dexter rockets out—ears pinned, nails skidding—then shoots through the busted front door like he's on a mission from God.

I chase him.

He plants himself in the yard, hikes his leg on a bush, and glares at me like:

What are you waiting for, asshole? Let's go get her.

"Good thinking, little buddy," I mutter. "Let's go get our girl."

I grab his stuff—bottled water, ritzy dog food, treats—and stuff them in a bag.

Dexter peeks back in, tense and ready, shooting me an impatient ruff.

"Yeah, yeah, I'm coming."

I sling the bag, scoop him up, bolt for the SUV.

Behind the wheel, heart pounding, I barely fasten my seatbelt before Dexter claws into the passenger seat.

He plants himself, paws on the armrest, tail stiff with determination.

A Rottweiler next door looks sketchy. Dexter barks like he's ten times bigger.

"Seriously, Dexter?" I growl, slamming into reverse. "Pick a fight your own size."

He gives a snooty ruff and stares out the window.

I grip the wheel tighter, blood boiling.

Wherever she is—whoever has her—

They just made the biggest mistake of their miserable fucking lives.

I don't know how I make it across the city without crashing, but when I skid into the courthouse lot, I'm half out of the car before it's in park.

Dexter under one arm, overpriced dog food swinging from the other—we look like the world's weirdest getaway crew.

Some poor lawyer's briefcase explodes. Papers fly and I hurdle the mess.

"Sebastian!" I roar.

Across the lot, Poppy's best friend—glasses slipping, coffee in hand—turns.

He lights up immediately, waving like we're meeting for brunch, not like I'm barreling toward him like a missile.

"Sebastian Elias Tréviot Ignatius Blaire the Third at your service, Detective," he chirps.

I'm on him in two more strides.

"Have you heard from Poppy?" I bark.

Sebastian's whole body stills.

The smile drops like a mask slipping. He's smart enough to know: if I'm asking, something's wrong.

"No, honey. She's been a little depresso espresso. We were supposed to have dinner tonight."

The words hit me sideways like a bullet I can't brace for.

But there is no time to think on it.

I grab the ridiculous coffee out of his hand and fling it toward the nearest trash can—it splatters across the sidewalk in a sad arc.

"Okay, so we're choosing violence."

I shove Dexter and the bag of supplies into his arms before he can say more.

"Watch him for her," I snap.

Sebastian fumbles the bag and the wriggling dog.

"Hold on Miss Ma'am—what's going on—"

But I'm already gone.

Running.

Pushing through the courthouse doors like the devil himself is at my heels.

Security's shouting, drawing weapons, because apparently hurling myself over the scanner like a deranged athlete is frowned upon.

"BLACKWOOD!"

Rourke's voice cuts through the chaos.

I barely glance back—my godfather's waving the guards off, flashing his badge like a shield.

He's jogging after me, red-faced, already sweating.

I don't wait.

I sprint for the precinct side, shoving through the halls until I skid into the locker room.

God bless the old man—he used to be lethal.

Now he's braced against a locker, wheezing like he needs a defibrillator.

But by the time he gasps out my name again, I've got my locker open, phone in hand.

And my whole world freezes.

A missed call.

Poppy.

My chest caves in.

She called—and I didn't answer.

There's a voicemail, three minutes long.

I sink onto the bench, elbows on my knees.

My hands shake as I bring the phone to my ear and hit play.

The recording crackles to life—static and breathing, the faint shuffle of movement.

Then a sharp voice cuts through.

"Matthews!"

Poppy. High-pitched. Frantic.

A struggle follows—grunts, crashing, the unmistakable sound of a fight.

"Mother fucker," I snarl, the words ripped from my throat, echoing through the empty room.

A sickening crack. A hit. I know they struck her.

My grip tightens until the phone case splits in my hand.

Then—so quiet I almost miss it—

My name.

Declan.

Barely a whisper, but it slices through me like a blade.

There are more footsteps. Muffled voices. Fading.

A deep one snaps, "Forget the phone. Let's get her to the house."

I sit frozen, listening to the last minute and a half of silence.

Like if I replay it enough, I can drag her back to me.

The voicemail ends.

Matthews.

She said a name.

Poppy doesn't do anything without a reason.

I run it through my head—names, cases, connections—

Nothing clicks.

Rourke's voice cuts in again, face flushed, hands on hips.

"What the fuck is going on, Declan?"

I don't answer. I already know.

"The evidence board."

I take off like a shot, boots pounding.

I slam through the war room door.

The board glows under harsh fluorescent lights, covered in sticky notes and string.

I scan—fast looking for hot pink: persons of interest.

I rip notes down until—

"YES!"

Alex Matthews.

I scan her notes.

There's an address. A house tagged HOLDING – New Transports.

A place they branded the girls. Drugged them. Kept them like livestock.

My hands shake so bad I nearly rip the paper.

I check the timestamp on Poppy's voicemail—and it feels like a cleaver through my chest.

They've had her for hours.

I swear a part of my heart dies.

Rourke's voice barks from behind me.

"I will shoot you if you make me run across this fucking precinct again. What the fuck is happening?"

I turn, stuffing the address in my pocket.

"They took Poppy."

The words hang between us like a noose.

Rourke's jaw ticks. "You know we have protocols."

I stop at the door, facing him full-on.

"I love her. I'm doing what I have to do to get her out."

My voice is low. Steady. Dangerous.

"If you send uniforms, be prepared to visit me in Rikers."

I hold his stare.

"You never saw me leave. You don't know she's missing."

A long silence.

"Well, if that's the case, then I've earned a cigarette." Rourke walks away. "And you're not telling your Godmother."

Bless him.

I'm out the door before he even sits.

I throw myself into my SUV, tires screeching as I rip out of the lot.

Dexter's empty seat beside me feels like a promise.

I'm coming, Poppy.

And God help anyone who tries to stop me.

I park two streets away and kill the lights before the engine finishes its death rattle.

The house looms ahead, tucked into the shadows like it's waiting.

I go the rest on foot, gun low but ready, every muscle wound tight, thrumming with rage I barely recognize.

Not the hot kind. Something colder. Heavier. The kind that drives a man into Hell to get her back.

I check every window. Empty.

No movement.

No lookouts.

No one waiting to pull the trigger.

The front door swings open, the wind nudging it like a taunt.

This is too easy.

Either someone inside is an idiot—or it's a trap.

I slip in, gun sweeping each shadow.

Living room.

Kitchen.

Empty.

Nothing but the sound of my heartbeat.

It's too quiet. Too still. A weight pressing on my chest.

Fear would be a mercy.

This is worse. If she's not here, she could be anywhere. That thought almost drops me.

No. Not yet.

In the main room, something catches my eye—a fireplace flanked by bookshelves.

There—just visible in the dust—scuff marks.

The shelf swings out. It's a hidden door.

I start yanking books, rough and impatient, prayers rattling in my chest.

Please.

Finally—a click.

The shelf creaks open.

A tunnel. Dim light bleeding from around the bend.

I move into the dark without hesitation, gun ready—but nothing prepares me for the war inside my chest.

Every step feels like walking a wire strung over a pit.

One wrong move and I lose her.

The tunnel curves tighter. At the end, a door looms. A small window cut into it—just high enough to see through.

I close my eyes and swallow hard, pushing back the nightmares that flash behind my eyes.

The one I can't stop seeing is her—dead.

With a breath, I adjust my grip and look through the small window of the door.

As soon as my eyes land on the room inside, I forget how to breathe.

Poppy.

She's facing away, frozen.

Covered in blood.

Wearing only an oversized shirt.

I push the door open quietly.

She's alone.

"Poppy," I whisper—like a prayer.

She flinches, body rigid.

First thing I see: a handsaw dangling from her hand, blood dripping.

Second—she's shaking.

I look past her.

A man lies strapped to a metal table. Chest cut open, heart resting in his lap.

Throat carved into a jack-o-lantern smile.

Above him, a cracked mirror hangs—aimed down.

A twisted design meant for torment because she pined his eyelids open. She turned it back on him.

Made him watch his own torture.

God knows how many girls had to endure that same sight.

And somehow, in the middle of all this blood and horror, it's the most righteous thing I've ever seen.

"Lollipop," I breathe.

She turns slowly, and for a second, I think she won't recognize me.

Tears streak her blood-spattered cheeks, eyes glassy, distant. Then—

The saw clatters to the floor.

She stumbles toward me, arms outstretched, broken sobs tearing free.

I'm already moving, pulling her into my arms like if I don't hold tight enough, she'll vanish.

She crashes into me, clutching my jacket, shaking so hard it rattles my bones.

"You're okay," I whisper again and again—a mantra I'll kill to keep.

"I've got you."

She falls apart, hands fisting my vest.

I pull back just enough to frame her face, brush blood from her jawline.

"Are you hurt?" My voice comes rougher than I mean.

She shakes her head—fragile. But the tremble says it all—shock, adrenaline, exhaustion.

I spot a stack of towels in the corner, probably meant for the victims they processed here like cattle.

I grab one, wet it from a jug of bottled water, and bring it back with hands steadier than I feel.

Gently, like she's made of glass, I wipe the blood from her face, her arms, her throat.

She lets me, eyes closed, breathing slow—like she's trusting me to put her back together.

"It's theirs," she whispers.

"The blood?"

She nods, opening her eyes.

I glance past her and finally see it—the pile tucked behind the far side of the room. A grim, jagged assembly of body parts.

Arms. Legs. A severed head.

Recognition punches me straight in the chest.

"Is that...?" I ask, squinting at the blood-slick face.

Her voice is flat. "Was."

Bastard worked courthouse security. We passed him daily.

"You know," I wipe under her eyes, "you think you know someone."

She breaks just enough to smirk. It's not much—but I'll take it.

I toss the towel. I can't hold back anymore. I need to taste her.

My mouth finds hers—she's just as starving.

"I thought I lost you forever," I rasp against her lips. "I

thought—" My voice breaks. I shake my head. "Even if you hate me, you're still mine. I should've protected you."

She pulls back to meet my eyes.

"I could never hate you."

Tears well and my eyes burn.

"I love you." She rests her forehead to mine and my breath catches.

The entire world tilts on its axis.

For a second, I think I imagined it—some hallucination from the part of me that's been breaking, waiting.

But she says it again.

"I love you."

And I'm gone.

Every bone in my body goes weightless.

I've whispered this moment like a prayer, too afraid touching her would ruin her.

But she loves me.

Not the detective. Not the mask.

Me.

The man who stalked her. Obsessed over her.

Fell the second she looked at me in that courtroom and flipped my whole goddamn world.

I cup her face like she's sacred, like she might vanish if I'm not careful.

My voice cracks.

"You have no idea what you just did to me."

She blinks and I kiss her before she can ask.

Slow. Reverent.

Like a sinner kissing the altar he burned to feel holy again.

When I pull back, our foreheads touch, breath ragged.

"I've loved you since the day I met you.

Maybe even before that.

Maybe in every life I never got to have."

I swallow.

"You say you love me, and I don't care if it's wrong or broken or fucked—

I'm yours."

I walk us back until her legs bump the exam chair.

Our mouths never part.

"I want to show you something," she whispers, kissing my jaw.

She takes my hand, sliding it lower, guiding me between her thighs.

"I was always yours," she says. "Now I'm yours forever."

The heat sears through the thin fabric.

I feel something there. A raised edge.

She parts her legs without shame, only fierce devotion.

I drop to my knees, reverence washing over me.

The second I see it, my breath shatters.

A letter.

Carved into her inner thigh.

A "D".

My fucking initial.

I trace the mark with my finger—so lightly she shivers.

Lust floods my body, throat tight.

I press my lips to the raw wound.

She moans—soft, broken—fingers threading through my hair.

"You're perfect," I whisper. Another kiss. And another.

I can't stop.

Standing, I kiss her mouth again, messy and deep, while she slides her hand into my pants.

I press my forehead to hers, panting like I've just fought a war—and maybe I have.

My voice breaks as she fists my cock.

"Mark me."

Her hands falter.

"Mark me, Poppy," I breathe. "Put your fucking mark on me. I'm yours. Forever."

I see the moment it hits her—that truth.

That I don't care how deep her darkness runs.

Because mine was always waiting for her.

52
Poppy

I slide to my knees in front of him, not to worship—but to claim.

Declan leans back in the exam chair, legs spread, arms resting at his sides like he's forcing himself not to reach for me. The muscles in his thighs are tight. His breath is already uneven. He looks like he's waiting to be devoured—and trying to enjoy the wait.

His cock is flushed and heavy, already leaking at the tip. I wrap my hand around the base, slowly, deliberately, and stroke once. His whole body jerks.

"You're beautiful like this," I murmur, my voice soft and certain. "Needing me."

His jaw flexes. He says nothing—but his eyes are on fire.

I kiss the tip, slow and teasing. Then I drag my tongue along the underside and feel the shudder ripple through him.

"Poppy..." His voice is low, cracked, barely hanging on.

I take him into my mouth, smooth and unhurried, my lips wrapping around him as I slide him deep. The taste of him—salt and heat—fills my senses. I hum around him, and he groans like I've pulled the soul right out of him.

I don't rush, setting the pace.

Slow, purposeful strokes. I let my tongue swirl and press. I suck him like it's the most important thing I'll do tonight—because maybe it is.

He holds on to the headrest behind him with everything he has.

When I pull back, breathless, I let my lips brush the tip again. My voice is silk and steel.

"You'll come when I say. Not before."

His chest rises in a sharp inhale, but he nods.

"Good boy."

I take him again—deeper now. I want him to fall apart for me. Not because he's lost control, but because I'm the one who has it.

His breathing is ragged now, head tipped back, throat exposed. I watch the way his hands clench, muscles flexing with the effort not to grab my hair, not to thrust into my mouth.

He's desperate.

And I'm not done yet.

Still kneeling, I rise just enough to strip off my shirt. It sticks slightly to my back—blood, sweat, maybe memory—but I don't pause. I let it fall to the floor without looking away from him.

His eyes drop immediately to my bare chest. He groans—low and guttural—like the sight of me actually hurts.

I hook my thumbs into the waistband of my panties, slowly peeling them down over my hips, my thighs, until they puddle at my feet. I step out of them, unhurried, letting him take it all in.

Then I drop to my knees again.

Naked. Bare. Bloody. In control.

His cock twitches at the sight, and I stroke him once—just to remind him what he can't have.

Yet.

I take him into my mouth again, sliding him deep while my hand trails down my own body—between my thighs, where I'm already soaked for him.

I moan around his length as my fingers find that perfect rhythm, soft circles that match the movement of my mouth. His whole body goes tense.

"Jesus, Poppy," he grits out. "What are you doing to me?"

I pull off him with a slow, wet pop.

"Ruining you," I whisper, lips brushing his tip.

He jerks—just barely—and I know he's close.

I suck him again, slow and filthy, tongue swirling, fingers still working myself until I'm whimpering around him. My thighs tremble, slick pooling beneath me, the edge of an orgasm cutting through and breaking around me.

I work him hard, moaning through my own pleasure.

And just when he starts to lose it—hips lifting, jaw clenching—

I stop.

I let him fall from my mouth, aching and wet, twitching between my fingers.

He groans like I stabbed him.

"Not yet," I murmur, licking my lips. "I want you perfect when I mark you."

His eyes darken into pools of desire.

And I smile because he knows I mean it.

His gaze follow me as I move toward the fire, every step slow, deliberate, lit by orange flicker and shadow.

The iron glows red in the flames, the metal stamped with a letter small and perfect.

A "P".

I grip the handle, steadying my breath as I lift it out, the heat radiating toward my skin like a challenge.

When I turn around, Declan is exactly as I left him—sprawled in the cracked leather chair, cock standing thick and flushed, every line of his body drawn tight with restraint. Waiting. Wanting.

I walk to him, naked except for my certainty.

"You're sure?" I ask. The iron doesn't tremble in my grip now.

His voice is low. Steady and unshakable. "Brand me."

He doesn't blink. Doesn't flinch.

I climb onto him slowly, straddling his lap, my slick heat sliding over the length of him. He groans through clenched teeth, eyes burning into mine, hands fisting the arms of the chair like he's one second from losing it.

I reach between us and guide him to my entrance. He's hot. Heavy. Barely held back.

And then I sink down onto him in one slow, perfect motion.

The stretch is blinding. The feeling—too much, too good. He fills me completely—body and soul.

At the same moment, I press the iron to his chest.

The hiss of scorched skin cuts through the air.

His breath punches out hard. Eyes squeezed shut. Sweat beads at his temple—but he doesn't move an inch.

Doesn't stop me.

His hands clamp onto my hips like anchors, pulling me tighter against him, burying himself as deep as I can take.

"Poppy," he gasps—like it's a prayer, a curse, a thank-you.

The P sears into his flesh, just beside the inked cranes above his heart. It's red and angry, raw and permanent.

And mine.

I toss the iron to the floor. I don't care where it lands.

All I care about is him.

Our mouths crash together—hungry, uncoordinated, gasping. We drink each other like lifelines. I bite his lower lip and he groans into my mouth. His hands are wild now—gripping my ass, sliding up my spine, tangling in my hair like he's afraid I'll vanish.

But I'm not going anywhere.

I start to move, rocking my hips against him. Slow. Deep. Deliberate. Every thrust drags his piercing against that sensitive bundle of nerves, and stars detonate behind my eyes.

My nails dig into his shoulders. He groans louder.

"I like this," I whisper, breathless. "The way it feels."

His voice is wrecked. "I got it for you. So you'd feel it every time you fucked me."

Something inside me cracks. The devotion. The sheer knowing. That he'd do that—alter his body just so I'd feel him more. So I wouldn't forget.

So I'd want more.

"I've watched you," he confesses, his teeth scraping down my throat. "For a year. I used to come to the sound of your moans. Your vibrator humming. Your fingers between your thighs."

A cry of pleasure spills from me, thick with heat and hunger and the smallest, sweetest ache of belonging. Shame and desire war inside me, but shame doesn't win.

Not tonight.

He thrusts up harder, faster. I meet him stroke for stroke, my body greedy, frantic. The sound of us fills the room—wet, obscene, gorgeous. Our gasps. Our curses. Our need.

"You think you're riding me right now," he growls, "but

you've owned me since the first time you smiled at me in court."

It hits me all at once.

The branding. The way he looks at me like I'm the center of gravity. The man who has always held the power giving it to me like it's a gift.

My orgasm tears through me, sudden and violent—like lightning. My whole body locks down, every muscle tightening as I cry out his name.

Declan.

I collapse against him, trembling, my mouth pressed to his neck as he pushes me through it.

One last thrust.

Then another.

He spills inside me with a guttural groan, his head dropping back, his entire body shuddering beneath mine. He clutches me like something holy, like I'm the only thing anchoring him to this world.

And maybe I am.

We don't move for a long time. We just exist. Tangled together in a room built for violence but made sacred by what we've done here. What we've chosen.

His hands slide up my back, then down again, holding me to him like the world might disappear if he lets go.

"You okay?" I murmur into the curve of his neck, brushing my lips against his damp skin.

He laughs—wrecked and breathless. "You branded me and rode me like a stolen car. I'm fucking incredible."

Then I pull back just enough to look at the mark.

His chest is red, blistered in the shape of my first initial. Right above his heart. Where the cranes fly.

I press my fingers gently to the wound—his breath catches.
"You're mine now," I say softly.
He looks at me like it's the first time he's ever seen sunlight.
"I always was."

53

Declan

Another crime scene no one would ever know existed.

Two more traffickers gone and buried—two fewer stains on the earth.

Hank Mayfield was now officially listed as *wanted* in connection with the trafficking ring, a neat little note in the file that would gather dust until they assumed he'd fled the country to avoid justice.

Alex Matthews, on the other hand, was shuffled into the chaos of the raids—reported as a casualty during a gunfight at another site.

No body to find. They'll think he was taken to the wrong morgue and likely labeled a John Doe. No one will look for him.

And my Sunshine? My Lollipop?

My beautiful, bloody, perfect girl?

She's free to slay another day.

After we showered, changed, and ate—because Poppy insisted she couldn't be expected to function without food— we made it to the courthouse just in time to witness the grand spectacle of Sebastian chasing Dexter across the front lawn, flailing a nearly empty bag of treats like a man facing the apocalypse.

Poppy barely had to raise her voice, calling his name once.

Dexter froze mid-chaos, his snaggletooth pointing at her like a compass finding true north.

She knelt with her arms out and laughed—really laughed—and I swear it was the only sound that mattered in the entire world.

Sebastian staggered up, silk ascot untucked, mopping sweat from his forehead like he was crossing the Sahara.

"Girlie-pop," he gasped, hand over his heart, "I have to tell you. Your little beast is an asshole."

He turned to me, arching a single judgmental brow.

"Don't judge me, Detective Hottie."

I shrugged, reaching down to pluck the bag of treats from his hand and tossing one toward Dexter.

It bounced cleanly off his snout when he missed the catch and hit the ground with a pathetic flop.

Dexter gruffed at me, staring like I'd insulted his entire bloodline.

"No offense taken," I said dryly. "He's a total asshole."

Sebastian fanned himself, making eyes at Poppy like he couldn't believe I actually spoke.

"But he grows on you," I added with a smirk, watching Dexter immediately sit like a perfect angel at Poppy's feet, begging for another treat like he hadn't just staged a one-dog rebellion across government property.

Sebastian narrowed his eyes, assessing both of us. Then he smiled—the kind of slow, wicked smile that spelled nothing but trouble.

"Um, diva," he said, voice pitching into an obnoxiously high sing-song.

His eyes darted between Poppy, then to me, then back to Poppy, his grin practically nuclear.

"You're forgetting to tell me something."

Poppy froze.

Sebastian leaned in close, stage-whispering so loudly that I was pretty sure half the courthouse lawn heard him:

"You have a freshly fucked glow about you, girlie. Please— *please*—tell me Detective Hottie finally broke your dry spell."

If Poppy could have launched herself into low orbit to escape, she would have.

The shade of pink that flooded her cheeks was spectacular.

She waved her hands frantically, making strangled noises, glaring at Sebastian like she was mentally setting him on fire.

I crossed my arms over my chest, biting back a grin.

Yeah.

Mine.

And the whole damn world was gonna know it.

Currently, Poppy is doing one of my favorite things— riding my face like the most graceful, filthy little equestrian the world's ever seen.

Another thing she hadn't experienced before.

Another thing I was all too happy to gift her.

She's gorgeous like this—wild and desperate, her thighs trembling against my jaw, her slickness coating my mouth as she chases another high I'm hell-bent on giving her.

"Please, Declan," she gasps, voice wrecked, almost broken. "I can't take it anymore."

I lift my eyes to hers, lock us in that sweet standoff I love too much.

"Say it, baby," I growl before dropping my mouth back to her clit, sucking her hard. "Be my nasty girl."

It's the soft whimper that does it—the way she breaks when she finally gives in.

"Eat my pussy like the whore you are, Declan."

The filthy words barely leave her mouth before I'm devouring her—ruthless, hungry, like she's the only thing that's ever mattered.

She leans back, bracing herself on my chest, hips rolling in frantic rhythm, sobbing in relief as she falls apart for me.

I lap up every drop, moaning against her, so fucking aroused it's embarrassing—and it doesn't even matter.

I'm coming in my pants, grunting, dry-humping nothing like some depraved teenager just from the taste of her.

It launches her into another orgasm, a shuddering, writhing mess above me.

Poppy leans forward, gripping the headboard, riding my face harder, smearing herself across my tongue without shame.

And this time she doesn't need coaxing.

"Are you coming just from eating my pretty pussy?" she pants, voice wrecked and sweet and utterly lethal. "Keep sucking, baby, just like that."

Head thrashing. "More." Panting galore. "Don't stop."

More filth pours from her mouth—each word a brand on my fucking soul.

She finally slides down my body, straddling me, licking her release off my mouth like she's claiming every inch of me.

"That may go down as one of the hottest things I've ever experienced," she says, breathless and smiling against my lips.

I grab her hips, grinding her against my still-hard cock.

"Not hotter than you riding my dick with your brand on

my chest," I mutter, making her blush and bite her lip like she's already planning her next sin.

I flip us over, pants open, cock out, and slide into her pulsing cunt.

Home.

Right here with her, just like this—I'm home.

When my pink-clad goddess has been well and properly fucked, we get dressed—barely coherent, still smiling like idiots—and head to her mom's for Sunday dinner.

To absolutely no one's surprise, her mother loves me right away.

Maybe it's because I helped fix her crooked mailbox before she even finished introducing herself.

Maybe it's because I didn't flinch when she gushed about a shadow-wielding prince and I asked about the physics of the shadow orgy with actual interest.

When she says the words "shadow daddy," I get several ideas that'll involve a trip to the adult toy shop.

Over dessert, I'm sitting against the wall flipping through this so-called masterpiece. Poppy perches next to her mom on the couch, clearly building up the nerve to say something.

Her voice is soft when she finally speaks.

"I just want you to know," she says, "I look up to you. I admire you—for the strength it took to do what you did. To stop him. To protect other girls."

Her mother's expression is warm but puzzled.

"You did the right thing, Mom. Even if it was hard. You were brave, and I hope you never regretted what you did."

Poppy's voice cracks a little. I see her biting it back.

And I'm just sitting there thinking I shouldn't be here for such a personal conversation.

She's talking about her mother murdering a man, for Christ's sake.

"Hold on, dear." Her mother looks hesitant. Perhaps suspicious. "What do you think happened?"

Poppy shakes her head at the absurdity of the question, as if her mother should know what she's referring to.

"Mother, I know you *killed* him." She whispers the word like it's a curse.

Her mother pauses—for way too long—and then... laughs.

I stiffen, book frozen mid–page flip.

Poppy looks at me wide-eyed, panic creeping in.

"Oh, honey," her mom chuckles, waving a dismissive hand. "I didn't kill him."

Poppy blinks. Once. Twice.

"What?" she croaks.

Oh my God.

"No," her mom says brightly, like we're discussing cookie recipes. "I talked to his mother."

"His mother?!"

Poppy and I say it at the exact same time.

Her mom nods, settling back with her cup of coffee like she didn't just detonate the entire foundation of Poppy's psychological architecture.

"Yeah. He was the son of a judge. Not the one assigned to the case, but one who stuck his nose in where it didn't belong. I overheard them arguing through the vent in the courthouse bathroom during the trial."

"A judge," Poppy repeats faintly, her hands curling into the couch cushions.

Her mother smiles. Stands up to clear dessert plates like she didn't just blow up Poppy's world.

"Well, what judge?"

"It's water under the bridge now. No use digging up old ghosts."

She laughs again as she walks into the kitchen, humming under her breath.

Poppy turns to me, face pale, like she's still trying to process what just happened.

I don't move.

Because I know my Lollipop—

She won't be able to sleep until she knows who it is.

Not with a lead dangling in front of her, ripe for the taking.

Sure enough, fifteen minutes later we're slipping old Al a covered plate of lemon bars, and the ancient night security guard beams at us like we've handed him the keys to the kingdom.

He waves us through with barely a grunt.

We're speed-walking through the dark halls, our footsteps echoing off marble and tile.

Poppy's practically vibrating next to me—near manic, brilliant, a storm with nowhere safe to land.

"I think I put something together," she says, words tumbling out fast as her beautiful brain shifts into overdrive.

My hand hovers near the small of her back, ready to catch her if she burns too hot and crashes.

"When I was slicing and dicing that last degenerate, I wanted some info too," she mutters, voice grim. "He started mumbling about the missing eighty-threes."

I lift a brow as we turn a corner, heading toward the records room.

"Missing eighty-threes?"

"Yeah," she says, almost tripping over her own feet in her hurry. "He was delirious. Blood loss. Whatever cocktail I injected into him. But before he started singing Taylor Swift at the ceiling, he said—'everything you need is in the missing eighty-threes.'"

I bite back a grin.

God, I love her.

We reach the heavy security doors to the evidence archive. I punch in the code while she bounces on her toes beside me, practically sparking like a live wire.

Inside, it's colder, the fluorescent lights humming low overhead. Rows of labeled boxes line the metal shelving units—organized by case number.

She points upward, her finger trembling with excitement.

I follow her gaze—and feel a low, dangerous thrill run through me.

"Well, I'll be damned," I murmur.

The serial numbers painted on the rows start with eighty-three.

The eighty-threes.

Sex crimes.

Someone's been systematically making case files vanish—specifically those tied to sexual assaults.

Someone powerful.

Someone desperate to cover old sins.

And if Poppy's right—and she usually is—then if we can find out which cases are missing, we can find the common thread tying them all together.

And maybe, finally, tear down the bastard sitting at the top of the pyramid.

She turns toward me, eyes wild, cheeks flushed, every inch of her lit up with purpose.

I can't help it.

I spin her around, press her back against the nearest evidence table, and crash my mouth onto hers.

Her gasp is swallowed by my kiss, her hands fisting in the front of my shirt.

"Have I told you how fucking sexy your genius is?" I growl against her lips.

She giggles—sweet and wicked—and it hits me right in the chest, knocking the air from my lungs.

I'm so hard it hurts. I'm so fucking in love with her I can't see straight.

"Maybe once or twice," she teases, dragging her hand down my abdomen to my cock, squeezing hard enough to pull a low, wrecked groan out of me.

"Let's get to work," she whispers, eyes sparkling like stars shot through with sin.

We break apart reluctantly, boot up two computers, and pull the first of the digital logs.

The first missing case?

Her mother's.

I look at her, and she looks at me, and in the silent crackle of the air between us, we know—

This is it.

This is where everything begins to unravel.

54

Poppy

The courthouse after hours is a different beast.

Gone is the buzz of voices, the clatter of heels, the occasional chuckle bouncing off the marble walls.

Now, it's just my footsteps.

Sharp. Echoing.

Each one slicing through the silence.

I hug my bag tighter, hurrying toward the stairwell. The overhead lights flicker, buzzing like they resent me.

It's fine. Totally normal. Not creepy at all.

A door slams somewhere behind me. I freeze.

"Hello?"

My voice vanishes into the empty hall.

Nothing.

I glance over my shoulder, heart thudding against my ribs.

No movement. Just still shadows pretending to behave.

Just get to the car.

I walk faster. My heels click too loudly.

Outside, it's worse.

The air is thick. Heavy.

The courtyard, bright this morning, is now drowned in shadow.

The nearest streetlamp is dead—perfect.

The only one out in the whole lot.

Every shadow feels like a threat. I grip my bag and move faster, scanning the dark.

Footsteps. Behind me.

Closer. Steady.

I whirl.

Judge Carter stands five paces away.

Relief punches through me.

"Goodness, you scared me, Your Honor."

He smiles—warm, and harmless. But not tonight.

"You shouldn't be out here alone," he says. "These lots are dangerous. Come. Let me walk you."

"That would be great, thank you."

We walk. Small talk flows—easy and empty as I nod along.

At my SUV, I open the trunk, glance back and smile, thanking him.

Then I feel it.

The shift.

The gleam in his eye.

The way he moves—subtle. Predatory.

He's not expecting it when I spin and jam the syringe into his neck.

Quick and clean.

He sways toward the trunk.

"That's it," I murmur. "Nice and easy."

His hand flails—slow, clumsy—but he's already falling.

I guide him in like a dutiful little nurse.

Pull the tarp over him and slam the hatch shut.

"Easy peasy." I wipe my hands together.

The drive to St. Pete's feels surreal.

I keep glancing in the rearview mirror like he's going to Houdini his way out of the trunk.

But he's out cold. Snoring like a chainsaw under a tarp.

The hospital looms ahead, abandoned on this side due to renovation. In a few weeks, this whole wing will be demolished.

Poetic, really.

The same place where I was dragged out, trembling and terrified.

And now I'm dragging him in.

Full circle.

I pull into the narrow service entrance, headlights off.

My supplies are exactly where I left them: the maintenance stretcher, the heavy-duty locks, the tarps in Room 402.

It takes more upper body strength than I want to admit, wrestling his dead weight onto the stretcher.

He slumps sideways, nearly sliding off, and I hiss, yanking him upright.

I over-correct, and his head bangs the side of the car with a deep thunk. "Oopsie! Sorry."

I heave him in place. "You're heavier than you look, you bag of judicial garbage," I mutter, tightening the straps across his chest.

I don't rush. I savor it.

Every click of a buckle and every tug of a restraint.

The elevator creaks as it climbs.

I'm half convinced it's going to drop us both, but fate isn't that merciful.

The lights on the fourth floor are dead.

Only the exit signs glow, bleeding red.

Room 402 waits like an open mouth.

I wrestle the stretcher inside and kick the door shut.

The tarps crinkle. The metal table gleams. The smell of bleach bites—freshly cleaned, courtesy of yours truly.

A crime scene no one will ever see.

After changing, I secure him to the table, locking down his wrists and ankles with zip ties.

Pink... obviously.

A second injection, this one from a different syringe, will keep him just the way I want him.

Frozen. Quiet.

But feeling everything he's about to endure.

And now, a little something before it's time to wake up our special guest.

I retrieve a vial of smelling salts from the prepared tray, cracking it under his nose with a little more force than necessary.

Judge Carter glares—or tries to. Hard to do without eyelids.

I wave up at the mirror, smiling like a game show host.

"Hi, Grandpa. Can I call you Grandpa?"

I let him see the tray. Tools lined up. Silence stretching like elastic.

I walk slowly around him, scalpel glinting under the low emergency lights, trailing it lightly across his skin just to watch him flinch.

"I'm going to tell you a story, Grampy."

I can tell he tries to grunt out a swear but my cocktail is keeping him paralyzed.

Precious little left of the big, bad judge now.

Just flesh and fear. And soon–nothing.

"I bet you're wondering why you're here."

His eyes scream yes.

I lean closer, resting a hand on his wrist. No pressure. Not yet.

"It's not just the trafficking. Or the payoffs. Or the girls you fed to politicians like appetizers."

I tilt my head, letting it land.

"It's personal."

I let that word bleed.

"Your son raped my mother."

A breath catches in his throat. Denial flickers but the lie doesn't last long.

"You couldn't risk being caught trying your own blood," I say softly, like a lullaby. "So you stepped back. Pulled strings. Buried it deep where you thought no one would find it."

I tap the scalpel to his nose, then trail it down his hand—light, teasing.

"But I did."

And then I slice.

A clean line down the side of his hand—the one he used to sign away so many fates.

It hisses as it parts, skin peeling like paper.

"And when the risk was gone, you didn't stop. Not once you saw how easy it was to make it disappear."

I unwrap each finger like a delicate present. No screams. Just pitiful, wet noises.

"Bribery." I hum, sliding down his arm. "Evidence suppression. Victims turned to inventory.

You turned the court into a rape mail-order catalog."

"But why wait for the perfect cases? Desperate rich boys needing a clean verdict, so their bright futures don't get," I air-quote, "ruined by one bad decision."

I roll my eyes and peel off a layer of pink surgical gloves, revealing the fresh set underneath.

With the bone forceps, I grip his pinky.

Snap.

Onto the tray.

Then the next.

"No, why not expand the biz? Start a trafficking ring."

Snap

"Excuse cases. Let a criminal organization become your infrastructure."

Snap.

"Host dinner parties where sleazy politicians pay $150 a plate to rape drugged girls cuffed in corners."

Snap.

"At first, I thought my mother's case was the turning point. That she killed her rapist to keep him from stalking her."

Snap.

I hold his thumb like a party favor and laugh—genuine amusement bubbling up. A thought interrupts my villain monologue.

"This is the funniest thing... I actually believed she killed him, and it led to this spiraling episode of hysteria where I accidentally became a serial killer. It was a whole vibe."

His thumb joins the rest of his sausagy digits. I move to the next hand.

A flick, and I sever the tendons.

He wheezes and his pupils widen likes he's losing focus. I tap his face, mock-gentle.

"Focus, old man. The story gets juicy."

The truth was worse.

"She overheard you arguing through a vent at the courthouse. She figured it out—her rapist was a judge's son, and he was going to get away with it.

She ran. For years.

And when she finally got desperate, she didn't go to the police. She went to your wife."

All fingers are accounted for, lined up like neat little ducklings.

He gurgles. I keep going.

I slice through the soft meat at the back of his ankle—the Achilles tendon.

None of the victims he helped could run. Neither can he.

Side note: I've always loved the story of Achilles. So angsty.

Now, where was I?

"But your wife wasn't his mother, was she?" I purr, dragging the scalpel down his thigh. The meat opens like a zipper.

"His real mother was *your* rape victim."

I use clamps to get a grip and tug the skin back. It resists, but the slide is *chef's kiss.*

"High school girl. Fourteen."

The next thigh gives less resistance. Noted.

"You celebrated passing the bar by getting drunk. You picked up high school hitchhikers. Then you came back and raped one—and gave her a souvenir. A baby boy."

He tries to move his mouth. Nothing.

The pain must be a lot by now.

"And when the rapist apple didn't fall far from the tree, you had to cover it up.

Not for him. For you.

Because if anyone dug too deep, they'd find your sins."

Scalpel down. Next layer of gloves off.

"But when my mother went to your wife... she figured it out. And when your wife realized she was married to a monster, she did what any proper society woman would do—stabbed him to death, then smiled like a good little wife while she kept your tuna noodle casserole warm."

I grab the sheers and cut away his shirt, baring his torso.

"I always did wonder why Judge Maxwell hated me. But now I know. Judge Maxwell is your wife. Kept her maiden name and helps keep things quiet for you." I tisk and shake my head. "What a couple you two make. A murderer and a rapist both casting judgement on everyone else but yourselves."

I release a deep breath and with it, my disgust.

"But don't worry," I say sweetly. "Detective Blackwood—my very scandalous, very," my face gets hot, "sexy boyfriend—and I are going to tie up all the loose ends."

In our research, we've found the Judge has developed a penchant for mutilation these days.

Probably due to a little problem... down there. (Winky face)

So, do unto others and all that jazz.

"We're going to dump the evidence. Make sure every news station knows what kind of Judges you and your wife were."

My scalpel slices around his shriveled, pepperoni-looking nipple.

Ugh. I use pliers to avoid the jiggle when I flop it onto the tray. Gross.

We can't have uneven chesticles—so, on to the next.

He tries to jerk. Still... nothing.

I smile wider.

"Your son is dead. There will be a manhunt for you. Sadly, they won't find you."

Barf. Jiggle nipple number two hits the tray. I shiver.

It's like rubbing a chalkboard with your hand and I hate it.

"They'll find a man burned like a marshmallow who

matches your description—next to your wife, who'll die in a tragic murder-suicide at your burned-out mansion.

You'll be the coward who shot her, lit the match, and took yourself out."

I crouch eye-level.

"Tragic, don't you think?"

I grab the pink-handled switchblade—a gift from my honey-cakes.

Slay Responsibly engraved on the blade.

"Now that everything's out in the open, it's time for your punishment."

I whistle *Here Comes the Sun* as I work.

A curved scalpel glides behind his eye, through fat and ligament.

He's twitching. I'm guessing this is excruciating.

My turkey baster—modified with a wider mouth—sucks the little beauty right out.

Hmm. Greyish blue. Not the vivid blue I have, thankfully.

I got my eyes from Mama.

The second orb suffers the same fate. I set my baster down, now full of the eyes of a man who will never prey on another woman.

He'll never walk toward another human auction, sign a release order, or tell another lie.

And soon, he won't breathe the same air as the girls he hunted.

He can't see me—his eyeballs are in a turkey baster—but he can hear me.

"187 cuts. One for every scratch my mother left on your son while he raped her."

I lost count around sixty-four. Had to start again. Rookie mistake.

Mental note: work in batches of ten.

It's cathartic, really. The chaos.

The slicing. The release.

I nick his neck with the scalpel, just enough to start a slow bleed into the bucket.

Testing a new method—so my little murder room doesn't look like a Tarantino film.

No need to rush. We're on my schedule now.

And it's much tidier this way.

"You'll be gone soon, Grandpappy." I switch to the bone saw.

"Thank you—for having a hand in creating me. The swift arm of justice that'll find more monsters."

It's louder than I expected, and for a second, I have to pause to re-angle my arms.

Another note to self: build upper body strength.

Also invest in an electric saw maybe.

The hands go first. Then each arm.

I use a blowtorch to cauterize the wounds so we can keep this nice and slow.

Feet next. Legs in two portions.

He died sometime between me taking his little piggies to the market and his right femur.

I wrap the pieces in red biohazard bags, sealed tight.

The zip ties go in a dish of disinfectant. I have plans for those.

After bagging the tarps and sterilizing my tools, all that's left are discarded gloves and bubblegum-pink coveralls.

Amazon lightning deal. Gotta love it.

Everything goes in a rolling garbage bin. Fitting for this piece of T-rash.

I change into pink scrubs, knot my hair, and wheel the party to the incinerator.

I don't flinch pressing the button. As I watch flames consume what he built on the backs of broken girls, I just smile.

With the doors shut and fire blazing, I pull out my phone.

Search: *origami heart tutorial*.

Murder's done so, may as well do crafts while the evidence disappears.

Fifteen minutes later, I'm crouched on the floor, shaping zip ties into something almost... delicate.

A pink heart—sharp-edged, a little crooked but not bad for my first one.

I hold it in my palm and look it over. I love it.

Finally, the peace that silences my mind settles like cool water over fire.

There's no static. No racing thoughts.

Just calm.

It used to scare me—how much I liked this part.

The stillness after.

Now? I'm going to let it in.

This peace is mine too.

Ping.

DECLAN: on my way.

I step out of the hospital's abandoned wing as his SUV glides to the curb like fate knew I needed a ride.

It gleams under the lights—sleek, black, smug with secrets.

An unholy chariot of domestic bliss.

And there, in the passenger seat, is my other ride-or-die.

My little homicide homie:

Dexter.

He's perched upright on the armrest with his snaggletooth on proud display, pink bandana crooked around his neck like he just came from brunch with scandalous secrets and a mimosa buzz.

His tail wags so hard when he sees me, his whole booty wriggles out of control.

"My boys," I whisper, smiling wide.

Declan steps out, something behind his back.

"I have a surprise for you," he says, voice low and warm.

He pulls it out—a small white paper crane.

The first time he left them for me, he was just a shadow.

Now he's the one waiting in the light.

I don't say anything. I just reach into my pocket and place the zip-tie heart in his palm.

He smiles. "Hold that thought."

He opens the back door, rummages in the floorboard and pulls out a mason jar.

He drops the heart inside and seals it.

"There," he says. "The first of many."

It's true. There are more names. More monsters. I'm going to need more jars.

"You're really okay with this?" I ask.

He shrugs. "I'm okay with anything that involves you."

My throat tightens. Not with guilt or fear.

Just that strange ache of being seen—and loved—for exactly what I am.

He opens the door and I climb in.

Dexter hops into my lap, tail thumping.

Declan gets behind the wheel, glancing at me like I'm his religion.

"You good?"

I nod. "Better than good. Settled."

Declan watches me closely. He's always watching. Not like before—obsessive, shadowed—but with that steady, reverent gaze that says *you're safe now. You're mine now. I'll carry whatever you can't.*

"What now?" he asks, voice low.

"I'm starving."

"For?" He casts his hands out. "Me, perhaps?"

He eyes me hungrily. "I'm getting a very strong Nurse/Patient roleplay vibe here, and it's doing it for me."

I deadpan.

"Cheeseburger. Extra pickles. Fries. And a chocolate milkshake the size of my chef's knife. Stat."

He laughs—deep, real. Takes my hand, kisses my knuckles.

"How could I say no to the love of my life?"

He pulls out, one hand on the wheel, driving in that way that makes his forearm send Morse-code arousal signals to my lady bits.

His other hand rests on my thigh, fingers curling tight.

He doesn't look at me when he says, "You're the only thing I've ever done right."

I study the man who hunted me, saved me, loved me.

"I'm all yours, McPerky," I say, sliding my hand over his. "And I'm not going anywhere."

"Oh, I know that." He winks. Squeezes my thigh like letting go might kill him.

As we disappear into the night, the weight of it all behind us, I feel it settle in my bones.

Not peace—but something better.

Power.

And love.
Dark. Twisted. And all ours.
"Hey, what do you think of my very own incinerator?"

Epilogue
Poppy

Two Years Later

Mariela's still glowing when I slip back into the hospital room, her husband, Javier, hovering protectively at her side like he might fend off germs with his bare hands.

And in his arms? The world's newest little queen—wrapped in a pink blanket like destiny stitched her from stardust and sugar.

"She's perfect," I whisper, kissing Mari's forehead.

Mariela grins, exhausted but radiant. "Thank you. For everything."

I set a small gift bag beside the stupidly large bouquet of roses and the onesie I picked out weeks ago—white, with tiny gold lettering:

Future Attorney – Winning Arguments at 2 a.m.

Right on cue, the sweet bundle of joy grunts. Her face turns an alarming shade of purple, and sounds from the demonic tar pits of Mordor bubble in her tiny diaper.

Javier recoils, yanking his hand back like the baby just detonated. Mari bursts out laughing—then winces, clutching her stomach. "Ow. Totally worth it."

I squeeze her hand, soaking in the warm, fragile tenderness before stepping back.

The night Mari nearly slipped away flickers like a ghost in my mind—but today?

Today she's here. Whole. Laughing. Alive.

Proof that sometimes the ugliest things we do can leave something beautiful behind.

I wipe a tear as I step into the hallway, breathing deep.

Walking to the parking deck, every step reaffirms I've made the right choices.

A bit unorthodox? Yes.

Slightly illegal? I plead the Fifth.

Worth it? Abso-stinkin'-lutely.

The elevator dings and spills me into the parking garage.

I step out—still reeling from baby snuggles—when everything inside me slows.

The air thickens. Heavy, like a held breath and I know I'm not alone.

A shiver crawls down my spine. The hairs on my neck rise.

Every instinct sharpens to a blade's edge: *Run.*

I keep walking, careful not to rush.

My hand tightens on my bag strap, knuckles white, but I stay composed.

Just a woman looking for her car.

My eyes scan every corner. Every shadow.

Up ahead, a flicker behind a concrete pillar—barely a whisper of movement—but it lights my nerves on fire.

My heartbeat stutters. So do my steps.

I double back a few times, eyes sharp, and breath ragged.

At the stairwell door, I grip the handle in one smooth, unhurried motion.

I slip inside—and bolt down the stairs.

Halfway down, the door above explodes open with a crash.

Adrenaline floods my veins.

I don't look back. I grip the rail, bag strap digging into my shoulder as my flats pound the steps.

Footsteps follow. Steady. Measured.

Each one echoes like a gunshot.

My lungs burn. My heart slams.

The dim lighting stretches every shadow.

Boots strike concrete. Closer.

Panic flares. I focus on the door.

Just as I reach for it—

A thud.

He's jumped the railing.

I burst through the door, cool air slapping me across the face.

A hand nearly grabs my shoulder but I slam the door behind me and smile at the deep cry of pain.

Ha. Take that.

The door dumps me into the hospital's under-construction wing—a maze of skeletal walls and unfinished corridors.

Plastic sheets sway from the ceiling like specters.

My foot catches on a loose cable—I stumble. One flat slips off. I kick the other away, choosing speed over protection.

I duck behind a stack of crates, pressing to the cold surface, steadying my breathing.

Every sound is louder now—the rustle of plastic, the creak of beams—then I hear him.

A low chuckle slithers through the air, chilling my spine.

"You're fast, baby. But I still have two minutes to catch you and fuck you the way I want."

A pause.

"Two minutes is such a long time, don't you think?"

I clamp a hand over my mouth.

Two more minutes. I just need to reach another floor and hide.

I can do it.

Spotting a partially open door, I make a plan: reach it, barricade it, buy time.

I inch forward, my muscles taut, nerves on fire.

Peeking around the corner, I see nothing and exhale.

Turning back toward the doorway, I scream.

He's there.

A black balaclava.

The white Punisher skull.

His fist tangles in my hair and slams me into a beam. Breath leaves me in a rush, but instinct kicks in. I jab his throat, knocking him back.

I bolt again, barefoot, heart pounding.

But he's faster.

He catches me like I weigh nothing, slamming me to the ground so hard stars burst behind my eyes.

Pain flares up my spine, but rage burns hotter.

I fight like a woman possessed—writhing, clawing, landing an elbow to his jaw. Blood soaks the white threads of the skull design.

I grin, wild and feral, savoring the small victory.

"Stop squirming, Sunny," he warns, voice rough.

He straddles me, crushing my arms to my sides. I buck, but it's useless. He cages me in.

The rip of fabric splits the air as he tears open my sundress. His knife flashes—slicing through lace. Cool air rushes over my skin.

He chuckles, noticing my thighs squeeze shut.

"One minute left," he murmurs, almost sweet.

The knife trails down my neck. His other hand rips my panties away.

I feel the nick of the blade on my thigh—a warning.

Then his fingers slide through the heat between my legs. Slick. Soaked. Betrayal pools in my gut.

He lifts his mask just enough to reveal a blood-smeared smirk.

"I won," he says simply.

I want to deny him—bite, kick, scream—but he licks his fingers, groaning low.

"Look how wet you are," he purrs. "You love playing our game, little Lollipop."

His hoodie hits the floor in one aggressive motion, his body all tense lines and sin. His hands fumble with his pants, freeing the thick length of him—hard and leaking.

Without warning, he grabs a fistful of my hair and drags me up, forcing his cock between my lips.

"Open your fucking mouth."

My arms are pinned beneath his thighs as he rocks his hips forward. One hand braces on the floor beside my head, holding me still.

He's merciless, pushing until my throat spasms, tears sliding from my eyes. I gasp, my nails scraping at his jeans.

"Take it," he growls. "Take it like a good girl. I want to feel your throat cry for me."

Each thrust steals my air. Heat pulses through me, shameful and sweet. My scalp aches, but I won't beg.

He pulls out with a wet sound, strands of spit and pre-cum still connecting us. Tilting my chin, to meets the molten green blaze of his stare.

"That's not where I want to come," he rasps, wiping away a tear. "Not today."

He slides down my body like a man possessed. His mouth finds the scar carved into my thigh—the "D" I gave myself for him.

He licks it. Bites hard enough to make me cry out. Bruises devotion into my skin like he wants to live inside the wound.

"I love that you're mine," he growls.

Then he's wrecking me again—cruel fingers, a merciless mouth.

He brings me to the brink... then pulls away. Again. Over and over.

I sob, trembling, desperate.

"You like this, don't you?" he murmurs. "You like when I make you beg. When I ruin you the way you need."

I shake my head. Denying it.

He slaps my thigh, grabs my chin.

"Don't fucking lie to me, Lollipop. Say it. Beg like the sweet whore you are."

The fight drains out of me when he sucks my clit—leaving only the truth.

"Please, Declan," I sob. "I need it—I need you."

He rewards me instantly.

No teasing. Just what I begged for—hard, brutal thrusts that tear sobs from my chest.

I shatter, climax barreling through me like a wrecking ball.

But he's not done.

He flips me onto my hands and knees.

A dark chuckle. "Oh, what do we have here?"

He nudges the pink plug I slid in this morning... a shameful hope.

His fingers twist it. "Did my little slut hope to get her ass fucked today?"

I whimper, nodding.

He doesn't rush. Just strips me open.

One hand dips back to my pussy. He tugs the plug free with a wet pop.

"You're so fucking needy," he grunts, reaching around me and retrieving a packet of lube from his pants pocket.

Fisting his slick length, he drizzles lube down my crack. Then he's there, sliding his way in.

I sob his name, the stretch obscene as he moves in slowly.

He strokes my clit, pulling me from pain into something else.

Then he thrusts deep, each punch stealing my breath.

"Your slut pussy is feeling left out," he murmurs like a promise. "I made something for you."

I hear the buzz of a toy turning on.

It's huge and I realize—it's him. A silicone dildo made from a cast of him.

"It's the Shadow Daddy." I feel his smirk. "And you're going to love us fucking you."

He slides it in, fixing a sucker around my clit and I nearly pass out. The pressure too much, the pleasure cataclysmic.

I'm split open, filled everywhere—his cock, the toy, the overwhelming rush of sensation flooding through me until I can't tell where I end and he begins.

My orgasm tears through me like a wildfire, dragging a ragged, broken sob from my throat.

Declan's hips stutter as he groans my name, thrusting deep one last time as he spills inside me, claiming me the way he was always meant to.

I collapse into the floor, panting, trembling, every nerve ending shattered and raw.

He leans over me, brushing sweaty hair from my face, pressing a kiss to my temple.

"I love you so much," he says, the words rough and reverent against my mouth.

"My sweet girl," he murmurs again, so low it vibrates through my bones.

"You're mine, little killer. Mine forever."

I smile, my lip split and throbbing from where he caught it earlier.

"I know," I whisper.

And I do. God, I do.

For a while, we just lie there in the ruins of what we made —our bodies marked and stained, blood and sweat dried to our skin like a second layer of devotion.

But eventually, I shift, crawling up and curling against his side.

"I have something to show you," I murmur, voice low and wicked.

Declan tilts his head, suspicion sparking instantly. He knows that tone. That look.

From the shredded remains of my sundress, I fish out something small.

His brow lifts. "Now where exactly were you hiding that, baby?"

"My dress had pockets."

Because listen: trauma, orgasms, potential felonies... none of it excuses ignoring the holy announcement that a dress has pockets.

It's law. I don't make the rules. I just obey them.

I crawl back over him slowly, savoring the way his cock thickens against my thighs as my dripping center drags along him.

He groans, head dropping back against the floor with a thud. "You're gonna kill me."

"That's the dream," I purr.

When I finally hold out the black-and-white paper, he blinks like I've hit him with a hammer.

He squints. "Sunny... that's an ultrasound."

"I know," I say, all sweet and innocent as I straddle his hips.

He stiffens like he's preparing for impact. "Wait—"

I flash him a wicked grin.

"That little rascal," I say, "knocked up the neighbor's dog."

Declan freezes. Blinks again.

"Dexter?" he says, voice cracking.

I nod solemnly. "Dexter."

"But—" He flails a hand, grasping for sanity. "She's a Rottweiler, Poppy. How the fuck did he even—he's got stumps for legs and a Napoleon complex!"

"Apparently not where it counts," I shrug with faux primness.

There's a beat of stunned silence between us before we both burst into laughter, collapsing against each other like lunatics.

"He's gonna be paying doggy child support for the rest of his life," Declan manages between gasps.

"Good," I mutter darkly. "He should've wrapped it."

Declan barks out a laugh, warm and wild and perfect, as I grin down at him.

"Do we get to keep one?" he asks, hope flickering behind that wicked smirk.

I blink. "A puppy?"

He nods, stretching beneath me like a satisfied beast. "I think Dexter earned visitation rights at least. And maybe a cigar."

I laugh, low and warm, but before I can tease him back, his expression shifts—just slightly.

Declan shifts beside me, brushing a thumb across my bruised lip like he's trying to soothe the place he marked.

"Oh," he says casually, like it's a grocery list item. "Your houseguest woke up. Just before I left."

I raise my eyebrows in excitement. "The new restraints you made for me are like a dream."

He stands, towering over me like sin in human form, tucking himself back into his jeans with a grunt. A smile of mischief tugging the corners of his mouth.

"Just wait till you see the new pink chrome tools I got for you."

He helps me stand and pulls my favorite chapstick from his pants pocket.

How did a girl get so lucky?

He pulls a black duffle tucked between the crates and gets me fresh leggings and an oversized pink top.

He leans in and kisses my shoulder—warm, reverent, filthy in all the best ways.

"I'll make dinner," he murmurs against my skin. "While you do your thing."

I turn to him fully, brows raised. "What's on the menu?"

"Meatloaf sound good?"

"Meatloaf is perfect." I kiss the tip of his nose and bend down to put on my pink tennies.

He grabs my wrist, halting me.

His eyes roam me all over again—wild, reverent, hungry.

"And when you're all done downstairs," he murmurs, voice gone dark and low.

"Sweet Lollipop–You're dessert."

Thank you so much for reading! If you enjoyed this story, please leave a review.

Check out the other books in the Accidental series:
That Time I Accidentally Took Over the Mafia
A **Why-Choose, Second Chance** dark romantic comedy.

And...
That Time I Accidentally Killed the Wrong Guy
A **John Wick** *meets* **Weekend at Bernie's** dark romantic comedy.

Up next in the *Accidental* Series

That Time I Accidentally Killed The Wrong Guy

**"They call her Saint.
But she's never been one for forgiveness."**

They call me Saint.
Not because I save lives—because
I end them. Clean.

But one bad hit changed
everything.
I killed the wrong mark, and now
I'm the contract.

The Guild put a price on my head
so high, every assassin on the
planet wants a piece of it.

I've got 48 hours to figure out who
set me up, and not die in the
process.

My name's Saint James.
And if you're coming for me,
you better bring backup.
A lot of it.

For updates and announcements sign
up for Rebekah Sinclair's newsletter

www.RebekahSinclairWrites.com

Welcome to
The Black Ledger

Where every desire has a price...
and every contract is final.

The Black Ledger
Billionaires

Check Out www.RebekahSinclairWrites.com for more!

More Works By

Rebekah Sinclair

THE
FORGOTTEN GODDESS

A completed Series available on Kindle Unlimited

GREEK MYTHOLOGY

URBAN FANTASY

FATED MATES

STAR-CROSSED LOVERS

She is the goddess time forgot

He is the god that never
stopped looking for her

More Works By

Rebekah Sinclair

RETURN to AVALON

A New Trilogy Coming 2025

The Fae Queen is a traitor
So the realm has selected
a new one... a mortal.

ENEMIES TO LOVERS

THE CHOSEN ONE

DARK FAE

ARTHURIAN LEGENDS

NORSE MYTHOLOGY

www.ingramcontent.com/pod-product-compliance
Lightning Source LLC
Chambersburg PA
CBHW061032310726

48969CB00004B/922